"Faessler excels at drawing characte[...] memorable."

Publishers Weekly

"*Everything in the Window* is a great pleasure to read, and a great pleasure to recommend."

Canadian Reader

". . . a winner . . . certain to keep the reader glued to its pages."

London Free Press

". . . an impressive piece of work . . . sardonic humour, compassionate insights and – above all – a gift for characterization."

William French,
Globe and Mail

". . . a sad story wonderfully told . . ."

Ottawa Citizen

". . . a host of fascinating characters . . ."

Windsor Star

"Faessler has a gift for comedy, but her writing can also create pain . . . Shirley Faessler writes very good stories."

Edmonton Journal

". . . earthy, gritty and realistic . . ."

Canadian Jewish News

"Every character in this novel is a clearly defined individual . . . a book of real people in real situations that many readers will identify with."

Lethbridge Herald

". . . wistful and nostalgic . . . always entertaining."

Matt Cohen,
Hamilton Spectator

Shirley Faessler has a distinguished reputation both as a novelist and as a writer of short stories which have been published in the *Atlantic Monthly* and the *Tamarack Review* and broadcast on the CBC.

The author's writing has appeared in eight Canadian and American anthologies. "A Basket of Apples" and "Lucy and Minnie" were included in the Distinctive Stories category in *The Best American Short Stories.*

Shirley Faessler was born in Toronto. She has travelled widely in Europe and the United States, and for a short time worked for the *Daily Herald* in London, England.

Shirley Faessler

Everything in the Window

New Canadian Library No. 159

McClelland and Stewart

Copyright © 1979 Shirley Faessler

0-7710-9302-0

The Canadian Publishers
McClelland and Stewart Limited
25 Hollinger Road, Toronto

For Jim,
and for Bernice

One

Sophie Glicksman was seventeen when Billy James came to work for the YW-YMHA. Everyone in Junior Class, of which Sophie was a member, was smitten by the 23-year-old blue-eyed, golden-haired athlete. They flirted with him on the gym floor, cavorted in the pool, and in the locker room lamented the fact that he was a *goy*. "If only he was Jewish," they sighed.

Sophie, who was an office employee at the YW-YMHA with fringe benefits use of the pool and gym, did not participate in the carry-on over the new instructor. She was in love.

Two months before at a fund-raising dance given by the Zangwill Literary, Social & Athletic Club of which she had recently become a member and co-editor of its bi-monthly mimeographed two-sheeter, she had met and fallen in love with Ronnie Swerling, a young radical, dedicated and good-looking.

Sophie, ninety-eight pounds, black hair, slim legs and a full bosom, had no confidence in her looks and no notion whatever of her attractiveness. At dances, which she loathed going to for fear of being a wallflower, she hid out half the time in the Ladies'. Or, wearing a disdainful look, would circle the dance floor smoking a cigarette in a holder. Who could approach her? Usually some lame duck would blunder over and attach himself to her.

For a change she had been addressed by a good-looking, intelligent boy.

"What's an intelligent girl like you doing with a reactionary chauvinistic outfit like the Zangwill Club?" Ronnie said as they were rhumbaing to "The Lady in Red."

"Why reactionary?" said Sophie who didn't know the meaning of chauvinistic.

He proceeded to tell her about the class struggle. All evening they dipped and glided and swayed, Ronnie all the while extolling the USSR, expounding on the decadence of capitalism and foretelling the imminence of the proletarian revolution. When the band struck up the last dance he held her close and lectured her for her disavowal of class origins. "You don't belong to the bourgeoisie. You're a workingman's daughter." (Too late she regretted having told him her father was a collector.) "You should be proud of your working class background," he was saying to Sophie who loathed every aspect of it. "Zionism," he scoffed. "A homeland for the Jews. 'Next year in Jerusalem' is okay for your *bubbeh* and *zaydeh*, not for people of our generation. The struggle is here and now." He had told her he was a member of The Young Communist League.

"Why did you come to our dance if you're against Zionism?" Sophie asked.

"Out of curiosity. Just as I might have gone to a dance given by Jehovah's Witnesses. Or the Doukhobors."

They spent an hour over coffee and sat for an hour longer on Sophie's verandah. He said he would give her *The Iron Heel* by Jack London. "That'll be an eye-opener for you." When he kissed her good night he called her comrade.

For fear of waking her father — who would give her hell for being out so late — she took off her shoes at the door and tiptoed up to her room. She switched on the light then took up the hand mirror from her dresser and studied her face, taking note for the thousandth time of the slight cast in her right eye, turning it inward to a fifteen-degree angle.

"You have a habit of looking down when you speak," Ronnie had said when they were having coffee. "Why do you do that?"

When Sophie was little she was called "cock-eyes" by kids in the schoolyard. Now in her seventeenth year she was still conscious of the squint, and the habit of looking down when speaking to someone persisted. On streetcars, in restaurants, in public waiting rooms, she kept her eyes on a book. It was by sheer effort of will that she was able to look anyone (except family and intimates) in the face when speaking to them.

Sophie put the mirror down, her heart constricted a moment by the memory of a childhood agony. Now for chauvinistic. . . She opened her dictionary at the C's. Chauvinism: bellicose patriotism, foreign jingoism. . . She cleared a space on the dresser and began composing a letter to Avrom Bochner, the 19-year-old president of the Zangwill Club. "Dear Av, I have long felt myself to be an alien ear of corn in your midst." (She paused to admire her opening sentence.) "Our cause, a homeland for the Jews, is chauvinistic, a piece of unmitigated jingoism."

At three in the morning she was still scratching away. Sheet after sheet had been scrapped but she was satisfied now with the final draft, particularly with the ending which read: "You and I belong to opposing classes in the economic and social scheme. I am the daughter of a collector, something I neglected to mention on my application form when I joined, and my place is with the proletarian element or the working class if you like, to which I am proud to belong. I will be joining The Young Communist League so naturally I will not be in the club rooms next Monday to help with the stencilling. In closing I request that you be good enough to expunge my satiric poem 'Shalom, Shaindl, Shalom' from the forthcoming issue of *The Zangwill*."

Two

Next day when the Glicksmans were eating supper Ronnie, without warning, came to the house with a copy of *The Iron Heel*.

"Excuse me for barging in," he said standing in the kitchen door. "I tried the bell but it doesn't work."

Glicksman, who was sitting with his back to the door, pushed his glasses up to his forehead and turned to see who it was.

"This is Ronnie Swerling, a friend of mine," Sophie said, and Ronnie came forward to shake hands. Mrs. Glicksman offered her hand and invited him in Yiddish to take a chair.

"Don't let me interrupt," Ronnie said, and took a chair by the door.

It was at this time of day with the late-afternoon sun highlighting every defect from the water-stained cracks in the ceiling to the worn linoleum blistered and rucked up under the sink that the kitchen looked its most squalid. Even the chair Ronnie was sitting in was rickety, its missing rungs never having been replaced. And Sophie, despite last night's indoctrination, felt her face getting red.

A week later she was a member of The Young Communist

League. Under Ronnie's tutelage she read *The ABC of Communism, Ten Days That Shook the World*, and for love of him even ploughed through Bukharin's *Dialectical Materialism*. She joined Ronnie in picket lines, distributed pamphlets with him, attended lectures on political economy, and together they peddled *The Worker* outside factories and on the streets of downtown Toronto.

Two months after Sophie became a member Ronnie was chosen by the National Committee to go to New York as representative of the YCL in Canada. He would be away five weeks or more, attending lectures and labour seminars.

One night at supper Glicksman, having finished with the paper, turned his gaze on his daughter who was sitting glumly at table. "Funny I didn't see nothing in the paper," he said. "I thought your boyfriend went to New York to blow up the Statue of Liberty?"

"Very funny," said Sophie.

With Ronnie away everything had gone to pieces. Meetings were dull, her work at the Y a bore and life at home was insufferable.

Thinking of the four more dreary weeks to be put in before Ronnie's return, she was taken on the sudden with a distaste for the chore assigned to her this evening; she was to help out with a jumble sale at the Labour League. Instead, she went to the Y and pulled a shoulder muscle doing push-ups. After class the instructor took her to his small office off the gym floor and massaged her shoulder, leaving the door ajar. She was last out of the locker room and when she came out of the building, there he was at the corner. He inquired about the shoulder, then invited her for a cup of coffee.

Sitting opposite him in the restaurant booth Sophie observed what a lovely blue his eyes were, the evenness of his teeth, and his hair which was the colour of gold. "I never worked with girls before I came to the Y," he was saying. "I was scared stiff the first time I took your class and I'm still nervous. Does it show? But I'm not nervous with you — you're more natural than the other girls. And the prettiest." Complimenting her, he blushed.

He was enthusiastic about his work. "It's the best-paid

11

job I've ever had and everyone's so friendly and generous."
He showed her the wristwatch he was wearing, a gift from
one of the men in Business Men's Class who owned a jewellery store. The suit he had on he had got at wholesale price
at a factory owned by one of the men. "You'd never know
they're such wealthy men, they're so friendly. And so generous."

Generous Jewish capitalists. He's not very progressive in
his thinking, thought Sophie.

When they left the restaurant she wouldn't let him walk
her beyond the top of her street, three blocks from her
house. "My name would be mud if we were seen together,"
she said.

"Why?" he asked.

"Because you're a gentile," she replied.

Next morning the instructor in T-shirt and shorts came up
from the gym to Sophie's office. "How's the shoulder?" he
asked. She said it was fine. He took a pencil from her desk
and rolled it between his palms. "I'm through at eight tonight and I thought if you weren't doing anything—"

"I'm supposed to be going to a meeting. I belong to the
YCL."

"What does that stand for?"

"The Young Communist League."

"Are you a bolshevik?"

She laughed. "I don't carry any bombs on me if that's
what you're worried about. I may not go to the meeting,"
she said. "If I don't I'll be at the corner of the Y at eight
o'clock."

"I'd appreciate that," he said.

At eight o'clock he came running down the steps of the
building, with his head turned to the corner. "I was hoping
you'd be here," he said, drawing her arm through his.

She abruptly pulled her arm away. "We're surrounded
by Jews. My name'll be mud if we run into anyone I know,"
she reminded him.

"I'm sorry," he said. "I forgot."

They walked several blocks and when they were clear of
the district Sophie asked, "Where are we going?"

"Wherever you like. What do you feel like doing?"

"I could eat something."

"That suits me fine," he replied.

They went to a restaurant where Sophie ordered a western sandwich.

"That's my favourite too," he said and ordered one for himself.

He told her he was not used to living in a big city. "I've met a lot of people since I came to the Y and they're all very friendly — but I feel lonely most of the time."

"You haven't met the right kind of people, that's why you feel lonely. The people you've met belong to a different class, they're the bourgeoisie. They don't consider you their equal, and you're not. Don't be fooled about how friendly they are. As a workingman you're their paid lackey."

He could be moulded into good material for the YCL, Sophie was thinking. A physical instructor, a clean, good-looking Anglo-Saxon free of racial prejudice. Except for a couple of Ukrainians, a Czech, a Finn, the members in Sophie's branch of the YCL were Jewish. To introduce someone like Billy James would be a feather in her cap.

"What are your political views?" she asked.

He said politics was not exactly his strong suit. "I've never been able to work up much interest in politics."

"Well, you should," she said. "As a workingman you should know something about the injustices of the capitalist system we live under. You looked shocked when I told you I was a Communist. A couple of months ago I was just as ignorant about communism as you are. All I knew about communism was that old joke — what's mine is mine and what's yours is mine. I'll lend you a book to read. *The Iron Heel* by Jack London. That'll be an eye opener for you."

Three

During a break in classes next day Billy came to Sophie's office to pick up *The Iron Heel*, and a week later coaching her in the pool to do the dead-man's float he said he had finished reading it. "That was a very interesting book. I really enjoyed reading it."

"Would you like to join the YCL?" she asked.

"I'd like that very much."

The following Friday, the night he was to be put up for membership, Sophie went down to the gym at closing time and told him she didn't think it was such a good idea after all.

"Your bosses are very right wing. It could cost you your job if they found out you're a member of the YCL."

"You're a member and you haven't been fired."

"I'm just the office girl. They don't care about my opinions. You're the physical instructor. You attend board meetings, you're important to the organization."

"I was looking forward to seeing you tonight," he said, disappointed.

"I'll skip the meeting. We can go to a movie if you like."

"I'd like that very much. Can we have supper together?"

"It's Friday. I have to go home for supper."

They met outside the movie theatre. Sophie, having arrived a few minutes early, had already bought her own ticket.

"Just get one ticket," she said. "I've already bought mine."

He bought a single then offered her the money for hers.

"Put your money back. That's another bourgeois conception — that the man must always pay."

After the show they went to a restaurant for a hamburger — Sophie paying for hers — then strolled to Queen's Park, Billy talking of his early interest in sports. They found a bench, the instructor dusted the seat with his pocket handkerchief and they sat down. Hesitantly he offered a cigarette, expecting she'd say she'll smoke her own. She accepted. Next minute he moved closer and put his arm around her. "You're very sweet. I'm usually shy with girls but I'm not shy with you."

He's a fast worker, thought Sophie. Shy with girls, what a line. She'd had experience of their tactics before, these *shkotzim*. Last year holidaying at a small hotel in Huntsville she had fallen in love with a gentile boy who worked at the hotel as a handyman and trucker. He too made out he was shy but on their second date he tried to get his hand up her skirt.

Jewish boys on the make were gropers and feelers too but they never let their hands stray lower than the bosom. At least not in her experience. The two or three she had necked with had not tried anything as crude as getting their hand between your legs. . .

"A penny for your thoughts," Billy was saying.

"I was making ethnic comparisons," she replied.

"What does that mean?"

She laughed. "It means exactly nothing. It's a dumb thing to do and I should know better. People are people."

He turned her face and put his lips to hers. "I've been wanting to do this for a long time," he murmured. Sophie, returning his kiss, kept her legs crossed.

With his arm around her he told her about his family in Galt. "This is the first time I've been away from home and I get very lonesome for my family." He had two sisters, both younger than him, a father and a stepmother. His mother had died ten years ago when he was thirteen. "She died of galloping consumption," he said. "The last two years of her life she was bedridden and hemorrhaging a lot but wouldn't have a doctor. She was a Christian Scientist. My grandmother on my mother's side was also a Christian Scientist but she died of natural causes, she was very old. Dad was very broken up after Mother died. He just couldn't pull himself together. He started drinking and lost his job. Fortunately for Dad, Mother had a very close friend, an unmarried lady about the same age as Mother. She took Dad in hand and made him pull himself together. They were married two years after Mother died. She's been our stepmother since I was fifteen."

"Isn't that a coincidence! I have a stepmother too," said Sophie. "I was four when my mother died and my sister was seven. I don't remember much about my mother but I remember the day of the funeral. I have a vivid recollection of that. A lot of people were in the house. A lady cried over me, she called me *yesemeleh* — that's Jewish for orphan — and gave me a handful of pennies. My father remarried when I was five and my sister was eight. I knew the new woman was my stepmother but it was not till I was about eight or nine — when I began reading fairy tales about wicked stepmothers — that I pitied myself as a stepchild. I envied kids who had their own mothers. I felt myself to be a second-hand kid. . ."

After their mother's death Sophie and her sister Bella were shunted around, singly or together, from one family to another; friends of their stricken father, who took them in out of compassion. After the traditional period of mourning, Glicksman, still mourning, went to a marriage broker in search of a wife to make a home for his motherless children. The matchmaker took down the particulars and recorded in his lists: Avrom Glicksman, Roumanian immigrant, 34, widower, two children, eight and five. Refined man, speaks a good English, also educated in Hebrew. Makes a poor living, no bargain.

Also a new entry on the matchmaker's lists was Chayele Simon, Russian immigrant, 38, single. Peasant type, uneducated, no beauty.

16

"I have somebody who might fill the bill," the matchmaker said to Glicksman. "But if she is the right person for you or if she will suit your taste, that's another question."

To which Glicksman replied, "I am a broken man. The right person for me will be an honest woman with a good heart."

The matchmaker contacted Chayele's uncle (who three years before had emigrated his niece) and told him about Mr. Glicksman, a widower with two kids. "Your niece will not exactly be falling into a pit of honey," he said. "But let's face it, she is not such a great catch herself."

The meeting took place at Chayele's uncle's house, with the family on hand to size up the suitor. The family's opinion was that he gave himself too many airs for a pauper. They talked against him, called him a *mamaliga-eater*. Only in Chayele's eyes did he find favour. But she was not counting her chickens: the word had to come from him. The word came, and a week after the meeting they were man and wife.

Billy was moved, listening to Sophie's story. "That's a very sad story. Was your stepmother unkind?"

Sophie laughed. "No, it was the other way around. Bella and I gave her a hard time. What about your stepmother? Do you like her, do you get along with her?"

"Yes, we get along very well. She's been wonderful. I never think of her as my stepmother, neither do my sisters. Mary was nine when Mother died, and Louise was eleven. Mary's nineteen now, and Louise is twenty-one. I think they've forgotten their real mother, and I have too in a way. I mean I never think of her. You see, I can't think of her without remembering the last two years of her life. The blood-stained towels and pillow slips and the terrible fights with Dad about refusing to see a doctor. My two aunts joined forces with Dad. They tried to talk sense into her. And there were some terrible sessions — I used to hide in the shed."

He brought out his handkerchief and wiped his forehead. "Whew! I don't know what got into me sounding off like that. I hope I didn't talk your ear off?"

Next morning when Sophie woke late from a heavy sleep, she experienced on first consciousness an obscure sense of

17

loss, as if someone dear to her had died in the night while she slept. She held herself still a moment and tried, by concentrating on yesterday's events, to locate the cause of this inexplicable sense of bereavement. Slowly the dream she had just come out of shaped itself and took visual form in her mind's eye. . . A wasted Billy James lying naked in a barn on a pile of straw with a bloodied handkerchief pressed to his mouth, while two blond-haired little girls were hopskipping around him, singing "Polly Put the Kettle On."

She lay back with a sigh of relief and gave her thoughts over to her date last night with Billy James. The kiss, recalled, gave her a shiver of pleasure. Her reverie was suddenly broken by her mother calling from the foot of the stairs, "Sophie? Six eggs will be enough?"

"What are you talking about? What eggs?"

"You told me to cook eggs. For the picnic, you forgot?"

Oh God, the picnic. She groaned aloud. Her spirits sank at the prospect of spending the day with a truckload of comrades, not a single one (with Ronnie away) in whom she had any interest.

"Six eggs will be plenty," she called, then got out of bed and rummaged through her clothes closet looking for a pair of slacks. Riled at her own untidiness, she cursed the closet for its disorder. When she came downstairs her mother was at the sink running cold water over the hard-cooked eggs. Mrs. Glicksman transferred the eggs from the pot to a plate, earning for her efforts a baleful look from her daughter. All but one of the eggs were cracked, glutinous whites bulging from the shell.

"What's the matter?" her mother asked, having caught her daughter's look.

"You've ruined them, that's all," she answered in Yiddish. To her mother Sophie spoke Yiddish, to her father, English. "I should know by now that if I want anything done right I have to do it myself."

Glumly she crammed into a paper bag the eggs, the bagels, the Philadelphia cream cheese, the tin of Millionaire sardines, the apples and bananas, all provisioned by her mother for the picnic. She then took up the bag, and its bottom collapsed.

"Oh God!" she wailed. "What kind of bag did you give me?"

"Shh!" said her mother. "You'll wake up Pa. Let him sleep." Heavy, clumsy of movement, Mrs. Glicksman stooped to gather up the scattered lunch.

"Leave it!" said Sophie. "Find me another bag."

Glicksman, wakened after all, came to the kitchen as Sophie was repacking the lunch. He was in his combinations and with a sense of propriety towards his womenfolk, his hands were cupped at the crotch.

"What's going on here?"

For answer his daughter grabbed the repacked bag and ran from the kitchen, flinging over her shoulder: "I'm just about the unluckiest person in the whole world!"

"What did she say?" Mrs. Glicksman asked; and Glicksman, laughing, gave her the Yiddish translation.

Sophie ran all the way to the Labour League, picnic lunch clasped to her bosom, shoulder bag thumping her thigh, and arrived on the scene as the truckload of picnickers was ready to depart; the tailgate was being put up. Fagey Shiffron, a bossy comrade whom Sophie particularly disliked, said, "You're late, comrade, we were going to leave without you."

"Comes the revolution Sophie will be on time," said Milan, the Czech comrade. Squatting, he took her by the armpits and hoisted her up. The tailgate was put up and they were on their way, a tightly packed load of comrades standing and singing with clenched fist salute the "Internationale." Sophie's heart lifted. She felt an easing of tension, an onrush of goodwill towards every last one of them, including Fagey Shiffron. These were her people, workers, the salt of the earth. She lifted her voice and sang along with them: *Banker and Boss Hate the Red Soviet Star/ Gladly They'd Build a New Throne for the Czar; John Brown's Body; I'm Spending My Nights in the Flophouse. . .*

The YCL load arrived at the picnic grounds simultaneously with a truckload of Party members; among them were several small children who began clamouring for the picnic as soon as they were set down. Tables were spread with newspaper and the food was communally set out. Sophie apologized for the eggs. "My mother overcooked them. . . "

The image of her mother clumsily stooping to gather up the scattered lunch came suddenly to her mind. Her spirits on the instant sank from high to low. The fullness of feeling she had experienced a few minutes ago evaporated. She regarded with displeasure the noisy children who were permitted to grab from the table anything they wanted, and observed that their behaviour was not lost on a group of nearby picnickers, gentile people. No wonder we arouse anti-Semitic feelings, she thought; she was ashamed to be connected with them. She picked out one of her mother's cracked eggs and walked away eating it.

Milan, eating a salami on rye, followed. "What's the matter, comrade? You have a heavy look on your face like you just lost your best friend."

"Someone just walked over my grave," she replied.

The Czech finished his sandwich then sat down on a grassy mound beneath a tree. "Don't be sad," he said, taking her hand and pulling her down beside him. "Be happy, comrade."

He was tall, his teeth were small and wide-spaced with a display of gum when he laughed, and his skin was bad. "Smile," he coaxed; and she smiled for him. "Do you like me?" he asked.

He's kind of nice, she thought, trying to work up some enthusiasm. "I hardly know you," she replied, "but I think you're a sensitive, understanding person."

A feeling of repugnance came over her when he pulled her to him and kissed her on the mouth, but not wanting to hurt his feelings she returned the kiss.

He stroked her face, brushed her hair back and playfully tugged her ear lobes. "Can I tell you something?"

"What?"

"Your ears are dirty." With his finger he traced the rim of her ear. "Only here, on the outside."

Her face grew hot. Controlling an impulse to slap his hand away, she rose quickly to her feet. "Let's go back."

He followed a pace behind her. "You're very quiet, comrade. You're not mad at me?"

Drop dead, she fumed inwardly. Clown, insensitive goon.

"I'm not mad," she brought out. "I don't feel like talking, that's all."

When she got home her mother was on the verandah, sitting in her chair with her head bent to the peeled apple she was scraping at with a spoon. Toothless but for a few side and back teeth, it was the only way she could eat an apple, which she loved.

"You had a good time?" she asked.

"Not bad. The eggs were okay, Ma. The shell was cracked but inside they were fine, just right."

"The eggs. . . ? Oh, the eggs." She spread her fingers over her face and laughed. "A great talent to cook a few eggs."

"I'm thirsty. Make some tea, Ma, will you."

"With pleasure." Flattening her hands on the verandah railing for leverage, she rose from her chair.

Proceeding to the kitchen, she began talking to herself, a habit she had fallen into from a condition of advancing deafness and also because she was alone so much. "With pleasure," she said, passing through the hall. "The eggs? A great talent to cook a few eggs." Musing, audibly mulling the few words she had spoken to Sophie, she filled the kettle and set out a cup for Sophie's tea and a glass for hers.

Upstairs, Sophie with her hair swept back was leaning into the dresser mirror. One glance at her ears and her hand automatically scratched at the back of her neck — a reaction to chagrin, embarrassment, an old habit left over from childhood. When her mother called her to come down for tea, she was leaning over the bathtub washing her ears. The basin taps didn't yield any water and Glicksman who washed the same way — leaning over the tub — was still saying as he had six years ago when they first moved to the house: "I'll have to get hold of a plumber."

"When are we going to get those taps fixed?" Sophie demanded, sitting down to her tea.

"What taps?"

"Upstairs. The taps in the sink, for God's sake."

Mrs. Glicksman pushed the teapot to Sophie. "I'll remind Pa. Take a cup of tea."

Four

Sophie woke Monday morning with a feeling of certainty that a letter from Ronnie would be in the post. In the five weeks he had been away he had written official letters to their branch of the YCL which were read aloud at meetings by Fagey Shiffron, but nothing personal to anyone. There was no reason, aside from pure psychic intuition, to fix on the hope of a letter, but the feeling of confidence that she would hear from him today kept mounting, so strong she could feel it in her bones.

Leaving for work a few minutes past nine, she saw the postman on their side of the street. On seeing Sophie, he riffled through the mail then handed her a letter postmarked New York. She was longing to open it on the spot, but it was late. She slipped the letter into her handbag and ran to work.

Mr. Rosenberg was sitting at her desk, sorting mail. He rose, yielding her the chair. "You'd better get started on the membership dues, Sophie. They should go out today," he said, moving to the door.

Mr. Rosenberg closed the door, and Sophie opened her letter. A few lines was all it contained. As the needle to the magnet, her eye was instantly drawn to a line halfway down

22

the page. "Hold on to your hat," it read, "I'm a married man." Without reading further she turned the letter face down on the desk. After a time, when her heart had resumed its normal pace, she took up the letter and read as follows: "Dear Sophie, I've been up to my ears in meetings, lectures, seminars and social activities. Our American comrades are very friendly and hospitable to a degree, but their knowledge of Canada and our work here is rather limited. Some of them have never even heard of Toronto. Now for news of a more personal nature. Hold on to your hat — I'm a married man. I was married two weeks ago. My wife is a gentile girl, active in the movement, and very intelligent. Some legal formalities pertaining to Canadian citizenship for my wife have to be ironed out before I can bring her to Toronto. Till then, yours in comradely affection, Ronnie."

Before beginning on the membership dues, Sophie inserted a sheet of paper in the typewriter and wrote as follows: "Dear Ronnie, We must be telepathic. Your letter arrived this morning, the very morning in fact that I had come to a decision about withdrawing from the YCL. I am in total accord with the aims of the movement (to better the lot of the working class) but I am *personally* not in accord with its membership. I have not been able to establish one iota of sympathetic or intellectual contact with anyone in the YCL. At the risk of being labelled a Parlour Pink, I hereby tender to you, the president of our branch, this, my official resignation from the YCL." Having signed herself "Yours sincerely, Sophie," she put the letter in an envelope, addressed it, and started on the membership dues.

Five o'clock and the day's work was done. Sophie was clearing her desk when the instructor in street clothes, very handsome, and taller than she remembered, came to the office.

"Did you have a good weekend?" he asked.

"Very nice. And you?"

"I didn't do much — I kept thinking of you. Well, not all weekend," he said, smiling, "but most of it. Will you be coming to class tonight?"

"I hadn't thought of it. Maybe."

Sitting opposite him in a restaurant booth after class, Sophie was saying, "I dreamt about you the other night."

"What did you dream?"

"It all took place in a barn. Your sisters were in the dream too. You were grownup but they were just little kids. You were lying on a pile of straw and—" Having witlessly embarked on the telling of that dreadful dream, she concluded with, "That's all I remember. Let's talk about something else."

"Okay, you begin."

"You asked me if I had a good weekend and I said very nice. Well, I didn't have a good weekend at all, it was ghastly. And to top it all, this morning I had a letter from my boyfriend — well, not really my boyfriend but sort of. I was expecting a love letter. Instead he wrote to tell me he got married two weeks ago, and so here I am at the tender age of seventeen a jilted woman, discarded, thrown away like an old shoe."

"You have a wonderful way of expressing yourself."

She shrugged. "But let there be no moaning at the bar," she said, pleased with the sophisticated image of herself she had created. "There are plenty more fish in the sea."

She took a cigarette from his pack; he struck a match and Sophie, nonchalantly covering the back of his hand with hers as he held the flame, observed with dismay that — for a woman of the world — her fingernails were none too clean.

"Do you know what I did over the weekend?" Billy said. "I wrote a long letter home and told my people I was seeing someone. I told them all about you and said that I'd been seeing a lot of you — which was a little white lie. I also said that being in love I wasn't so lonely anymore." He couldn't make out from Sophie's expression how she was taking this. "I did say, though, that it was a little one-sided because I wasn't sure that you. . . " He was shifting uncomfortably, rapidly losing ground. "I said I *thought* you liked me."

"I wouldn't be here if I didn't — but you shouldn't have done that. You forget that I'm Jewish," she said, not as glib as before. "Did you tell them I was?"

"That wouldn't mean anything to them. We didn't know

any Jewish people in Galt except for one old man, a peddler who used to come around to buy old clothes. The kids on the street used to chase him and call him Sheeney — excuse me for using that word. I was just a kid myself, my own mother was still alive. I didn't know what the word meant but it made me mad to see an old man being treated like that and I used to get into a lot of fights with the kids over it. That's the only contact we ever had with Jewish people."

"Well, your family may not be prejudiced against Jews, which is unusual, but my people are against gentiles. Well, not exactly prejudiced but they'd have a fit if they knew I was going out with one."

He leaned forward to whisper, "A girl's been trying to get your attention. I think she's coming over."

Next minute Ruby Stitsky was at their table. "Hello, there," she said to Sophie, ignoring Billy who had risen. "Long time no see. Where've you been keeping yourself?" Sophie shrugged and Ruby, as if aware suddenly of another presence, turned a coquettish glance on Billy. "Or need I ask?"

She would show up now, thought Sophie, and reluctantly made the introductions. "This is Billy James, our new instructor at the Y, and Ruby Stitsky, an old school chum."

Ruby held up two fingers, crossed. "We were like this." She slid in next to Sophie. "Am I butting in? Say so if I am. I can take a hint."

Sophie reached for her handbag. "We were just leaving."

Ruby put a restraining hand on her arm. "Stay another minute. I'm expecting Lou. He should be here any minute. He'll be tickled pink to see you, Soph. It's been ages."

Ruby's intrusion was bad enough; Lou's was unthinkable. Fastened like a stinger in the skull was the memory of a humiliation she had suffered in his presence a little over a year ago. Ruby had arranged for Lou, whom Sophie had not yet met, to bring a boy for her chum and the four would go on a date to Sunnyside. Sophie, nervous of a blind date, went over to Ruby's at the appointed time, dolled up in her best dress. She was introduced to Ruby's new boyfriend Lou Epstein, and shortly after, Phil, Sophie's blind date, arrived. He gave Sophie the once-over, then said to Lou, "Can I see you for a minute?" and Lou followed him to the hall.

Phil kept his voice down; Lou's came over clear as a bell: "I just met her. I didn't know she was cockeyed." A muttered reply from Phil, then Lou's voice: "Come on, be a sport, she's Ruby's best friend." Phil audibly came back with: "Look, I didn't come out on a blind date to earn a *mitzva*." Next came the sound of footsteps and the closing of the front door.

Lou rejoined the girls, dancing and shadowboxing. "Let's go, girls. Let's get cracking."

Ruby, putting a final touch to her makeup, noticed they were three instead of four. "Where's Phil?" she said. "Where is he, the shmo?"

Lou came up with a fast explanation. Phil, he said, just remembered that he had a message to do for his old man. "He said we should go ahead and he'll meet us at the fountain in about half an hour." He sent a glance to Ruby; she was quick to catch on.

Sophie, her face on fire, begged them to go without her. "Please. I don't mind. Really."

Ruby put an arm around her, making it worse. "Don't be like that, Soph. Who needs him? If he shows he shows, if not not. We can have a good time without him."

And Sophie dragged along with them to Sunnyside. Lou treated them to hot dogs, cokes, chips; they played games, fished for prizes, bowled. Sophie, trying to keep up a front, could not remember when in her life she had been so miserable. They rode on the Ferris Wheel, Lou sitting between them with an arm around each. At the Tunnel of Love, Sophie balked, refused to ride with them. Lou bought tickets for two; Sophie, waiting outside, bawled.

All this happened over a year ago. Since that time, Sophie had not been seeing much of Ruby except for once in a while when they stepped across the street, one to the other's house, for a cup of coffee, their conversation invariably reverting to a rehash of school days. Otherwise, they had nothing to talk about; they had branched out in different directions. She had seen Lou three or four times since the Sunnyside episode. In conversation she was unable to meet his eyes. When obliged to bring up her head in acknowledgement of a remark made directly to her, she felt her eye turning in. For this reason, and for the word cockeyed he had spoken over a year ago, the very sight of Lou was hateful to her.

She shook her arm free of Ruby's hold. "It's late, I have to be home. Give Lou my regards—"

Too late. Ruby had caught sight of her boyfriend coming through the door and was already on her feet yoohooing and waving. Billy rose at Lou's approach. "Meet my fiancé, Lou Epstein," said Ruby. Billy, offering his hand, gave his name.

Lou sat down and turned his attention to Sophie. "Long time no see. How are you, Sophie?"

Her answer "I'm fine, thanks" was given to her empty coffee cup.

"I'm so hungry I could eat a horse," said Lou. "Ruby?"

"Thanks a lot but no thanks, I ate at home. Order for yourself."

Sophie got up. "It's late, I have to be home. I'll be seeing you," she said to Ruby. Telling Lou good-bye, she spoke to the wall.

Outside Billy suggested a walk to the park. "It's still early. You don't have to be home yet, do you?"

"No, I only said that to get away. The sight of Ruby depresses me out of my mind. She reminds me of everything I want to forget."

"She said you used to be best friends. At least that's what—"

Sophie cut in. "I don't know why she keeps harping on that. That was years ago, we were just kids. She's become very coarse. She behaves like a tart. And that loathsome Lou Epstein — the very sight of him nauseates me!"

He looked at her in surprise and as they proceeded slowly to the park, she sensed a subtle change in atmosphere.

Wanting to make up for her unbecoming outburst, she began telling him about the blind date. She thought to make an amusing anecdote of it, something to divert him. Recalling it vocally she got very worked up. The word cockeyed was a stone in her throat, it was an effort to get it out. "Sixteen," she said, coming to the end, "and bawling outside the Tunnel of Love like a five-year-old."

He was deeply moved. "That's very cruel," he said. "You have beautiful eyes. That's the first thing I noticed about you. There's a slight little turn in but it's cute."

She wished he'd get off the subject.

It was dark when they got to the park. They found a bench and sat on it over an hour, necking. Half-past twelve they were at the top of Sophie's street.

"Are you my girl?" he asked in parting.

Five

After that they started dating regularly. They saw each other almost every day and Sophie, taking care not to be seen with him anywhere too near her neighbourhood, met and took leave of him four blocks from her house. The nights he worked late they met for a cup of coffee or to sit a while in the park; it was late fall but the weather was still mild. Saturdays they spent the day together. At the Island on rented bikes he taught her to ride a wheel. At the roller-skating rink he coached her on cutting corners. Picnicking on the Humber he taught her to paddle a canoe.

Riding a wheel, paddling a canoe — these were pleasures of a kind not known to her before. And for once she had a real boyfriend, someone who dated her exclusively and never looked at another girl. Ruby had always been the popular one; she started dating when she was fifteen. Sophie was almost sixteen before she was taken any notice of by a boy. That was Ben Ruskin, a 19-year-old medical student whose parents kept a grocery store on their street. Ben was an intense, dark-complexioned short little guy with black hair and thick eyebrows that met across the bridge of his nose. He used to help out in the store and waiting on Sophie would flirt with her over the counter. One night he asked if she would come out with him. He was nothing to get excited about, but a date was a date. An appointment was made for the next night at eight and Sophie dressed in her best met him outside the grocery store. He took her on a long walk through the University grounds and talked Darwinism to her. Sophie, wearing her sister's high heels, came home with crippled feet.

Next came Avrom Bochner, the 19-year-old well-dressed president of The Zangwill Literary, Social & Athletic Club, and editor of its paper. He kissed her one night when they stayed late in the club rooms stencilling, and Sophie fell in love with him. He told her she was the brainiest girl he had ever met but he never dated her or even kissed her again. Then Ronnie. But not even Ronnie had been a real boyfriend; he was popular in the YCL and everyone wanted a piece of him. He had shown a special interest in her but as it turned out it wasn't a romantic interest, it was a comradely one.

Ben Ruskin had talked Darwinism to her, Avrom Bochner talked Zionism, and Ronnie, Marxism. Billy James talked love.

One day when they were passing a store on Yonge Street Billy said he wanted to buy a present for his sister. He asked Sophie to select something from the window display. "And don't worry about the price," he said. "The sky's the limit. I got paid today."

Sophie admired one thing and another then selected a handbag made of stillborn calfskin for thirteen ninety-five, almost half of his week's pay. He went into the store and came out with the handbag wrapped in tissue. "It's for you," he said, smiling. Next payday he went on his own to the store and bought her the compact she had admired. A week later, a charm bracelet. "You're my girl," he said. "I'm going to buy you everything in the window."

One Saturday — running from the rain which had come down suddenly to spoil their picnic at Long Branch — they came across an abandoned woodshed to shelter in. Billy spread the picnic rug and they lay down together on the floor, first time for them in such an intimate embrace.

"I can feel your heart," he whispered, his own beating wildly against hers.

They lay in each other's arms, stupefied with desire. Sophie abruptly pulled away. "My dress is getting creased," she said. She took off her dress and lay down with him in her slip.

"You shouldn't have done that," he murmured. "You'll get me all worked up."

Strongly sexed and with a burning curiosity to know "what it was like" she whispered, "I'm not afraid, Billy. Go ahead if you want to."

He immediately got to his feet, pulled her up and gave her her dress to put on. "I don't want to do anything bad," he said. "Let's get married, honey."

They rode solemnly home on the streetcar, silenced by the words that had been spoken. It was dark when they reached the street where they usually parted. Seeking to prolong the leave-taking, Billy said, "We'd better start making plans. Let's go someplace where we can talk."

A voice suddenly broke in on them. "Hi, there!"

It was Ruby on the arm of her boyfriend Lou. Lou clapped the instructor on the shoulder. "I'm thinking of joining the Y, Billy. I want to brush up on my breast stroke."

"Very funny," said Ruby. "How about the four of us going for a coffee, Soph?"

"No, thanks," said Sophie. "I have to go home."

"And I was just leaving," said Billy.

"What's with this guy?" said Lou. "Whenever you see him he's just leaving."

A streetcar was approaching. Billy cast a despairing glance at his girl, waved to the couple and ran for the car.

They walked Sophie to her door. Ruby, hanging onto her arm, wouldn't let go of her. "I want to talk to Soph a minute," she said to her boyfriend, and giving him a fast kiss sent him on his way.

"What do you want to talk to me about?" said Sophie irritably.

"You don't have to get on your high horse with me,"

Ruby replied. "I know you from way back, don't forget. What I want to talk to you about is for your own good. Are you going steady with that *shaygets*?"

"God, you come out with some crude expressions."

"What's crude about calling a *shaygets* a *shaygets*?"

"It's the way you say it that makes it sound crude. I've been seeing a lot of him, if that's what you mean by going steady. He asked me to marry him," she couldn't resist bragging. "And what's more, I'm considering it."

"Soph! You must be out of your mind."

"Why? I'm in love with him."

"In love with him," Ruby scoffed. "Not that I blame you, he's a living doll. But that's not love, Soph. He's a *goy*, you're infatuated. Look how many times I thought I was in love — with Jewish boys — and it turned out to be infatuation. With Lou, I'm sure. If you're serious about getting married to him all I can say is you're asking for trouble. For one thing it'll kill your parents. And aside from everything else, a Jewish boy makes a better husband."

Ruby's advice didn't count for much but Sophie lay awake, nonetheless, mulling it over. A Jewish boy makes a better husband. Since when? She hadn't noticed anything remarkable about the Jewish husbands at the Y or on her street. It'll kill your parents. That was the most ridiculous thing Ruby had come out with. They'd get over it. It would be wonderful to get away from that miserable house. With the two of them working they'd be able to afford a nice apartment. Instead of Sophie, the girl in the office, she would be Mrs. Billy James, wife of the handsome instructor, someone to be taken into account. But to marry a *goy* — did she dare do it?

A week later on a Saturday at one o'clock they were married by the Reverend R. A. Foster, a minister they had found in the yellow pages of the telephone directory. The minister's wife and sister-in-law stood in as witnesses while Sophie spoke her marriage vows, thinking all the while: If Pa finds out he'll kill me.

After the ceremony they walked hand in hand to a nearby restaurant for lunch. Billy ordered a full-course meal; Sophie, out of sentiment, ordered a western sandwich.

She bit hungrily into her sandwich — she hadn't eaten anything yesterday, for worry — and when he told her he had reserved a room at a downtown hotel, her appetite left her. She
had been anticipating this day, had lain awake nights luxuri-
ating in an out-and-out voluptuousness, but now that the
realization of every erotic imagining was actually at hand, she
was scared.

"It's still early, Billy. Can't we go someplace first?"

He showed her passes he had been given for a baseball
game at Sunnyside.

"I'd like that. I've never seen a baseball game," she said,
and they boarded a streetcar for the double-header at Sunnyside.

It was getting on for seven when they left the park to
come back downtown. At the approach to the hotel, Sophie
felt perspiration gathering in her armpits. Billy paused at the
entrance to wipe his perspiring forehead. "Won't it look
funny if we check in without luggage?" he said.

They went looking for a suitcase, which they found in a
second-hand store a block away from the hotel. Retracing
their steps he began worrying about the lightness of the case.
"The bellboy takes it up to the room, he'll know it's empty,"
he said.

They stopped at a newsstand; he bought an assortment of
newspapers and magazines and weighted the case.

Like thieves they slipped out of the hotel early Sunday
morning so that Sophie could get home before her parents
were awake. They took a streetcar and said a quick good-bye
three blocks from her street. "Can I call you after work?" he
asked, and Sophie, running, called back "Yes."

She took her shoes off at the door, slipped upstairs, took
off her clothes and got into bed. She lit a cigarette and lay
back, giving her thoughts over to her bridal night. . .

She was shy of undressing with the light on so they undressed with the light off and groped in the dark for the bed.
The quick excitement of lying naked in bed legally man and
wife overwhelmed them. But Sophie at first contact panicked. "There's something wrong with me, Billy," she said, "I

can't do it." Which resulted in a cooling off of ardour on his side. He took her in his arms and comforted her, and then made another try. "It's this damn bed," said Sophie irrationally. And so they left the bed and sat a while on a chair smoking a cigarette, gathering strength for coming to grips with it again. And so it went all night; it was almost dawn before the bridegroom, in humiliating defeat, gave up.

"I'm sorry," he said miserably, "but it's not your fault, it's mine," and adding further to his shame, confessed that he had never been with a girl before.

Billy telephoned after work. "I'm at the corner of Major and College. Can you come out for a while?"

"I'll be there in ten minutes," she whispered.

They were shy meeting at the corner and walked self-consciously to the park without speaking. They sat on a bench and spoke of impersonal things, like two strangers sharing a seat on a train.

Sophie after a while said dejectedly, "It's getting late. I'd better be going."

When it came to parting at Major and College he took her hands and held them tightly gripped in his own. "This is terrible — I love you so much," he said, then drew her to him and they clung briefly to each other, forlornly embraced.

Monday the instructor came early in the morning to the office, with a prepared excuse for business there. Mr. Rosenberg had not come in yet; Sophie was alone. She rose from her desk, they stepped behind the filing cabinet and with the alarming possibility of Rosenberg's imminent arrival, exchanged a nervous kiss.

"Don't come to class tonight, honey. I won't be able to keep my mind on my work if you do," he said, his blush matching hers.

They met after class and sat in the park necking.

And that's how it went the next few days: a stolen kiss in the office, a nighttime necking session on a park bench, loving words, yearning glances over coffee.

Saturday, when they had been married a week, they met downtown at noon and the instructor, provisioned with a box lunch, took his wife to his room on Jarvis Street. Things went better this time and early Sunday morning — in celebration of his success — Billy saw his wife to the top of her street in a taxi. They met again that night when he was through work, and proceeded to his room.

"We won't have to sneak in. I told my landlady I was married. She wanted to know when you'd be moving in," he smiled. "I told her we were keeping it secret for a while."

"Did you tell her why?" she asked, doubtful of her welcome in a gentile house.

"No, I didn't think you'd want me to. I just said it was for personal reasons."

Sophie stopped going to classes at the Y. The instructor was her husband; pride of situation and a sense of apartness as his wife would not permit her to playact the role of just another girl in Junior Class. Instead of going to class Monday night, she went to his room to wait for him. Saturdays she came early to the room, freshly bathed and in clean underwear. They made love first, letting the coffee get cold. Like a regular married couple they shopped for groceries; Sophie cooked bacon and eggs, held her knife and fork as he did and patted her mouth with a napkin. Sundays it wasn't so easy to get away early. Her father seldom left before two or three in the afternoon so she stayed in her room marking time, waiting for him to go for his Sunday game of dominoes with his friends. First thing when she got to Billy's room she took off her clothes and put on the Japanese kimono he had bought for her at that store on Yonge Street. Waiting for him — Sundays he worked from ten to eight — she read, played the radio and roamed the large room, taking pleasure in its tidiness and in her own clean-smelling self. She liked opening his clothes closet, and his drawers which were kept so neat you could take inventory without disturbing the disposition of his socks, handkerchiefs, shirts, shorts. She loved this time to herself; it gave her a sensuous pleasure to touch his things, wrap his scarf around her neck, slip her arms through the sleeves of his dressing gown.

At home the mother remarked the change in the younger daughter. "Like a little lamb," she reported to her husband. "You don't hear a sour word from her. It must be," she reflected, "that he came back from New York, the bolshevik. Runs every night to a meeting like a wild thing."

35

Six

Sophie woke one Saturday morning, three months after they were married, and lifting her head felt a queasiness in her stomach and a rise of nausea. She ran to the bathroom and leant over the toilet bowl, retching and vomiting. Dizzy afterwards and weak in the knees, she sat on the rim of the tub moaning, "Oh God."

Throat raw, face in a sweat, she roused herself and went downstairs to phone her husband. "I'll be there in half an hour. Be prepared for bad news."

The instructor had an anxious time of it waiting for his wife. Be prepared for bad news. . . She had a flair for dramatizing; it could be that she had a run-in with her sister or a quarrel with her father. A few days ago she had mentioned the delayed period but had spoken lightly of it. "If I'm pregnant, I'm pregnant. I'll simply tell my people I'm married and that'll be that." A day later there was a change of mood. "You'll lose your job at the Y, my father will close his door to me, we'll be driven out like lepers. We've been too happy, Billy. I have a strong presentiment that the axe will fall. The gods are jealous of mortal happiness."

He stood inside the door listening, and presently heard her step.

36

"I'm pregnant," she announced, flinging open the door.

He took her in his arms. "That's wonderful news. I was hoping that's what you were going to tell me. Now you'll have to tell your people and I'll write home to mine. We'll be together all the time, Soph, it'll be wonderful. We're husband and wife, for heaven's sake. We should be living together. We're going to be parents. We should be proud instead of pretending we're not married."

Sophie doubted that she could stand up to the ordeal of telling her father. "Keep talking, Billy, you give me courage. I feel strengthened listening to you."

He kissed her. "That's nice. I'm nowhere near as smart as you."

They stayed in bed all day and into the night, the instructor from time to time getting up naked from bed to make them a sandwich. Sophie, watching, felt in herself a deep and abiding love for him. He's my true love. He cares for me and I care for him.

Half-past twelve they were on the street, talking over the course of action he had outlined. First thing tomorrow she was to make the news known to her parents.

"Don't get excited," he said. "Try to keep calm. I think you'd better pack a suitcase tonight so you'll have it ready. Just tell them you're a married woman now and your place is with your husband."

Too soon they were at the corner of their customary meeting-and-parting place. "Stick to your guns, honey. Don't weaken — and for heaven's sake, stop scratching your neck."

After a troubled night's sleep she woke early Sunday morning, and immediately felt sick. She hurried to the bathroom; the door was shut. Gagging, stomach heaving, she banged frantically on the door.

"Wait a minute," said her father. "What are you in such a hurry?"

Unable to check the rise of vomit, she stumbled back to her room and vomited in the wastebasket.

Glicksman, coming from the bathroom, stopped at her room to look in. His daughter, flushed, gulping air, was sitting on the edge of the bed mopping her face with a towel.

"What's the matter with you?" he asked.

"Something I ate last night. It didn't agree with me."

"Come downstairs, I'll give you a little cognac, it'll settle your stomach," he said, and she followed him downstairs.

"I couldn't do it, Billy," Sophie was saying. This was Sunday night; he had come home from work expecting to find his wife moved in. "I felt better after the cognac and I was getting up the nerve to tell him but he didn't give me a chance. He started looking for lemons to make me a hot lemonade and got mad at my mother because there were no lemons in the house. He went out to buy some. All the stores in our neighbourhood were closed but he found a place. He looked so *old* squeezing the lemons, I didn't have the heart. I couldn't do it, Billy."

He sighed. "Putting it off isn't going to make it any easier."

"I'll do it tomorrow. Tomorrow," she said resolutely, "no matter what happens." Her face paled. He was alarmed to see her sink weakly in a chair holding a hand to her heart. "I go weak in the knees just thinking of it," she said. "Feel my heart."

She pondered the method of approach and finally decided the best way would be to tell her mother and leave it to her to tell the father. "That's what I'll do. I'll tell her in the morning before I go to work. My father will be gone by then. He gets home early Mondays. By the time I get home from the office he'll know and we can sit down and discuss it like two rational human beings."

Next morning at nine-thirty when Billy was getting ready for work he heard a thumping on the stairs, then a bang on the door. It was Sophie, lugging a heavy suitcase. "I did it!" she announced triumphantly, and next minute was in his arms weeping a flood of tears. "God knows how they'll take it. Wait till my father finds out I'm married to a gentile. How will I ever get through this day!"

He gave her two aspirins. "You're hysterical. Calm down, honey, and tell me what happened. I have to be at work soon."

She gulped the aspirins then went to the mirror to have a look at herself. "I'm a wreck! I'll have to phone Mr. Rosenberg and tell him I won't be in today."

"Honey, please, tell me what happened."

"I was up all night packing and writing a letter to my father. I didn't have the nerve to tell my mother. I just gave her the letter and told her to give it to my father when he comes from work. She wanted to know where I was going with the suitcase. I told her I was taking some things to the cleaners. They'll know when he comes from work. It's in the lap of the gods now!"

Sophie had in fact been up all night packing and writing a letter to her father. The letter was a plea for forgiveness — with a line or two plagiarized from *I Am a Woman and a Jew*, a library book written by a lady in the same fix.

"Dear Pa," she wrote, "You have had many blows in your life and now Fate decrees that I, your daughter, must deal you yet another one.

"Please don't worry about me thinking I've done God knows what. I am well and happy. With your permission I would like to go into a little preamble before giving you my news.

"You are my father and I love you. I may not have shown my love any more than you've shown yours for me over the years. Now that I am mature I realize that it was your rage against life with all its cruelties that inhibited you from demonstrating the love that was locked in your heart. I realize the sacrifices you made. To give us a home you married an uneducated woman inferior to you in intelligence. Please don't take this as a disloyalty to Ma. She is a good woman and I feel very close to her in spite of her shortcomings.

"Not to keep you in further suspense, this is my news. I am a married woman. Three months ago without your knowledge or sanction I married Billy James. He is the physical and swimming instructor at the YW-YMHA, twenty-three years old and a gentile. You are not a religious man, Pa, so I beg you to keep an open mind. We Jews chafe under the designation Kike, Sheeney, Hebe, but are we ourselves innocent of racial prejudice? The *goy*, we say, which is derogatory and insulting. My husband is a gentile who is utterly devoid of anti-Semitic feelings, a paragon amongst men, kind, gentle, considerate, and I am fortunate in having his wholehearted love. To complete my happiness I need only your forgiveness, and Ma's. Forgive me, Pa. Don't close your door to me. If my own flesh and blood turns against me, what am I to expect from strangers?

"Your loving and contrite daughter, Sophie."

Seven

Sophie stayed away from work that day, the day after and the next, waiting for a telephone call from her father. She kept the door of their room ajar, listening with a trembling heart for the phone downstairs in the main hall.

Worn out and beside herself with anxiety, she went down eight o'clock the evening of the third day and telephoned Ruby. "It's me — Soph. Can you keep a secret? I did it. I'm married, Ruby."

"Oh my God!"

"I'm sick with worry. I don't know what's happening at the house. I left a letter for my father. It's three days, Ruby, and I haven't heard from him. Go over to my house, please, and find out what's happening there before I go out of my mind."

"I'll go right over. Where can I get in touch with you?"

Sophie gave her the telephone number and the address. "Call me right back. I'll never forget you for this, Ruby."

In an hour's time Ruby was knocking on the door. Billy opened; she gave him her hand. "Congratulations," she said breathlessly, then embraced her friend and took a chair. "I've just come from your house. I'll tell you everything. Let me catch my breath first."

Ruby took a deep breath. "Your mother can't stop crying. Your father stayed off work two days. He's threatening to commit suicide. . . " Sophie paled. "Don't worry. People who threaten never do it. He says with a disgrace like this he'll never be able to hold his head up again. But he blames himself. He said he should have been more strict with you."

Sophie bridled; she regained her colour. "Should have been more strict with me," she said indignantly. She turned to her husband. "He gave me a belting when I was *sixteen*, Billy, for coming home late from a party." She appealed to her friend. "You remember, Ruby?"

Ruby sighed sympathetically. "Be that as it may."

"What else did he say?"

"He told me to tell you he'll phone you tomorrow after supper." She rose. "I'll be going now. I left Lou sitting in my house."

The following evening after supper they heard the alarming signal — two long and one short buzzing in the hall.

"That's him," said Sophie, her tongue dry with fright. "Come down with me, Billy. He might want to talk to you."

They hurried downstairs and Sophie picked up the phone. "Hello, is that you, Pa?"

"I have one word to say to you," he replied. "What's done is done and it's no use to cry over spilt milk. I have inquired about your husband at the Y and I have heard from them that they hold him in great respect. But the fact still remains he is not a Jew. If he is willing to become a Jew, we have something to talk about. If not, my door is closed to you. Discuss it with him and I'll be by your place tomorrow seven o'clock," he said and hung up.

"Oh God!" Sophie wailed replacing the receiver. "He's suddenly become a pious Jew and. . . " She stopped — the word Jew like the sting of a bee on her tongue — and glanced nervously around, wondering if she had been overheard. "Let's go upstairs."

Back in their room and safe from eavesdroppers, she continued. "He's suddenly become religious. He's suddenly become a pious Jew and wants you to become one too. It's enough to make you laugh. My mother knows from nothing.

42

She's religious because she's scared of God. She goes to synagogue once in a while but she can't read the Siddur. She can't even read or write a word in Yiddish. She's been in this country umpteen years and has only learned to speak a dozen words in English. But my father can do all these things — Hebrew, Yiddish, English. He knows Jewish history, he knows the Talmud backwards, but that doesn't make him a religious Jew. He goes to synagogue once in a blue moon to keep up appearances and not to shame my mother. But he's an *atheist*, for God's sake! I've known that since I was fourteen."

Glicksman came to them the following evening seven o'clock sharp. He courteously extended a hand to his son-in-law, placed his fedora on the mantel shelf, and with eyes lowered and hands locked behind his back, paced up and down the room. A wisp of a man with a navy-blue suit shiny in the pants, he began at last to speak.

"I am a poor man," he said, "but I tried my best all my life to make a living for my family and to bring up my children right. I had many hard knocks in my life. My first wife died a very young woman. An intelligent woman, we were sweethearts from the time we were children in Roumania. I was a young man when this happened and I felt like to die myself. But I had the responsibility to bring up my two children. . . "

Sophie's throat tightened. She advanced a step. "Sit down, Pa."

He waved her away and continued talking.

Life had dealt him many blows, but never one as hard as this. For himself, he didn't care. He couldn't care less what the neighbours or even the relatives would have to say. He was indifferent to criticism; he wouldn't give two cents for people's opinion of him. But his wife — that was another story. She unfortunately did not have his independence of opinion and to her this was a bitter disgrace. True, she was an uneducated woman. Ignorant, you might say. But she was a kind woman with an understanding heart and a noble soul.

Noble soul — Ma should hear this, thought Sophie. Whenever her father got upset about one thing or another he would say to his wife that she was incapable of understanding what was bothering him because she had the soul of a peasant.

"And for this reason," he concluded, "I feel we have to show her a little consideration. We have to do what she wants."

"I'll do anything you say," said Billy emotionally. "I'll become a Jew. My people aren't very religious. They won't even have to know — they live in Galt."

Glicksman took his fedora from the mantel shelf. Sighing in the manner of a man who had been broken on the wheel for his belief, he said to his son-in-law, "It's not such an easy thing to be a Jew. Think it over before you do anything," then shook hands and left.

Billy James took hardly any time to think it over. He telephoned his father-in-law next day and told him he was ready to become a Jew. He arranged for a substitute gymnast to take his classes for a week, and went with Glicksman to a Mohel to be circumcised. He came home by taxi, crippled with pain. His wife wept over him.

A week later, companioned by Glicksman, Sophie and Billy were remarried by a rabbi. Renamed Abraham, Billy was given *I Am a Jew Because* to memorize, and Maimonides' *Guide for the Perplexed* to read.

The rabbi then called Sophie aside. "Your husband looks to me like a very fine man," he said. "I spoke to him private and he understands the children will have to be brought up according to the Jewish faith." Jokingly, with his index finger he gave her a gentle prod in the stomach. "Or have you got already a little *goy* in there?"

The instructor shook hands with his father-in-law, took leave of his wife with a kiss, and warily — as if walking on eggs — set off for work. Watching his cautious, measured gait, Sophie felt a rise of bitterness against her father. Executioner, she said to herself, and couldn't bear to look at him as he accompanied her to her streetcar stop. "Don't say anything for a while, Pa," she said, averting her eyes. "Don't tell Bella yet, or Aunt Hannah. I want to keep my marriage a secret a while longer. I told Ruby not to say anything either."

"What's there to be ashamed? Your husband is a Jew now."

"That's got nothing to do with it," she replied hotly. "I wouldn't be ashamed if he had remained a gentile. Less ashamed than I am now in fact because the whole thing is a mockery. My husband is led like a lamb to the slaughter and gets himself circumcised. All that suffering," she said tearfully. "The rabbi says a few words over us in Hebrew and Billy James the gentile becomes Abraham the Jew. I know this wasn't Ma's idea, it was yours. And that's really hypocritical from a man who's supposed to be an atheist."

A rush of angry blood reddened his face. Struggling to control his temper, he stooped to his shoes and engaged his shaking hands in retying a shoelace. Then he straightened and regarded his daughter.

"You are very clever," he said. "But what you know is only from books. You have a lot to learn yet about life."

He looked so old. His face with stubbled grey on the chin was a face of skin and bone, with a pair of watery blue eyes. Sophie put her hand on his sleeve. "I didn't mean that, Pa. I'm not feeling well these days and I get worked up over the least little thing. I'm not ready to face people yet. You told Ma I was pregnant?"

"She knows. Why don't you phone her at least?"

"I will. Soon as I get home."

"So what shall I tell your sister? She knows you're not in the house. I'll have to tell her something."

"Tell her I'm out of town. Tell her I'm in Oakville taking a short refresher course in secretarial work. Good-bye, Pa. Here comes my car."

A lie comes so quick to her lips, he thought, watching her board.

Sophie telephoned her mother from a drugstore call box where — relieved of the worry of eavesdropping *goyim* in the downstairs hall of the rooming house — she was able to speak freely in Yiddish to her.

Eight

Her bouts of morning sickness continued. Griping, debilitating seizures, there was no letup to them. She had to quit her job. She lost her taste for cigarettes; the smell of cigarette smoke made her violently ill. Billy went outdoors to light up. That didn't help. She could smell it on his clothes and was sick the minute he put his nose in the door. So he smoked at the Y between classes. She was beset by all kinds of quirks. One day on a streetcar when she was sitting opposite a woman in a yellow coat, she felt her stomach begin to heave. The colour yellow was making her sick; she had to get off the streetcar.

Now that he had become a Jew, Billy was diligently reading and making notes of the points set forth in *I Am a Jew Because. Guide for the Perplexed* was heavier going; reading it, he found himself more perplexed. Despite a busy schedule at the Y, he found time to attend the rabbi an hour a day for lessons in the Aleph Beth. Glicksman became a member of a second synagogue (one not too near his own neighbourhood) and they went together, the born Jew and the technical Jew, each with his prayer shawl and phylacteries in a velvet bag. Billy James, the blond, blue-eyed athlete, champion swim-

46

ming and diving medalist, submitted to every requirement made of him. He was a sincere convert and kept up his studies without flagging. It was Glicksman who tired of the whole rigamarole first.

One night, instead of readying himself for synagogue, the instructor settled in with the sports page of the daily paper.

"What's the matter?" said Sophie. "No Shul tonight?"

"Your father says it's not necessary to go to church every day," he replied. (Abraham the converted Jew still referred to the synagogue as the church.) "He says it's not even necessary to go every Saturday unless you're a — I forget the word he used."

"Tzadik?" she prompted. "Chassid?"

"One of those words," he said.

Sophie's absence from the house had been accounted for. Her father, as she had requested, had put out a story that she was out of town taking a refresher course in secretarial work. It was not till a month after her morning flight that it was given out by him, with her assent, that she had married a gentile boy who was now a Jew.

The first telephone call was from her sister Bella. "What's this I hear?"

Quick on the defensive, Sophie replied, "Any objections?"

"Well, if you're going to be like that, good-bye!" said Bella and hung up.

Later in the day, a call from Aunt Hannah. To begin, she expressed herself of the opinion that Sophie had done a very risky thing by marrying a *goy*.

"That's a nice expression coming from you, Aunt Hannah."

Her aunt hastily corrected herself. "I said it without thinking. I meant to say gentile. I understand from your father that he is a very refined boy?"

Silence. Aunt Hannah resumed. "Your father is a very good judge of human nature and if he says your husband is refined I respect his opinion."

"Thank you."

"But you'll find, my dear Sophie, that in every gentile, no matter how refined he is, there is a lit-tle bit of anti-Semitism—"

"Oh, for God's sake, Aunt Hannah, what does he know of anti-Semitism. He never met a Jew before he came to Toronto. The only Jew he ever came in contact with when he was a small boy in Galt was an old ragpicker who used to come around to their house to buy old clothes."

"You see?" said her aunt. "Already the connection is made in his mind between the ragpicker and the Jew."

"If you're going to talk like that I'm going to hang up."

"Don't get excited, Sophie. I'm a little older than you, so have a little respect. What I'm only trying to point out, if you'll give me a chance, is that they are different people from us, the gentiles. We are open people, we speak what's on our mind. You know that expression 'What's on the lung is on the tongue' — that's us. But they are not open people. You can't tell from their expression what's in the heart. They keep things to themselves and it builds up. So you'll have to be very careful, Sophie — your temper. You'll have to learn how to control yourself. Don't give him a chance to say to you: Jew."

Now that the news of the marriage was made known to Sophie's family, Billy wrote to his people in Galt and received a congratulatory reply by return post. The letter, signed Mother and Dad, expressed the wish that they would meet Billy's wife "in the not-too-distant future."

"Let's go this Saturday," he said, eager to show her off. "They'll love you, honey."

"Did you tell them I was Jewish?"

"No, I never thought to. I didn't tell them I was either," he said, laughing.

"I didn't expect you to tell them you were — but why didn't you tell them I was Jewish? Tell me — honestly."

"Because I never know whether you want people to know," he said wearily. "You don't want them to know here that you're Jewish but if you want my family to know I'll tell them."

Moodily, without thinking, he lit a cigarette. Sophie gagged and ran to the bathroom. He flung the cigarette out of the window, and it was decided the trip to Galt would have to wait till she was feeling better.

In a few weeks — except for intermittent and fairly mild attacks of morning sickness — she was feeling better. The smell of cigarette smoke stopped bothering her and the colour yellow was just a colour like any other. Instead of coming home to an unmade bed and a quickly-got-together meal, Billy was coming home to a tidy room, a nicely laid table, a casserole from *The Joy of Cooking* in the oven, and a loving wife with a settled stomach.

Every second day she went to the drugstore call box and telephoned her mother. "Come Friday for supper," Mrs. Glicksman kept coaxing. "I didn't meet my new son-in-law yet and I didn't see you for a long time."

Sophie kept promising. She was proud of her handsome husband and wanted to show him off to the family, but dreaded bringing him to the house. She shrank from the thought of laying open to him that dump of a place she had come from. She kept postponing, but in the end there was no help for it: they set out one Friday night for the house on Bellevue Avenue.

"The house is an awful mess," she said, trying to prepare him. "It's terribly neglected. I suppose I could have done something about it while I was living there but you get so discouraged, there's so much to be done you don't know where to begin. It's like knocking your head against a brick wall," she said gloomily. "So you end up by shutting your eyes to everything and pray for the day that you can get the hell away from it. My father isn't lazy. He's a hard-working man but when it comes to any one of the million things that any ordinary man can do around a house, he's hopeless. You can hire someone but he doesn't really care what the place looks like. He's got dozens of friends and he's out half the time playing cards or dominoes at someone else's house. My mother stays home all the time but she doesn't notice that the place is falling apart, she thinks she's living in a palace. And compared to where she came from it probably is. She comes from some prehistoric little village in Russia. They used to bring the calf in the house to keep it warm. She isn't lazy either. She works hard but she's a terrible housekeeper. Meeting her for the first time she'll probably strike you as being — well — kind of primitive. She can be very irritating but she's a kind-hearted woman with pity for everyone except herself."

Glicksman was in the hall to greet them. "Welcome to my house," he said, shaking hands with his son-in-law. "Come in, please, and you'll meet the rest of my family. I mentioned to you my wife doesn't speak English very well?"

Mrs. Glicksman, in her clean Friday-night apron, hair smoothed down with water and knotted in a bun, ducked her head when she was introduced and gave him her hand, looking somewhere to the left of him. As he was being introduced to Sophie's sister Bella, her husband Henry and their little boy Philip, she went to the kitchen and stood in the doorway, scrutinizing him through narrowed eyes. Glicksman excused himself, stepped over to his wife and speaking quietly gave her hell in Yiddish for "acting like a barbarian." She got busy with her pots and he rejoined the company.

Sophie observed the new cloth on the table and the paper napkins — that must have been Bella's doing. She also observed the mismatched chairs, the twin windows with their yellowed lace panels, the faded wallpaper — one wall displaying last year's calendar with three puppies lapping curdled milk, another wall hung with a picture that came with the house: Mary Queen of Scots in majestic raiment kneeling with the lace-capped head to the executioner's block.

Mrs. Glicksman, who had been cooking since Thursday, went all out serving supper that first Friday night to her new son-in-law. She had made chicken soup with farfel, chopped liver, *gefülte* fish, a meat-and-barley *cholent*, hamburgers with mashed potatoes, a carrot *tzimmes*, a compote of dried apricots and prunes, and a honey cake to eat with lemon tea.

This Friday she did not sit down with her family. Busy delivering the various courses she ate her supper in the kitchen, on the run between heats, so to speak.

Bella brought the first course to table, the chicken soup, ceremoniously serving the guest of honour first. Everyone began as soon as his plate was put down. Billy, waiting for his hostess to come to table, let his soup get cold. Sophie nudged him. "Begin, Billy, don't wait." She observed him ladling aside the globules of chicken fat on the surface of the soup, the minute spoonfuls he brought to his mouth. When her mother came to clear the plates, Sophie took up her husband's plate and handed it to her half full.

"He doesn't like chicken soup?" she asked her daughter.

"It's too fat for him," Sophie replied. "Don't worry about it, Ma, he'll get used to it."

It was with the *gefülte* fish that he really came a cropper. Stunned by the taste, he bolted a mouthful and reached for his water glass.

"Don't eat it if you don't like it," Sophie said.

"It's nice," he replied. "I do like it."

He drank slowly from his glass of water then speared a morsel of fish on his fork and gazed at it with an unbelieving stare. Sophie took up his plate and went to the kitchen with it. Her mother was dismayed; *gefülte* fish was the tour de force in her culinary repertoire. "He doesn't like my fish?"

He picked at the *cholent*, taking over-nice little bites from the tip of his fork. But he liked the hamburgers. "Soph, tell your mother they're really good."

After serving the compote, the tea and the honey cake, Mrs. Glicksman took her customary place at table beside her little grandson. She responded affectionately to his chatter, sipped tea from her glass and never once took her eyes off her new son-in-law. Shortly after supper, Sophie rose and Billy got to his feet.

"What are they running away?" Mrs. Glicksman asked of the table in general.

Sophie told her they were going to a movie. Billy shook hands with his father-in-law, gave his hand to his mother-in-law, then bent his head to kiss her on the cheek. Mrs. Glicksman quickly brought her hand to her cheek and looked shyly away, blushing like a girl.

"What did you think of my family?" Sophie asked him.

"They're very nice, I like them. Your mother's very shy. She blushed when I kissed her."

"She nearly fell over," Sophie laughed.

"Shouldn't I have done that? Is there something in your religion?"

"If my father were a rabbi there might be something against kissing his wife. It's just that we're not a kissing family. I don't remember when I kissed my mother last, or my father. What did you think of the house — pretty gruesome, isn't it?"

"It's not all that bad. You exaggerate everything, Soph. It's the food that bothers me, all those spices — whew!"

"What did you think of him?" Sophie asked, speaking to her mother next day on the phone.

She was captivated. His eyes were bluer than Pa's, his teeth were like pearls. A beautiful boy, a diamond. "He gave me a kiss, you saw? Come next Friday for supper, I'll make him *cocletten*. He likes them."

"Make his separate. Leave out the garlic."

Nine

They continued going Friday nights to the parents for supper
and in July when Sophie was full in the belly she came to
dread the walk down her street with neighbours on verandahs
taking the evening air. Her gaze fixed straight ahead, she
walked stiffly beside her husband without taking his arm.

"I loathe coming down this street with my stomach stick-
ing out. It's like running the gauntlet. I can just imagine what
they're saying."

"That's ridiculous, honey. There's nothing to be ashamed
of, we're married."

Mrs. Glicksman became used to having her new son-in-law
at the table. She lost her shyness with him, joked about her
English and even tried to teach him a word or two in Yiddish.

As for Sophie's father, he doted on his son-in-law. Friday
nights he attended his every word as if listening to an oracle.
He fell over himself lighting Billy's cigarette.

At first this was pleasing to Sophie, but after a while she
became uncomfortable at the attention paid him. The parents were devoted to the first son-in-law, Henry, but with the
instructor at the table he was hardly given the time of day.
Here was her mother laughing at a Yiddish word spoken by

Billy, laughing with her head thrown back, exposing a gaping mouth. Ashamed of her missing teeth — though you couldn't get her to go to a dentist — she always put a hand over her mouth when she laughed. Giddy, thought Sophie, just plain giddy. Here was her father bolting from the table to fetch Billy a glass of water and polishing the kitchen tumbler a full minute before putting it under the tap. It bothered her to see her people dancing about him; you'd think she had married the Prince of Wales. Truckling to the *goy* was the thought that came to her mind.

Shortly before Sophie's confinement, it was decided by the couple that it would be impossible — with a baby — to continue in their attic bedroom at Mrs. Todd's on Jarvis Street. Billy hunted furnished apartments but rents were sky high, way beyond his means.

One Friday night at supper Mrs. Glicksman said to her daughter, "What's the matter with moving in here? You'll take back your bedroom, you'll have a toilet on the same floor, a kitchen downstairs and a yard to put the baby out when it's nice weather. Pa will be glad, I will be glad and you won't need to pay rent."

Sophie made no reply.

"Ask him," Mrs. Glicksman said, pointing to her son-in-law. "Tell him what I said."

"I don't need to ask him," said Sophie, glumly incising her paper napkin with a fork. "I don't think it's a good idea to live with your parents after you're married."

"What parents? When parents?" her mother replied. "When is Pa home? True, I'm home all the time but you'll see, you'll be glad to have somebody in the house to leave the baby with when you go out."

No response from her daughter. She appealed to her husband, "You tell her. She'll listen to you."

"Don't interfere," he said sharply. "Don't tell people what to do. Let them make up their own mind."

Speaking Yiddish, they might as well have been speaking Greek as far as Billy was concerned. He looked questioningly from one to another.

Bella, taking over, addressed him in his own language. "My mother suggested to Soph that you come here to live rent

54

free. Personally I think it's a very good idea. It'll give you a chance to save for furniture, then you can look around. Unfurnished apartments are a lot cheaper."

The instructor agreed with his sister-in-law. "That's a marvellous idea," he said to his wife. "I'll save on carfare too. The Y's a five-minute walk from here. We can give our notice tonight and move in next week."

"Would that be all right with you?" he asked his father-in-law.

Glicksman glanced at his daughter: the bleak entreaty in her eyes caused him to hold off a second before replying. "You are very welcome in my house," he finally came out with. "And my daughter naturally is welcome also. But better to talk it over between you before you do anything."

They talked it over that night in bed.

"The thought of moving back to that house depresses me out of my mind," said Sophie despondently.

"Oh, come on, honey, it's not that bad."

"You don't know what you're saying, it's terrible. My mother talks about the back yard — you've never seen our back yard, it's a jungle. She throws slops out there and fifty million cats come around. I wouldn't dream of putting a kid of mine out there."

"If that's all that's bothering you I'll clean it up."

"That's not all that's bothering me. I never told you how miserable I was in that house. I never brought a friend home, except for Ruby. I used to be ashamed even when a crummy neighbour dropped in. My mother's a sloppy housekeeper and she's got some terrible habits — I don't want to talk about them. Friday nights for a couple of hours is okay, you don't notice things so much, but to live there is terrible. I hate that house. It's been a misery to me ever since I can remember. That's one of the reasons I married you, to get away from that dump."

"You exaggerate everything, honey. You married me because we were in love," he said. "I think we should give it a try, just for six months. We need so many things with the baby coming and six months rent free would be a load off my mind. But if you feel that badly about it, I'm not going to talk you into it."

She remembered the circumcision. He cut himself for me. "Okay," she said, "I guess I can put up with it for six months." Her face was flushed and she was near tears.

He put his arms around her. "I appreciate that, honey. I know how you feel but it won't be so bad with me there."

Next morning when he went down to give a week's notice, she wished desperately that she had not given in. It won't be so bad with me there. . . It'll be worse, she reflected. If she had spoken openly last night she might have persuaded him against the move. She had mentioned her mother's sloppy housekeeping, her terrible habits, but had been unable — for shame — to speak specifically of these things. Her mother's lack of personal cleanliness, for one thing. She used to take a bath regularly — Fridays usually, after the day's work — but now that she had put on so much weight she was frightened of slipping in the tub so she washed herself down once a week from a bucket of water which she took to her room. Except for Fridays there was an emanation from her of a strong body odour. She drank a lot of tea and because it was hard for her to climb the stairs she had taken recently to urinating in the back yard. In the winter she used a pail in her room; in the summer, unencumbered of the bloomers she wore in the winter, she took to the yard and emptied her bladder standing upright with her legs apart.

First time Sophie caught her at it she raised hell. "Is that what you've been doing out here, peeing!"

Abashed, Mrs. Glicksman swore no. Swore no despite the puddle at her feet and the splattered shoes.

Sophie could not bring herself to speak of these things to her husband. Apart from shame on her mother's behalf she felt that she herself was in some way implicated, that the shame in some way was attached to her too. She dreaded the move back. He would see her as a familiar, an intimate of the house he saw her in for only an hour or two on Fridays, and she would stand revealed to the man who all these months had been holding doors for her, jumping to his feet, proudly escorting her on the street as if he had a princess by his side. With the mother's unclean habits laid open to him, the daughter, she felt, would be lessened in his eyes.

Ten

Early one morning two weeks after the move Sophie suddenly sat up in bed; something peculiar was happening to her. Next minute the bed was flooded with water. Billy, who slept naked, sped downstairs to the hall telephone. Hearing the commotion, the parents emerged from their bedroom. They made a weird-looking trio: Glicksman in his combinations, his wife in some kind of *shmata* she used as a nightdress, and the instructor bare-naked at the phone.

The taxi arrived and Mrs. Glicksman stood in the hall wringing her hands. "God help her, a dry birth."

Sophie was put in a room with a Mrs. Palter, who the day before had been delivered of her fourth child, a ten-pound boy; and a Mrs. Friedman, who had been delivered of her second son, an eight pounder.

"Your first?" Mrs. Palter asked Sophie.

"Her first," said Mrs. Friedman. "What a question. She looks like a baby herself. How old are you, dear?"

"Eighteen," said Sophie.

Mrs. Friedman was astounded. "Would you give her eighteen years?" she said to Mrs. Palter.

"Did I look any older at eighteen? Let me tell you what

57

happened," said Mrs. Palter settling back on her pillows. "I was twenty-one when I had my first. My husband brought me in and right away they start to wheel me in the operating room — not the delivery, the operating room. They got mixed up with the records in the office. They were looking for a girl fifteen years old who was supposed to come in for an appendix operation and they thought I was her, that's how young I looked with my first."

"Is it hard having your first baby?" Sophie asked.

"It depends," replied Mrs. Friedman.

"God forbid you should have the same experience I had with my first. I wouldn't wish it on my worst enemy," said Mrs. Palter. "Let me tell you what happened. My husband brought me in around five on a Monday morning. I told you how they wheeled me in the operating room? Anyway, they saw right away I wasn't a 15-year-old girl, I was in my first stages of labour. This was on a Monday five A.M. Comes Tuesday night and I'm still kvetching. They thought they'll have to give me a Caesarean, my husband was going out of his mind. Wednesday three in the morning — hello, I popped. With my second I nearly dropped it in the elevator. You can never tell."

"I had my first very easy," Mrs. Friedman said to Sophie. "And God willing, you'll have yours easy too."

"But it's still painful?"

"It's not exactly a picnic," Mrs. Friedman replied. "But after it's over you'll forget the whole thing. You won't even remember the pain."

"My mother said I was going to have a dry birth. What does that mean?"

Mrs. Palter raised herself from her pillows. "How does she know?"

Sophie told them about the early-morning flood.

Mrs. Friedman said, "You broke your water already?" Noticing Sophie's alarm she quickly put in, "But that's not serious."

"It doesn't help," said Mrs. Palter. "A dry birth she'll have to work twice as hard."

This drew a sharp rebuke from Mrs. Friedman. "What do

you need to tell her all these *boobeh mysehs*?"

"Isn't it better she should be prepared? They don't put you under right away, don't forget."

Just then the nurse entered bearing in each arm a fat baby. The mothers let out cries of delight. Teasing, the nurse brought them to Sophie's bed and lay them beside her.

"Aren't they a pair of beauties?" she said.

In Sophie's eyes they looked gross. "They're beautiful babies," she said, smiling.

The mothers received their babies to the breast and suckled them amidst cries of "*Zeendeleh, tateleh, zaideleh.*"

Mrs. Friedman raised her head and smiled encouragingly at the expectant mother. "You're taking a lesson? Wait, you'll see what a beautiful feeling you'll get when you'll hold your baby in your arms for the first time."

Mrs. Palter glanced up. "Mother love is the most beautiful experience a human being can have," she said kissing the bald baby hanging on her tit.

"I cried from joy," said Mrs. Friedman.

"Me too," said Mrs. Palter.

Billy returned at noon and was introduced to his wife's roommates. He extended a polite hand to each, then took a chair by his wife's bed and began anxiously questioning her.

"Nothing yet, Billy, not even a twinge. I've made a pest of myself all morning, driving Mrs. Palter and Mrs. Friedman crazy with questions about childbirth. But they've been very patient. I was lucky to be put in this room."

The instructor sent the ladies a grateful glance.

Suddenly Sophie became aware of the abrupt cease in conversation between the two women who had not stopped chattering all morning. Both were on propped elbows, giving her husband the once-over.

In an hour his visit was over, and as he took leave of the ladies, Sophie noticed the deference they accorded him. She recognized in their manner that extra politeness reserved for the *goy*.

He was hardly out of the room when Mrs. Palter said, "What does he do, your husband?"

"He's a physical instructor, he works at the Y. The Jewish Y," she put in quickly. "That's where we met. I used to work there too."

Mrs. Friedman took a comb to her hair. "You make a nice-looking couple," she said, combing her hair and mirroring herself in Mrs. Palter's eyes. "You so dark and him so blond."

Sophie's pains began early in the afternoon. In the throes of labour the worry that her husband had been sniffed out for a *goy* fled from her mind. In the evening she was carted to the delivery room where she laboured till midnight giving birth to a black-haired little girl weighing a meagre six pounds.

Billy, who had been hanging around for hours, was given a view of the baby and permitted a few minutes with his wife.

"She's beautiful," he said emotionally. "What are we going to call her?"

"Emma," she replied, slipping back into sleep. During the last week of her pregnancy she had been reading *Madame Bovary*.

"Emma, that's a nice name," he said, relieved she hadn't decided on Isadora, which was also a projected name if the child were female. The book before *Madame Bovary* had been *My Life* by Isadora Duncan.

Next morning Sophie waited impatiently for her baby to be brought to her. "What's keeping them? What are they doing with her?" she fretted.

"They'll bring her, don't worry," said Mrs. Palter. It was at least an hour since the other two babies had been brought to their mothers.

The nurse appeared at last with Emma in the crook of her arm. She was about to put the baby beside its mother when Mrs. Palter called from across the room, "Bring her over here, nurse, let's have a look at her." The baby was detoured to permit the ladies a glimpse.

"She's so little," Mrs. Palter remarked.

And Sophie was overtaken by a mingling of anxiety, resentment, anger; the overriding emotion, a bristling pride. "Bring her to me," she said sharply to the nurse. "I haven't seen her yet."

"What are you so touchy?" said Mrs. Friedman, who only yesterday had been her good friend.

Sophie made no answer; she was scrutinizing the living breathing black-haired little human at her breast, the miracle of it so overwhelming that later she could not say whether she had or had not experienced that beautiful feeling of mother love promised by the ladies.

Billy came on his lunch hour with two dozen roses, and her father came in the evening with chocolates.

"Why didn't your mother come?" she was asked later by Mrs. Palter.

"She never goes anywhere," Sophie replied.

That night after lights out she heard her roommates whispering to each other. "I asked the nurse," said Mrs. Palter, "and she told me."

Mrs. Friedman drew a deep sigh, then said in a whisper loud enough to reach Sophie's ears, "As if there aren't enough Jewish boys to go around."

Miserably, Sophie wished she had booked into any hospital but the Mount Sinai. It was because her cousin Miriam, Aunt Hannah's 21-year-old daughter, was a nurse at the Mount Sinai that she had decided to have her baby there.

Sophie was in hospital six more days, every day a misery to her. Her roommates had stopped speaking to her altogether; they behaved as though she didn't exist. They spoke to each other, leaning across their beds to whisper, their intention to hurt and belittle unmistakably and cruelly deliberate.

At noon of the second day Billy came to visit, and to him they were sweet as pie.

His wife, face flaming, made him draw the curtains. Curtained off, he asked her, "What's the matter, honey?"

"I can't stand the sight of those two hypocrites!"

"Shh! They'll hear you. You're so changeable. You liked them — what happened?"

"They've turned on me like a pair of snakes. They *exude* hate."

"Why?"

"I don't know and I don't care."

When her father came she hid him behind curtains. She

shielded her sister and brother-in-law from view. Aunt Hannah was concealed from sight. Ruby and Lou came to visit; she made them draw the curtains, then told them the whole story. "Pay no attention," said Ruby, "they're ignorant." When the visit was over Lou drew the curtains apart, and as they were leaving he called mischievously from the doorway, "See you in church, Soph." Sophie could have killed him.

Her cousin Miriam looked in several times and found Sophie curtained off. "Why do you keep the curtains drawn?" she asked.

"Because of those two women. They keep whispering. It's like poison gas seeping in the room."

"It's all in your imagination. Post-natal depression, that's all it is. You need some air. You don't want to make yourself sick," she said, and professionally drew the curtains apart.

But the whisperings were not in Sophie's imagination. They whispered behind their hands to visitors who came in packs to see them, and all without exception turned to have a look at Sophie. One of their visitors, an old woman with a shawled head, actually came right to her bed. "Very nice," she said in Yiddish. "I'm sure this is great *nachess* for your parents. I pity them whoever they are."

A quick-tempered retort rose to Sophie's tongue but she refrained from giving it utterance. "I won't answer back," she said in Yiddish. "My parents brought me up to respect old people."

The instructor knew nothing of this. The glances at his wife he took to be admiring ones; she was so young to be a mother, and so pretty. The morning he came to take his wife and baby home, he brought chocolates for the tattletale nurse who had been the cause of his wife's misery, and bade an amicable farewell to Mrs. Palter and Mrs. Friedman who were "staying a couple of days extra for post-natal."

Sophie said good-bye to no one, and her husband, in the taxi, reproached her for rudeness.

Eleven

The first week they had the baby home, they trembled over her. She lost an ounce the second day and this scared them out of their wits. She was such a tiny thing, they feared they wouldn't be able to sustain life in her. They kept vigil by the baby's cot, listening for the sound of her breath.

Sophie after a while became acquainted with her child's needs and gained confidence in her ability to care for her. She lost her fear that the baby might slip away from her.

Not so Billy; he continued nerved up. A whimper from the child brought him to her side in alarm. A sneeze sent him scurrying from bed. He was up two and three times in the night to check the thermometer he had brought for the bed-room wall. One minute he was putting extra covers on the cot, and at the next reading removing them. At a quarter to two in the morning he was changing the baby's diaper, ready-ing her for the two A.M. feeding. Sophie, half asleep, nursed the baby while he timed the feeding; ten minutes at the right breast, ten at the left. At five forty-five he was out of bed again for the six o'clock feeding.

He searched out newspaper items pertaining to infant mor-tality. "Listen to this, Soph. . . " A two-month-old infant had slipped beneath its loose bed coverings and its life was snuffed out. Loose bed coverings — he had Emma's so securely fastened with mammoth diaper pins at both sides of the cot you had to be a Houdini to extricate her for a change of diaper.

Once a week — Sunday morning before going to work — he wrote to his family, and received by return post a chatty letter written by the mother, usually ending in expressing a desire to see the baby.

"We should go, Soph. It's not fair, Emma's almost three months old," he said.

Sophie kept promising.

One day a letter arrived in which the mother said in closing: "Dad and I are thinking of taking a trip to Toronto. Ha."

That decided Sophie. "I'd die of embarrassment if they came here. Write and tell them we'll come next Saturday."

The following Saturday they set out with three-month-old Emma for an overnight stay in Galt. The train was draughty and Billy worried the baby would catch cold. They kept changing seats till they found one halfway down the coach away from the doors. There, he felt a draught coming from the window. He gave her the baby to hold while he caulked the windowsill with newspaper.

"Do you think they'll like me?" Sophie said, nervous of meeting her in-laws. "You told them I was Jewish. . . ?"

He took the baby from her and rearranged its wrappings. "It'll be a miracle if she doesn't catch cold. We never should have brought her out in this weather."

They taxied from the station and paying the driver he let some change slip through his fingers into the snow. He gave her the baby to hold and knelt, fishing with bare hand in the snow for sunken nickels and dimes. Sophie, keyed up and nervous of meeting his family, exclaimed, "Oh, for God's sake, Billy, let it go!"

Billy's father opened the door to them. Father and son greeted each other with a handshake and punch on the chest. Sophie received a kiss on the cheek. The mother came to the hall, smiling. Taller than her stepson, she bent her head to kiss him then turned to her daughter-in-law. Sophie awkwardly returned her mother-in-law's embrace with a misplaced kiss which landed on her neck. Blushing, she offered the baby.

The sisters, Louise and Mary, blond and blue-eyed as their brother, were sitting side by side on a small sofa in the living room. They rose, kissed their brother, gave their sister-in-law a shy smile and stepped forward to admire the baby in their mother's arms. The baby was then handed back to her daddy who took her upstairs to the cot he had slept in as an infant.

"We may as well sit down," said the mother, leading her daughter-in-law to a deep-seated chair upholstered in mohair. After a long pause with smiles exchanged all round, the mother inquired about the train journey. "I hope it wasn't too hard on the baby?"

The father asked his daughter-in-law's permission to light a pipe.

"Please do," she replied. "I love the smell of a pipe." Her voice sounded phoney in her ears.

The mother remembered the lovely window displays in the downtown stores when she had visited Toronto some time back; and Sophie, who loathed shopping downtown and never went unless there was no help for it, enthusiastically agreed. "Especially at this time of year with all the fantastic Christmas displays," said Sophie who had not been downtown since the baby was born.

The mother sat with folded hands in her lap, smiling at her daughter-in-law. The sisters exchanged smiles. The father, puffing on his pipe, took a secret glance at the clock on the mantel shelf. Sophie wondered what her husband was doing upstairs. If my face freezes like this I'll be smiling the rest of my life, she thought.

He returned at last and the sisters trooped out to lay the table for lunch.

"Well, son," said the dad, "how does it feel being a father?"

To which his son soberly replied, "It's a great responsibility. I'm just beginning to appreciate what you and mother must have gone through."

Louise appeared to tell them lunch was ready.

Sophie picked at her cold cuts and potato salad, hardly knowing what she tasted, she was so engrossed observing her husband at home with his family. She listened to their politeness of address to each other and marvelled at her husband speaking in an idiom she had not heard him use before. Speaking of his child he referred to her as "a little tyke."

Louise and Mary cleared the dishes and the couple went upstairs to attend to their baby. Billy readied the baby and gave her to his wife, together with a wad of moistened cotton wool. Suppressing irritation at his finicky attention to detail she accepted the cotton wool and gave each nipple a fast swab. He took a chair and glanced at his watch to time the nursing.

"What did you think of my family?" he asked.

"I was very uncomfortable with them. Are they always like that?"

"What do you mean?"

She paused, giving herself time to consider her answer. "Well — you don't speak to each other like a family who've been living together all your lives. You speak to each other as if you were strangers. Like people who happen to be sitting beside each other on a bus or in a train. I was afraid to open my mouth in case I said something too personal."

"That's ridiculous."

She could tell he was offended. "Oh, come on, Billy, don't be like that. I didn't say anything insulting about them. It's just that I'm not used to being with people like that."

He rose from his chair and lit a cigarette, which normally he avoided doing with the baby in the room. "Well, they're not like your family," he said, moodily staring out of the window.

"What's that supposed to mean?"

He turned. "Oh, honey, let's not quarrel."

"I'd be interested in knowing what you meant by that remark."

He shrugged. "I've never mentioned this before, but you don't realize what a shock I got when I met your family for the first time — everyone talking at the same time, no one passing things at table. . . " He passed a handkerchief over his face. "And other things," he concluded vaguely.

She felt the milk curdling in her breast. "Like what?"

He moved quickly from the window and knelt by her chair. "Let's not quarrel," he said, encircling mother and child in an embrace. "I'm used to your family now. These things don't bother me anymore. And you'll get used to my family when you get to know them."

Louise's boyfriend came for supper — Roger Hall, a slim, pale-faced fellow with big ears. He brought a box of chocolates for the mother, and a jigsaw puzzle for his girlfriend. Louise exclaimed excitedly over the gift, and Sophie remembered her husband telling her of his sister's passion for jigsaws.

At supper Sophie observed the effort her husband was making to draw her into the family circle and acquaint her through good-natured table gossip with absent members of his family.

"How's Aunt Margaret?" he asked his mother, and hardly waiting for a reply told his wife, "Aunt Margaret is Dad's sister-in-law. She was married to Dad's older brother who passed away. . . How long ago, Dad, since Uncle Dan passed away?"

"Twelve years now," the father replied.

"Aunt Margaret's very well," the mother said. "She came for lunch last Sunday and actually walked all the way from Wyndham Street. She's very spry for her years."

"Aunt Margaret was a little older than Uncle Dan," the instructor informed his wife. "How old would she be now, Mother? Eighty?"

"She'd have to be at least that. Poor dear, her appetite isn't what it used to be. But she's still very fond of chocolates," the mother said with a mischievous glance at the daughters.

This elicited a fit of giggles from the girls. The father spoke sternly. "Now now, girls, none of that."

"What were your sisters giggling about?" Sophie asked her husband when they were upstairs attending to the baby's six o'clock feeding. "Something about your Aunt Margaret being fond of chocolates—"

"Oh that. It's just a family joke. The girls get a kick out of it and so does Mother, but it probably won't strike you as being very funny."

She put the baby to her breast. "Tell me anyway."

"Well," he began dubiously, "Aunt Margaret has a lot of funny habits. Uncle Dan left her well provided for but to hear her talk you'd think she was on the point of starvation. She stints herself on food, she loves chocolates but she's too stingy to buy them. Mother always offers chocolates when she comes to visit and Aunt Margaret always refuses. Mother pretends to put them away — that's part of the game — and Aunt Margaret just about has a fit. 'Well, maybe I will,' she says, 'but just a teeny weeny one,' and invariably takes the biggest one in the box."

"Is that all? From the way your sisters were laughing I thought it would be something hilarious," she said, and knew before the words were out that she had made a mistake.

The smile left his face. He bent forward in his chair and with elbows propped on knees and chin resting on his fists stared with a disheartened gaze at the floor. "You've made up your mind to find fault."

"I'm not trying to find fault. I'm sorry, don't be mad at me."

He kept his eyes on the floor.

"Why are you so hostile to everything I say!"

Her sharpness of tone caused a disturbance in the baby; it lost its hold on the nipple and let out a wail. That brought his head up. "Watch what you're doing, you're upsetting the baby."

"I'm a stranger in this house," she said mournfully, "and you're not doing anything to help."

"You're not a stranger in this house, you're my wife. My family were looking forward to meeting you. They were prepared to like you but you're not giving them half a chance."

They were prepared to like her; that, precisely, was the rub. She had been welcomed and courteously received, but any ordinary girl he might have brought home as his wife would have been just as welcome. That was the rub, their inability to distinguish between her and any ordinary girl.

When they came downstairs, the family was grouped

around the table, and Louise, sitting in Roger's lap, was working at the jigsaw puzzle. The father brought two more chairs to the table. "Whoever invented jigsaw puzzles must have had Louise in mind," he said.

Roger, craning behind his girl's shoulder, spoke for the first time to Sophie. "She's a whiz at them," he said proudly. "I couldn't put one of those things together to save my life."

Louise was playing a lone hand. Her father had bet a dollar with Roger that Louise, with no help from anyone, would complete the puzzle in an hour flat. She played fast, her eye was quick, her fingers swift in fitting the pieces together. She was a magician at the jigsaw.

The puzzle was completed four minutes before the hour was up. Roger made a big to-do about paying up. Performing a Chaplinesque mime of penury he searched his person, showed the lining of empty pockets, and with everyone laughing took off his shoes and found a dollar there.

The mother made a pot of coffee and brought a chocolate cake to table. Roger was given a glass of ginger ale to go with his cake. "Coffee keeps me awake," he said to Sophie; his second remark to her that evening.

The father asked his son what it was like living in a big city, and Billy replied, "People aren't very friendly in a big city. I was very lonely till I got to know Soph."

"Holy smoke tempis sure fugits," said Roger, looking at his watch, and went to the hall to fetch his coat. He shook hands with the men and gave his future mother-in-law a kiss on the cheek. Louise saw him to the door and received as chaste a kiss on the cheek as he had given her mother.

Sunday morning after the baby's ten o'clock feeding, Billy said to his wife, "Honey, you don't mind if I go to church with my family?"

Sophie looked up from packing the baby's things. "You must be kidding."

"They expect me to," he said uncomfortably.

"But you're a Jew."

"Oh Lord, they don't know I've become a Jew. They expect me to go to church with them when I come home."

"You don't have to tell them you've become a Jew. Tell

them you've lost your faith. Ask them to pray for you," she said, snapping the case shut.

He sighed. "I don't know why you're trying to give me a hard time."

"What's the matter with you, Billy, can't you take a joke? I was just kidding. I don't mind if you go to church."

Twelve

They were late getting home and Mrs. Glicksman envisioning sickness, accident, was in the hall when they arrived, anxiously peering through the window. She stepped aside to permit them entry and Billy, fretting because the baby's six o'clock was overdue, brushed past his mother-in-law and carried his baby upstairs, denying her even a glimpse of the child.

"Come on, hon," he called. Sophie had stopped to speak to her mother. "I've got a class at seven." He had arranged for a substitute coach to take his classes till seven.

Angered at the rebuff to her mother, Sophie called up, "Put her down and go to work. I can wipe her ass," she added with deliberate crudeness — to pay him out for the affected manner she had felt obliged to assume in the presence of his over-polite family.

He came down the stairs wearing a hurt look and Sophie, ascending, passed him with her nose in the air. As soon as he left, her mother called from the foot of the stairs, "Sophie, he's gone. Bring her downstairs to nurse."

Sophie brought the baby down and gave her to her mother to hold while she unbuttoned her dress. "You had a good time?" Mrs. Glicksman asked, stroking the baby's head.

Sophie put the baby to her breast. "Not bad."

"They're a nice family?"

"They're very nice."

"A big family?"

"Just the parents and two sisters."

"Nice-looking girls?"

"Very nice-looking. They look like their brother."

"They're a rich family?"

"Rich — the father works in a factory and rides to work on a bicycle."

"The mother keeps a clean house?"

Sophie turned a sullen, forbidding look on her mother. "Everybody's house is clean except ours."

Mrs. Glicksman regretted the question; a clean house was a touchy subject with her daughter. She lowered her head and began twirling her thumbs. Sophie observed the movement of her lips; she was talking to herself. Musing, ruminating, withdrawn to the private world she inhabited, she was mulling over the unfairness of her daughter's accusation. I don't keep a clean house? What do I do the whole day, read a book to pass the time? Sit on my hands waiting for my servant to come and clean my house? Is there even a corner of this house that doesn't know the feel of my hand? she silently asked her twirling thumbs.

She did work hard and was, according to her lights, a good *balaboosteh*. She didn't laze around; she rose early and went to bed late. She cooked, she cleaned, she washed, she ironed; in a house there was always something to do. Friday, with the Sabbath meal to prepare and the house to clean, she was up at dawn. Before taking anything in her mouth she attended to her stove. She gave it a good shake-down, ashes and live embers spilling to the floor. Bunched-up newspaper, sticks of wood, coal — all at the same time — would be crammed in the stove and a match set to it. A second match, a third; in no time the kitchen was dense with smoke. With the fire finally caught she swept up the ashes then filled the kettle, talking all the while to herself. Maybe she'd make a *ghiveci* for a change? Her husband was fond of *ghiveci* (a Roumanian dish he had taught her to make). With the kettle on the boil she'd make a pot of tea then cut from the Sabbath loaf two thick slices of bread. "There," she'd say, sitting down to her tea and bread, "I've earned my breakfast."

By mid-afternoon with the Sabbath food prepared and pots boiling over on the stove, she went about putting her kitchen in order. Scooping up from the table spilt salt, onion skins, potato peelings, egg shells, she carried them in relayed lots to the garbage pail under the sink. Then she scoured the oilcloth-covered table, rubbing in an abrasive powder, wiping it off with a wet cloth and leaving the surface gritty. Next came the sweeping of the floor. She swept in circles, her broom going around and around, and what wasn't ground underfoot was harried and driven into corners. Water was then drawn into a bucket and the floor was washed by pushing an old broom around with a wet rag under it. When finished, the floor was dry in some places and wet in others. Newspaper was put down, soaking up the wet parts. After the kitchen, the dining room got a going over.

Her labours completed she would take a chair and fanning herself with the lifted end of her apron, survey her handiwork. "Done," she'd say, taking a satisfied look around. "Finished. The Czar may step in."

Mrs. Glicksman took a wary look at her daughter. The baby had fallen asleep at her breast and Sophie's expression, a while ago sullen and unyielding, had given way to a softer expression. Maybe now it was safe to speak?

"They made a fuss over the baby?"

"They said she was cute."

"Cute?"

She gave her mother the Yiddish translation of cute.

"That's all they said?"

Sophie rose, cradling her baby. "They don't get excited about anything."

In the beginning Billy tried his best to put that neglected rundown house in order. He was always at something — patching, painting, plastering, hammering. Defunct washers were replaced and for the first time in Sophie's memory taps stopped dripping. Broken sash cords were replaced and for once you could put up a window without a stick or empty pop bottle holding it. In the dining room he stripped the walls of its peeling paper, plastered the cracks, sanded them, then primed the walls and painted them canary yellow. He stripped the floor of its worn linoleum and painted the boards a jade green. Sophie waxed the floor, laid down a numdah rug and warned her mother about slopping things. She waxed the knickknack shelves he had knocked together from knotty pine and filled them with an assortment of doodads from Kresge's. The yellowed lace panels were thrown in the garbage and in their place she hung the twin windows with curtains of brightly patterned cotton. (Her mother retrieved the lace panels and shortened them to fit her bedroom window.) Billy took down the picture of Mary, Queen of Scots and hung in its place a Maxfield Parrish print (a gift from his mother). He took up the cracked linoleum from the kitchen floor, filled a bucket to the brim with swept-up dirt, then painted the kitchen walls and ceiling and laid new linoleum on the floor.

"He has a pair of golden hands," said Mrs. Glicksman admiringly, and a day later was tracking slopped water on the newly laid linoleum.

Sophie's days were given over to domestic chores, the care of the baby and the monitoring of her mother. She was up and down the stairs twenty times a day. Attending her baby, she hollered from upstairs, "Ma! Wipe your hands before you go to the phone, the receiver stinks of herring." Washing diapers on a washboard in the bathtub she'd leave her wash and come running downstairs. "There's something burning on the stove, can't you smell it!" Coming down for a quick bite she'd land into her mother again. "You spilt sugar on the floor. How can you walk on it without noticing? What's this grease doing on the table? What's that stink? Oh, for God's sake, you left the back door open — there's a pile of catshit in the summer kitchen!"

Whatever Sophie put her hand to she did with thoroughness and total absorption. She gave the same care to scraping stools from the baby's diaper as she did to ironing her husband's shirts. Except for Friday nights when they ate with the family, she served her husband separately cooked meals.

On weekdays Glicksman and his wife ate in the kitchen and Billy — on a clean cloth kept especially for him and on dishes kept apart for non-kosher food — sat down in the dining room with his wife. She gave him casseroles from *The Settlement Cook Book*, poached eggs, bacon, creamed vegetables, chicken à la king, creamed salmon, baked potatoes, and for dessert, which he loved best of all, she served up jello with whipped cream, puddings, junkets, prune whips. And when they went to bed he lay down in a room as clean as the one they had come from at Mrs. Todd's.

"Moving back here wasn't such a bad idea after all," he said. "Admit it, honey."

A clean room was nothing remarkable to him; to Sophie it was a novelty. A change of sheets every week was to him routine, to her a luxury. As a child she had not been taught to brush her teeth; she didn't own a toothbrush, neither did Bella. She was never bothered by her mother to keep herself clean or to take a change of underwear, so she had not cultivated habits of personal cleanliness. In this respect she was no different from other kids in the neighbourhood; they were a scruffy lot too. She was almost thirteen before it was brought to her attention that cleanliness is next to godliness.

This happened one Monday morning in grade eight under Miss Lapp, a tall, thin, old-maid teacher with black hair and white long-fingered hands.

Miss Lapp was chalking the morning's lesson on the blackboard when she stopped suddenly and turned to face her class. "There is a bad odour in this room," she said sniffing air. "An unwholesome, unwashed odour." She folded her arms over her flat chest, fingers meeting behind at the shoulder blades. "What virtue is held to be next to godliness?"

A class of thirty-six girls and not a single hand went up.

"Cleanliness," said Miss Lapp. "Cleanliness is next to godliness," she said, fingers drumming her shoulder blades. "How many of you washed before coming to school this morning?"

All hands shot up.

"Put your hands down. Those who had a bath over the weekend, raise your hands."

A consolidated show of hands.

"Put your hands down. Someone is telling an untruth. Probably more than one judging by the obnoxious odour in this room. Who are the guilty ones? Raise your hands."

Nobody's hand went up.

"Very well," said Miss Lapp, "let's get to the bottom of this." Hugging herself closer she told the girls they were to come to her desk one at a time. "We'll begin with row one. Becky Soskin, you first."

One by one they came to Miss Lapp and spread their hands on the square of white towelling she had placed on her desk. She inspected their hands, their elbows, and some had to lift their heads so she could look in their nostrils. Everyone had to unfasten or pull away from the neck the dress or blouse she was wearing, and exhibit a portion of underwear. All were smelled and sniffed at by Miss Lapp, an immaculately clean lady herself.

Waiting her turn Sophie was scratching the back of her neck raw. She couldn't remember when she had changed her underwear; that her feet were dirty she knew for sure. So far no one had been made to take off his shoes. Please God, she prayed, approaching the desk, don't let her make me take off my shoes and stockings.

Sophie was lucky. She was thirty-fourth in line and with the morning almost over Miss Lapp was fagged, used up. "Your hair needs washing," she said. "It's as black as mine but nowhere as clean." She took hold of a lock of Sophie's hair and gave it a punitive pull. With a skeletal forefinger she then took a half-hearted poke at Sophie's bosom. "And you should be wearing a brassiere."

Tuesday morning Sophie came to school with feet still dirty but hair washed and bosom flattened down with a lisle stocking she had pinched from her mother and bound herself with, knotting it behind. This gave her a little hump in the back but at least she was fairly flat in front.

A month later when she went down at recess to use the lavatory, she discovered a bloodstain on her pants. Her heart began to beat very fast and she sat a long while on the toilet, trembling. Ruby came to see what was keeping her.

"Soph? What are you doing in there? The bell's ringing."

"I've got my first period," Sophie replied, pulling squares of toilet paper from the metal dispenser to form into a pad.

They returned to class and Sophie sat at her desk till half-past three, on one haunch, with her legs crossed.

She and Ruby walked home together, Ruby a few paces behind her chum. "It's okay, Soph, nothing shows. You don't get a heavy flow with your first period."

Sophie went upstairs first to clean herself, then came down and told her mother. "My time has come."

"So soon?" said Mrs. Glicksman sighing. "Where do the years go?" Then she went to her bedroom and returned with an old towel. "You're a woman now. You'll have to keep yourself clean," she said offering the towel.

When Bella came from work she was informed by her mother that her sister had become a woman. (When Bella finished public school Glicksman had laid out eighty dollars for her to take a stenographic course at Shaw's Business Schools. She was now working in an office and paying board at home.)

Bella went up to her sister who was lying in bed. "Why are you in bed, have you got cramps?"

"No. Ruby said I wouldn't have a heavy flow with my first period but I'm bleeding like a stuck pig."

Bella went to her room and came back with a sanitary belt and Kotex. "Here, fix yourself up. Keep yourself clean when you have a period, wash before you change your pad. There's a girl in our office—" Bella pinched her nostrils.

From that time Sophie began to keep herself clean; cleaner than before, that is. Leaning over the bathtub with a soaped face cloth she washed herself all over every other day. The supply of hot water depended on the kitchen stove and in winter with the stove going all the time you could take a bath without depleting the supply; but she was impatient of a bath, it was quicker to take a wash leaning over the tub. But she didn't go altogether without bathing; she found time every second or third week to fill the tub and immerse herself altogether.

It was not till the move to Mrs. Todd's that Sophie, spurred by her husband's example, took herself in hand. At Mrs.

Todd's the bed was made as soon as they were out of it. She mopped and dusted and cleaned and pulled open her drawers a dozen times a day for the pleasure of seeing her things clean and tidily stacked. She got in the habit of taking a bath every day. It felt good to be clean; she wondered why she had been resisting it so long.

The move back to the house on Bellevue Avenue had a demoralizing effect on her. It took a day-by-day vigilance to keep herself up to the mark. But she did it, for about three months, then slid back into former habits. She went back to taking a quick wash leaning over the tub and scrubbed her feet under the running tap. True, there was now the care of the baby, whom she kept scrupulously clean, so there was no time for lolling in a tub. But she found time for other things. She found time for reading a book, time for returning it to the library and bringing another one home to read. She found time for policing her mother, a futile occupation ending with Mrs. Glicksman muttering to herself in the kitchen. She washed and ironed her husband's white gym shorts, T-shirts, handkerchiefs, shirts, jockey shorts, her own wash piling up in a corner of the clothes closet. She took fifteen minutes to iron a shirt of his but never found time for the minute it would have taken to sew a button on a blouse of hers.

Thirteen

In April when the baby was eight months old Billy undertook to clean up the back yard. It was a back-breaking job, hacking, slicing and chopping at that jungle of weeds. Mrs. Adilman, the neighbour to the right, stood at the fence praising his efforts: "Very nice, Mr. Billy. Soon we'll be able to see daylight here." Mrs. Oiffer, the neighbour to the left (known on the street as the Sly One), put in her two cents' worth. "It'll be a regular park. You'll be able to have a picnic in the yard," she said giving Mrs. Adilman a wink.

"Who knew we had such a beautiful yard?" Mrs. Glicksman said, and continued throwing leftovers to the cats and slipping out to empty her bladder.

"All that work for nothing," Billy said despondently. "Can't you speak to her, Soph?"

This was on a Friday night; they were going to have supper out then go to a movie.

"Forget it," she said, "it's hopeless."

"Hopeless is right," he returned, then muttered under his breath, "filthy woman."

Just then the baby began to cry and Sophie hurried to the room she now slept in.

During the baby's breast feeding, which lasted six months, she had been kept in their room. Two months ago when she was weaned, Glicksman, who was night watchman for a tobacco plant, had of his own accord given over for the baby's use the back room upstairs (formerly Bella's) which he had been using to catch a few hours daytime sleep before going to work.

Sophie turned the baby on her side and as she began to push the cot slowly back and forth to rock her asleep, a delayed anger rose in her. Filthy woman — that's great coming from him. I give her hell, Pa gives her hell—

She went back to the bedroom. "Filthy woman," she said wrathfully, "that's great coming from you. I give her hell, Pa gives her hell, we've got her jumping at her own shadow — and all on account of you. You haven't a clue what her life has become since we moved in. She knows you can't stand the sight of her. She keeps out of your way, didn't you ever notice that? Filthy woman! She goes shopping on swollen feet to buy fresh vegetables and fruit, not for herself or Pa, for you!"

Sophie went back to the baby, who was still crying. "Go to sleep," she said sternly to Emma, and returned to the bedroom.

"She keeps the stove going day and night so that I'll have hot water for the baby's wash and your wash and doesn't say boo about the coal bill which is twice as high as it was before. The milkman's bill is double what it used to be, and who drinks the milk? Not them — you and the baby. And my father pays it without a murmur — he's so honoured to have a gentile living in his house rent free."

She went back and forth from the baby's room to theirs, discharging in relays an accumulated load of grievances.

"You're chummy with my father and you even condescend to say a word to my mother now and then. But she's not dumb. That look in your eyes doesn't fool her. And what about me! Do you think my life is a picnic? You're at the Y basking in admiration and I'm at home washing shitty diapers, thinking up menus, battling my days through to keep things nice for you. . . I'm not even twenty years old!" she wailed, and went back to her baby.

Billy came cautiously to the room; Sophie was sullenly pushing the cot back and forth. "I'm sorry—" he began.

"Don't tell me you're sorry because it gives me a strict pain in the ass to hear it. My father goes to work with his head split open from the noise on the street so that our kid can have a room to herself." Saying, "That too you take for granted," she gave the cot a violent push. The baby let out a cry, and Sophie received from her husband a stinging slap on the cheek.

She put an unbelieving hand to her face. "You hit me! That settles it!"

She sped to the bedroom, grabbed from the clothes closet whatever came to hand, crammed it into a suitcase and ran out of the house. She didn't stop running till she got to College Street; there she stepped into a delicatessen to eat a corned beef on rye.

Now what? She wasn't in the mood for a movie. Maybe she'd go to a hotel and stay there all night; let him worry. Fifteen minutes later she was booked into a room at the downtown hotel where they had spent their wedding night. With her unpacked suitcase on the bed, she lit a cigarette and gazed at herself in the dresser mirror. The hotel that had seen the beginning of her marriage was now witnessing its finish; the drama of the situation made her cry. She stubbed out her cigarette and stood a while staring bleakly out the window. Nobody in the world knows where I am. I could die here and they wouldn't know where to find me. The thought of herself isolated, cut off from the world, brought fresh tears to her eyes.

It was too early to go to bed; she wished she had brought something to read. She remembered having seen a magazine rack in the lobby so she took the elevator down in search of something to read. Two women with a lot of makeup on were kibitzing with the desk clerk, and a man in a short-sleeve sports shirt was standing at the window, looking out. She bought a magazine then deliberated a few seconds — go back to that godforsaken room, or sit a while in the lounge in the company of human beings?

She went over to a small sofa by the wall, sat down and opened her magazine. The two women soon left and Sophie became uneasy; she could be taken for a pickup sitting alone in the lounge of a downtown hotel. The thought was hardly formulated when the man in the sports shirt was sitting beside her, offering a cigarette from a pack of Camels.

"No, thank you. I'm not a pickup," she said severely.

He laughed. "Don't you think I can tell the difference?"

Sophie accepted a Camel.

He told her he was a shoe salesman from New York and was in Toronto placing his line with some of the smarter shoe stores. Her small foot he judged to be a sample size. Then he noticed the wedding ring on her finger. "Don't tell me you're married. You don't look old enough."

"Not only married but the mother of an eight-month-old baby."

The salesman whistled.

She told him she had had a quarrel with her husband. "I'm a runaway wife," she said glibly.

"Runaway wife, that's cute."

He said he was glad he had run into her. "People on the whole aren't very friendly in this burg. Don't get me wrong. I'm not knocking Toronto. I like the business I'm getting but people on the whole—" he concluded with a shrug.

"Are people in New York friendlier?"

"Much."

Eleven o'clock and he was still talking. Sophie said it was time she was getting back to her room. Time for him too, he said. They took the elevator up; his room too was on the fifth floor. He invited her to have a nightcap with him. "Just one," he coaxed, holding the door, and she preceded him into the room. She looked around for a place to sit; the only chair in the room held his suitcase with a topcoat draped over it. "Make yourself at home," he said. "Sit on the bed."

He took a bottle from his suitcase, brought two glasses from the bathroom and poured in each glass a good-sized drink. "Say when," he said, holding the water jug.

"I take mine neat," said Sophie, reaching for the glass. She swallowed the whiskey in one gulp.

The salesman whistled.

The whiskey burned her throat, sent her head spinning and

loosened her tongue. "My husband would have a fit if he could see me," she giggled. "Our wedding night was spent in this hotel but I don't remember what room we were in or even what floor we were on."

"You had your mind on other things?" he said, putting himself beside her on the bed.

"I shouldn't be telling you this — you're a comparative stranger — but our wedding night was a fiasco. In fact I was still a virgin a week after we were married."

"Boy, what a *shlemozzl* you must of married."

Sophie wondered if he was Jewish. There *was* a Jewish cast to his features. She rose on unsteady legs. "Thank you for the nightcap."

He shoved her back on the bed. "Stay a while."

The next minute he had shucked his pants and was on top of her, pulling up her skirt. She struggled, she writhed and squirmed. "Please let me up."

"Relax," he said. "Don't be so hard to get along with." Breathing heavily he held her down with one hand and pulled off her pants with the other.

Sophie was struck with terror at the transformation in the man; he had become a beast, a rapist, there was murder in his eye. "Please let me up," she begged, twisting and turning to keep him from getting at her. "Let me up! I'm a Jewish girl," she wailed, pleading racial immunity.

When that didn't stop him she sank her teeth in his arm, drawing blood. He let out a cry of pain and hit her a clip with his elbow. Leaving her pants on the floor where he had thrown them, she ran for the door and tried to unbolt the lock but couldn't get it to work. She turned her back to the door and faced him. "Let me out! I'll scream! This is statutory rape!"

Sucking blood from his arm the salesman hiked up his boxer shorts, came to the door and unbolted the lock. Then he turned her around and with a vicious lift of the knee gave her a swift kick in the behind, calling after her as she ran down the hall, "You lousy little cock-teaser!"

Sophie opened the door to her room, grabbed the case from her bed and took the five flights running, her face burning at the name he had called her.

It was after twelve when Sophie got home. Billy was in bed, reading Glicksman's daily. He put down the paper and gave her a searching look. Sophie's hand automatically crept to the back of her neck. If he asks where I've been I'll say I went to a movie.

"Have you had anything to eat?" he asked.

She nodded and withdrew her hand from her neck.

"Come to bed then."

She undressed behind the closet door so that he wouldn't see she wasn't wearing pants, hung her dress on a hanger, threw the brassiere she had been wearing over a week in a corner of the closet, and got into bed.

"That was nice," he said after they made love, and ruefully added, "You said some terrible things to me, honey."

"I didn't mean them."

He kissed her, put out the light and before long was asleep. She lay awake a long while, caressing his arm which was around her waist. Suddenly she switched on the light and shook him gently by the shoulder. "Billy, wake up." He groaned and turned on his other side. She shook him again.

"Wake up, Billy. It's important, our future life depends on it." He didn't move. "Emma's life depends on it," she said, and at once he was awake. He sat up and glanced uncomprehendingly around the room. Then he lay back. "What's the matter with you, Soph? Emma's asleep. Why did you wake me up?"

"There are certain things we have to talk about, Billy. We've got to get out of this house."

"Oh Lord, what a time to bring that up. Can't it wait till tomorrow?"

"No, tomorrow I might not feel as desperate as I do right now. I might let it slide again. Billy, our marriage is heading for the rocks."

He sighed. He closed his eyes. "If only you wouldn't exaggerate everything."

She gave him a wallop on the shoulder. "Sit up. I want you to listen to me."

He propped his pillow behind his head. "Why's our marriage going on the rocks? What put that idea in your head?"

"You slapped my face."

He kissed the slapped cheek. "I'm sorry."

"I know you're sorry, that's not what I'm driving at. What I'm trying to tell you is that this house is having a terrible effect on you and you don't even realize it. You — a gentleman — to slap his wife in the face? It's all on account of living in this house. You're not the same Billy James you were when we were living at Mrs. Todd's. And I'm not the same either. The things that *eat* at me in this house and you're not even aware of them. My mother peeing in the yard, Mrs. Oiffer laughing at her, and even the Adilmans, they're so friendly — it's Mr. Billy this and Mr. Billy that, but don't kid yourself, they're terrible hypocrites. To them you're still the *shaygets* that Glicksman's daughter married and it gives them something more to laugh about."

"They know I've become a Jew."

"Oh, come on, Billy, such a Jew as you've become. I'm not criticizing you, you're as good a Jew as my father is. It's the house that's jinxing us. Especially me. At Mrs. Todd's I took a bath every day, I looked after my underwear. Here I've become a slob the way I used to be before you knew me. You don't notice these things about me."

Saying, "Wait, I'll show you something," she got out of bed and rooted round the floor of the clothes closet. "Look at my brassiere!" she cried, holding it aloft like a banner.

Fourteen

To save their marriage they went next morning after breakfast in search of a place to live. After looking at several
places, none suitable and all highly priced, they came across
a FLAT TO LET sign in the window of a nice-looking house
on Palmerston Boulevard. A middle-aged woman with a wrinkled neck and dyed black hair opened the door to them.
"With pleasure," she replied to their request to see the flat,
and led them into a hall with a highly polished floor. Following her up the carpeted staircase, Sophie whispered, "She'll
want a fortune."

They were shown three lovely rooms, Sophie commenting
admiringly and Mrs. Little, the landlady, modestly acceding.
Finally the burning question, How much? They were stunned by the figure she named; they had been asked twice as
much for places which couldn't compare with this.

Billy put his hand in his pocket. "That's very reasonable."

"But only to the right people," said Mrs. Little.

The instructor withdrew an empty hand from his pocket.

"We can give you references," Sophie offered.

"I don't need references, I go by my instincts. I like you
people and the place is yours if you are willing to overlook

a couple of little inconveniences. You'll have to share a bath-room. There's only one and we use it too. But we're a small family — just myself, my husband and our son Harold who is sixteen. A very intelligent boy with a high I.Q.," she said, smoothing back a strand of lacquered black hair. She moved to the bathroom and knocked sharply on the door. "Morris?"

The door opened and Mr. Little emerged, a short stocky man with a bald head and a folded newspaper under his arm. Billy, giving his name, extended a hand. "The other incon-venience," Mrs. Little was telling Sophie, "is that our son Harold occupies a room on this floor."

Alcoved in the wall on the bathroom side was a closed door. "This is my son's room," said Mrs. Little lightly tap-ping a red fingernail on the door. "He's a very studious boy and very shy. You won't know there's another person on the floor." She looked to her husband for confirmation. "Morris?"

He inclined his head. "Absolutely."

Mrs. Little put her arm through her husband's. "Come, Morris, we'll leave the young couple while they make up their minds," she said, and they descended the stairs arm in arm.

"What do you think?" Billy said to his wife. "I say we should take it. We'll never find a place like this."

Sophie put her finger to her lips. "They're Jewish," she whispered. "They don't speak with an accent but I'm sure they're Jewish. I think we should tell them you're a convert-ed Jew. I'd hate to move in and then have them start whis-pering behind our backs."

"It's more important to tell them we have a baby. We didn't say anything about having a child."

Mr. and Mrs. Little met with them at the foot of the stairs.

"We love the flat," Sophie said, "and we'd like to take it but we think you should know—"

"We have a baby," Billy interposed. "She's only eight months old but she's very good."

Mrs. Little smiled. "We love children. It'll be a pleasure to have a baby in the house. Morris?" Confirming, her husband gave her a bald nod.

"Another thing you should know — my husband is a converted Jew," Sophie blurted, her face getting red.

"We are not narrow-minded people," said Mrs. Little. "The couple before you, the husband was white and the wife Japanese. Morris?"

Sunday morning after Billy left for work, Sophie dressed the baby for an airing in her pram, then went down to the kitchen to speak to her mother. "I have to tell you something," she began. "We're going to move, Ma. We found a place yesterday, three nice rooms, very cheap."

Mrs. Glicksman put down her glass of tea. "I said to Pa something is going on." She lowered her head and put her hands in her lap. "His doing," she said to her twirling thumbs.

"Why do you blame *him* for everything?"

Her mother raised her head. "When?" she said bleakly. "When are you going to move?"

"In about two weeks. We'll have to buy furniture first."

She wheeled the baby to the park then sat on a bench with pencil and paper, making a list of what they'd need. Everything. Bed, bedding, towels, dishes, cutlery, pots and pans, curtains, carpets, a new bed for Emma, a kitchen table, chairs, a chesterfield suite. She wondered how much money they had in the bank. She never asked and he never said. Nine months rent free, he must have saved something. It came to her — not for the first time — that he was odd about money. Not exactly stingy but kind of secretive.

She wheeled the carriage home and parked it on the verandah, leaving the baby asleep. Passing through the hall she heard her parents in the kitchen. They were sitting opposite each other at the table and as soon as she made her appearance conversation between them ceased.

Glicksman pushed his glasses to his forehead. "Ma tells me you're moving. What's the matter, aren't you comfortable here?"

"Of course we are but that's got nothing to do with it. We've been living here long enough free, gratis. It's time my husband had the responsibility of paying rent instead of parking here with his family like a *schnorrer*."

"That's why you're moving? You can start paying rent here."

"Very funny," his daughter replied.

"Where are you moving?"

"To Palmerston Boulevard, just above College."

"Let me hear a word too," said Mrs. Glicksman, looking from one to the other.

"They're moving to Palmerston Boulevard," her husband said in Yiddish.

She looked aghast. "Where?"

"Palmerston Boulevard," he repeated. "That's not in Siberia. It's a fifteen-minute walk from here."

Later in the day Billy telephoned from the Y. "Did you tell them?" he asked.

"Yes, they know now. How much money have we got in the bank?"

"Why?"

"What do you mean, why?" she said irritably. "We'll have to buy furniture and a lot of other things. I thought I'd go downtown tomorrow but I can't just start buying without knowing what we can afford."

"I have to go, hon. We'll talk about it when I get home. Don't make supper for me. I'll be late tonight. There's a board meeting."

When he came home at half-past ten he heard his wife talking with her mother in the kitchen. "Soph?" he called from the hall. "I'm going up to bed. Will you be long?"

"I'll be right up," she replied, then turned to her mother who was saying, "The house without Emma will be like a tomb. She's the light of my eyes, Sophie. The joy in my heart."

"It's not the end of the world," said Sophie. "You'll see her Fridays when we come for supper and I'll bring her over during the week too. You'll see enough of her, don't worry."

Her husband was in bed when she came up, a worried expression on his face. "How much will you need?" he asked.

"I don't know. We're starting from scratch, we need everything. It'll take a lot of money. How much have you got in the bank?"

He shrugged. "About six hundred."

"Is that all?"

"A bit more," he said cautiously, "but we can't leave ourselves strapped. What if you get sick, or Emma? Doctors' bills come high."

"Don't be so pessimistic, Billy. We'll worry about that when the time comes."

"I might get sick," he said glumly. "Then what?"

"You're healthy and you're as strong as an ox."

He sighed. "I'm beginning to be worried about my physical condition. I'm getting stale, Soph. I can take three gym classes in a row without getting up a sweat, and that's not a good sign."

Leaving Emma with her mother, Sophie went downtown next day to buy the things they would need. She was an unpractised shopper; with no patience for pricing, comparing, selecting, the six hundred was used up before she was halfway through her list. The rest, including a fourposter bed, was bought on time. With everything on her list accounted for, she went down to the coffee shop before going home, to tot up what she had spent. A fortune.

"Good Lord, Soph, you must have gone haywire," said Billy, examining the duplicate bills. "A coffee table, a wardrobe, a *fourposter*." He wiped the sweat from his forehead.

"I thought you said you couldn't work up a sweat?"

"That's not funny, Soph. How are we ever going to pay for it?"

Though worried herself, she said, "Don't worry about it, Billy, we'll manage. We've got twenty-four months to pay."

Three days later around eleven in the morning, there was a call from their landlady. "Mrs. James? This is Mrs. Little."

"Yes?" said Sophie.

Silence on the phone, then a deep intake of breath. "I'm a nervous wreck. There's a delivery at the door every half hour. It's raining and they come in like bulldozers with wet shoes, tracking dirt through my hall. And if I say a word they're rude to me. I'm getting one of my migraines. That will finish me for the day. They said there's more to come but I won't be able to go to the door. I'd like you to be here as soon as possible and attend to it yourself. Please." She hung up.

90

It was pouring when Sophie arrived, and a van was parked in front of the house. Going up the verandah steps she noticed two pairs of men's shoes near the doorsill. Wiping her own shoes on the mat, she rang the bell, though the door was open, and stepped into the hall.

Two shoeless truckers were easing the fourposter up the stairs. The first man, halfway up, was advancing backwards; the second man, facing him, was four steps below; and immediately behind him, progressing step by step, was Mrs. Little directing the operation.

Forehead bound in a white cloth, "Please," she was exhorting, "please be careful. You're scraping my wall! Lean the bed over to the left a little. That's too far! You'll break my banister."

The bed manoeuvred at last to the landing, the truckers asked, "Where's it to go?"

"Morris!" Mrs. Little cried, and Mr. Little with a folded newspaper under his arm emerged from the bathroom. "What's the m-m-matter?" he stammered.

"Show them where the bed goes," she snapped.

With the back of her hand pressed to the cloth on her forehead and eyes half closed, she descended the stairs mimicking her husband's speech defect, opening and shutting her mouth like a fish out of water: "What's the m-m-matter?"

It was not till she was at the foot of the stairs that she saw her new tenant in the hall; an ill-timed arrival, an unlooked-for audience to her show of nastiness.

Her face coloured. "There's no living with me when I get one of my migraines. I'm just not the same person. I must lie down, will you excuse me?" She paused to wipe finger marks from the newel post with a duster from her pocket. "You'd better go up, dear, and tell them exactly where you want the bed placed."

The following Saturday the flat was ready for occupancy. After breakfast Billy went upstairs to pack and Sophie stayed down to tell her mother they would be moving in a couple of hours. "We might as well, Ma, the place is ready for us."

Mrs. Glicksman put down her glass of tea and rose from her chair. "I'll wake up Pa. He doesn't know you're moving so soon."

"Let him sleep. It'll take a while to pack. You'll wake him up before we leave," Sophie said, lifting the baby from her highchair.

"Leave her here," said Mrs. Glicksman sharply. "Go, leave her here till you'll get ready. Let me fill my eyes at least."

Sophie settled the baby back in her highchair and went up to help her husband with the packing.

When she came down, Glicksman was sitting at the table with the child in his arms, and his wife sat silently opposite, staring at the twirling thumbs in her lap. She glanced up at Sophie's approach.

"What's the matter?" said Sophie, taking a chair next to her. "You act like you're sitting *shivah* for us."

"Bite your tongue," her mother said sharply.

Billy came to the kitchen and told his wife he had called a cab. "But they won't take the carriage or highchair. I'll have to come back for them."

"Wait a minute," said Glicksman. "I know a man, I play pinochle with him. He's a small mover. He has a little truck and if I ask him he'll do me a favour. The only thing is you'll have to wait till tomorrow. He's a religious man, he doesn't take his truck out on Saturday."

"Don't bother, Pa," said Sophie. "We can do without the carriage for a day, but not the highchair. Billy can come back for them." She held her hands out for the baby. "Give her to me, I'll put her coat on." She dressed the child and gave her to her mother to hold.

"I'm not good at making speeches," Billy was saying to Glicksman. "But thank you. Thank you for everything." Glicksman courteously inclined his head. "For nothing," he demurred. Billy turned to his wife. "Soph, tell your mother I appreciate everything."

"He says," Sophie began, but her mother didn't wait to hear her out. She smiled at her son-in-law and ducked her head in acknowledgement; she understood without knowing his language that a courtesy was being directed to her.

The front door was suddenly thrust open and the bellow "Taxi!" resounded through the hall.

Mrs. Glicksman gave the baby to her daughter, and solemnly they all proceeded to the hall. "Good-bye, Ma," Sophie said, patting her on the shoulder. Mrs. Glicksman covered Sophie's hand with hers and held it pressed to her shoulder. Then she took the baby's hand and kissed it. "Take good care on her."

When they arrived at their new lodgings, the door was opened by the 16-year-old son. "I'm Harold," he announced, "scion of a long line of Littles." Holding the door he made them a sweeping bow. "Welcome to the family manse." Then called over his shoulder, "Mother, they're here."

Mrs. Little came to the hall. Fingernails freshly done, she held her arms at her sides. "Welcome," she said and excused herself for not offering her hand. "My nails are wet."

Harold dropped his eyes to his mother's red nails. "With my father's blood," he said. His mother gave him a cuff with her elbow. "Don't show off," she said, and turned her attention to the baby. "What a beautiful child." She stretched her neck, bringing her face close to the baby's. "You're going to grow up to be a little heartbreaker," she said gaily; and Emma, gazing solemnly at Mrs. Little, burst into tears.

Fifteen

Sophie unpacked Emma's things first, then made her bed and put her bottle on to warm while Billy, with the child in his lap and a tin of baby food before him, was coaxing her to eat her lunch. Used to being fed sitting in her highchair, Emma turned her head away at every spoonful offered. "Don't force her," said Sophie, taking the baby from him. "I'll put her down with her bottle, that'll satisfy her. She'll sleep for a couple of hours. Meantime we can get a few things unpacked."

That done, Sophie began making up the fourposter, and Billy, standing on a kitchen chair, tackled the hanging of the venetian blinds. Working quietly they were startled by the sound of Emma's bottle landing on the floor: flinging her bottle over the side when she was finished was a habit recently acquired. "She's so sweet when she does that," Billy whispered, pausing to cast a loving glance at his daughter. Sophie, absorbed in tucking in sheets, nodded absently, then looked up at the sound of footsteps padding along the hall.

It was Mrs. Little. Feet shod in satin mules with feathered pompons, she stood in the door with her hands clasped at her bosom. "What happened?" she asked, taking a tiny step into the room. "I thought somebody fell."

Sophie, plumping new pillows, assured her no one had fallen. Billy turned his head. "It was only the baby's bottle." Courteously he descended from his chair, leaving the venetian blind hanging aslant. "She throws it over the side of the bed when she's finished with it," he explained.

Mrs. Little's eyes went to the bottle lying on its side, a few drops of milk oozing from the nipple onto the highly polished parquet floor. "And the noise doesn't wake her?" she asked, advancing a few steps into the room. Once in, she moved quickly to the bottle and picked it up. Stooped and holding the bottle with one hand, she withdrew a piece of Kleenex from her pocket and took a swipe at the droplets of milk. Then she straightened, smiled at the instructor and held out the bottle to him — Sophie noticing that her eyes had dropped to the level below his belt. She turned abruptly to the door. "Don't let me hold you up," she said, gaily waved her hand and was gone.

Billy cast his eyes down to where the landlady's gaze had lingered. "Whew!" he said, drawing a relieved sigh. "I thought my fly was undone."

"She was looking, wasn't she?" said Sophie. "I thought it was only my dirty mind. You know, Billy, I remember reading somewhere that compulsive cleaners — you saw how she couldn't resist wiping up that drop of milk — are sexually frustrated women."

"That doesn't make sense. It doesn't follow that good housekeepers are sexually frustrated women. She happened to look at my fly, by accident probably. One thing sure," he said soberly, "she's a very house-proud woman. We'll have to watch ourselves," and got back on his chair. "Good Lord!" he said suddenly. "Come and see this."

On their side of the street, about three or four houses away, was Glicksman. He had on his new suit and his good fedora, and was wheeling his granddaughter's carriage, pausing as he approached to scrutinize the house number through his dollar eyeglasses. Beside him, carrying the highchair, was a 13-year-old boy, fat, with a buttery complexion and a head taller than Glicksman.

"Who's that with him?" Billy asked, and Sophie, peering,

laughed. "It's Moishe Titty, for God's sake."

Moishe, whose surname was Ceifets, lived with his family across the street from the Glicksmans. The nickname Moishe Titty had attached itself to him because it had taken his mother four years to wean him off the breast. Two or three times a day during the summer months, when Moishe was almost four, Mrs. Ceifets, a big woman, would sit herself on the verandah, bare her breast and call in a sing-song voice to Moishe, playing in their front yard with the kids: "Moishe! Titty! Titty, Moishe. Titteee!" Moishe would leave the kids, jump up on her lap and take the breast to his mouth. Finished, he'd wipe his mouth with the back of his hand, jump off his mother's lap and rejoin the kids in their play.

Sophie moved away from the window. "Leave the blind. Let's get downstairs before my father rings the bell."

The highchair and carriage had been set down flush with the doorsill. Standing a few feet from the edge of the verandah was Moishe Titty, gazing obliquely at the quarter in his open hand. "What's the matter?" Glicksman was saying. "A quarter isn't enough? When I was a boy your age. . ."

Unaware of his daughter's and son-in-law's presence, he proceeded to give Moishe Titty an abridged account of how he, Avrom Glicksman, a boy of thirteen, had to walk two miles from where he lived in Focsani, Roumania, to the vineyard where he worked from sunup till sundown, tamping down grapes in his bare feet, his broken shoes tied around his neck for fear they'd be stolen. And his pay for the day's work? Six lei and a loaf of bread. "You know how much six lei is, Moishe?" The boy shook his head. "Six cents," said Glicksman righteously. "And a quarter isn't enough to carry a highchair a few blocks?"

"I didn't say nothing," Moishe Titty said, pocketing the quarter and backing away. "I didn't expect you'll gimme more than a dime or fifteen cents."

"Where did you dig up Moishe Titty?" Sophie asked, laughing.

A look of disapproval crossed her father's features. Crudeness of speech offended him, especially in a woman. "Call him by his right name," he said.

"That was very thoughtful of you," Billy said. Feeling in his pocket, he skirted the highchair and carriage which were blocking the doorway, brought out a quarter and offered it to his father-in-law.

"Please," said Glicksman, making a gesture of refusal with his hand.

"Please take it," said Billy.

Her husband pressing the quarter on her father brought an angry flush to Sophie's cheeks. "Put that quarter away," she said sharply. "You're insulting my father."

Embarrassed, Billy glanced briefly in his wife's direction, then lowered his eyes and gazed at the quarter which lay like lead in his hand. Glicksman looked at his shoes and muttered, "Don't fight." Sophie began scratching her neck and they stood there all three, mired.

Making the first move, Billy put the quarter in his pocket and took hold of the highchair. "I'll take this up first," he said.

Sophie dropped her hand to her side. "Come up and see our place, Pa?"

"Not now, you spoiled everything. I wouldn't be comfortable," he said and turned to go down the steps.

Sophie stepped around from behind the carriage and put her hand on his arm. "How did I spoil everything? What did I say that was so terrible?"

"It's not what you said, it's the way you looked. If Ma looked at me like that it would make me feel like a nothing."

"How can you compare me with Ma?" Sophie said stubbornly.

"I don't compare you with Ma, she's a better woman. You could take a lesson from her how to respect a husband."

Sophie, standing with her back to the door, noticed that his eyes had shifted from her face and were now concentrated at a point beyond her head. He suddenly bared his head. Face relaxed, fedora held in one hand against his chest, he stood in courtly attention at the approach of Mrs. Little.

"Oh!" she said. "The door was open and I thought—" She retreated a step. "Excuse me."

Thankful for the leavening presence of a third person,

Sophie put in quickly, "Don't go, Mrs. Little. I'd like you to meet my father, Mr. Glicksman."

Barricaded behind the carriage, the landlady reached her hand across its top and offered it to Glicksman. "Glick means luck. Glicksman means lucky man. *Are* you a lucky man?" she said, leaving her hand in his a second longer than necessary.

Glicksman smiled. "I wouldn't say *un*lucky."

"I think I recognize that accent. See if I can guess what part of Europe you're from," she said, tapping her lips with a red-tipped finger.

Glicksman's smile broadened. "From three words?"

Assuming a little-girl-like ruminative pose, she laid her finger along her cheek and said, "Say three more words."

"One two three," he said teasingly.

His vexation with his daughter had subsided; the last trace of displeasure had left his face and his manner now was skittish, flirtatious. This kind of behaviour on her father's part was altogether outside Sophie's experience of him. She was embarrassed for him. To put an end to his foolishness, she said matter-of-factly, "My father comes from Roumania."

"Roumania! You come from a very romantic country," said Mrs. Little, touching her hand to her dyed head.

"*And* an anti-Semitic one," Sophie said severely.

"King Carol. His love affair with Lupescu," the landlady went on, paying her tenant no heed. "To give up a queen for a junk dealer's daughter. They say he'll even give up his throne if he has to."

"A queen, yes," said Glicksman. "A throne he will not be so anxious to give up. He will fight and if the Iron Guard steps in—" he shook his head—"it will cause a lot of trouble for our people."

That didn't faze her. "And your music!" She hummed a few bars from Enesco's Roumanian Rhapsody. "It was nice talking to you," she said. Then she stepped into the hall calling over her shoulder, "Auf wiedersehn."

Glicksman put his hat back on his head. "Auf wiedersehn," he mused. "She comes from Austria?"

"I don't know where she comes from," Sophie said crossly. "Are you coming up?"

"I told you no." Saluting his daughter with a touch to the brim of his hat, he turned and went down the steps.

"Where's your father?" Billy said, coming down for the carriage.

"He went home, I guess. I asked him to come up but he wouldn't."

"I didn't mean to hurt his feelings," he said tonelessly.

She was about to tell him the fault was hers but the aggrieved look he was wearing put her out of patience. Without saying anything, she went up the stairs and he, following, ascended backwards, pulling the carriage up step by step on its back wheels.

Attaining the landing, he left the carriage and looked in the kitchen, where his wife was unpacking dishes. "Where do you want me to put the carriage?" He spoke dispiritedly and the expression on his face was that of a long-suffering put-upon man.

For answer she bunched a crumpled sheet of wrapping tissue in her fist and threw it angrily to the floor. "First my father picks a fight with me, and now you're sulking."

"Shh! They'll hear you downstairs," he cautioned.

"Why are you always so afraid of people hearing us!" she demanded; then added mournfully, "It's our first day here and we're quarrelling."

He moved quickly to where she was standing and put his arms around her. "I'm sorry. Let's not quarrel," he said, and lifted her head for a kiss. "You flare up at me so often I get the feeling sometimes that you hate me."

She kissed him on the cheek and on the mouth. "I love you. I always say 'Bless you' to myself when you sneeze. I'll bet you don't say that when I sneeze?"

He admitted guiltily that he didn't, then he pressed himself against her and whispered, "Let's initiate the four-poster."

She smiled, considering; then very positively shook her head. "There's too much to do, Billy. And there's shopping to be done. We didn't bring any food."

He was not put off by her refusal. He could tell by her tone that she was already half-persuaded. He held out his hand to her. "Come on, honey, I'll do the shopping afterwards," and they proceeded to the bedroom, the captor leading his willing captive by the hand.

With the screen bought for that purpose, he screened off the sleeping child and began to undress. Sophie got out of her dress, then took off just what was necessary and got into bed wearing her bra, garter belt and stockings.

"What are you doing?" she said as he stooped to his socks. "You don't have to take your socks off unless you intend to stay in bed the rest of the day."

He laughed and got into bed with his socks on.

They lay embraced a while, and as he was unfastening her bra, murmuring, "Take it off," their ears were assailed by a vibrant, whirring noise.

"What's that?" said Sophie, sitting up.

She got out of bed and opened the door a crack. A cylindrical-shaped vacuum cleaner, trailing a long cord, had been set on the landing at the head of the stairs and Mrs. Little, a few steps below, was vacuuming the carpeted stairs, tread and riser. Sophie shut the door and began to get dressed.

Billy got out of bed. "What are you doing?"

"She's vacuuming the stairs," said Sophie, getting into her dress. "You must have left marks dragging the carriage up." Her hand was on the knob. "I'll have to at least offer to do the stairs."

"That's not fair. You've got me all worked up." Just then the baby woke and set up a wail. "Oh Lord," he groaned, "that does it."

He went to the baby, she went to the hall. The noise of the machine subsided and there was silence except for their voices, his wife's and Mrs. Little's. Then the machine started again, and Sophie was back in the room.

"I insisted on doing the stairs but she wouldn't let me. She said she doesn't mind housework, she enjoys it."

The baby had stopped crying and Billy with only his socks on was walking the floor with her in his arms, crooning, comforting her.

"And you know something? I believe she actually does enjoy housework. Talk about sexually frustrated women, she's rampant! You should have seen her flirting with my father."

100

Her husband eased the child from his shoulder and held her at arm's length, her face level with his. "Bad noise all gone now. Smile for Daddy?"

"Might as well talk to the wall," Sophie muttered and flounced out of the room.

She took Emma from him when he came to the kitchen and settled her in her highchair with a biscuit. "I'll make up a shopping list," she said, took up her pencil and sat listlessly down to a scratch pad she had been doodling on.

He sat down beside her. "What's the matter, Soph?"

"I think it was a terrible mistake to move here. We've got ourselves in debt. It'll take years to pay for all that furniture. And that woman. If she's going to get busy with the vacuum every time we take the carriage up or down the stairs. . . "

"There must be a place downstairs where we can keep the carriage. I'll ask. Come on, Soph, tell me what to get, I'm hungry."

She tore off the scratched piece of paper, reversed it to its clean side and held her pencil poised. "And that bathroom," she said gloomily, "it looks as if it's never been used. It looks like a model bathroom in a display window. How am I going to keep Emma from splashing? Is she going to come running up with a rag every time I give Emma a bath? That woman is going to be impossible to live with. We won't be able to call our souls our own in this house. I should have known that the day our furniture was moved in. I told you she made the movers take their shoes off? — what are you *doing*?" she said irritably.

Billy, who had been sitting half-turned in his chair with his profile to the door, had taken hold of her arm, his fingers digging warningly in the fleshy part above her elbow. He rose suddenly to his feet. "Come in, Mrs. Little," he said, smiling, and Sophie, grasping the awful significance of his warning, sat with her back to the door as if turned to stone.

"I hope I'm not interrupting?" said Mrs. Little, stopping at the door. She was carrying a silver tea tray with a pot of coffee on it, cream and sugar, a plate of sandwiches and two pieces of cake. "A little welcoming lunch for my new tenants," she said, offering the tray.

101

"That's very kind of you," said Billy. He took the tray and set it on the table. "Soph?" he said; she was still sitting with her back to the door.

She got up from her chair. "Thank you. Thank you very much. I was just saying to my husband that if we didn't get some food in soon we'd both starve," she brought out in a rush.

Smiling, Mrs. Little said, "*Bon appetit*," and proceeded to the stairs.

Sophie ran after her. "Oh, Mrs. Little, my father wanted to know if you come from Austria?"

"Austria? Why? Do I speak with an accent?"

Sophie shook her head. "Oh no! You haven't got a trace of an accent," she said earnestly.

She returned to the kitchen and shut the door behind her. "How long was she standing here before you saw her? What was I saying? Did she hear me?"

"Calm down, Soph."

"Don't tell me to calm down!" she said angrily. "Answer me for once. Haven't you any understanding of how I feel?"

He looked her way a second and said quietly, "Don't talk to me like that, Soph. I have feelings too." He lifted the baby from her highchair and sat down with her in his lap. "When Mrs. Little came up, you were saying we wouldn't be able to call our souls our own in this house," he said evenly. "I saw her coming and tried to warn you but you kept right on."

She wrung her hands. "Where was she when I said she made the movers take off their shoes?"

"At the door."

She moaned and sank into a chair. "I feel sick."

He reached over and took her hand away from her neck. "I don't think she heard anything, she didn't act like it."

"Are you sure?"

"I'm sure of it. If she had heard anything, she wouldn't have been so eh—"

"Casual?" she prompted. "Unruffled? Suave?"

He nodded to all three words. "Pour the coffee, hon. Let's have a sandwich. That cake looks good."

Later, after the baby had been fed and put to bed for the night, they sat down to a meal of boughten food which Billy, who had done the shopping without a list, had picked up in a hurry before Saturday closing time. He ate with appetite; she picked at her food.

"What's the matter, hon?" he asked.

She put down her knife and fork. "I'm not a fit mother. That child should be taken away from me."

"Soph! Don't say things like that. It gives me the heebie-jeebies." She had probably been impatient with Emma while he was out shopping, scolded her, perhaps, and now it was on her conscience; he wished she wouldn't dramatize the least little thing. "Finish your supper," he said.

She poked aimlessly at her food. "It's our first day here and I've quarrelled with my father, I've quarrelled with you, I insulted Mrs. Little behind her back — I'm sure she heard every word I said — and when you were out shopping I got so mad at Emma for being cranky I could have killed her. I actually lifted my hand to hit her."

He gasped.

"It took all my control not to. I hollered at her and she cried."

He gathered up the dishes and put them in the sink. "You're overtired. Come to bed," he said, drawing her out of her chair.

He opened the door to the bedroom. "I'm going to brush my teeth. Cheer up, hon." He gave her a squeeze. "We've got a date."

She was in bed when he came back. He undressed and got in beside her. "I love you," he whispered.

She lay inertly in his embrace. "You wouldn't if you knew what I was really like. I'm a miserable person."

"No, you're not. You're my own sweet wife."

He rocked her in his arms and sang softly in her ear: *"We'll ride through clo-ver and proudly we'll explain, Mister and Missus is the name/ We'll phone all ov-er, to Tom and Dick and Mame, Mister and Missus is the name/ And then to your peo-ple and my peo-ple we'll write this way/ We're wed-ded and we're head-ed for hap-py days."*

He was tone deaf, unable to carry even a simple tune, and his voice, which always gave her the giggles, now for some reason saddened her. His atonal rendition of the buoyant tune came to her as a poignant lament, reflecting the deepest faults in her nature. She wanted to weep for having shamed him before her father, for having brought an innocent child to tears. She wanted to weep for the hard-earned money she had squandered on furniture, for the sweat on his brow when he wrote the cheque, for the pain he had suffered for love of her to become a circumcised Jew. Impulsively she brought his hand to her mouth and kissed it.

"Hey!" he cried, and drew his hand away, embarrassed.

He turned off the bedside lamp and took her in his arms. "Soph? Let's do it a different way."

"How?"

"With you on top."

He nestled close and told her he had heard some guys talking in the locker room. "They said there's at least a hundred different ways." He nudged her. "Are you game?"

Sophie knew all about the different ways (from books). A hundred was an exaggeration but she wasn't about to argue the point. "You're the boss," she said demurely; and the instructor, tipped by the guys in the locker room to a whole new world of erotica, pulled his wife on top and showed her how to do it a different way.

They went to sleep in each other's arms, a change from spoon fashion, their customary way after making love. Having mastered an unpractised feat to the satisfaction of both parties, the instructor soon fell tranquilly asleep, while Sophie (a book-learned debauchee from way back) drowsed languorously in his embrace, her thoughts on one thing and another.

The room had suddenly grown cold. Wind rattled the venetian blinds and as Sophie went to shut the window a light came on in the hall and the door blew open. Looming in the doorway was Mrs. Little. She had on a black velvet evening cape and her head was turbaned like a Mohammedan. *"Bon soir,"* she said, drawing on long evening gloves. "Where's my silver tea tray?"

Sophie, naked, drew her knees together, folded her hands and modestly covered her place. "In the kitchen," she said.

"There's more in the kitchen than meets the eye," said Mrs. Little mysteriously; and Glicksman came dancing out of the kitchen.

A prancing bacchant in rundown shoes with a bottle of wine in his hand, he jigged the length of the hall to where the landlady stood. "For you," he said, proffering the bottle of wine he had made himself. "Old World courtesy," she said, and gave him her gloved hand to kiss. He goggled and slipped his hand in her bosom between the folds of her evening cape. Then Harold appeared out of nowhere, swinging a lariat round and round over his head. Grinning, he flung out the noosed rope and spun it menacingly over Sophie's head. She squeezed her eyes shut as she felt it encircling her neck. "Please! For God's sake!" she cried, her voice expiring in her throat. She worked her fingers inside the rope, tried desperately to loosen the tightening knot, and woke gasping for breath, with the feel of the rope round her neck. Forehead in a sweat and heart pumping agitated blood, it took a sustained second or two before she realized that the noose was only her sleeping husband's arm encircled round her neck and pressing in slackened repose against her windpipe.

Gently, not to wake him, she put his arm away from her neck. He groaned, turned over and murmured, "Don't be afraid, sweetie" (his pet name for Emma). Then he stirred restlessly, drew up his knees and shuddered.

He was having a bad dream too, though he said he never dreamed. She shook him by the shoulder. "Wake up, Billy." He didn't respond so she leaned over and put on the bedside lamp.

He sat up with a start and stared at her as if she were someone who had come unbidden to his bed. Then he said querulously, "Why did you wake me up?"

"You were having a bad dream."

"I wasn't, it was a sweet dream. I was teaching Emma to swim. She was swimming like a seal and diving. . . I've been thinking about teaching her to swim before she learns to walk. They have no fear of water at that age."

"I had an awful dream. A nightmare," she said and proceeded to tell him her dream. "You know, Billy," she concluded, "I read somewhere that we make our own dreams."

"How do you mean?"

"Yours was simply a wish-fulfilment dream. Mine was a little more complex. I mean that part about my father — I told you about Mrs. Little flirting with him on the verandah? What I didn't tell you was that he was flirting with her too. It was embarrassing to see my father making a fool of himself — but more to the point is that the picture of my father cheapening himself must have impressed itself on my subconscious — and that's why I dreamt what I did about him putting his hand in Mrs. Little's bosom."

"Oh, come on, Soph, that's kind of far-fetched."

"No, it isn't. The subconscious is the dominant part of our whole mental process. I don't think I'll ever feel the same about my father again."

"That's ridiculous. Your father is a very moral man."

"I'm not saying he isn't. The moral side of my father is the other side of the coin. I told you how strict he was in his upbringing of us? We didn't dare show ourselves in a petticoat, not even when we were little kids. He's never told a lie in his life, at least not that I know of, and he never uses a swear word, not even in a temper. And he's always been very courteous to women. He tipped his hat to me on the street when I was still a school girl. But he goes to extremes. Tips his hat to me when I'm thirteen, and gives me a licking when I'm almost sixteen for coming home late from a party.

"And there's something else I haven't given much thought to before," she said reflectively. "My father and mother — my own mother — were childhood sweethearts. He was very broken up when she died and the only reason he married again was to make a home for his children. And yet he was able — while he was still mourning the wife he loved — to go to bed with a woman he was not in love with and have sex with her. My mother — I mean my stepmother — had a baby a year or two after they were married. It didn't live long, two days, I think. It was a little girl."

"You've never mentioned that before."——

"I never think of it. I suppose my subconscious shies away from it."

"What was wrong with the baby? Why did it die?"

"It was born without breath and the doctor slapped it with his rubber gloves on — to make it breathe — and the baby died a day or two later, its body terribly bruised."

"That's dreadful. Wasn't there an investigation? What did the death certificate say?"

"The baby was born at home. Poor people, immigrant parents, the mother illiterate — who knows what the doctor wrote on the certificate. He could have put anything down."

"How do you know the baby died of bruises? There may have been other causes."

"My mother's cousin was there when it happened. She was in the room when the baby was born. I don't remember my father being around. He was probably at work — it happened during the day. I remember my mother dragging herself along the hall holding onto the walls, going into the bedroom and coming out again holding her stomach. She was in labour. I didn't know anything and I must have laughed at the faces she was making because I remember Bella telling me not to laugh, that Ma was going to have a baby. Then my mother's cousin came with a doctor. The doctor bawled my mother out for not being in bed. My mother went into the bedroom. My mother's cousin went in too and after a while I heard the baby cry. I never saw the baby but a day or two later I knew it was dead."

"That's an awfully sad story. Poor little mite."

"Poor Ma. Maybe she still mourns it, who knows? A child of his — she worships him."

Sixteen

"If you want Ma to enjoy herself," said Bella, "don't ask Aunt Hannah. You can have her and Miriam another time."

"It's my first entertainment," Sophie said. "I wanted it to be a family affair."

The sisters were on the telephone, discussing the dinner Sophie was planning to give in a week or two. "Take my advice," Bella resumed, "don't ask Aunt Hannah."

"Ma doesn't dislike Aunt Hannah," Sophie argued.

"She doesn't dislike her but she'll have a better time if she isn't there."

Mrs. Glicksman and her sister-in-law did not see much of each other. They chatted on the phone frequently but rarely visited. Aunt Hannah phoned once a week to inquire about the state of her brother's health, her sister-in-law's, and the children's. Mrs. Glicksman in turn inquired about her health and Miriam's. The topic of health satisfactorily discharged, their conversation veers to the weather, household affairs and the alarming day-to-day rise in the cost of comestibles. Eggs are up three cents a dozen, milk is going up. Bread next, they conjecture, potatoes.

Glicksman was married almost a month before he told his

sister he had taken a second wife. Hannah wept for her dead sister-in-law who had been a close friend of hers, then she dried her eyes, embraced her brother and said, "You have done a sensible thing. Children need a mother and a man needs a wife."

When he told her he had been married almost a month, she was hurt. Why had he kept it from her so long? Why indeed had she not been invited to the ceremony — an only sister.

"I didn't get married in a ballroom," he replied. "I went to a rabbi, without music."

Who is the woman? Hannah wanted to know. Glicksman gave her a brief sketch of Chayele's background. A homeless woman, hard-working, uneducated, a few years older than himself.

Hannah was appalled. "I hope you didn't make a mistake, Avrom."

To which her brother replied, "She is a human being. She's not a parcel from Eaton's which I can take back and say I made a mistake."

A week or so later when Hannah met her sister-in-law, her worst fears were confirmed: her brother had acted too quickly in his choice of a second wife. Immovably stubborn, impatient to give his children a home, he had rashly taken a woman who was markedly inferior to his first wife. But Hannah kept her peace. To spare her brother pain, she said nothing. Just once she essayed an unasked-for opinion and was quickly silenced by his temper. Another time in a quieter moment he said to his sister, "What's done is done. The tears I cried could fill an ocean, but they could not bring back the dead from the grave. She is a good woman and tries her best for me and the children, so don't start comparing her with Becky. Treat her with respect."

As for Chayele, she counted herself the luckiest woman in the land that Glicksman had chosen her for his wife. From a lowly situation — an old maid, servant in her uncle's house — she had miraculously become mistress of her own home and wife of a man she respected and adored. Glicksman had acquainted her with his first wife's talents, her intellect, and Chayele mused on them constantly. But she did not repine or claim for herself parity with her predecessor; she knew she was not in any way the equal of the woman she had succeeded. But she had not snared him by trickery. She had not represented herself to be something she wasn't. He had not been spelled, dazzled, or blinded; he came to her with open eyes. She blessed him every day of her life and thanked God that he had not looked further.

Hannah loved her brother and pitied his misfortunes. "Becky would turn in her grave," she grumbled to her friends but in behaviour to her sister-in-law she could not be faulted. She was friendly, open, communicative. Yet there was something in Hannah's manner, something Chayele could not describe or give a name to, that made her uncomfortable. She was easy enough with her on the phone, but not face to face. In Hannah's presence she became awkward, clumsy of movement, harder of hearing, and self-consciously aware of her missing teeth. When she married Glicksman she had had an almost full mouth of teeth, poor teeth which began to loosen a year or two later, during her pregnancy. One day she lost a front tooth biting into an apple. A second tooth was lost in a piece of bread. And that's how her front teeth went, a lower, an upper, embedded one by one in a potato, a piece of meat.

Hannah, who lived in a gentile neighbourhood, came once in a while after shopping at the Jewish market, to look in on her sister-in-law before going home. . .

The door is not locked and Chayele is always at home, but Hannah knocks and waits politely to be admitted instead of going right in. Chayele going to the door recognizes through the curtained window the pillbox hat her sister-in-law wears, with a tacked-on dotted veil covering the upper half of her face from forehead to nose, and tied in a bow at the back.

"Hannah!" she exclaims, her greeting overly warm. She wrests the shopping bag from Hannah's hand. "Let me! Go in, Hannah, go in." She draws up a chair and wipes it off with her hand. "Sit down, Hannah." She offers tea, coffee, a glass of fresh buttermilk, something to eat. "A piece of cheesecake, Hannah? I baked it this morning, feel it's still warm." Hannah wants only a cup of tea. The tea is made, Hannah asks for a slice of lemon, and Chayele, getting deafer

110

by the minute, puts milk out to go with the tea, and cuts into her cheesecake for Hannah to taste.

They sit at opposite ends of the table — Chayele with a lump of sugar in her mouth, sipping tea through it from a glass; Hannah drinking hers from a cup, with milk in it instead of lemon. She overpraises the cheesecake which lies on her plate three-quarters uneaten. She leans forward. "Chayele, I tell you this as a friend—" Chayele knows what's coming. "You should get your teeth fixed. It would make you look ten years younger. I think we are the same age, but who would guess?" She puts her thumbs in the corners of her mouth, lifts her upper lip and displays for Chayele's inspection a partial which she herself wears. Chayele stares at her sister-in-law's nose; the lifted upper lip has puckered the dotted veil, resulting in a cluster of black dots thick as fleas around Hannah's nostrils.

Hannah takes her thumbs out of her mouth, finds a scrap of paper in her handbag and writes on it the name of her dentist. "Tell Avrom to take you to my dentist," she says, and gives Chayele the scrap of paper. Chayele puts it in her pocket, Hannah takes her shopping bag and they go to the door together. "Forgive me," says Hannah, "but a woman who is married to a man a few years younger should not let herself go." She speaks openly, the advice she gives her sister-in-law is for her own good, but there is a look in that veiled eye that eludes Chayele, a look she cannot give a name to — and while she would not go so far as to say that she had given tea to an enemy, she feels she has not given it to a friend.

Chayele returns to her kitchen, takes the scrap of paper from her pocket and puts it in the stove. "My sister-in-law speaks with fleas in her nose," she says to herself, and busies herself getting supper for her family.

A few days after the sisters had spoken on the phone, Sophie telephoned her mother and told her not to make supper the coming Friday.

"I want you and Pa to come to our place. Bella and Henry are coming too."

Her mother remained silent a second. "Sophie," she said hesitantly, "I'm not the one for parties, for suppers—"

111

"Don't start that," said Sophie. "Let me talk to Pa."

"He went out someplace. I'll tell him when he comes home. Do me a favour," she said, "let Pa come without me."

"What do you mean you won't come? That's an insult to me. Tell Pa you're both coming to our place for supper next Friday. Six o'clock," Sophie said and hung up.

Mrs. Glicksman hung up the phone. Talking to herself, declaring she was not the one for parties, suppers, she went to her bedroom and took from the closet hook her going-out dress — worn twice — a brown crepe with sequins at the neck, which Glicksman bought her five years ago to wear to Bella's wedding. She wore it again a year later to go to Philip's *bris*.

She was a few pounds lighter then, but even so she had to squeeze herself into a corset to wear it. She laid the dress on the bed, pulled open several drawers and rummaged through them till she located the whalebone-stiffened corset, rolled up and lying where it had been put four years ago. She unrolled the corset and spread it on the bed. A misery to wear; maybe if she took a few of its bones out she'd be able to draw breath at least.

Glicksman came home towards evening. He was in very good humour. He had spent a pleasant few hours with his cronies, had won four dollars at double-deck pinochle and was looking forward to his supper, his appetite sharpened by the three glasses of wine he had drunk. Hanging his coat on the hall rack, he heard his wife cursing to herself in the kitchen. "A black year on it!" she was saying. "The cholera take it!"

Three hours before, when he left for a game of cards, she was happily preparing a meat-and-potato stew for his supper. He hung his hat on the rack and proceeded to the kitchen, wondering what had gone amiss.

First thing that caught his eye was his wife's corset draped over the back of his chair, pruned, its bones lying in a heap on the seat. The table was spread with a folded-over sheet, and laid out on it was her brown crepe dress, its neck puckered and denuded of sequins. The iron she had been using lay on its side; and with a knife in her hand she was scraping at the layer of crushed sequins lining the flat of the iron. "The devil take it," she muttered, flung down the knife and went to the stove. She took the lid off the stewpot and let out a wail.

Glicksman made his presence known. "You burnt my supper?"

She started and pressed her hand to her heart. "You're home?" She hastily returned the lid to its pot and began recounting word for word her telephone conversation with Sophie.

Saying he was hungry, he took the lid off the pot and bent his head to the stew, sniffing. "When are we going to Sophie's," he asked, "Friday?"

She nodded. "Six o'clock."

"This is only Monday," he said. "What were you in such a hurry to get ready that you burnt my supper?"

She fanned her hand over the stew, inhaled its fumes and swore as God was her witness that his supper was not burned. Then she took her dress from the table and held it up for his inspection. "I spoiled my dress."

"The neck looks funny," he remarked. "You ironed away the beads?"

Without saying anything she put the dress back on the table, gathered up the corset bones and threw them in the garbage pail under the sink. She put the iron aside on an up-ended saucer, laid her corset on the dress, rolled up the sheet and went to her bedroom, corset and dress bundled under her arm.

Glicksman was not an insensitive man; he understood her distress at having spoiled her dress, and regretted that he had commented jokingly. He sat down at his place, put his glasses on and opened his paper. But he was unable to concentrate. Passing through his mind was the recollection of an afternoon he had taken off from work to go downtown and find a dress for her to wear to Bella's wedding. He remembered her pleasure when he brought it home, how she had left the table several times during supper to look at it. He recalled how pleased and flustered she was, blushing like a girl when he told her the day of Bella's wedding that she looked nice in it. There was no vanity in her, she constantly made nothing of herself, but a woman after all was a woman, and he understood intuitively that the dress, though unworn four years and gathering dust on a closet hook, meant something to her. He seldom complimented her and, for all he knew, the dress he had selected was, in her eyes, a tribute, an unspoken acknowledgement of her worth as a woman.

He waited a while longer for her to come and give him his supper, then he put down his paper and went to the bedroom.

She was sitting at the window in the darkening room. Her head was bent to the dress, which was spread on her lap, and she was picking at the few mangled sequins adhering to its neck.

"Why are you sitting in the dark?" he said, and switched on the light.

She raised her head and looked at him. Then she got up from her chair and took her dress to the closet. He heard her saying to herself, as she hung it on the hook, that she wished the earth would open up and swallow her altogether, hide her forever from the sight of everyone.

"Don't talk like a child!" he said angrily. "The earth to open up and swallow you — what kind of talk is that!"

Leaving her in the closet he went to the telephone and called Bella, who was handy with a needle. "Ma had a little accident."

Bella screamed.

He explained the nature of the accident. "Do you think you will be able to fix it? If not, I'll go downtown tomorrow and look for something else."

Bella thought that would be a waste of money. How often and where would she wear it? "I'll go downtown Friday morning and find a trim for the neck."

"Go tomorrow. Please. She is very upset."

Bella sighed and said she would, though it was inconvenient. Her father thanked her and hung up the phone. Then he went to the bedroom. His wife was putting on a clean apron. "I just spoke to Bella," he said. "She'll be able to fix your dress. Come and give me my supper. I'm hungry."

Seventeen

Five o'clock Friday afternoon Mrs. Glicksman, corseted, dressed in the brown crepe (the damaged neck cleverly concealed by a Bertha collar), was standing in bare feet at the kitchen table, while Glicksman, barbered, wearing his new suit, sat in his chair with a heap of her lisle stockings in his lap, sorting them to find two alike. Grumbling that she always left everything till the last minute, he at last found two stockings that matched. She went to the bedroom to put them on, and he went to the shoemaker's to pick up her shoes, which he had left there two days before to be stretched.

The shoes she had become accustomed to wearing were the ones Glicksman bought for her, soft-soled Romeo slippers with elasticized sides. Hannah had observed on one of her visits that her sister-in-law was ruining her feet wearing a soft-soled shoe with no support. She drew Chayele's notice to the corrective shoe she herself wore — an Enna Jettick. Chayele said if Hannah would be so kind as to write the name of the shoe on a piece of paper, she would tell her husband to get them for her. Knowing this would lead to nothing, Hannah said she would look after it herself; it so happened she was going downtown the next day. Chayele was made to take off her comfortable Romeo slippers and put her foot down on a piece of paper. Hannah, with a pencil in her hand, knelt on the floor and drew an outline of the foot, to get the proper size. She brought the shoes to her sister-in-law the next day, and Chayele, dismayed at the sight of the stiff unbending shoe, thanked her profusely.

"You will thank me by wearing them," Hannah said. "Wear them an hour or two every day till you break them in."

And Chayele dutifully wore the crippling shoes an hour every day for about a week. Then she put them in the closet where they lay till the day of Bella's wedding. She wore them to the wedding because she knew Hannah would be there; and she was wearing them to Sophie's because she was reasonably sure Hannah would be there too.

Glicksman came back from the shoemaker; his wife was sitting on the edge of the bed. He put the shoes on her feet and laced them up. "How do they feel?" She took a few cautious steps and glanced down at her feet. "Good," she said. "Nice."

It was still too early to go and they sat in the kitchen, Glicksman with a newspaper and a glass of wine, his wife, feet planted solidly on the floor, twirling her thumbs in her lap.

Bella and Henry, in their apartment, were also idling time. Philip was on his father's lap looking at a comic book. Henry, with his arm around the child's waist, was drinking coke from a bottle. Henry was a coke addict. His day began with a coke; he shaved with his right hand, holding a coke in his left. He drank a coke before breakfast, at meals and at least six more in between.

Bella was admiring a cloisonné vase she had bought for her sister, a house-warming present. "Do you think she'll like it?" she asked her husband. "I spent enough on it."

He nodded absently.

"You know," said Bella, "I don't understand Sophie."

"Oh?" said Henry, not a very talkative man.

Sophie's whole purpose in giving a family dinner, she told

him, was to get Ma out of the house. "Which is very nice, and she's going to a lot of trouble making a three-course dinner. She's been on the phone every second day and yesterday when she phoned she said her shopping was all done except for the chicken and she didn't have time to go to the Jewish market. She said there's a Loblaw's around the corner from their place and that's where she was going to buy her chicken. I said that wouldn't matter to me or you or even Pa, but what about Ma? 'Ma won't know the difference,' she said."

Henry glanced significantly over his son's head. "Little pitchers," he cautioned.

"I said *I* wouldn't serve ickenchay that wasn't osherkay to Ma even if she didn't know the ifferenceday," said Bella.

Sophie, meantime, with Mrs. Little helping, was setting up for dinner. Sophie was laying a four-place setting on the kitchen table, which was covered with a white cloth, and Mrs. Little was laying a three-place setting on a card table covered with a rose-patterned cloth. Setting up two tables was Mrs. Little's idea. Earlier in the afternoon when she came up to see if she could help, Sophie was setting seven places at the kitchen table. Mrs. Little said they'd be crowded, six adults and a child sitting at a small kitchen table. With that she went downstairs and returned with the card table, the rose-patterned cloth and salt and pepper shakers.

Sophie had become very friendly with her landlady in four short weeks of tenancy. They called each other by their first names, and were more like sisters than landlady and tenant. They went shopping to the market together, Mrs. Little wheeling Emma. Leaving Emma asleep in the carriage, they would sit down to a cup of coffee and an exchange of views on marriage, love, sex, and the human condition in general, each admiring the other's insight and originality of expression. Citing their own experiences and libidinous thoughts from adolescence upwards, they spoke candidly of things that would make a sailor blush.

It was during one of these soul-searching sessions that Mrs. Little confided in Sophie her habit of looking at men's flies. This was one night around half-past eight when Emma was asleep, Billy at work and Mr. Little and Harold at the movies.

117

The ladies were upstairs having a cup of coffee. . .

The confession made, Mrs. Little sets down her cup and waits for her confidante's response.

"That's interesting," says Sophie. "Is there a sexual connotation?"

"Not that I'm aware of. It's simply a compulsion that I can't control. I look at men's flies — any man." She laughs. "I even look at the laundryman's fly, and you know what he looks like. Put a man in front of me and my eyes are drawn to his pants."

"Penis envy?" Sophie offers.

Mrs. Little ponders a moment. "No, it can't be that. I even look at Mr. Little's fly and I know what's behind there. Nothing."

Sophie stares.

To clarify her meaning, Mrs. Little props her elbow on the table and holds up her little finger.

Sophie lets out a shriek of laughter. Mrs. Little's shoulders begin to shake. Coming home at that moment, Billy finds his wife leaning back in her chair with her legs drawn up, hugging her knees to her chest. Mrs. Little is wiping her eyes and both women are rocking with laughter.

The day of the family supper, the instructor made short work of his five o'clock swimming class, but he was delayed clearing the tank and got home later than he had promised. Running up the stairs, he smiled to hear Emma in her bath, squealing with laughter. The bathroom door was ajar and Emma, immersed to the waist, was slapping water at the plastic duck which Harold, on his knees, was spinning round with his forefinger.

Harold was a thin boy of medium height with light hair, narrow face and a long neck. He was vain of his intelligence, spoke affectedly with an over-nice enunciation and had a disconcerting habit of jutting his head forward before he spoke, like a rooster getting set to crow.

"That will do, Emma," the instructor said, coming into the bathroom; the smile had left his face. He lifted his daughter out of the tub and wrapped her in her towel.

Harold rose from his knees. "Mrs. James asked me to

watch her," he said, leaning over the tub to pull the plug.

"Thank you," Billy said stiffly and went to the kitchen with Emma in his arms. His wife was at the stove, fussing over her pots. "Soph," he said, speaking in an agitated whisper, "I wish you wouldn't ask Harold to look after Emma."

"Then you should have come home earlier," she said testily. "Emma likes to play after her bath and I didn't have time to watch her, so I asked Harold."

Just then Harold emerged from the bathroom. Billy waited till he was safely out of earshot, then he continued: "I don't like that kid, he's a creep. He always manages to be around when Emma is having her bath. The thought that he might touch her makes me sick to the stomach."

Sophie pulled open the oven door and bent her head to the chicken stew. His fears, his womanish fussiness where Emma was concerned, irritated her. She thought it unsuitable in a man.

"What are you afraid of," she said unpleasantly, "rape? Put a chastity belt on her." She slammed the oven door shut.

He could have hit her. To hear her use the word rape in connection with their nine-month-old daughter sickened him; and anger, an emotion which did not come readily to him, swept over him now with such force that his hand tingled with a desire to slap her. He moved away from her. She observed how shaken he was and cursed herself silently for her quick tongue.

She drew his attention to the card table. "That was Jessie's idea. She said we'd be crowded, six adults and a child. . . "

He turned away and leaving her mid-speech went to the bedroom with his daughter in his arms. She went after him to make it up. Emma had been put on their bed and he, still in his coat, was leaning over the child, getting her into her nightclothes. He said gravely, "I don't want to make an issue of this, Soph, but doesn't it bother you — I mean good Lord! you're the child's mother — doesn't it bother you having a young punk hang around your naked baby girl for the kick he gets out of it?"

Passing through her mind as he spoke was the picture of Harold on one knee outside the bathroom door, his eye at the keyhole, peeping at his mother who was having a bath. This happened one morning as she was coming up the stairs. Catching sight of her on the landing, he bent to his shoe and made as if he were tying a shoelace.

She was glad now that she had not mentioned this incident to her husband. She had saved it for Jessie.

When they sat down to a cup of coffee after Billy went to work, Sophie began by saying, "Jessie, let's talk about the Oedipus complex. In your opinion, is there any validity in the theory that a male child develops libidinous feelings towards his mother from the time he's three years old?"

Mrs. Little, with a cup of coffee in one hand and the other in her bosom fondling her breast, said after a moment's consideration, "Broadly speaking, I would say no. That's a Freudian theory. He reads sex in every impulse, every act and every thought that comes to one's mind. I don't go along with it, Sophie. I think he must have gone overboard reading *Oedipus Rex*. According to Freud, if a boy kisses his mother on the cheek he wants to go to bed with her."

"But just suppose — for argument's sake — that you discovered something in Harold to substantiate the theory of the Oedipus complex? How would you react to that?"

Mrs. Little withdrew her hand from her bosom. "I think my maternal instincts would be so repelled that I would be incapable of taking an objective view of it."

Sophie closed her mouth and kept to herself what she had seen outside the bathroom door.

Watching her husband leaning over his baby, the gentle care he took easing her arms into her nightdress, the loving kisses he bestowed on the child's feet and knees, she said: "I don't think Harold gets a kick out of seeing Emma naked. He's an only boy, he grew up without sisters, it's a natural curiosity, that's all."

Hearing the sound of a car drawing up, Sophie went to the window. A cab was parked at the curb. Her father, with the neck of a paper-wrapped bottle protruding from his topcoat pocket, was standing beside the driver, and all that was to be seen of her mother who was backing out of the car was her rear end. Her head and shoulders were beneath the roof of the car, one foot was on the floor of the car and the other was suspended behind her, seeking a foothold.

When Sophie opened the door, her mother and father were slowly making their way up the verandah steps. With no railing to cling to, Mrs. Glicksman was holding on for dear life to her husband's arm. Gaining the landing, she put her hand to her heart. "Oh my dear one," she said, seeing Sophie. "Oh my dear one," she repeated, shaking her head.

They proceeded to the hall and Mrs. Glicksman, holding onto her husband's arm, stopped at the foot of the stairs, dismayed at the sight of the staircase. Two red patches appeared on her face.

"Are you all right?" Glicksman asked.

She nodded. "Give me a little minute."

"Go!" said Glicksman to his daughter. "Bring her a glass of water."

Sophie sped along the hall to Mrs. Little's kitchen. Both came hurrying; Sophie with a glass of water, Mrs. Little bringing a chair. Glicksman withdrew his arm from his wife's grasp and took off his hat. "This is my wife," he said, then told his wife in Yiddish that the lady she was being introduced to was the *baleboosteh*. Mrs. Glicksman ducked her head and offered her hand. Mrs. Little set down the chair and took Mrs. Glicksman's hand in both of hers. "It's a pleasure to meet you," she said. "I've heard so much about you from Sophie." Mrs. Glicksman smiled politely and looked at her husband for intelligence. He explained what the lady had said.

"Here, Ma," said Sophie, offering the glass, "drink some water."

Mrs. Little seized hold of the chair and, skirting around Mrs. Glicksman, set it down behind her. "Sit down, dear," she said, putting her hands on her shoulders from behind. Mrs. Glicksman, feeling the pressure of the *baleboosteh*'s hands on her shoulders, did not know what was happening; she had not heard the invitation to sit. Mrs. Little caught sight of her husband poking his head out of the kitchen door. She beckoned to him. "Come and meet Sophie's parents."

Mr. Little shook hands with Glicksman then leaned towards Mrs. Glicksman, offering her his hand. Sophie at that moment excused herself and slipped away.

Mrs. Glicksman could not understand what was taking place. Her daughter had thrust a glass of water in her hands, exhorting her to drink; the landlady had forced her to sit; now Sophie disappears and leaves them in the hall to visit with the landlord and landlady. All three were talking and she sitting in their midst did not understand a word that was spoken. The landlord and landlady smiled at her from time to time, and every time they looked her way she took a sip of water; like a performing bear, she thought to herself. She was hoping they would soon make an end to the talk when Glicksman turned abruptly to her and said, "We are keeping these good people from their supper," as though she were the one dallying.

The doorbell rang. Mr. Little admitted Bella, Henry and their little boy.

Bella took alarm at seeing her mother sitting at the foot of the stairs with a glass of water in her hand. "It's nothing," said Glicksman. "She got a little bit winded walking up the steps," and introduced them to the Littles.

The pharmacist went over to his mother-in-law and took from his pocket a round little pillbox from which he extracted a pill. "Take this, Ma," he said, "and swallow it with a drink of water."

Then her grandson climbed on her lap. She gave him the glass to hold and sat there while the Littles were becoming acquainted with the new arrivals.

Mrs. Little was struck by the resemblance between the two sisters.

"Sophie is the image of her mother, my first wife," Glicksman said. "But when they were little. . . "

He was interrupted. "I have to go to the toilet," said Philip, jiggling in his grandmother's lap with his hand on his crotch.

Mrs. Little hastily took the glass from Philip and his mother hurried him up the stairs, with Henry following. Glicksman gave his arm to his wife and they proceeded up the stairs. Sophie and Billy were waiting to receive them. Glicksman gave his son-in-law his hat and coat, taking first from his pocket the paper-wrapped bottle of brandy. Sophie, helping her mother off with her coat, bent her head to hear what she was whispering. Then she stepped over to the bathroom and rapped sharply on the door. "Bella? Is Philip going to be long?"

Leading Philip by the hand, Bella came out of the bathroom with her nose in the air. Bella was offended. A few minutes before, she had presented Sophie with the cloisonné vase in a pretty gift box. Her sister took the lid off and with one quick look inside, said, "It's lovely, thank you," and dumped it in the baby's carriage. Just like that, as if the present she had been given was a dollar *tsatske* from Woolworth's.

Sophie, showing her mother in, told her sister to go to the living room. "Pa brought a bottle of brandy. We'll have a drink before supper."

Glicksman was standing at the window with Emma in his arms, and Henry was sitting in a corner of the chesterfield with his head bent to the floor. Bella took a critical look around the room with its Axminster rug, glass curtains, plush chesterfield with armchair to match, tapestry-covered wing chair and a console model De Forest Crossley radio.

Sophie certainly doesn't believe in stinting herself, she thought.

Sophie came to the living room, escorting her mother by the elbow. As soon as his wife was settled, Glicksman handed her the baby. Billy came with a tray bearing the bottle and six small glasses filled with brandy. Drinks were passed and when Henry was served he refused apologetically.

Bella pursed her lips. "You know Henry doesn't drink," she said coldly to her sister.

Sophie clapped her hand to her mouth. "I forgot to get cokes. Go to the drugstore, Billy, and get some cokes."

Henry got up. "Don't bother, Billy, I'll go," but his nose began suddenly to bleed and he sat down again and put a handkerchief to it. Bella told him to lie down and he stretched out on the chesterfield with his head in her lap. Billy went to the kitchen and returned shortly with ice cubes packed in a tea towel. Henry put the bloodied handkerchief in his pocket and applied the ice-pack to his nose.

Bella, cradling her husband's head in her lap, noticed how thin his hair was getting on top. As he removed the ice-pack for a second, two thin streams of blood trickled slowly down his upper lip. His nose, Bella noticed, was beginning to look just like his mother's, long and pinched.

"Your nose is still bleeding," she said crossly. Then turned to her sister. "I think we'd better go home."

"Well I like that!" Sophie exclaimed.

"Why are they quarrelling?" Mrs. Glicksman asked her husband. "Two sisters."

"Two cats in a sack," he replied. To Bella he said, "Don't spoil the party. Have some consideration for Ma, how often does she go out?"

Bella muttered under her breath that he was always taking Sophie's side, which Glicksman pretended not to hear. Then she held out her glass to be refilled. Sophie took up the bottle, filled her sister's glass and her own.

Bella raised her glass. "Let's cheer up."

"L'chaim," said Glicksman, raising his glass. "Take a drink, Chayele."

The atmosphere was still a little tense, and Bella feeling it was her fault, said to her sister, "We met your landlady. She seems to be a very friendly woman."

"She's wonderful," Sophie returned enthusiastically. "I knew you'd like her."

Bella sniffed, took a sip of brandy and said, "I didn't say I liked her. From the way you've been raving about her I didn't expect to see a middle-aged woman with a ton of makeup on her face acting like a girl of eighteen."

Sophie bridled. "I didn't know you had such a malicious streak in you."

"Thank you," Bella returned, then said irritably to her mother, "Look what the baby's doing to your collar."

Emma had a portion of the lacy border of the collar bunched in her fist and was holding it to her mouth and drooling on it.

Mrs. Glicksman kissed the top of the baby's head. "Leave

her," she said, "it doesn't matter."

An angry flush spread over Bella's face. "It matters to me. I was the one who dropped everything and went chasing downtown to — oh what's the use of talking. Nothing matters where Bella's concerned," she said accusingly, and burst into tears.

Henry sat up and put his arm around her shoulder, resting the ice-pack on his knee. Seeing his mother cry, Philip began to cry. Then Emma began to cry. Billy took the baby from his mother-in-law and walked the floor with her, patting her on the back. Bella lifted Henry's arm from her shoulder and fled from the room; they heard the bathroom door slam.

Mrs. Glicksman uneasily smoothed her collar down several times, bent her head and began unhappily twirling her thumbs.

Glicksman poured himself another brandy. "What are you so upset about?" he said to his wife. "It's the brandy talking. Don't you remember how they used to be at the Seder? Sophie drank wine and laughed, Bella took a sip of wine and cried."

She raised her head. "I remember," she said, smiling. Then she spread her hands on her knees and glanced down at her feet.

"Your shoes hurt?" he asked.

"A little bit," she admitted. "It's nothing."

Glicksman knelt and untied the laces of the constricting shoes and eased them off her feet. She heaved a sigh of relief, passed her hand over her mouth to wipe sweat from her upper lip, and began to worry that she would not be able to get the shoes back on again. "So you'll go home in bare feet," Glicksman said. Then he went to the hall and took her Romeo slippers from an inside pocket of his coat which was draped over the banister. "I knew you'll have trouble," he said, returning with her comfortable shoes.

"God be with you," she said.

"Give me your foot," he said crossly.

She leaned back in her chair and extended a swollen foot, murmuring a blessing on his hands.

It was getting on for seven and Bella was still in the bathroom. Henry's nose had stopped bleeding; Philip was back at his comic books; Emma had been put to bed; Glicksman was making conversation with Billy, who kept looking at the mantel clock; and Mrs. Glicksman, eased of pain, was contentedly twirling her thumbs and wondering when they would eat.

Sophie, having twice watered the chicken stew to keep it from drying, got up from the hassock where she had been sitting impatiently tapping her foot and regretting the day she had conceived the idea of giving a family dinner, and rapped on the bathroom door. "Bella? What are you doing in there? Everybody's starving."

Bella opened the door. Eyes red from crying, she drew her sister in by the arm, sat down on the rim of the tub and began crying all over again. Wiping tears from her face with the back of her hand, she said pathetically, "What's happening between us, Soph? Pa called us two cats in a sack and that really hurt me. It made me realize how far apart we've grown. We never talk without arguing and it's not my fault, Soph, it's yours."

Sophie held her tongue. Her sister was touchy, excitable and argumentative. Disagree with Bella on the most inconsequential point and her back was immediately put up.

"You pick on me for the least little thing," she went on. "We never used to be like this, we used to love each other. I remember the day our own mother died, you were only four so you don't remember but—"

"I certainly do! I have a vivid recollection of the day she died."

"There you go!" said Bella, puffed eyes blazing. "You're always ready to argue with me."

The sisters seldom spoke of their childhood; they steered clear of the subject for the simple reason that once in a while when one or the other was stirred by some incident to a nostalgic reminiscence of the past, an argument invariably ensued. . . Let Sophie say she remembered their father coming to visit them at the orphanage with a bag of jelly beans, and Bella would say: "Pa brought oranges." Sophie said she remembered the yard they played in, all kids dressed alike in grey dresses; Bella claimed: "We wore our own clothes."

"I'm sorry, Bella, what were you going to say?"

"Nothing," Bella replied. "I'll only get another argument from you."

Sophie promised not to interrupt, and Bella resumed: "You can't possibly remember the funeral because you weren't there. Pa took you to that family across the street, I've forgotten their name. When we came back from the funeral I went across the street and brought you home." She lowered her head and clasped her hands between her knees. "And that night when you were asleep I cried over you. I pitied you for being without a mother and I cried over you." She raised her tear-stained eyes. "I didn't pity myself for being without a mother, I pitied you."

Impulsively Sophie sat down on the rim of the tub beside Bella and put her arm on her shoulder.

Bella stiffened. She held herself in embarrassed silence, shoulders yoked in her sister's self-conscious embrace. Then she rose, moved briskly to the door and said, "Let's eat."

The guests were summoned and seated according to Mrs. Little's plan: Bella with her family at the card table, the parents at the kitchen table. Sophie filled the soup plates and Billy brought them to table. There was no conversation. Bella's crying spell had cast a sombre atmosphere over the party.

Mrs. Glicksman broke the silence by praising the soup. "It's good," she said, ladling soup made from a chicken whose neck had not known the *shochet*'s knife.

"Delicious," said Bella with a sly look at her sister, and broke into peals of prolonged slightly hysterical laughter.

Henry glanced uneasily at his wife and cautioned her to control herself.

They ate and drank and Bella, with a kind of feverish animation, talked throughout the meal. She had something to say to everyone. To her brother-in-law she told the story of the banana that had been given to their stepmother by someone on board ship when she was emigrating to Canada by cattle boat.

"She had never seen a banana before in her life and she ate

127

it skin and all," said Bella, smiling at her mother.

Surrounded by smiling glances directed at her, Mrs. Glicksman understood that she was the cause of their amusement, and it pleased her. "They're laughing at me?" she asked her husband, and he told her they were laughing at her having eaten a banana without peeling it. Unused to being the centre of attention, she became shy and spread her fingers over her face.

With supper over, and Bella still talking, Mrs. Glicksman rose and began gathering up dishes. Piling them one on top of another, she carried them to the sink held against her chest, a teetering lopsided pyramid. Sophie, fearful for her new dishes, told her, "Leave them, Ma."

Bella got up and shooed her mother away. "You're not the servant here, you're a guest."

Billy led his guests back to the living room, and Bella stayed behind to help her sister with the dishes. Left by themselves, a feeling of constraint came over them. Sophie washed, Bella dried, and neither one spoke: the moment of shared closeness in the bathroom had left them a little embarrassed with each other. A bicker, a wrangle was the normal course of encounter between the sisters. A quarrel was an everyday affair, dismissed from mind with a last-word accusal from Bella, a grumble from Sophie. But an unaccustomed gesture of tenderness was not so lightly disposed of; it lingered in the mind and in some way divided them. Dishes were passed from one to the other in silence.

Bella put down her towel and took up the brandy bottle. "Let's have a drink."

Sophie said, "Please, Bella, don't have any more brandy."

"Why not? I'm restless, it'll relax me."

"It won't relax you, it'll only make you cry."

"Are you implying that that's why I cried? Because I had a drink of brandy?" said Bella aggressively.

"I'm only repeating what Pa said," Sophie said cautiously. "He said I used to laugh at the Seder when I drank wine, and that you used to cry."

"Pa gets everything wrong," said Bella, pouring brandy. "*I* was the one who laughed, you used to cry."

Eighteen

"I can't find it in my heart to forgive him," said Mrs. Little.

This was one Saturday morning early in July. Billy had taken Emma to the park; Mr. Little was at the Jewish Home for the Aged visiting his old father; Harold was at the library; the ladies were upstairs having their morning cup of coffee. The topic this morning had to do with the devious nature of man, and it had come out in the course of conversation that Mr. Little, who was an insurance salesman, had had a brief fling two years before with a public stenographer to whom he had sold a life insurance policy.

"Infidelity is in the nature of man," Mrs. Little went on. "Schopenhauer deals at great length with it in one of his works. . . Easy enough to accept in theory, Sophie, but not so easy to accept when it happens to you."

Sophie loved this kind of talk. "True," she agreed. "Not even the philosopher is proof against toothache."

Mrs. Little withdrew her hand from her bosom and lit a cigarette. "How well you put it."

"Jealousy," she resumed, "is made up of divers emotions. Indignation at the betrayal of trust, a sense of insult, wounded ego — you name it — but the overriding emotion is fear of loss."

Her face had become very pale and her hair dyed the colour of soot looked blacker than ever. Her hand trembled as she put her cigarette to her lips.

"Morris Little," she said contemptuously. "I was afraid of losing *him*."

"Well—" said Sophie uncertainly, "that's understandable, Jessie. He's your husband."

"I despise him," she said unemotionally. Then she leaned back in her chair and very slowly shook her head. She drew reflectively on her cigarette; her hand had stopped trembling. "I don't despise him. I have a bitter feeling in my heart." She leaned forward. "Relentlessly bitter, Sophie, for the indignity he subjected me to. But it's myself I despise for the humiliating things I did. I mean after I found out."

"How did you find out?"

"Pure chance."

Her husband, she said, was a good insurance salesman despite his stammer, and he was out at all hours calling on clients, prospects and cases. "He always phoned if he was going to be late, and I never gave it a thought." One afternoon she was getting a suit of his ready for the cleaners. She went through his pockets first, as she did with her own things, and in one of the pockets she found a folded handkerchief. "Inside that handkerchief," she said, "were three rubber safes. I can't describe my emotions, Sophie. I just stood there in the bedroom in a kind of catatonic state, my mind a total blank. 'How dare he!' I kept saying over and over like an idiot. I felt a desperate need to do something to relieve me of my violent emotions." Her face had regained its normal colour and her hand had stopped trembling. Watching Sophie closely, she said, "I laid his pants out on the bed, took a scissors to them and cut them into shreds. Then I unfolded the handkerchief and laid that on top, with the three french letters prominently displayed." Her mouth tightened. "That will be a sight to greet him when he comes home, I thought, and my head miraculously stopped aching."

From having attended Mrs. Little with wholehearted sympathy, Sophie was unable for the moment to meet her eyes.

After a short silence Mrs. Little shrugged her shoulders and said, "I suppose you're shocked?"

Sophie looked up but could not find words to answer.

"You are. I can see it in your eyes, they're a dead give-away. I'm disappointed in you, Sophie. I've credited you with a mature intelligence and a capacity for understanding which you do not possess."

"Please don't say that, Jessie, it's not true."

"You talk like a mature woman," Mrs. Little conceded, "but you're still a child, a fledgling, unbruised by life."

"You're mistaken," said Sophie with dignity. "I know what it is to be betrayed. I was rejected by someone I was deeply in love with before I met my husband," she said, and went on to tell the story of Ronnie Swerling, whose name for the life of her she could not at the moment recall. "I wept when his letter came telling me he was married. I wrote him an embittered letter, full of venom, and that night. . ." The night she had spent necking a full hour or more on a park bench with Billy James she described as an anguished night, her pillow wet with tears.

She topped up Mrs. Little's coffee and her own. "What happened when Mr. Little came home?"

"He didn't come home till late. It was after one. Harold came from school at half-past four and he could tell at a glance that something was wrong. He's very sensitive to my moods. I didn't mean to say anything to him but I couldn't contain myself. 'Your father's been whoring around,' I said. He was shocked, naturally, to hear me use such a word. I made him come to the bedroom and when he saw what was laid out on the bed he called me a bitch."

Just then Cecile La Flamme, a 17-year-old French-Canadian girl who came once a week Saturdays to clean, came running up the stairs. "*Madame?*" she said, standing in the door. "I have finish *cuisine; et maintenant?*"

Mrs. Little turned. "So soon?" she said irritably. "Did you do the windows, the cupboards?"

The girl stared uncomprehendingly.

"*Fenêtre, buffet,*" said Mrs. Little impatiently.

"*Oui, madame.*"

"Do the bedroom. Turn the mattress over before you

131

make the bed. And for heaven's sake be careful with the vacuum cleaner. Don't yank it around and bang it up against the furniture, move it gently."

"*Oui, madame,*" said Cecile, and ran down the stairs.

"They're hopeless," said Mrs. Little. "They've no understanding of electrical equipment."

"I don't think she understands English very well."

"She understands well enough when it suits her purpose. Stubborn is the answer. And she's a poor cleaner, not a patch on her aunt Marie."

Cecile lived with her aunt, Marie Sorel, who was the former cleaner, a married woman with four children ranging in ages from seven to two.

Cecile was a hard worker, eager to give satisfaction. She had learned to cope a little with English, but she was easily confused and fear of misunderstanding made her perspire. She was plainly frightened of Mrs. Little, and in her presence was nervous and clumsy.

Sophie wanted to hear what happened when Mr. Little came home to a pair of cut-up pants with three french letters prominently displayed on top. She glanced uneasily at the clock. Billy would be home soon with Emma; there was lunch to get. "What happened when Mr. Little came home?" she asked for the second time.

Mrs. Little stubbed out her cigarette and folded her hands in her lap. "When we began our conversation about jealousy I remarked, if you recall, that jealousy is made up of many emotions but that the overriding emotion is fear of loss. . . "

Mr. Little had come home very late. When it got to be one o'clock, she panicked.

"I panicked, Sophie. Men in their middle years experience a change of life, as women do in the menopause, and they have been known to walk out of their homes without a word, in search of rejuvenation. Usually with a woman younger than his wife," she said, drawing in her mouth.

She had lived with Mr. Little eighteen years and knew him to be a responsible man, a homebody, and common sense should have told her that he was the last man on earth to fly the coop; but in the grip of fear, she was incapable of rational reasoning. After calling her a bitch, Harold had gone up to his room without saying another word. It was apparent, from that strange look he had given her, that he was concealing something. She ran up to his room and flung open the door. He was in bed reading. "Where's your father?" she demanded. His answer shocked her: "Enjoying himself, I hope."

She crumpled and fell on his bed in a state of collapse. He told her to pull herself together. Then he very coolly advised her to get rid of the pants she had cut up. "That's a castrating act," he said.

Was she to say nothing then when he came home? she asked her son. Did a wife who had served her husband well have no right to express *some* indignation at his infidelity? He agreed her indignation was not entirely unreasonable. "Bawl him out," he said, "act like a jealous woman. That'll bolster his ego if he has any left. It'll make him feel like a man instead of an appendage around the house."

A faraway look came into Mrs. Little's eyes and she sat a moment caressing her neck with her fingertips. Then she said, "Harold is an extremely intelligent boy with an exceptionally high I.Q. and I did as he advised me. I wrapped the pants in a newspaper and put them in the garbage."

The contraceptives she put in her pocket, folded up in the handkerchief as she had found them. Then she made a pot of coffee and waited for him to come home. When she heard him at the door she began to tremble all over, her heart beating so hard it was an effort to draw breath. He asked what she was doing up so late, and she said she was waiting for him; she thought he had been killed, run over. He said he should have called. He was out with the district manager having a few drinks and didn't realize how late it was getting to be.

"You've been with a woman," she said.

A foolish grin spread over his face. "Aw, J-J-Jessie," he said; that was the first time he had stuttered over her name. He put his face close to hers and blew out his breath for her to smell, to prove he had been drinking with the district manager.

She brought out the folded handkerchief and shook its

contents out onto the table. "Here's the evidence," she said. "Who is she?"

He stared at the tumbled contraceptives then turned his gaze on her and stared with bulging eyes as if she were a performing prestigidator. Then he sat down in the chair next to hers and said without stuttering, though his face had become white as paper, that he had been with a woman, but she meant nothing to him, absolutely nothing.

She was a woman to whom he had sold a life insurance policy. She had been married only three years and her husband had been killed a few months before in a car accident. She cried when she told him the story, and he felt sorry for her.

"So you took her to bed?" said Mrs. Little. He hung his head. "How old is she?"

He didn't know her age; he said it would be hard to guess because she was a slight little thing, an itsy-bitsy woman.

"Did you ever in your life hear a more asinine description?" Grimly amused, Mrs. Little pressed her lips together in a tight smile. "I threw the book at him. I made him get on the phone to his itsy-bitsy woman. I told him to tell her the party was over, that his wife knew about it and there would be trouble if he ever saw her again."

Mr. Little went to the phone and called the woman's number. "This is Mmm-mmm. . ." he said, unable to pronounce his own name. Mrs. Little took the receiver out of his hand. "This is Mrs. Little," she said. "Morris Little's wife. My husband's lost his tongue so I'll speak for him—" The woman cut in on her: "You've got one hell of a nerve phoning at this hour."

The gall, the audacity of her! Mrs. Little lost all control of herself. She screamed at the woman and threatened violence if she didn't lay off her husband.

"We engaged in a verbal sparring match, hurling insults at each other. She called me a witch, I called her a whore. She told me to go and — it's a word I can't bring myself to say." Mrs. Little lowered her head. "She told me to go and f-u-c-k myself," she said, tracing the rim of her cup with her forefinger. She looked up. "Can you conceive of me using an expression like 'lay off my husband,' screaming like a fish-wife and trading insults with a public stenographer who sounded like a common street woman?"

"You were under stress," Sophie offered.

"That doesn't excuse me," said Mrs. Little, refusing to take comfort. "I, Jessie Little, to participate in a name-calling brawl with a common, filthy-mouthed woman?" She sat a while regarding her confidante with brooding eyes, then she put her handbag under her arm and rose. "I have some shopping to do," she said, and went out of the kitchen with her head bent to her chest.

Sophie ran after her and caught her by the arm. "I'll come with you, Jessie."

"That's sweet of you," said Mrs. Little. "I get emotionally stirred up talking of that time, and I don't feel like being by myself — but what about the girl's lunch?"

"I'll leave a note for Billy. He can get it for her."

Nineteen

Cecile came at nine Saturday mornings and worked till four, stopping half an hour for lunch. Seven weeks ago, when she came for the first time, Sophie had insisted on paying her share for the cleaning of the bathroom and the upstairs hall. But Mrs. Little wouldn't hear of it; she said if Sophie would give the girl her lunch that would be enough.

Cecile was shy coming up for lunch that first day, and ate with her marcelled head bent to her plate. She had a healthy appetite, eating bread with everything, including a jello mould topped with canned peaches.

She was less shy the following Saturday, and came eagerly up for lunch. The third Saturday, she and Sophie began exchanging lessons over lunch. Cecile knew more English than Sophie knew French, but Sophie was a quick learner. Cecile was under the impression that Sophie too was under madame's thumb. Thinking they were in sympathetic accord — where Mrs. Little was concerned — she was moved several times during lessons to malign the mistress of the house. Complaining of Mrs. Little, Cecile forgot her English and spoke her abuses in French. Half the time Sophie made out what she was saying, and half the time she didn't.

Sophie was late getting home from shopping with Mrs. Little. Coming up the stairs, she glimpsed Cecile through the bathroom door which was slightly ajar. The girl was on her knees. Dress hiked up and tucked in at the waist, she was scrubbing behind the toilet bowl.

Billy was at the sink, washing up. "Soph," he said, speaking in a whisper, "I think that girl's in trouble — and I mean *trouble*."

He told her Harold had come home while he and Cecile were at lunch; that he came upstairs with a pile of books under his arm and went to his room. The girl left her lunch, got up without a word and went to his room. "I could hear them talking in French. She was crying and he was trying to hush her. Then he went out and left her in his room crying."

"Cecile gets upset very easily," said Sophie. "She was probably crying over something Jessie may have said to her this morning. I'll go in and speak to her."

Sophie poked her head in the door. Cecile turned on her knees and covered her face with dripping hands. "Oh, Sophee," she moaned, rocking, her head bent to the bucket. "Oh, Sophee."

"What is it, Cecile? What's the matter?"

The girl uncovered her face. "*Je suis enceinte*," she said in a whisper.

Sophie stared.

"*Je suis enceinte*," she repeated; a despairing wail.

Sophie shut the door. "I understand. Keep your voice down, madame is home. You have a boyfriend? Are you engaged?"

Cecile shook her head. "*Non*. 'Arold," she said, jerking her thumb towards his room. "'E 'as done it." She got up from her knees and took hold of Sophie's hands. "I am honest girl," she said with Sophie's hands clasped in her wet ones, "and 'e tells 'e 'as not done it."

Sophie released her hands from the girl's grasp, and said, speaking slowly and distinctly, "Cecile, Harold is sixteen years old — you are seventeen years old — he is Jew — you are Catholic — he cannot marry you even if he was more old."

"Not for *mari*," she said, wiping sweat from her face with the floor rag. "*Mais il est responsable* — I must 'ave money."

For an abortion? Sophie wondered. A Catholic girl; hardly likely. She took a stab at it. "For doctor? To make *fini* the baby?"

Cecile recoiled. "*Non*! I 'ave confess to priest. 'E 'as place for me but I must 'ave money. 'Elp me, Sophee, speak for me."

"Look, Cecile, we can't talk here. When you finish work, go to the Golden Arrow — you know — that restaurant at corner where you take streetcar? I will come there for rendezvous with you and we will talk, *comprenez-vous*?"

Cecile nodded. "*Merci bien*," she said and got back on her knees to finish scrubbing.

Sophie went to the kitchen and shut the door behind her. "She's pregnant," she announced.

The instructor let the towel drop from his hands. "Good Lord! I thought there was something fishy going on — is it Harold?"

"Yes, but he denies it, that's what she was crying about. She needs money and wants me to speak for her, but I don't know whether she meant I was to speak to Harold or his mother. Anyway, I'm meeting her at the Golden Arrow when she's through work."

Cecile was sitting in a booth at the back of the restaurant. Sophie got herself a cup of coffee at the counter, took it to the girl's table and sat down opposite her.

Cecile put down the slice of bread she was buttering and took a sip of her chocolate milk. "I am honest girl, Sophee." The declaration made, she followed with an outpouring of French: Sophie interrupting to say, "*Lentement*, Cecile, *lentement* — speak English."

Cecile, speaking partly in English and partly in French, began by telling of the parish priest she had been to see a week ago Monday, for confession. She confessed she had become pregnant by a boy, son of the house where she worked one day a week, cleaning. He absolved her from sin and said she was not to go back to that house again, thus avoiding further communication with the son. What could she say to her aunt as to why she had quit? She must tell her aunt the truth, said the priest. She told him that her tongue would dry in her mouth. He said if she would give him permission, he would speak to the aunt. Further, he would find a place for her when her time came, in a Catholic hospital. They would take her in without money, meantime she would not be without a home. She asked the priest would it be permissible to go this Saturday for the last time to clean. He said, yes, he could trust her.

This morning when she was cleaning downstairs, it made her heart tremble to think that the priest at this very moment was speaking to her aunt. They were poor people, tante Marie and oncle Claude, and it made her heart ache that she would be living off them till her time came. She thought to herself if she could make a present of money to them, she would not feel so bad. And so she spoke to Harold when he came home from the bibliothèque, and asked him for money.

"'E tells 'e 'as not done it, Sophee, and 'e will not give me money."

"It is possible that he tells he has not done it because he has no money to give you. Harold does not work for a living, *il est étudiant*."

"'E 'as money, Sophee. *Il est juif, n'est-ce pas?*"

Sophie stiffened. "Do not speak like that, Cecile, it is insult. *Moi aussi*," she said, jabbing her bosom with her thumb. "*Je suis juive*."

The girl stared in disbelief. Then she covered her mouth and moaned behind her hand, "*Excusez-moi*."

Sophie got up. "I will speak to Harold. I cannot promise to get money but I will try."

"I don't know anything about the law," Billy said after she had given him a rundown of her conversation with Cecile, "but he's a minor and I don't think he can be held responsible."

"Then his parents must assume responsibility. It's a moral obligation. She's not asking him to marry her. All she wants is a few dollars to give to her aunt and uncle because they're poor people. But if Harold claims he didn't get her pregnant, what's to be done? If it comes to a showdown Jessie will take his word against hers."

Sophie went down the hall to knock on Harold's door.

"Harold? It's me, Mrs. James. Can I speak to you for a minute?"

A second or two passed, and no sound from within. Then Harold's voice, precise in diction: "I'm sorry, Mrs. James, but you've got me at a critical time. I'm doing a paper on *War and Peace* for English Lit."

Sophie tried the door; it was locked. She gave it a bang with her fist. "Let me in!"

He came running and opened the door, just partly. "I'm sorry, Mrs. James, but I can't spare the time."

She put her arm through the partially open door, shoved him back and thrust her way in, pulling the door to behind her.

"This is an unwarranted intrusion."

"Save your breath to cool your porridge," Sophie said — an expression she had come across recently in a book. "Let's get down to brass tacks — Cecile's pregnant."

He jut his head forward. "*Mea non culpa.*"

"Don't give me that fancy talk. Speak English."

"I am not guilty," he crowed.

She gave him a tight smile. "You've just given yourself away. I haven't accused you."

He smirked and made her a deep bow. "Touché."

It was going to be easier than she thought. "Look, Harold, she's a simple girl, it's criminal to take advantage of her. All she's asking is a few measly dollars."

"How much, precisely?"

"She didn't say and I didn't ask."

He said the most he'd be able to scrape together would be thirty-five, perhaps forty dollars. He would have the money Monday noon. "But the mater must know nothing of this, agreed?"

Sophie gave him her hand to shake. "Agreed."

Around half-past eight Mrs. Little came knocking on their door, which was partly open. The radio was playing soft music, Sophie was in the armchair with a book, and the instructor was studying a manual on synchronized swimming.

Mrs. Little took a tiny step into the room. "You look so cosy. Am I intruding?" She said she had come to invite them downstairs for a game of bridge. Billy warned Mrs. Little that he was a clunkhead at cards and would probably ruin their game. She said not to worry, she would partner him, and they descended the stairs, the landlady with her arm through Sophie's.

Mr. Little, sitting at a card table set up in the kitchen, rose to receive them. Mrs. Little dealt the first hand, and opened the bidding with a diamond. Sophie, sitting under her hand, bid a spade. Billy frowned at his hand and passed. Mr. Little upped his partner's bid to two spades. Mrs. Little called three hearts; Sophie responded with three spades; Billy smiled apologetically at his partner and passed; Mr. Little took his partner's bid to game in spades. There was no further bidding. Mr. Little carefully laid down his cards one at a time, as if he were handling sticks of dynamite, till all thirteen (duds except for the Jack of spades, King and Queen of clubs) were exposed in four neat rows. Sophie's hand was meagre enough; his was a disaster. She'd be lucky if she were set only three.

"We're in for trouble, Mr. Little," she said, looking from her hand to his.

"The fah-fault is mine," he returned amiably.

Just then the doorbell rang. Mr. Little got up. "Suh-saved by the bell," he said, and went to see who it was.

They heard the sound of a woman's voice, hesitant, quiet-spoken; then a man's voice, strident, harsh. Next came the sound of footsteps approaching the kitchen, and Mr. Little returned with a man and a woman.

The woman, short and tubby, wore a summer print with puffed sleeves, ankle socks and sneakers, and on her head a kerchief tied under the chin. Her companion, a husky, thick-shouldered man with a flattened nose and belligerent expression, had on a white shirt open at the neck and rolled up at the sleeves and baggy pants belted at the hips.

The pair positioned themselves inside the kitchen a few feet from the door.

"Excuse me," said Mr. Little to no one in particular, and hurried out of the kitchen.

Mrs. Little put down her cards and rose from her place.

"Marie!" she exclaimed, rushing over to the woman. "What a pleasant surprise! How is the new baby, *l'enfant?*" Without waiting for a reply she said in the same breath, "And this gentleman I take it is your husband, *votre mari.*"

Marie, the former cleaner, dropped her head. "*Oui, madame,*" she said, gazing at the floor.

Mrs. Little turned to the man, offering her hand.

Ignoring the outstretched hand, he fastened his eyes on her with an insulting, openly contemptuous look. "You make ruse, madame," he said. "Claude Sorel is honest man. 'E will not take your 'and."

Mrs. Little's face went white. "How dare you! You come to my house uninvited, I receive you in a civil manner and you dare to insult me."

"I 'ave not come for *visite*, madame, I come for business. *Pour affaire,*" he said, insolently looking her up and down.

Mrs. Little crossed her trembling arms over her chest. "And what may I ask is your business with me?"

Sorel put his hands in his pockets and squared his shoulders. "Your son is *seducteur*. 'E makes tricks on innocent girl. 'E 'as done injure to Cecile. She is *enceinte* from your son."

Mrs. Little turned her head to the card table, where her guests were sitting like statues, and flung up her arms. "Sophie! Mr. James! Am I going out of my mind?" Then she turned to Sorel. "As I understand it," she said mockingly, "you have come to my house to inform me that my son is *père* to Cecile's unborn baby."

"*Oui.*"

"You're drunk!" she spat out at him.

Sorel took his hands out of his pockets. "That's for sure — for courage to speak *en face* with ugly woman."

She regarded him a moment with intense loathing, then darted out of the kitchen shrieking, "Morris! Harold!"

The instructor looked to his wife. "Let's get out of here, Soph, I don't want to get mixed up in this."

The words were hardly out of his mouth when the Littles appeared; Mrs. Little in the lead, Mr. Little side by side with his son.

"You will make your accusation to my son," said Mrs. Little, squaring up to Sorel, "and in the presence of my husband."

Sorel looked at Harold a long minute, then he spat on the floor. "*Maudit bâtard!* You 'ave done trick on Cecile. She 'as baby from you."

Harold cast a glance at the glob of spit on the floor. "You are mistaken, *monsieur*," he said, meeting Sorel's gaze with unblinking eyes. "I am not guilty. *Ce n'est pas moi.*"

Sorel shook his fist in Harold's face. "Okay, tell name. *Qui?* 'Oo 'as done it?"

Harold shrugged, jut his head forward. "*Cherchez-le.*"

Sorel brought his fist down on Harold's head with a blow that sent him sprawling.

His mother screamed.

Mr. Little helped his son to his feet.

Sophie went over to Mrs. Little, put her arm through hers and drew her into the hall. "Jessie," she said, holding her firmly by the arm, "this is going to be an awful shock to you."

She told her of her meeting with Cecile at the Golden Arrow, and of her confrontation later with Harold.

"He denied it at first, but later he admitted it and asked me not to say anything to you. But now that it's come out in the open he's frightened, that's why he's lying — Jessie! are you all right?"

Mrs. Little had gone limp; her knees were giving way. She gazed at Sophie with unfocussed eyes, as if she had been dealt the blow on the head. She drew in a deep breath, and with a wrench of her arm freed herself of Sophie's hold and leaned against the wall to keep from falling.

Sophie advanced an anxious step. "Jessie!"

Mrs. Little shrank back. "Don't touch me!"

Breathing heavily, she regarded Sophie with the look of loathing she had turned a few minutes ago on Sorel. Then she drew herself up. "Come with me," she said, and Sophie followed her to the kitchen.

She swept past the Sorels and interposed herself between her husband and son. "Please be seated, Mr. James," she said

143

to the instructor who had risen, and he sat down. She turned her head to Sophie. "You say my son admitted to you that he is the guilty party?"

Sophie's hand went to the back of her neck. She drew it quickly away and mumbled, "Yes."

She turned to Harold. "You're putting me in an awful position, Harold. Please tell the truth, there's no point in denying it now."

Harold paused, jutted his head forward and said, "I can only say to you now as I said to you before — *mea non culpa*, I am not guilty."

Sophie turned to her husband. "Billy! Didn't I tell you that Harold admitted he was to blame?"

Billy lowered his gaze to the card table and muttered, "Please, Soph, don't drag me into this."

She cast a murderous glance at his lowered head, then turned again to Harold. "If you are innocent," she said, why did you offer to give me forty dollars to give to Cecile?"

Sorel looked at his wife. "*Quarante dollar*," he sneered.

"Blackmail," Mrs. Little screamed. "I might have known that was the purpose of your call, Monsieur Sorel. There is a law against assault and battery. I will have you up in court."

He inclined his head. "*A votre service, madame.*"

Mrs. Little put a protective arm on her son's shoulder, and ordered the Sorels to leave. "If you do not leave my house this instant, I will call the police."

Her face turned pale; she sagged suddenly, her arm dropping from Harold's shoulder. "Morris," she moaned, tottering. He caught her before she fell. With his arms around her middle he hauled her backwards to the nearest chair, her feet dragging the floor.

Sorel offered his arm to his wife and they left without a backward glance. Sophie took a hesitant step towards Mrs. Little. Mrs. Little made a gesture of dismissal. "Please," she moaned, "spare me."

Sophie left the kitchen with her face on fire; the instructor said a polite good night and followed his wife upstairs.

Twenty

Sophie put the light on in the kitchen and sat down, drumming her fingers on the table. Billy took the chair next to her. "Soph," he began, and reached for her hand.

She snatched it away. "Don't speak to me."

He sighed. "I knew there'd be trouble if we got mixed up in this."

"If we got mixed up in this — you didn't get mixed up in anything. You made me out to be a liar. I should have known better than to appeal to a politely bred *goy* whose policy is hush, lower your voice, somebody might hear you."

"There's no point in trying to reason with you when you're in this frame of mind. I'm going to bed."

He woke in the middle of the night and found himself alone in the fourposter. He went looking for her. She was lying asleep on the chesterfield with her clothes on, the light from the floor lamp shining full in her face. He eased her shoes off her feet, turned off the lamp and went back to bed. When he came to the kitchen next morning, Emma was in her highchair with her bottle, and his wife, dress rumpled and hair uncombed, was cooking his breakfast cereal.

It upset him to see her dishevelled appearance. He wanted

to apologize for having chickened out on her, but was afraid of getting off on the wrong foot again and so he said nothing. He got up when he was finished, kissed the baby and said uneasily to his wife, "I'd better get going."

She put her arms around him. "I didn't mean what I said to you last night."

"Forget it, hon. I should have spoken up, I'm sorry about that."

"It wouldn't have helped. I realize that now. That lousy kid. I should have known that Jessie would take his word against anyone's, but I didn't think she'd turn on me like that. Oh God, what can I say to her to make it up?"

He gave her a comforting pat on the shoulder. "Least said soonest mended," kissed her and left for work.

Two minutes later he was back again. "Read this," he said, offering the folded piece of notepaper he had in his hand.

"Dear Mr. & Mrs. James," the note read, "I, Mrs. Little, in conjunction with my husband, Mr. Little, are desirous of repossessing the premises you occupy on the second floor of our house. We request therefore that you remove your furniture, your accoutrements, and your presences, as soon as possible. In view of the circumstances brought about by Mrs. James, we do not feel obliged to give a month's notice which you, as monthly tenants, are entitled to. Yours sincerely, (Mrs.) Jessie Little."

Sophie's heart began to beat very fast. She had to sit down. "Did she give you this?"

"Yes. She was on the verandah. She must have been waiting for me."

"Phone the Y. Tell them you're not coming in today."

"I can't, Soph."

"Then I'll phone them."

She lifted Emma out of her highchair. "Put a clean dress on her and put her in her carriage. Take her bed apart. We're not staying here another night."

She raced down the stairs. He heard her at the hall phone. "Pa, we're moving. We're coming home for a few days until we find another place." There was a pause. "Don't ask me any questions," she said and hung up. Then she phoned the

Y. "Mr. Rosenberg? It's me, Sophie. Billy can't come in to work today, he's got stomach flu. . . No, it's nothing serious. He wanted to go to work but I wouldn't let him."

She dropped the receiver and strode purposefully to the downstairs kitchen. Mrs. Little was by herself, sitting at the kitchen table with a cup of coffee and a cigarette.

Sophie stopped at the doorsill. "May I come in?"

Mrs. Little shrugged. "As you please."

She was without makeup. Her black hair hung down her back, and on her forehead was a bandage smelling strongly of vinegar. Her mouth without lipstick was a thinly incised line; her eyebrows, unpencilled, showed a few scattered hairs; and her eyes without mascara were bare of lashes.

Sophie took a chair opposite her. "Jessie," she said, "I'm sorry about what happened last night. I'd give anything to undo it. I'm not asking you to reconsider. If you want us to move we'll go. But I can't bear to leave this house with a feeling of ill-will between us. We've been such good friends. You've been my mentor, my—" She paused, overcome with emotion.

Mrs. Little stubbed out her cigarette, leaned back in her chair and put her hand in her bosom. "I've been a true friend to you, but you've been a false friend to me, treacherous and deceitful. I've nurtured an asp in my bosom," she said, feeling inside.

Sophie rose. "I've nothing more to say."

Billy was at the head of the stairs, standing beside the carriage with Emma dressed for going out. He put his hand in his back pocket, drew out a cheque and gave it to her. The cheque, for one hundred dollars, was made payable to Cash and signed Morris Little. "Harold gave this to me," he said. "You're to get the cash for it tomorrow and give the money to Cecile."

"I don't understand," said Sophie, studying the cheque.

"Harold said he'd explain everything. He's waiting for you."

She tapped on Harold's door and he opened right away. He ushered her in and shut the door.

"What's this all about?" she said, waving the cheque. "Is

147

this your father's signature, or did you forge it? I wouldn't put anything past you after last night."

"You do me an injustice, Mrs. James. The signature is genuine."

"I do you an injustice. You've turned your mother against me with your lies. We've been given notice to move, do you know that?"

He nodded unhappily. "Please, Mrs. James, let me explain. The mater," he said, "is a little touched in the head. It's a genetic inheritance. Her father spent his declining years in a loony bin. She's not certifiably nuts, she's an unhappy woman, neurotic, paranoid, but is able to function in what appears on the surface to be a perfectly normal manner. The pater is devoted to her, but she doesn't appreciate his devotion. I'm her pride and joy. She's in love with me, Mrs. James, her brilliant son. If I had admitted having had anything to do with Cecile, it might have sent her around the bend."

"What about this cheque?" she said. "Explain that to me."

"The pater is an understanding man. We had a confabulation after the mater went to bed and he very generously wrote me a cheque for twice the amount I asked for."

"It's lucky for Cecile that someone in this house has a conscience," said Sophie.

"One thing more," he said as she made to go.

Head lowered, he said he had not tricked Cecile as he had been accused of doing by Sorel. Of the two, it was he who was the virgin, not she. The second Saturday she came to clean she confided to him that she had a lover, a boy she had met at a church social. He was *très amoureux*, and they had done it several times in the back seat of his father's car in the garage. The third Saturday she came to clean, she did a fast cleanup of his room, then lay down on his bed saying she was *très fatiguée*.

He raised his head. "She offered herself to me—" he shrugged. "The flesh is weak. Now she claims she's pregnant and that I am to blame. You have a tender heart, Mrs. James, but Cecile is not the simple girl you've taken her to be."

"What do you mean? Are you implying she's pregnant by that boy in the garage?"

"My hands are not clean so I cannot give you a positive yes. All I can say is that on the three occasions I availed myself of La Flamme's favours, I practised *coitus interruptus*."

Billy was in the bedroom packing the baby's things. Her bed had been taken apart, its frame, bedspring and mattress leaning against the wall.

"You'll have to come back here and do the packing without me," Sophie said, coming into the room. "I don't ever want to see that woman again. We can't get a mover till tomorrow so you'll pack just what's necessary — our clothes, sheets, things like that. Everything else will have to go into storage till we find another place — except Emma's highchair, she'll need that."

He went down with the baby's chair and packed case and set them down at the foot of the verandah steps. When he came back, Sophie was in the kitchen combing her hair. She put the comb back in her purse. "I'll take Emma down, you take the carriage."

As they descended the stairs they heard a burst of music from the Littles' living room. The door was wide open and Mrs. Little, hair hanging down her back and forehead bound with a cloth, was leaning on propped elbows over the phonograph listening to Chaliapin singing at full volume an aria from "Boris Godounov."

The baby was put back in her carriage and they set out, Sophie wheeling the carriage, Billy carrying the highchair and suitcase. They walked a while in silence, then Sophie said, "You'll take that hundred-dollar cheque to the bank tomorrow and get a money order for it and mail it to Cecile. I don't ever want to see her again either."

"I can appreciate how you feel about Mrs. Little — but what have you got against Cecile? I thought you were sympathetic to her," he said guardedly.

"My sympathies were misdirected. Harold's a decent kid, she's the foxy one. And anti-Semitic."

When they got to the house, Sophie took the baby out of the carriage, and Billy followed her in carrying the baby's things. "God, what a mess," said Sophie, glancing around the kitchen.

A pot of cabbage borscht was boiling up on the stove, with its lid upside down. Beside it was a frying pan with hamburgers sizzling in chicken fat. The kitchen table was littered with potato peelings, onion skins, egg shells, spilled sugar, and on the windowsill was a *Yartzeit* commemorating the anniversary of the first Mrs. Glicksman's death. The pleated parchment shade Billy had bought to cover the bare bulb hanging by a cord from the ceiling was fly-specked, and attached to it was a strip of flypaper thickly covered with glued flies, a few still alive and buzzing. The pail under the sink was filled to the brim with kitchen garbage, and balanced on the rim of the sink and the back of a kitchen chair was a wooden board with a slab of wet flank steak, dredged with coarse salt, water dripping off the tilted board onto the floor.

Billy put his arms around his wife. "Don't let it worry you, hon, it's only a temporary measure." And left to do the packing.

The door to the summer kitchen stood open and Mrs. Glicksman, with an old broom worn down to the shape of a scythe, was sweeping up a mound of coarse salt. "A black year on it," she was saying, cursing the bag which lay split open on the floorboards. Intent, preoccupied, she didn't notice Sophie standing in the door with the baby in her arms.

The summer kitchen, a small windowless lean-to behind the kitchen, was used as a catchall. Bella's old coat, which hadn't seen the light of day in seven years, hung on a hook with its moth-eaten mouton collar. Leaning against Bella's coat was the leaky old boiler, at one time attached to the kitchen stove for hot water. The broken-down wooden icebox stood in another corner, and leaning against it was a ladder with its bottom rungs missing. A tumble of newspapers was on the floor; sticks of wood; a basket with coal in it for the stove; the pail Mrs. Glicksman used for her Friday night wash-down; a washtub with a washboard in it. A mop that hadn't been used for years was propped against the wall, and stuck to the floor was the old floor rag, clasped in the mop's rusted clamp. On a shelf running the length of one side of the summer kitchen were Glicksman's winter galoshes, a flatiron, an earthenware crock cracked down the middle, a scattering of candle ends, a tin of shoe polish, a grater, an old coffee pot with a hole in its bottom, a bar of kosher soap, and a large wooden bowl with a butcher's cleaver in it for chopping fish.

The summer kitchen door was open and Sophie could see through to the back yard. In a few short months it had become the jungle it was before Billy had put his hand to it. Three cats, replete with leftovers Mrs. Glicksman had thrown them, were dozing in the weeds, and a fourth cat, crouched, was sneaking up the steps that led into the summer kitchen.

Sidestepping her mother, Sophie strode across the floor and slammed the door shut.

Mrs. Glicksman started. "Sophie! You gave me a scare."

"Why do you leave the door open? The place stinks of catpee!"

"Why do I leave the door open. I forgot." She leaned her broom against the wall and held out her arms for the baby. "Let me hold her."

"Where's Pa?" Sophie asked, giving her the baby.

"Pa's upstairs making the baby's room ready."

Glicksman, a night watchman for a tobacco factory, worked five days a week from 6:00 P.M. to 6:00 A.M. He came home around half-past six and before going to bed spent half an hour or so in the kitchen reading the morning paper. Their bedroom was downstairs at the front of the house and Glicksman, a light sleeper, was kept awake by traffic on the street, kids going to and coming from school, peddlers calling their wares; so he had taken to using the back room upstairs, formerly Bella's. This was the room he had given up for the baby's use after she was weaned. When Sophie and Billy moved, he resumed use of the room where he could sleep without being disturbed by the noises on the street.

"And where will Pa sleep?" Sophie asked.

"Where will Pa sleep," said Mrs. Glicksman. "With me."

Sophie took Emma's sheets out of the packed case and went upstairs to make up the cot.

151

Glicksman, suspenders hanging from his pants, was sweeping the floor which he had scattered with wet tea leaves to keep the dust from rising. "What happened there that you're moving all of a sudden?" he said, seeing his daughter.

"Because she's crazy."

"Who? Mrs. Little?"

His daughter made no reply; he could see she was upset. "She seemed to me like a very nice woman. Educated," he said cautiously, "civilized."

"Civilized! She's touched in the head. Her own son told me that."

Sophie put the baby's sheets on a chair and went to the bathroom to use the toilet. A minute later she was calling from the bathroom, "What's the matter with the toilet? It won't flush."

Glicksman came. "Something is out of order." He took the lid off the water tank, put his hand under the ballcock and held it suspended. "I'll have to get hold of a plumber," he mused, waiting for the water to rise.

Later in the afternoon Billy returned by taxi with four packed cases and Sophie's library books. He unpacked the cases, hung his and Sophie's clothes in the closet and made up their bed. Shortly after six he put Emma to bed. Sitting beside the cot, waiting for Emma to finish her bottle, his eyes travelled slowly around the room. The floor, he observed, had been swept clean, but the baseboard was overlaid with ingrained dirt. The window had been washed and a freshly washed net curtain hung on it, still damp. The bed Glicksman had been sleeping in looked like an apple-pie bed, its lumpy surface covered with a faded chenille spread.

Billy sighed; his wife was not a very practical person. She had acted on impulse without considering the consequences, and look what a mess she had landed them in. It distressed him that Emma would be sleeping in this unsanitary room in a cot too small for her, till they found another place. But the fault was his; it was up to him to have taken a stand. He should have faced up to Mrs. Little and insisted on a month's notice which they were entitled to. He should have handled it himself instead of letting Sophie call the shot. Why hadn't he acted more forcefully? He was capable of making decisions on his own; he made decisions at the Y, he spoke up at Board meetings, he programmed swimming meets, conducted his classes with authority, and was respected for it. It was only with Sophie that he was incapable of asserting himself.

He was roused from his reverie by Emma throwing her bottle over the side. He waited a minute to make sure she was asleep, then went downstairs.

Glicksman was sitting in his chair with a glass of wine and the Sunday paper. Sophie was in her place opposite the window, with her nose in a book. At her end of the table Mrs. Glicksman, with the rim of a pot gripped in one hand and a fork in the other, was mashing boiled potatoes.

Mrs. Glicksman set down the pot of potatoes, took up a soup plate, filled it with cabbage borscht and served it to her son-in-law. Sophie reminded her mother that he didn't like borscht and moved the plate to her father's place. Mrs. Glicksman then put two hamburgers on a plate, and a mound of mashed potatoes. "He likes my *cocletten*," she said. "I made them specially for him." Sophie took the plate from her mother and set it before her husband. He cut into a hamburger, put a small portion in his mouth and laid down his knife and fork.

"What's the matter?" Sophie asked. "She made them specially for you — hamburgers to celebrate the return of the prodigal son-in-law."

He rose. "I'm sorry but I can't eat them. My stomach is churned up from all that commotion."

Sophie's eyes followed him as he left the kitchen. "Oh God, these hyper-sensitive types." Reaching for her book, she noticed her father shaking his head at her. "What are you shaking your head at me for!" she said, bridling. "Is it my fault that his stomach is churned up?"

Glicksman made no answer. He put on his glasses, folded his paper in half and ate his borscht behind it. Mrs. Glicksman served her daughter a plate of borscht, filled her own plate and the meal continued without comment to its finish.

Sophie got up and put her book under her arm. "That was a good supper," she said to her mother, and went upstairs.

Billy was sitting in the window seat. Slumped forward, head bent low, he was silently crying with his hands over his face.

She had never seen him in tears before and the picture of misery he presented caught at her heart. She sat down beside him. "What's the matter, Billy?" she asked, taking his hands off his face.

He took a handkerchief from his pocket and wiped his eyes. "I feel so blue," he said, then he dropped his head on her shoulder and fastened her arms around his waist. "Rock me, hon," he murmured.

Arms clasped around his waist, she rocked him from side to side, her body swaying in unison with his. Presently his head began to feel heavy on her shoulder. She rocked him a while longer then disengaged her arms from his waist.

"You must be hungry. You haven't eaten anything since breakfast."

He said he wouldn't mind something to eat; but nothing spicy, his stomach felt queasy. She offered to get him something from the neighbourhood ice-cream parlour. "What about a malted milk? And a piece of cake or something like that to go with it."

"I'd appreciate that," he said.

When she returned with a container of malted milk and two cup cakes, he was lying in bed on his back, his eyes roving the ceiling. He raised a naked arm and pointed a finger to the ceiling. "Look at those cobwebs, Soph."

Twenty-One

The following evening when Sophie was giving the baby her supper, her husband telephoned from the Y. "I've been trying to get in touch with you," he said, "but the line was always busy."

"I've been on the phone all day practically, trying to get hold of a mover. I got one finally but—"

"Soph," he broke in, "Dad passed away. Mother called from Taylor's Funeral Parlour in Galt around half-past one." He paused. "Hold the line a minute till I put someone in charge of the tank. I left it unattended," he said; there were tears in his voice.

He returned presently and told her that his father bicycling to work that morning had been run over by a truck. "He died of internal injuries, mercifully without regaining consciousness."

"I'm sorry, Billy. I'm terribly sorry."

"Thank you," he replied.

Sophie hung up the phone and stood a while in the hall. His mother, he said, had called at half-past one. How could he have taken classes knowing his father was laid out in a funeral parlour? He could have put up a notice on the bulletin board cancelling all classes. "Dad passed away," he said. The man had been struck down and killed!

She returned to the kitchen and said to her mother, "That was Billy on the phone. His father was run over by a truck and killed."

Mrs. Glicksman put down her glass of tea. "Killed?" A shudder passed through her. "An ugly death," she said. "He was an old man, your father-in-law?"

"He was about Pa's age, I think."

"Bite your tongue!" said her mother sharply.

Billy came home shortly after. He went over to his baby and kissed her. Then he took off his tie and told his wife that the funeral would be held Wednesday at two o'clock.

"That's the day after tomorrow," he said bleakly. He put his arms around her. "Oh, Soph," he sobbed.

Next morning, at Sophie's insistence, Billy telephoned the Y to advise Mr. Rosenberg that he would not be in to work until Thursday. He was reluctant to do this. He had already taken Sunday off. His wife had to steer him to the phone.

"I'm sorry, Mr. Rosenberg, but I — my Dad eh —" Hemming and hawing and standing on one leg like a stork he brought out in apologetic tones that his father had met with a fatal accident.

Three o'clock that afternoon they were at Union Station boarding a train for Galt.

When they got to the house the door was opened to them by Louise's fiancé, Roger Hall. He shook hands with his future brother-in-law. "This is a very sad occasion," he said, leading them into the living room. "The girls are at the funeral parlour but they should be home soon. They've been there all afternoon receiving visitors."

"How's Mother taking it?" Billy asked.

"Like a brick," Roger replied.

"And the girls?"

"They're bearing up. Louise is taking it rather harder than Mary, but on the whole they're all being very good. Your Dad was a wonderful man, Billy."

With an effort Billy brought out, "Was he badly bruised?"

"Not a mark on him. The injuries were internal and when

the men got him out from under the wheels your Dad was still conscious. 'Don't take me home, boys,' he said to them." Roger sat back and crossed his legs. "How's that for grit?"

Billy held out the baby to his wife. "Take her." They heard him going up the stairs, sobbing.

The baby began squirming and arching her back. Sophie put her on the floor. Presently they heard footsteps on the verandah. The mother and sisters, hatted, came into the living room.

"Who have we here?" said the mother. She stooped and gathered up the child in her arms.

Sophie went up to her mother-in-law. "I'm sorry," she said, offering her hand.

With the baby in her arms, she took Sophie in a one-arm embrace and kissed her on the cheek. Sophie then turned to Louise. "I'm sorry," she repeated. And when Louise embraced her without taking her hand, Sophie felt she was doing it all wrong. She should be kissing them instead of holding out her hand and blaring I'm sorry. Without offering her hand she kissed Mary and said she was sorry, then went upstairs to fetch her husband.

He was standing at the window. He went to the dresser mirror as she came in. "I can't go down like this, Soph. Look at my eyes."

"They're a little red, but it's not a disgrace to cry for your father."

Saying, "It'll upset them to see me like this," he went to the bathroom, ran the cold water tap over a face cloth and applied the cold compress to his eyes.

Sophie unpacked the case, hung up the clothes they had brought to wear to the funeral, and went downstairs.

Her mother-in-law with her hat still on was sitting in the sofa, Billy was beside her with his head bent and hands clasped between his knees.

"It's hard not to grieve for Dad," the mother was saying, "but you must try, dear." She rose as Sophie came in, and said, "Dad loved his family and wouldn't have wanted us to mourn him."

And Sophie who had not felt any emotional impact at the death of her father-in-law began to weep her first tears for him.

"I'm sorry," she sobbed. "I'm very sorry," and broke down completely.

Just then Mary came to the door. "Mother, did Aunt Margaret say she was—" Seeing her sister-in-law in tears, she paused in the doorway a second, then returned to the kitchen leaving her question suspended. Her mother followed her out, and Billy went over to his wife. "Don't, hon," he said, "you're upsetting everyone."

His mother returned to the room. "Supper's ready but we're waiting on Aunt Margaret. She's very late."

Billy smiled. "She's probably looking for something she's mislaid.

The mother explained to Sophie that Aunt Margaret was always losing things or mislaying them. "It's her age, poor dear. She gets herself into an awful tizzy. I've seen her hunt for a scarf that's around her neck," she said, and at the same moment the doorbell rang.

The mother went to the door and returned with a tiny woman dressed in a navy blue crepe redingote with a matching dress underneath. On her head was a large navy tam which she wore at a slant. Her face, high in colour, was puffy and wrinkled. She had an upturned nose and round brown eyes. The round eyes, tilted nose, tam set at a rakish angle with a pink ear showing through sparsely clustered grey curls — these features, combined with a withered skin, gave her the look of a Kewpie doll grown old.

On entering she pressed a gloved hand to her heart and apologized for being late. She exclaimed admiringly over the baby, embraced her nephew, then turned to Sophie.

"We speak of Billy and his wife quite often," she said, "but I'm afraid I've forgotten your name."

Sophie spoke her name and Aunt Margaret, perfumed with a sweet-smelling scent reminiscent of vanilla extract, embraced her niece and said she would not forget her name again.

She turned her eyes upwards and said that everything under the sun had conspired to make her late. Then, just as she

158

was getting off the streetcar, who should she see but Mrs. Ward!

"Lo and behold, there she was at the top of the street, wearing her winter coat — in this weather, Nell! — with only her nightie on underneath." She explained to Sophie that Mrs. Ward was a dear old lady who had become senile in the last few years. Mrs. Ward's senility, she said, had taken a very odd form. You never knew what she would do next. She sometimes forgot who she was, or where, and at other times could be quite keen. She was looked after by her daughter Marjorie who was very talented at the piano. Marjorie used to give lessons but when her mother was taken queer, she gave up teaching. "She takes in sewing, poor girl, so that she can be at home to look after her mother."

She turned again to her sister-in-law. "There she was, striding along on this side of the street, Nell, with a bouquet of flowers, cut from her own garden, I expect, and all of a sudden something told me she was coming here."

She said it was only when she saw the flowers that it dawned on her that Mrs. Ward, addled as she was, poor soul, was coming to pay her respects. Thinking of the disturbance a visit from Mrs. Ward would cause at a time like this — let alone the manner in which she was dressed — Aunt Margaret decided then and there to prevent her from coming in, if she could. "You know how obstreperous she can get when she's crossed."

Then the strangest thing happened. On seeing Aunt Margaret, Mrs. Ward made her a curtsy and offered the flowers. "I can't think who she thought I was — someone important, I expect — and she quite obviously had forgotten who and where she was."

She accepted the flowers (which she later put in a trash can, they were so badly wilted), and requested Mrs. Ward to please follow her. With that she turned about face and led her straight to Paley's Ice Cream & Confectionery Parlour. She sat Mrs. Ward down at the counter, ordered a banana split for her, and then had a word with Mr. Paley. He very kindly said not to worry, that he would telephone Marjorie to come and get her mother.

"She was such a clever woman in her day," Aunt Margaret

concluded. "Do you remember what a head she had on her, Nell? And the reader she was! Poor soul. The years have not dealt kindly with her." She touched her hand to her tam, said she would keep it on because her hair was a mess, and they went in to supper.

The girls, who were sitting at table with Roger between them, rose to greet their aunt. Aunt Margaret took her bereaved nieces — first Louise, then Mary — in her embrace, with no words spoken. To Roger, who had also risen, she extended a hand and absently inquired, "How is your mother?"

Billy, at his mother's request, took his father's chair, and when the mother had taken her place Roger sat down again between the sisters. Plates were passed to the mother, and when everyone had been served she put some food on her own plate, set aside the serving dishes and looked to her son. "Billy?"

He lowered his head. "For what we are about to receive," he recited, "may the Lord make us truly thankful. Amen."

Uppermost in everyone's thoughts was the man laid out at Taylor's Funeral Parlour. But no mention was made of him, nor was his name spoken. Food was taken in silence. After a time the widow remarked on the weather.

"The man on the radio said it has been the hottest day on record in forty years."

"It sure has been a scorcher," said Roger.

Passing his plate for a second helping, Roger praised the meatloaf. His future mother-in-law acknowledged the compliment. With set smiles on their faces the widow and bereaved daughters spoke at random of inconsequential things, each politely yielding when her remark or comment happened to coincide with the speaker's, their eyes bright with unshed tears.

Sophie marvelled that they could keep up this pretense. Here was her mother-in-law with a fixed smile listening attentively to her son sitting at the table's head in place of her husband, while he spoke of a swimming meet he had scheduled for next week in which his swimmers were to compete with the YMCA's team of synchronized swimmers.

And while in her thoughts Sophie pitied them because they felt bound, for the sake of form, to put on such an obviously painful show of make-believe, in her heart she scorned them for it.

Twenty-Two

Roger left shortly after supper. Billy and his mother went to the living room to talk over particulars of the funeral service. The girls washed up, Aunt Margaret dried, and Sophie, who had put the baby's bottle on to warm, sat with the child in her lap.

After Sophie had put the baby to bed with her bottle, she opened the suitcase they had brought and got out her diary. She read through several pages given over to unstinted praise of Jessie Little, then she took her Penman's from her handbag, sat down at the bedside table and — to finish for all time the Jessie Little episode — wrote in her diary the following two lines: "What a rude awakening it is to discover that you have reposed your trust, admiration and friendship in a frustrated semi-hysteric. With a friend like J.L. one does not need an enemy."

On a fresh page she wrote: "B's father was run over by a truck yesterday morning and died shortly after. B, his mother and sisters are stricken, naturally, by the death of a loved husband and father — but you'd never know it from their behaviour. Smiles and polite chit-chat is the order of the day. You may be torn apart inwardly, that's acceptable, but an

162

outward show of emotion or grief is not nice. I must say that I can't understand the *goyische* psyche. The fact that they are *able* to maintain this kind of restraint simply defeats me. When the girls were washing up after supper, they talked about what they would wear to the funeral tomorrow. They're going to bury their father, for God's sake! and they're fussing about what would be a proper dress to wear to his funeral."

She held her pen poised a second, then put it to the page. "Our people rend their garments," she wrote. Hearing her husband's steps on the stairs, she quickly returned her diary to the suitcase.

"Mother and I are going to Taylor's Funeral Parlour," he said, coming into the room. "They're staying open till ten, then the casket will be sealed." He sat down on the edge of the bed and began cracking his knuckles. "It'll upset me terribly to see Dad. Just to think of him makes my heart ache," and his eyes filled with tears.

"Then don't go. Your mother will understand."

He said his mother hadn't asked him to come with her but he felt he should go. People who hadn't been able to come during the day would be dropping in this evening and would expect to see him there. He kissed her and then went downstairs.

She got her diary out. "The charade continues," she wrote. "B just left for the funeral parlour. He'll be shattered to see the mangled corpse of his father laid out in an open coffin. But he went because it's expected of him." She put her diary away and went over to the baby's cot.

Emma had fallen asleep with her half-finished bottle clasped loosely in her fist. Sophie eased the bottle from the child's grasp and took it to the bathroom to rinse. Opening the bathroom door, she saw Aunt Margaret standing at the cabinet mirror. Her handbag and tam were on the toilet seat. With a pocket mirror in her hand, she was standing with her profile to the cabinet mirror, carefully spreading apart a few curls, intently probing, examining with the aid of her pocket mirror the side of her head that had been kept under cover by her tam.

She turned and saw Sophie standing in the doorway. "Do you want in, dear?"

Sophie retreated a step. "I just wanted to rinse the baby's bottle but it can wait."

"Come in," said Aunt Margaret, putting her pocket mirror back in her purse. "I was just looking at my poor old head. I burnt it," she said plaintively, like a child.

"You burnt your *head*?" Sophie exclaimed.

Aunt Margaret said she had curled her hair this afternoon before going to the funeral parlour and had let her curling irons get too hot. She put her hand to her head. "I burnt my scalp," she said, tenderly fingering between the curls.

Sophie put the baby's bottle in the sink and went over to the medicine cabinet. "Let's see if there's something here for burns."

She opened the cabinet door and found among the supplies nothing for a burn. "There should be something in Billy's first-aid kit. Let's go to our room." She gave the baby's bottle a fast rinse and they proceeded to the bedroom.

Aunt Margaret took a chair, putting her tam and purse on the floor by her feet. Sophie opened the suitcase and found her husband's first-aid kit alongside his shaving things. His kit, equipped to deal with exigencies, contained (in addition to a tube of Ozonol for burns) Fingertip Quik-Bands for cuts, cotton wool, bandage gauze, aspirin, lotion for eye fatigue, a gargle for sore throat, glycerin suppositories in adult and infant size for constipation, powders to relieve a dyspeptic stomach, a rubbing compound to treat aching muscles, and Absorbine Jr. for athlete's foot.

Sophie plucked a wad of cotton wool from the neatly rolled paper casing and squeezed a liberal spread of healing salve on it. Aunt Margaret separated a few scorched curls to show where the burn was, and Sophie applied the salve, spreading it gently on an inch-long burn.

Aunt Margaret sighed and said she had forgotten how nice it was to be fussed over. Dan had spoiled her dreadfully. He was a dear man and she missed him sadly. They were an ideally suited couple, she said, though she was a little older than Dan.

"Two or three years older, hardly worth mentioning." (Sophie remembered Billy saying Aunt Margaret was twelve years older than Uncle Dan.) "His mother raised the roof when she heard we were going to be married. She was dead set against the match. Dan said not to worry, she'd come around, but she never did. She was a crotchety old woman and the week before we were married she made a point of telling me to my face I would be robbing the cradle if I married her son, that I was old enough to be his mother. She said I was desperate to find a husband and, as *a last ditch stand* — those were her very words — I had won her son over by practising my old maid's wiles on him. As a matter of fact, I—"

"Old maid's wiles," Sophie interrupted, "that's a contradiction in terms."

Without comment, Aunt Margaret continued. "As a matter of fact, I had a lot of beaus. Last ditch stand indeed! I was a much-courted young lady," she said, reminiscently winding around her finger a curl on the good side of her head.

Sophie got up to light a cigarette.

"May I have one too, dear?" Aunt Margaret said.

"I'm sorry, I didn't know you smoked." Sophie offered the cigarettes.

Aunt Margaret said she didn't smoke very often. Dan had taught her to smoke. She didn't much care for it at first, but after a while when she got in the habit of having a cigarette after supper, she began to enjoy it.

She smiled. "Dan used to tease me. He called me his hoyden," she said. "But I never smoke in public places or when I'm visiting." Saying, "It's one of my secret vices," she drew on her cigarette and blew out a whiff, a puff of smoke. She asked did Sophie mind if she stayed a while longer. "I'm not quite ready for bed, and I do enjoy a natter."

"I won't stay long." She wagged a warning finger. "I'm an awful chatterbox — promise to shoo me out the minute I've overstayed my welcome?"

Sophie promised and Aunt Margaret, a tiny figure weighing a brittle ninety pounds or so, stooped with a creaking of joints to her bag and took from it a halved lemon wrapped in waxed paper. She undid the wrapping, laid the square of paper on the bedside table Sophie had put between their chairs, and sat down with the halved lemon in her hand. Saying she had read an article in the *Ladies Home Journal* three months ago which said a nightly application of lemon would in time lighten liver spots and might even erase them altogether, she began vigorously rubbing the halved lemon over the backs of her hands which were speckled with brown spots. She gave the back of each hand a good rubbing several times over, rewrapped the squeezed-dry half lemon, dropped it into her bag, then examined her hands, frowning.

"These ugly spots — but they are getting a bit lighter." She put her hands palms down on the table. "At least I think they are?" she said, inviting Sophie's opinion.

Sophie took a passing glance at the veined liver-spotted hands. "I wouldn't worry about them," she said. "They're not ugly spots, they look like freckles."

The old lady examined her hands again. "They can't possibly be mistaken for freckles," she sighed, "not on the hands of the old. They're commonly referred to as graveyard marks."

"How barbaric!" Sophie exclaimed.

"I have some dreadful nightmares about dying." A shudder passed through her. "I'm terribly frightened of it." This was said in a whisper.

Sophie asked, "Don't you believe in a hereafter?" Most church-going people believed in Heaven. Some, from the books she had read, couldn't wait to get there.

For answer Aunt Margaret asked of her, "Do you believe in an afterlife?"

Sophie poked a finger at herself. "I personally do not believe in an afterlife," she said, then wished she hadn't. "But that doesn't say there isn't one," she offered.

Hesitantly the old lady said, "I don't know very much about your religion but don't your people, I mean people of your faith—" she paused — "Jews," she finally brought out, "don't *they* believe in an afterlife?"

Sophie didn't care for the turn the conversation was taking. She was reasonably sure there was no prejudice in Billy's family against Jews, but Aunt Margaret wasn't very bright

166

and God knows what she might come out with next if they got on the subject of comparative religions.

"I can't speak for all," Sophie replied. "Some do and some don't."

"Is there a Heaven in your religion?"

"Of course. It's called Gan Eden, which means paradise. There's also a Hell. That's called Gehenna. My father doesn't believe in either. He says Heaven is a fairy tale, and Hell is what we endure on earth."

"Is your father an atheist?" Aunt Margaret asked, shocked.

Sophie shrugged. "He's more of a freethinker, a nihilist."

Aunt Margaret pondered freethinker, nihilist. "I'm afraid I'm not up on these words."

"Skeptic, agnostic," said Sophie. "He's not a God-fearing man for the simple reason that he doesn't believe in the existence of a Deity."

Aunt Margaret said in mildly reproving tones, "A non-believer, dear, is an atheist."

"Not at all. There's a great difference between atheism and agnosticism," Sophie said, not sure herself what the difference was.

Aunt Margaret murmured an understanding "Oh."

"Although he doesn't believe in an afterlife, he's not afraid of death. He says it's a dreamless sleep, an eternal never-ending peace with no headaches or worries."

"Your father must be a very clever man to have such thoughts," said Aunt Margaret respectfully.

"He is a clever man. And the remarkable thing is that he never had the benefit of an education. He's a self-taught man and can talk intelligently on almost any subject." On any subject, she said to herself, except how to make a decent living. "Neighbours come to him for advice on legal matters." Saying, "My father would have made a very good lawyer," she stubbed out her cigarette, excused herself and went to the bathroom. Sitting on the toilet, she reveried Lawyer Glicksman, a robed fiery-tempered five-foot-four man arguing a case in Osgoode Hall, giving the presiding judge what for. When she returned, the old lady was sitting with her head down, musing, hands folded in her lap.

She looked up. "I must try and keep in mind," she said, "what your father said about the hereafter being a dreamless sleep."

She said she wasn't afraid so much during the daytime. In the daytime she busied herself with one thing and another and seldom gave it a thought. It was only at night when she went to bed that this dreadful, un-Christian fear came over her.

"If I weren't alone, dear — if Dan was still alive I might not be so frightened of—" Unable to bring herself to utter the dreaded word "death," she substituted "it."

All at once she brightened. Saying she had brought something with her to chase away the blues, she leaned down to her purse and withdrew from it a paper bag from which she took a little silver cup and a small bottle labelled HP Sauce 8.5 ozs net. "This was Dan's christening cup," she said, setting the silver cup on the bedside table. She then uncapped the bottle. "I usually take a tot before going to bed. It helps me to sleep." (The small bottle, washed clean of HP Sauce, contained 8.5 ozs gin.)

She filled Dan's christening cup to the brim. "The cup that cheers," she said, sipping straight gin. "Will you have a little tot with me?"

"No, thank you, it'll just be wasted on me. I never have any trouble getting to sleep."

Aunt Margaret sighed. "Nor did I at your age." Holding her husband's christening cup lovingly in both hands, she took a sip of gin. "I'm beginning to feel drowsy but let's have a little chat before I turn in. Just a cosy little chat. Nothing intellectual, dear. You're far too clever for me, I won't be able to hold my end up."

Sophie pooh-poohed the notion of her superior intelligence and they sat a while in silence, Aunt Margaret sipping gin. All of a sudden her eyes filled with tears. She put her cup down and wept silently, holding a handkerchief to her eyes.

Sophie got up and put her arm clumsily around her shoulder.

The old lady dried her eyes. "I'm making a nuisance of myself, I'd better go to my room," she said, but made no move to pick up her things.

Sophie lit a cigarette and went back to her chair.

Aunt Margaret took a swig of gin. "I don't cry about it very often — at least not any more I don't. About Dan's death," she explained, noting Sophie's puzzled expression. She drummed her fingers abstractedly on the table, then she put the cup to her lips and took a sizeable swallow. "My gums are sore," she said. "I need new dentures. These are so badly fitted." Saying, "I'd better take them out for a while," she put down her cup, turned her back and took out her uppers and lowers and put them on the table, wrapped in her handkerchief. "That feelth better," she said, and settled back in her chair with a sigh of relief. She replenished her cup, sucked in a drop of gin and said apologetically, "I'm afraid I don't thpeak very well with my teeth out."

The baby began whimpering and stirring restlessly in her cot. Sophie said, "She's probably wet," and got up to change her diaper. She gave the baby a change of diaper, and went back to her guest. The old lady, sitting loosely in her chair with her head sunk to her chest, had fallen asleep. Sophie shook her gently by the shoulder.

She opened her eyes and gazed blearily at her hostess. "I've had a drop too much." Apologizing for dropping off, she capped the HP Sauce bottle which still held an ounce or two of gin and dropped it and Dan's christening cup into her bag which lay open at her feet, then rose unsteadily and bent to gather up her things.

Swaying slightly and half asleep on her feet, she made her way to the door, her bag grasped feebly in one hand, her tam in the other.

Sophie opened the window to its full to clear the air of smoke — Billy didn't like her to smoke with the baby in the room — then, as she was dumping the telltale cigarette butts into a paper bag, she noticed that the handkerchief Aunt Margaret had wrapped her dentures in was still on the night table; the old lady had forgotten to take her teeth.

Before five minutes passed, there was a knock on the door.

Wearing a sheer baby-blue nightgown, Aunt Margaret stood in the doorway, abashed at having forgotten her teeth. "Dan uthed to thay I'd forget my head if it wathn't properly thcrewed on," she said with a cupped hand over her mouth. Steadier on her feet now, she moved to the table, took up her dentures and stood a while with them in her hand, apologizing for making a nuisance of herself. As she stood there with the overhead light shining full on her, the closely fitted bodice of her sheer nightgown revealed an outline of her bosom where two little sacs — more like bean bags emptied of beans — hung from her chest.

Sophie was moved at the sight of the pitifully dwindled breasts, the caved-in mouth, the doll-like face with withered cheeks, the liver-spotted hands. They said good night at the door and Sophie, recalling with pity the old lady's fear of death, her aloneness, impulsively embraced her. "Sleep well," she said and kissed her on the cheek.

Twenty-Three

People were grouped in the lobby of Taylor's Funeral Parlour, conversing in hushed tones with the Reverend Jenkins and Mr. Taylor. On the arrival of the bereaved family, the officiating minister and the funeral director detached themselves from the group and came forward to receive them. The doors to the small chapel stood open and several people were seated in pews on the left side of the chapel, some with bowed heads, listening to an invisible organist rendering on an invisible organ "Beautiful Isle of Somewhere."

More people arrived and addressed themselves to the bereaved family. The son shook hands with all who approached and emotionally thanked them for coming. With a strained smile that never left his face, he gazed abstractedly around the lobby, his eyes once or twice falling on his wife without a flicker of recognition.

Roger came bounding up the steps and hurried over to Aunt Margaret. Bending from the waist, he said in an agitated whisper, "Marjorie must be out of her mind. She's bringing her mother to the funeral." He straightened himself. "If that isn't the limit," he said, then passed through the chapel doors and seated himself in the pallbearers' pew.

Aunt Margaret turned her head towards the entrance. "This must be one of Mrs. Ward's good days," she said to Sophie, "or Marjorie wouldn't dream of bringing her." Standing at a remove from the open doors, they watched the two women coming slowly up the steps.

Mrs. Ward, a tall gaunt-faced woman with a muscular twitch which spasmodically jerked her head upwards or sent it lolling crazily from side to side, was dressed in an autumnal coloured print. A parasol dangled from her wrist; on her restless head was a shallow crowned straw hat with a wide brim, and on her feet brown and white spectator pumps. Marjorie, a washed-out-looking woman shorter by a head than her mother, was wearing a plum-coloured dress with long sleeves, a close-fitting felt hat of no definable colour, and on her feet a pair of Mary Jane slippers.

On entering the lobby, both women came to a standstill, Mrs. Ward's head under the cartwheel hat bobbing this way and that. On seeing the curious glances they were attracting, Marjorie protectively drew her mother's arm through hers. Casting about with worried eyes for a friendly face, she was relieved to see Aunt Margaret coming forward to greet them.

Addressing herself first to Mrs. Ward, Aunt Margaret said how nice it was to see her. "And looking so well," she added, beaming.

Mrs. Ward stared at her a moment, then turned to her daughter and said in a stage whisper, "Who is this dwarfish person?"

"Behave yourself, Mother," said Marjorie sharply. "You know perfectly well who this lady is. She's Mrs. James — Mrs. Daniel James."

Mrs. Ward gazed down again at Aunt Margaret. "Mrs. Daniel James," she said, "nee Margaret Carruthers. We were classmates at senior high. I was—"

"What a wonderful memory you have," Aunt Margaret put in.

Commandingly, Mrs. Ward said, "Don't interrupt my train of thought." Her head suddenly steadied itself. Fixing an unwavering gaze on her former classmate, she said with pride, "I was valedictorian of our graduating class, if you remember."

"Indeed I do," said Aunt Margaret who couldn't recall the occasion. "Those were happy days, Mrs. Ward. We should see more of each other, there are so few of us left."

Mrs. Ward jerked her arm away from Marjorie's. "My daughter, a mistaken genius at the piano and an unskilled seamstress to boot, virtually keeps me a prisoner in my own house. By God's will I'm not enfeebled yet or she'd have me tied to the bedpost." Her head bobbed up, it was commencing its erratic cycle. "Here comes Billy James Junior," she said, pointing with her furled umbrella. "Will he deign to speak to us, I wonder."

He did more than just deign to speak to them. Each received a smile, a handshake, and as he had done with all, he thanked them for coming. Mr. Taylor came hurrying up to them. He put his hand on Billy's sleeve and pointed out that the lobby was rapidly emptying; the last of the people were now going into the chapel. The smile faded from the instructor's face. "I'm a little unnerved," he said.

"Understandably so," said Mr. Taylor, and they proceeded to the chapel with the undertaker in the lead.

He conducted the son to the front row pew, where his mother and sisters were already seated; Aunt Margaret and Sophie he put in the pew behind them. When it came to seating the Wards, Mr. Taylor found himself in conflict with Mrs. Ward who balked at being shown to a pew on the left side of the chapel. Mrs. Ward declared that she and her daughter, who was a distinguished pianist, were not of a mind to be pushed around or treated like gate-crashers, and with a toss of her head, sat down next to Sophie. Momentarily forgetful of the dignity of his calling, the undertaker raised his shoulders in a shrug, hurried down centre aisle and passed out of sight.

The invisible organist brought his final selection to a close, and the minister made his appearance through a side door and took up his position at the lectern.

The casket was centred on a platform about ten feet from the front pews. On its closed lid was the family wreath, and to either side of the coffin were floral tributes from friends and neighbours.

Mr. Jenkins glanced down with a sad smile at the occupants of the front row pew, then raised his head. Addressing the assembly, he began: "We are saddened and impoverished by the loss of a good man. . . "

Billy James, he said, was a warm, decent human being who would be remembered for his kindliness of heart and generosity of spirit. He was a man who was devoted to his home, his family, and loyal to his friends. He was a modest man who never put himself forward. Ungrudging of the other fellow's success, he wished him well, and was content with his own lot. . .

The eulogy over, his gaze returns to the widow and her children. He regards them gravely. Sadly he says, "We cannot halt the hand of time, or live again the past." And recites for their hearts' ease: "His gentle ways and smiling face/ are a pleasure to recall/ He had a kindly word for each/ and passed on beloved of all."

He bids the congregation to rise. He bows his head. "Our Father," he begins, and the assemblage intones the prayer with him. At the conclusion of the Lord's Prayer he steps down from the platform, walks a few paces down the aisle, and halts. Mr. Taylor joins him and they stand side by side with folded hands.

The six pallbearers — of whom Roger is one — make their way in single file up the four steps to the platform. Roger removes the family wreath from the coffin and places it beside a grouping of variegated summer flowers. The pallbearers then position themselves, three to each side of the coffin. At a nod from Roger the coffin is lifted and they proceed, taking extra care coming down the steps that it not be tilted in its descent.

A hush falls over the chapel.

Standing behind her husband, Sophie watches his face as he stands with head turned, his eyes on the slowly approaching coffin. There is no evidence on his features of grief. Knowing his pain, she marvels at his composure. If it were my father, she thinks — and on the sudden a vision of her father, shrouded, sealed in a coffin, presents itself to her. The coffin is borne slowly past and Sophie, overcome with emotion, experiences a foretaste of the pain she will know when her father's time comes. Her throat tightens; she tries desperately to hold back her tears, knowing the family will be upset if she cries. But the struggle is useless, she weeps uncontrollably, rooting frantically in her handbag for a handkerchief.

A sob bursts from Mrs. Ward, and the chapel is filled suddenly with an unearthly sound of blubbering, yammering, wailing. "Mother," Marjorie admonishes. Her mother pays her no heed. A profound grief, dredged up from some shadowy, unknowable source, is at the heart of Mrs. Ward's hubbubboo; she cannot be stilled.

But Sophie's crying fit is soon over; she gains control of herself as her husband with his mother on his arm, his sisters a few paces behind, join the procession down the aisle.

Mrs. Ward's clamour subsides and she respectfully steps aside to permit Aunt Margaret and Sophie precedence over herself and Marjorie in the procession.

As the coffin is being eased into the hearse, Billy turns to Sophie and suggests that perhaps she had better not come to the cemetery. "It'll upset you," he says. "Mr. Taylor will arrange for a car to drop you off at Mother's." Sophie realizes that her breaking down in the chapel had embarrassed him.

Around four in the afternoon when she was packing so that they could make the five o'clock train to Toronto, she heard the family returning from the cemetery, and presently her husband came upstairs. He picked the baby up from the floor and sat down on the window ledge with her in his lap. "I'm glad that's over," he said.

"I can imagine," said Sophie.

"Louise was marvellous," he said. "We were afraid she might break down, but she didn't. She was marvellous."

Full marks for Louise, Sophie said to herself. To him she said, "Why is it such a disgrace among your people to cry at a funeral?"

He got up. "Please don't pick on me, Soph. I feel badly enough as it is."

"I'm not picking on you, Billy, I know how you feel. I simply asked you a question."

"It's not a disgrace to cry," he said, "but there is such a

thing as self-control. There's some excuse for Mrs. Ward. She's mentally and emotionally unstable. I don't know what possessed Marjorie to bring her. She knows her mother can't be depended on not to behave badly." He went over to Sophie and put his arm around her. "I was a little upset when you began to cry. We were all trying so hard not to, and it wasn't easy. But it's all over now, let's stop talking about it." He told her to give him a shout when she was finished packing, and went downstairs.

She completed the packing, and before closing the suitcase she wrote in her diary: "Mrs. Ward, the town's crazy woman, and I were the only two who behaved badly at the funeral. 'Behaving badly' is the expression they use for crying at a funeral."

Twenty-Four

Billy's holidays, which began July 15 and ended July 31, were given over to a search for a moderately priced three-room apartment. Except for two Sundays when they took the baby and a picnic lunch to Centre Island, he and his wife set out every morning around ten, leaving Emma on the verandah securely belted in her highchair, with her doting grandmother to mind her.

Prompted by her husband, Sophie told her mother the first morning they set out that she was not to put the baby in her lap. "It's too hot, Ma. If she gets restless take her out of the highchair and sit her up in her carriage." The carriage had been left on the verandah for that purpose but when they returned at noon Mrs. Glicksman had the baby in her lap.

Next morning as they were going down the steps, Billy asked his wife to remind her mother not to take the baby out of the highchair, except to put her in the carriage. "Ma," said Sophie, stopping on the steps, "don't take her on your lap. If she gets restless—"

"Go!" said Mrs. Glicksman. She didn't need a second reminder. The look on her son-in-law's face when he found the baby in her lap yesterday had not gone unnoticed by her.

"Go!" she repeated, her face flushed an angry red. Though she spoke of herself as "one of God's frightened ones," claimed in fact that she was born frightened, she was capable nonetheless of sudden and sometimes even violent bursts of temper.

On August first, Billy went back to work. They had viewed numerous three-room apartments but hadn't found one to suit them.

"I could have told you that this isn't the time of year to look for an apartment," Bella said to her sister. "The only apartments to let at this time of year are the kind of places that people move in and out of every Monday and Thursday."

This was one Friday night after supper. Billy was upstairs putting the baby to bed; Mrs. Glicksman was in the kitchen washing up; Glicksman was at table with the evening paper and a glass of wine; the sisters were sitting over their tea; Henry was in a chair by the open window, nursing the last of his coke; and Philip was at his comics.

Sophie said, "We saw a few nice places, but the rents were exorbitant. The ones we could afford were places you wouldn't want to be found dead in. Even this dump is a palace by comparison."

Glicksman looked up from his paper. Slowly he pushed his glasses to his forehead and fixed his daughter with a stony look.

"Is that what you call my house, a dump?"

"It's just an expression, Pa. I didn't mean it."

He got up from his chair. "You are welcome in my house but I didn't send for you and I don't force you to stay." He drank down his wine. "So long as you are in my house I don't want to hear that word dump from you again," he said, and took his glass to the kitchen. They heard him telling his wife he was going to a friend's house for a game of cards.

Billy came downstairs as Sophie was saying to her sister, "After you've had a taste of living in a nice place it's very depressing to come back here. You wouldn't like it any more than I do if you had to come back."

Bella pursed her lips. "Probably not, but I'd try and make

178

the best of it. I certainly wouldn't sound off the way you did, calling the house a dump in front of Pa."

"Oh for God's sake, Bella," said Sophie irritably, "stop harping on that. I said it without thinking."

"That's your trouble right there. You should learn to think before you speak."

Sophie turned to her husband. "Is the baby asleep?"

He nodded. "That room's a sweatbox. She kept tossing and turning, poor little thing, and finally fell asleep. An electric fan would help but there's no outlet," he said glumly.

Bella said, "The building we live in is a little more modern than this house and it's hot there too." Her brother-in-law's complaints irked her. He's got a nerve, she thought, they move back to the house uninvited, pay no rent, Pa treats him like royalty and he complains about accommodation that he gets free of charge.

"Philip's bedroom is no cooler than the one Emma is in but it doesn't bother him." She got up from table. "Children don't feel the heat as much as older people. That's a known fact," she announced, then said to her husband, "Henry? Let's take Ma for a car ride before we go home."

"Okay," said Henry.

Billy looked at his watch and then glanced at his wife. She returned his glance with a shrug.

The mimed communication was not lost on Bella: she knew they had planned on going to a movie. She ordered her son to pick up his comic books, then went to the kitchen and said to her mother, "Take off your apron, Ma. We're going for a ride in the car."

Mrs. Glicksman seldom had the chance of a car ride — which she loved — but she shook her head and said she had a few things to do.

"What few things have you got to do?" Bella asked. "Sit here and look at the four walls?"

Her mother clasped her hands to her bosom. "Please, Bella," she said, "next time I'll go, not tonight."

"Why not tonight? Give me one good reason," Bella insisted.

For reply Mrs. Glicksman whispered, "They want to go to a show."

"That's too bad about them. What are you in this house, Bella said, raising her voice, "a servant? Their nursemaid? ' She went behind her mother, untied her apron, flung it over a chair and seized her by the arm. "You're coming for a ride in the car."

Sophie appeared in the door.

"Henry bought that car three months ago and you haven't invited her even once to go for a ride. But tonight, purely out of spite — to prevent me and Billy from going to a movie — you want to take her for a ride," she said in a voice unsteady with anger. She turned to her mother and told her to go for a ride.

Mrs. Glicksman sat down and folded her hands in her lap. In softer tones, Sophie told her they had changed their minds about going to a movie. "We're staying home anyway, Ma, you might as well go."

Bella sniffed. "Very noble."

Sophie shouted, "Shut up!"

Bella shouted, "You shut up!"

Mrs. Glicksman covered her ears.

Sophie drew her mother's hands away from her ears. "Don't be stubborn, Ma. Go for a ride, you'll enjoy it."

"Not now I wouldn't. Two sisters quarrelling — I lost my taste," she said, poured herself a glass of tea and took it to her bedroom.

Bella returned to the dining room. "Let's go," she said, and left without bidding her brother-in-law good night.

Sophie rejoined her husband.

"What was that all about?" he asked.

He had heard them wrangling in the kitchen but the only portion intelligible to him was Sophie's outburst, accusing Bella of spiteful motives in wanting to take their mother for a car ride; the rest, except for the sisters shouting at each other to shut up, was spoken in Yiddish.

"Bella said we're taking advantage of Ma, that we use her as a nursemaid. As if I'd begrudge my mother a ride so that we can go to a movie," said Sophie indignantly. She sat down and began drumming her fingers on the table.

He checked his watch. "We can still make a movie, Soph."

"We might as well," she agreed.

"It's very depressing to come back here after you've had a taste of living in a nice place," Bella said, mimicking her sister.

This was the following morning. Bella, spreading chopped liver on a kaiser roll, was putting up a lunch for Henry, who took his noonday meal at the drugstore. "You saw how Pa reacted when she called the house a dump?"

Just then the phone rang and Henry took the call. "I don't know anything about it," Bella heard him say, "wait a minute, I'll ask my wife." He turned to his wife. "It's the superintendent, he says he's located Philip's playpen and wants to know if he should bring it up to the apartment."

"Tell him not to bother, and thank him for his trouble."

Henry did as he was bid, and then asked his wife, "What did you want with Philip's playpen?"

"I promised it to Sophie. But she can whistle for it now, after calling me spiteful."

Later in the day she called her mother's house and said curtly to her sister who answered the phone, "Let me speak to Ma." Her mother came to the phone. "Tell my sister," Bella said to her, "that if she still wants the playpen, she's welcome to it."

"Couldn't you tell her yourself?"

"I'm not talking to her. If she wants the playpen let her phone Henry at the drugstore and he'll bring it over tonight after he closes."

Sunday morning Billy took the baby to the verandah and put her in the playpen, which Henry had brought the night before. A few minutes later Sophie heard him calling excitedly from the hall, "Come and see this, Soph!"

The baby was in a corner of the playpen, standing up and holding onto the rail.

"She stood up by herself, Soph." His eyes were alight with pleasure. "I wish I didn't have to go to work." He went reluctantly down the steps, cautioning his wife not to leave the baby alone just yet. "It's all new to her," he said, "she's apt to get frightened."

Sophie went upstairs to tidy her bedroom and when she

came out again Emma, far from being frightened, was having the time of her life. There were five kids on the verandah, the oldest about ten, a pale-faced girl with stringy hair. One of the kids, a boy of three with a round head, runny nose and wet pants, was in the playpen. Grasped in his hand was a popsicle which he was sharing with Emma; a lick for her, a lick for him.

Sophie lifted the three-year-old out of the playpen and set him solidly on his feet. He immediately began to cry. The girl with stringy hair took him up in her arms. "He's my brother. And you're a meanie," she said.

"Why am I a meanie?" Sophie demanded. "I didn't hurt him."

"You're a meanie because you won't let him play with the baby."

"He's got a cold. You had no business putting him in the playpen with a small baby when he has a cold. You should know better, a big girl like you," Sophie went on — and found herself arguing with a girl whom she now recognized as one of the several children belonging to the only gentile family on the street, and whose mother was referred to by the women on the street as a *nafka*, a *kurveh*.

The girl's mother, Mrs. Sheppard, a plump woman of faded prettiness, had come by these names because it was conjectured by the women that the driver of Brown's Bakery wagon, a husky man who called at her house with several loaves of bread three or four times a week (when her children were at school and her husband at work) and left his horse and wagon a good hour on the street before coming out again, was delivering more than just a few loaves of bread to her on his calls.

Mrs. Oiffer, who was called The Sly One behind her back, said the driver didn't even have to rein in the horse when he got to the *kurveh*'s house. "The horse himself knows where to stop," she said, and Mrs. Schwartz, who had a stubbly growth on her chin and was called The Beard behind her back, swore she saw the driver coming out of the *nafka*'s house, buttoning himself up.

They shared secrets, exchanged recipes, gossip, went marketing in threes and fours, tended each others' children when the need arose, and each poked fun at the other behind her back. Mrs. Schwartz would have been deeply hurt had she known she was called The Beard, as would Mrs. Oiffer at being called The Sly One behind her back. The group of intimates consisted of five women and not one among them had an inkling that she herself, when not in their midst, was not spared.

Sophie was in bed reading when her husband came home. He was upset when she told him about the kids pestering Emma.

"They just wouldn't leave her alone. The back yard would be ideal if it wasn't such a mess."

Gloomily he said, "Let alone the cats."

"They'd stop coming around if I could get my mother to stop feeding them."

"What a hope." He took off his clothes and went to the bathroom. (On their return from Galt they found that the toilet flushed without having to hold the ballcock suspended to fill the water tank; Glicksman had actually got hold of a plumber. But for the fact that he forgot to mention the defective basin taps, they too would have been yielding water.)

Billy returned to the bedroom. "I'll clean up the back yard next Saturday," he said. "I won't have a chance before then. And you'll have to speak to your mother about feeding the cats."

"I will. I'll be very firm," she said.

He got into bed and lay back with his hands behind his head, staring at the ceiling, and then said, "Your mother's a very stubborn woman. The only way I can think of that might stop her is to throw a scare into her."

Sophie put her book down. "What do you mean, throw a scare into her?"

"Don't look at me like that, Soph. I only meant that she'd be scared if she could be made to understand that it's dangerous to have strange cats around a baby. Emma could have her eyes scratched out. It's happened before, I'm not making this up. I've read of cases where babies have been mauled by cats."

Next morning Sophie told her mother that Billy was going to clean up the back yard so that the baby could play there, and that it was important that she stop feeding the cats.

"It's dangerous to have strange cats around a baby. Emma could have her eyes scratched out."

Mrs. Glicksman gasped.

"Only last week there was something in the paper about a baby being mauled by cats."

Her mother put her hand to her heart. "God forbid!"

"Never mind God forbid, stop feeding them. They'll stop coming if they don't get anything to eat."

Mrs. Glicksman swore as God was her witness that she would not feed the cats any more. She prayed God to strike her, her hand to fail should she throw them so much as a crust of bread. Rather than harm come to the baby, she would gladly witness with her own eyes the slaughter of every cat in the land.

Billy went to work on the four months' overgrowth in the back yard. Cutting, clipping, digging and shovelling, he filled three bushel baskets with weeds, catshit, grass, dandelions, giant sunflowers, rotting fish heads, slops, chicken bones.

And his mother-in-law stopped feeding the cats. When she had to go to the back yard, she took a broom with her to chase them. Instead of nourishment, they got whacks. But they were unshaken, they kept coming back. It took some time before they realized they had fallen on evil days, and thereafter they ran for their lives at the appearance of their former benefactress.

Twenty-Five

"There's no sense to it," Billy said. "With money being frittered away like that we'll never get ahead."

"It's not being frittered away," said Sophie. "We're paying off the Home Lovers, aren't we?" He shrugged. "What do we still owe?" she asked.

"Two hundred and eighty. At twenty a month, plus service charges, that'll take another fifteen months to pay off."

Bella said to her sister, "I don't know why you bought all that stuff in the first place — I mean without being able to pay cash for it. I don't know how you can stand being in debt. I wouldn't be able to sleep nights."

Glicksman looked up from his paper. "Don't mix in, Bella."

"Excuse me for living," said Bella. He was always siding with Sophie.

Glicksman was sitting at table with his paper and glass of wine, putting in time before going to his Friday night game of cards. Henry was sitting next to him, with part of his father-in-law's paper and a coke. Billy, his forehead creased in a frown, was scratching figures on a notepad. The sisters were sitting over their tea. Mrs. Glicksman was in the kitchen. Philip, who had a cold, had been left at home with a sitter.

Billy looked up from his notepad. "July, August, September, October, November, December, January," he said, ticking the months off on his fingers. "That's seven months now that our stuff's been in storage. At twenty-one a month that comes to—" he consulted his pad "—a hundred and forty-seven dollars." He took a handkerchief to his forehead. "That was a bad move, moving out of the Littles before we found another place."

Sophie slumped in her chair, letting her arms hang limp at her sides. "Moving there at all was a bad move. I wish to God that we'd never seen that Flat to Let sign in their window. That was an ill-fated day."

"Ill-fated day," said Bella. "Things might have worked out differently if you hadn't got so friendly with Mrs. Little." A warning look from her father failed to silence her. "You should have kept your relationship on a landlady-tenant basis instead of becoming *shmelkess* with her. That never works out."

Sophie drew herself up from her slumped position. "Let's go to a movie, Billy. It's getting claustrophobic in here."

Bella stood up. "Thanks."

She took up her cup and saucer, leaned across the table for Henry's empty coke bottle and went to the kitchen with them, telling her husband to get her coat. "We're going, Ma."

Mrs. Glicksman came away from the sink. "So soon?"

Glicksman stood to say good night to his daughter and son-in-law.

Henry said good night to Sophie and called up, "Good night, Billy," to his brother-in-law, who had gone upstairs to see that the baby had not thrown off her covers. Bella took leave of her sister with her nose in the air.

Glicksman put on his glasses and sat down, his eyes focussed severly on his daughter sitting opposite. "How many sisters have you got?"

The question was rhetorical; it so obviously required no answer but Glicksman stubbornly insisted on one when it was asked. And Sophie, equally stubborn, refused now to accommodate him. Instead of the usual "One" for reply, she propped her elbow on the table and made a fist of her hand, except for the forefinger which she held up in front of her face, the middle joint touching the tip of her nose.

That drew his anger. "Don't be so smart. I asked you a question." His eyes were icy blue behind the spectacles, and the expression on his face was the one she had come to fear as a child when he threatened to take his belt to her for talking back.

Refusing the mimed answer, he waits for a vocal one, his lips an unyielding line. And she, observing the obdurate face, the grimness of expression, recalls the power it had a long time ago to strike terror in her. But she is no longer a child. A married woman with a child of her own she is beyond reach of the violence his countenance threatens; and for some obscure reason, the chord it now strikes is pity.

"I asked you a question," he repeated, and received for answer a filially obedient "One."

Glicksman leaned intently forward. "Only one?" he asked as if taken by surprise. "Not three? Not four?" He took off his glasses and put them in his vest pocket. "Only one sister and you can't get along with her?"

To this question, he required no answer. They were playing a two-hander with Glicksman speaking all the lines; the only word in her part had already been delivered.

Glicksman stood to drink down the rest of his wine then took his glass to the kitchen. Sophie heard him telling her mother he was going out to play cards at a friend's. And heard her mother give him her blessing: "God be with you. Go in good health. And return in good health."

Thrice-blessed Glicksman passed through the dining room, shaking his head at his daughter in passing. He took his coat from the hallrack and made his exit forgetting to put on his rubbers.

Sophie went upstairs to see what was keeping her husband. The door to the baby's room was open, the light was on and he was standing beside the sleeping child, watching her. She tiptoed over and said in a whisper, "If we're going to a movie we'd better get started."

187

He said, "I don't think we should go out tonight. Look at the baby, she's running a temperature."

Emma had been cranky and restless all day. Her face high in colour, she was now lying on her side tranquilly asleep with her thumb held loosely in her mouth. Sophie leaned over the cot and passed her fingertips over the child's cheek, which was warm to the touch.

"She's cutting a new tooth," she told her husband, "and her temperature probably is a little higher than normal, but it's nothing to worry about." She looked at her watch. "Let's go if we're going, she'll be all right. You worry too much, Billy."

"I guess I do," he allowed, and followed her out thinking, I wish I could be like her; she takes the baby's upsets so calmly.

It was a short walk to the Playhouse but they were late getting there; the newsreel was over and *Of Human Bondage* had been on five minutes. There were no aisle seats (which Billy preferred in case of fire) and they had to take seats mid-row in the middle of the house: the worst possible seating, ideal for viewing but disastrous in a stampede for the Exit doors.

Billy was unable to put his mind to what was taking place on the screen; his thoughts kept reverting to Emma. They should never have left her alone in the house with a deaf old woman who probably wouldn't hear her if she woke up crying. His gaze kept shifting from the screen to his wife. Miserable himself for worry, he grudged her the pleasure she was taking in the film. He kept looking at his watch and returning his eyes to the screen, groaning inwardly, Oh Lord, how long.

His mother-in-law meanwhile was experiencing tenfold his anxieties.

When the baby woke, Mrs. Glicksman was sitting at the kitchen table with a glass of tea. Audibly mulling over the day's happenings, she admitted having oversalted the chicken soup. The girls complained, but her husband, bless him, made a joke of it; he asked if she was buying salt in bargain lots. Smiling at his wit, she put her spoon in the jam jar and treated herself to a heaping spoonful. She licked her lips, then slid her tongue over her teeth, the few she had left. She opened her mouth and with thumb and forefinger cautiously laid hold of the least firm of her few remaining teeth and experimentally jiggled it. She took her fingers out of her mouth and sighed: she was going to lose yet another tooth. She lifted her shoulders in a shrug. "I'm not such a picture it will spoil my looks," she remarked to her invisible auditor.

Suddenly she tipped her head back. Was that the baby? Deaf as she was, her hearing was acutely attuned to her grandchild's every vocal sound. She sat several minutes listening intently. A plaintive cry overhead brought her to her feet.

As quickly as she was able, she made her way to the stairs leading to the two upstairs rooms and bathroom. For her, the dozen wooden stairs which were narrow and walled on either side was a laborious climb. First she bent over and flattened her hands on the third from bottom step; then, with the thrust of her weight on her arms, she set one foot and then the other on the bottom step. Repeating the procedure, she flattened out her hands one at a time on the fourth step, and brought her feet to the second step of the ascent. Toiling, bent over, chafing at the slowness of her progress, she cursed the stairs: "A cholera take them. . . . Bubbeh's coming," she called to reassure the crying child, and gained at last the topmost step.

"Bubbeh's here!" she cried, and switching on the light went over to the baby's cot. The child had stopped crying. She lay inertly on her back; her face was flushed, her hair clung damply to her forehead, and there was vomit on her chin, neck, and on her nightgown.

Mrs. Glicksman let down the side of the cot and with the hem of her apron wiped off the vomit. She brushed back the baby's hair and laid her hand on her forehead; it was hot. The child was sick. She lifted the ailing child and walked the floor with her. The heat of the baby's breath on her neck frightened her. She returned the child to its cot, covered her, and stood watching as she dozed, waked, let out a feeble wail, dozed, and waked again, whimpering. She had never before seen the child like this. When would the parents be home? Murderers, to leave a sick child.

Her feet sore from standing, she sat down on Bella's old bed. If only she could do something. A sick child needed care. Sitting on the edge of the bed with the mattress sagging like a hammock under her weight, she cursed her helplessness. Anything, God forbid, could happen between now and the time the parents got home. Fearing for her grandchild, she recalled how swiftly the breath of life had been extinguished in her own child. A time-healed wound but remembered to this day with a stab of sorrow for the briefness of her sojourn, the child whom they had named Becky, for Glicksman's first wife. But it was the child Emma, growing up under her eyes, who had gained purchase on her heart with a firmer grip than the lost one had, her own child who had lain so briefly at her breast. She wrung her hands and prayed God to spare her grandchild.

Calling down the plagues of Egypt on herself for uselessness, it came to her all of a sudden that help *was* at hand. Mrs. Oiffer. She'd know what to do, having raised four children. All she had to do was bang on the adjoining wall and Mrs. Oiffer, whose bedroom was on the other side, would come running. Familiar with the habits of her neighbours, The Sly One knew that her next-door neighbour spent a lot of time alone; and you could depend on it that she'd know a bang on the wall was a call for help. Bella's old bed took up the length of the wall adjoining Mrs. Oiffer's; she'd have to move the bed to get to the wall.

She went to the foot of the bed and leaning over it grasped with both hands a corner of the iron bedstead. Panting, biting her lips, she put all her strength into the effort of moving the heavy bed away from the wall. As she straightened her aching back and paused for breath, she felt the loose tooth come away from its mooring. She spat it out and continued grappling with the bed till she had cleared enough space to admit her bulk between bed and wall.

Then she set to drumming with both fists on the wall, repeatedly calling in a loud voice, "Mrs. Oiffer!"

Shortly after Mrs. Glicksman had hit on this means of summoning help, the parents returned. On opening the door they were startled at the sound of a thumping from upstairs, followed by Mrs. Glicksman's cry "Mrs. Oiffer!"

Taking the stairs two at a time, Billy reached the baby's bedroom first. The big bed stood at an angle a few feet away from the wall, and his mother in-law was pounding the wall with her shoe, intermittently letting out an ear-splitting "Mrs. Oiffer!"

"Stop that immediately!" he commanded. But his voice (so seldom addressed to her) failed to reach her ear; she continued hammering the wall. "Make her stop that racket," he ordered his wife, and went over to the baby's cot.

Sophie reached over her mother's shoulder and grabbed the shoe out of her hand. "What do you want with Mrs. Oiffer?" she asked.

Mrs. Glicksman turned. "To give me a help with the baby."

Her clean Friday night apron was bunched and clotted at the hem with Emma's vomit. Her front hair had come loose. It hung in strands at the sides of her face which was flushed a violent red.

"You remembered you left alone a sick baby that needs care? Now you're home, look after her," she said angrily.

Sophie noticed a new gap in her mouth; her one remaining incisor was gone. "You lost a tooth," she informed her mother.

Mrs. Glicksman's hand went to her mouth. "I know." She glanced briefly at the floor. "The devil take it," she said and reached out her hand. "Give me my shoe."

"Aren't you going to put it on?" Sophie asked; her mother was stuffing the shoe in the pocket of her apron.

Mrs. Glicksman made no answer. Knowing that her presence in the room was not pleasing to her son-in-law, nothing could have induced her to take the time to put on her shoe, which she would have had to sit down to do.

For a woman who constantly made nothing of herself, who always put others' wants before her own, who spent hours alone in the house without thinking to feel neglected by her husband in whose shadow she existed, or to feel imposed on by her daughter who took it for granted that her services were there for the asking, she had an indomitable pride. Her pride would not permit her to prolong her stay by even another minute. With one shoe on and the other in her pocket, she made her way out of the room heavily treading the floorboards with a lopsided gait.

The instructor felt all the strength going out of him as he stood gazing down at his child.

"Soph," he called hoarsely without turning his head, "come here."

There was a feverish glow to the baby's cheeks; she was awake, fitfully turning her head from one side of the pillow to the other. She had worked her blankets off and they lay bundled at her feet. Her nightgown was rucked up; she had dirtied herself and a diarrhetic ooze was trickling down the insides of her thighs.

"I think we'd better get a doctor. There's one on Baldwin Street — God! why can't I remember his name!" It suddenly came to her. "Cherkover. Cherkover, that's right," she said, running out of the room.

She got the doctor's telephone number from Information. The telephone rang and rang and was answered at last by Mrs. Cherkover.

"Let me speak to the doctor," said Sophie. "Hurry."

"Wait a minute," said his wife. "He went to sleep, I'll have to wake him up. Hold the line."

Sophie held the line, trembling.

He came to the phone. "Who is it?" he asked, yawning.

"My baby's sick," she wailed.

When she returned to the room the baby's diaper had been changed and she was lying on clean sheets. Her husband, with his coat off, was sitting by the cot.

"The doctor will be here in half an hour," she told him.

He looked up at her. "If anything happens to that child," he said tonelessly, "I'll never forgive you for it."

She stared. He returned his gaze to the child.

Seeking to occupy herself till the doctor's arrival she went to the bathroom and washed some diapers she had left soaking in soapy water, rinsed them, hung them on the clothes-horse and went back to the baby's room. Emma was sleeping; he was moving the big bed back to the wall. He stooped suddenly and peered at the floor. "What's this?"

Sophie looked down to where his finger pointed. "It's my mother's tooth."

He reached his foot to the yellowed incisor and toed it towards her.

She picked up the tooth and took it to the bathroom to flush down the toilet. She returned to the room and they sat in silence waiting for the doctor, she on the bed, he with his back to her on a chair by the baby's cot. Keeping vigil over his child, he sat hunched, with arms folded across the top of the side railing: intentionally shielding the baby from her view, she thought.

The sick call had come from a neighbourhood address and Dr. Cherkover, a thin, narrow-shouldered man of medium height, his left cheek brutally birth-marked with a ragged patch of crimson extending from cheekbone to jaw, decided to walk the short distance rather than get the car out of the garage. As he approached the house, he took in at a glance the poorness of it. A one-dollar call, he said to himself.

Sophie had left the downstairs hall lit, and Mrs. Glicksman, peering through the front-door window, was at the door to receive him. "*Gut Shabbes*," he said on entering; she wished him a good Sabbath and a good year. He put his bag on the floor and took off his coat, asking in Yiddish, "Where's the baby?" She told him upstairs. He gave her his coat to hang up, picked up his bag and went upstairs wearing his galoshes.

"Anybody home?" he called coming into the room.

Billy got up from his chair. "I appreciate your coming so quickly, doctor."

The doctor stood at the baby's cot a while, rubbing his hands, blowing on his fingers. The chill off his hands, he took the vacated chair, let down the side of the cot and motioned the mother to undo the baby's diaper. He was gentle with the child but she woke and let out a wail as he was taking her temperature. He spoke soothingly to her, calling her *faygeleh*. She reached her hand to his face. He took hold of her hand and guided it to his blemished cheek. "You want to touch my beauty spot?"

"Her temperature," he told the parents, "is a little bit higher than normal. Give her a quarter of an aspirin every four hours. That should take care of it. Keep her on a bland diet for a couple of days — apple sauce, jello, farina — and don't give her any milk or orange juice." He closed his bag and stood up.

Billy asked, "What do I owe you, doctor?"

"A dollar."

"That hardly seems enough," Billy said. "Bringing you out on a cold night, and so late."

"All right, you talked me into it. Give me two bucks."

Going down the stairs he saw the grandmother at the foot, mutely searching his face. He told her not to worry; all that was wrong with the baby was a little fever from teething, and a loose bowel movement. Leaving, he said if his life were extended by a year each time her grandchild was to make kaka in her pants between now and her wedding day, he would live to be a hundred and twenty. She thanked him and bade him go in good health, invoking God's blessing on his healing hands.

"Go to bed, Soph," Billy said. "There's no sense in both of us staying up."

The baby had been given a quarter aspirin and had been sleeping soundly since without stirring. It was now one o'clock and the parents, in silence till Billy spoke, had been keeping an anxious vigil.

"Are you going to stay up all night?" Sophie asked.

"I might as well," he replied. "I'm not in the least sleepy and I'll have to be up at four anyway, to give her another dose of aspirin." He put his arms around her. "Go to bed, hon, you look all in."

She put her hands against his chest and thrust him away from her.

"What's wrong, Soph?"

"You have a short memory," she said coldly.

"I don't know what you're talking about."

"I'm talking about that intemperate threat you made when we were waiting for the doctor."

Intemperate threat? "I don't know what you're talking about," he said.

His colour had heightened but his eyes, she observed, were innocent of guile; he clearly was puzzled. "You said to me — to me, the child's mother — you said, 'If anything happens to that child, I'll never forgive you for it.' "

He sat down and put his hands over his face. "Oh Lord! I'm sorry, I didn't mean it. I was terribly upset, I didn't know what I was saying." He uncovered his face. "You're not going to throw that up to me, Soph?"

Twenty-Six

The door to Glicksman's house stood open and two men were hauling furniture out of a van parked in front and carrying it into the house. Grinning and ogling Sophie who was directing the operation, the movers, both husky young men, cheerfully positioned furniture as requested; Glicksman, with Emma in his arms to keep her out of the way, stood in the kitchen doorway, scowling at the men for their indecent glances at his daughter.

Acting on Bella's advice to save further expense of storage, Billy had sold the fourposter, the chesterfield and the wardrobe, paid off the Home Lovers, and was having the remainder of the furniture moved into Glicksman's house, as a temporary measure, while he and Sophie continued the search for a suitable apartment.

When it came to taking the kitchen table and chairs to the cellar — and the men asked Sophie to show them down — Glicksman stepped forward, gave her the baby to hold and said he would show them. When they brought the dresser in, Glicksman told them to take it upstairs. And to forestall further commerce between them and his daughter, he led them up himself to Sophie's bedroom. With the new dresser in the space cleared for it, he asked them to take the old one down to the cellar. To which they replied they were movers, not handymen; and with retaliatory satisfaction both men descended the stairs, leaving the old dresser standing. Glicksman followed them down and slammed the door shut after them.

On hearing the door, Sophie came from the kitchen where she was giving Emma her lunch. "Are they gone? I was going to ask them to take the old dresser down to the cellar."

"I asked them," said Glicksman irritably, "and they didn't want to do it."

Her brazen reply, "*I* should have asked them, they wouldn't have said no to me," angered him.

"Don't talk like a loose woman. It doesn't suit you," he said and didn't speak to her again for two days.

"I told you I was going to speak to Soph about it," Bella said to Henry.

He nodded. He was waiting for the lunch she was preparing for him to take to the drugstore.

"She said Billy keeps offering to pay rent and Pa won't take it. So I said if Pa the millionaire won't take rent from him, why doesn't he at least pick up the phone bill, the gas bill and the Hydro? I said he was taking advantage of Pa and she got mad at me. Which I might have expected."

This was one Saturday morning towards the end of March, exactly a year to the month that Billy had his furniture taken out of storage and brought to his father-in-law's house.

"I mentioned it to Aunt Hannah," Bella went on, "and she agreed that he was taking advantage of Pa."

Henry remained silent. Bella looked up from the bread she was slicing. "Say something."

Henry said, "I don't see that their being in the house makes any difference in the upkeep. Gas and electricity is probably a bit higher, but what you're not taking into account is all the work that he's put into that house."

"So he made some improvements in the house. Does that entitle him to live there rent free forever? Doesn't Pa pay rent? And aren't they taking up two rooms in the house he pays rent for?"

197

"And if they weren't living there, would Pa rent out the two rooms and have strangers in the house? You know he wouldn't, so their being in the house isn't doing him out of an income."

Bella considered this a moment. Then she said, "At least he'd have a bedroom where he could get some sleep during the day. Pa's a light sleeper. He doesn't get any rest in that front room with all the *tumel* that goes on in the street."

"So if Billy starts picking up a few bills, is that going to give Pa a good day's sleep?"

"It's impossible to have a discussion with him," Bella said to the wall, and handed him his lunch.

"What's there to discuss," said Henry, putting on his coat. "Pa wants them in the house, and so does Ma. It's company for her."

"Company for her. Ma talks to Soph and Soph answers or doesn't, depending on what mood she's in. And him. Does he ever speak a word to her?"

"What's he going to say to her? He doesn't speak Yiddish."

Later the same day Glicksman's sister Hannah was saying to him, "You're a stubborn man, God keep you."

"Please, Hannah," said Glicksman, "I came to see how you are, not to hear a lecture." His sister was laid up with phlebitis and he had come to visit.

"If they were living someplace else," Hannah continued, "wouldn't he have to pay rent? But I'm surprised more at Sophie than him, that she lets it go. Is her husband a *yeshiva bucher* that she brought him home for her father to support him?"

"How do I support him? Do I give them to eat? I don't give them to eat, and besides it's not strangers I'm keeping in my house. You talk like my son-in-law is a loafer in my house. He's a responsible man, Hannah, he looks after things. He fixed up the house with money from his own pocket. Enough, I talked it over with Chayele, and she feels the same way, not to take rent from him."

"Chayele. Chayele knows money doesn't grow on trees, and she knows that her husband turns night into day to make a living. But does she know the value of a dollar?"

"What does she spend on herself that she should know the value of a dollar," Glicksman said, running out of patience. Perhaps unfairly, but he felt that his sister — when the opportunity presented itself — could not resist taking a dig at his wife. "And if I'll take a few dollars from him," he went on, "is that going to make me a rich man? And another thing you have to consider, which is more important than a few dollars, is Chayele's condition. I go away from the house five days a week before six and I don't come home till six in the morning. Anything could happen to a woman that's alone in the house and practically deaf. It all happened for the best that they didn't find an apartment. When I go to work I don't have to worry that Chayele is alone in the house. I have to go now," he said, getting up from the chair by his sister's bed. Hannah offered her hand and, as was their custom on leave-taking, brother and sister formally shook hands and wished each other good health.

Hanging his coat on the hallrack when he got home, Glicksman heard Sophie saying, with an excitable ring to her voice, "It's not right! It's unprincipled!" Then a woman's voice, "Calm yourself, my dear. You're a very tempestuous young woman."

Glicksman hung up his hat and proceeded to the dining room, wondering what was going on. Billy, standing at the window, turned his head to him. Sophie stood before a woman who was sitting in the armchair. She turned abruptly to him and said, "The house is going up for sale, Pa."

"The house?" said Glicksman, bewildered.

"This house," said Sophie.

He stared at her. "My house?"

Sophie pointed at the woman in the armchair. "Her house. You're just a tenant here. She came here with the good news that she's selling the house." She then moved towards the hall and Billy followed.

Stunned, Glicksman looked at the woman in the armchair; an elderly woman wearing a brown felt hat with an upturned brim, a camel's hair coat, unbuttoned, and in her lap a brown handbag with gloves to match.

"Mr. Glicksman?" she asked.

He went over to her. "And the lady's name?" he asked. He had never met the owner of the house, nor did he know her name. He paid his rent to a Mr. Richardson, the owner's lawyer who had an office on Simcoe Street.

"Miss Burroughs," she said, offering her hand.

Shaking the owner's hand he caught sight of his wife standing in the kitchen doorway. Face flushed, she was frantically gesticulating behind the woman's back, summoning him to the kitchen. Glicksman excused himself and joined his wife.

"It's true?" she asked him in a voice hardly above a whisper. "She's going to sell the house?" He made no answer. Studying his face, she sat down and put her hands in her lap. Thumbs silently whirring, eyes smouldering, she cursed the woman sitting in her dining room. "A black year on her. The cholera take her." He turned without a word and went back to the dining room.

She sat in the kitchen listening to their voices, her face flaming up at the sound of the woman's voice. She covered her ears. Then uncovered them. The woman was still talking. She got up from her chair. She'd go to the bedroom, put herself beyond reach of that voice. She smoothed down her apron, smoothed back her hair, and moved towards the doorway, not noticing in her agitation that one of her *poditskess* had come undone and slipped to the floor. *Poditskess* was her name for the strips of cotton cut from the hems of her worn-out aprons and housedresses, which she tied below the knee to keep her stockings up.

Miss Burroughs looked up as she emerged from the kitchen. Glicksman, too, turned his head to her.

With head averted Mrs. Glicksman went by her husband and the owner of the house without a glance for either. And as she passed in silent dignity through the dining room, riding loosely on the instep and back of her shoe was the crumpled wide top of her lisle stocking.

"You've done wonders with this house," Miss Burroughs said, resuming where she had left off.

The last time she had seen the house was ten years ago,

she said, when it became vacant. She had had a series of bad tenants of all nationalities, and the worst of the lot were the tenants before Glicksman. An Irish family, they skipped owing her three months' rent and left the house in an awful condition. She had thought of making some repairs but had let it slide because it was just too discouraging.

"If I had known that a Jew — excuse me — if I had known that someone of your persuasion had rented the house, I would not have been so neglectful of repairs. You people do make better tenants and you've been an exceptionally good tenant, Mr. Glicksman. I feel badly about selling the house, but I'm afraid there's nothing I can do about it." She said this was one of four houses she owned, and that she was obliged, for private reasons, to sell all four.

Glicksman idly asked, "How much are you asking for this house?"

"Four thousand."

He smiled. "That's all?"

"The house is worth that," she said. Then frankly admitted that the house was in such good condition now, due to his care, that there would be no trouble selling it at that price.

Glicksman sighed. "My daughter and son-in-law — young people, it won't be hard for them to find another place. But for me and my wife it's a different story."

She said she was sorry and repeated that she was afraid there was nothing she could do about it. Businesslike, she then said that if there was any possibility of him being the purchaser she would make terms as lenient as possible.

"Can you give me some figures?" Glicksman asked. There was no harm in asking. "How much would you want for a down payment?"

"If you were the purchaser, four hundred dollars."

"That seems to me reasonable," said Glicksman who didn't have two dimes to rub together. "And the balance?"

She brought a pencil and slip of paper out of her handbag, went to the table and sat down beside the prospective buyer. Jotting down figures, she read aloud as she wrote: "Four hundred down. Balance thirty-six hundred. Five percent interest on thirty-six hundred is one hundred and eighty dollars. That, plus two hundred on principal, will come to three hundred and eighty dollars per annum." She looked up. "You can pay the three hundred and eighty dollars in two half-yearly payments of one hundred and ninety dollars each, or in quarterly payments of ninety-five dollars each. Which would you prefer?"

"Quarterly payments," Glicksman said without hesitation. He was paying twenty-five a month for rent; that came to seventy-five dollars quarterly. Ninety-five was only twenty dollars more. But where could he get hold of four hundred dollars? That was the question.

With the figures completed, Miss Burroughs handed the slip of paper to Glicksman and stood up to button her coat. "I'll have Mr. Richardson call you," she said, picking up her handbag and gloves.

"Not right away, please. First I'll have to discuss it with my wife."

"Naturally," Miss Burroughs agreed.

"How soon do I have to give you an answer?" he asked, seeing her to the door.

She said she had to have an answer in two weeks. That if he could not come to a decision in two weeks, the house would officially be put up for sale.

Sitting at the bedroom window, Mrs. Glicksman heard their voices in the hall. At the sound of the opening and shutting of the door, she thrust the curtain to one side and leaned into the window. Intently watching, she saw the woman who owned the house go down the verandah steps and get into a car parked in front of the house, the house in which she had been the *balaboosteh* for ten years.

Glicksman poured himself a glass of wine and sat down at the kitchen table to study the slip of paper Miss Burroughs had left with him. Where could he get hold of four hundred dollars? Maybe the bank would give him a loan. What bank? He didn't have any savings. Engrossed, he did not hear his wife's heavy tread in the hall.

"When do we have to pack up?" she said, coming into the kitchen.

"In two weeks," he answered, not thinking. His head was spinning.

"Vey is mir!" she wailed. *"Vey is mir!"*

Glicksman drank down his wine. Should he ask Hannah? A widow who lived on what Miriam brought in, how could he ask Hannah for money? Henry? Henry supported a widowed mother and owed money to the bank. He can't even afford steady help in the drugstore, how can I ask him for money?

Mrs. Glicksman filled the kettle and put it on the stove. Waiting for the kettle to boil, she paced the floor. Where would they find a place? In an upstairs flat — she with her crippled feet? Head bent, hands clasped on her stomach, she trod the kitchen floor talking to herself. Back and forth she went. With her stocking dragging.

I'll go to my boss, thought Glicksman. I'll ask Aaronowitz to give me four hundred dollars and take it out of my pay, ten dollars a week till it's paid up. But how could he manage the quarterly payments if ten dollars were taken out of his pay every week for forty weeks? He wondered how much he could get on his life insurance policy if he cashed it in. No, he couldn't do that. If something happens to me Chayele will be left without support. Should I approach Billy?

Sophie came down as her mother, abstractedly overfilling the teapot and slopping water on the table, was saying to herself, "With a *balaboosteh* downstairs, I'll have to go on tippy toe with my crippled feet." Seeing Sophie, "I'll take a knife to my throat," she said desperately.

"Watch what you're doing!" Sophie cried. "And pull up your stocking." To her father she said, "What happened?"

"She made me a proposition that I should buy the house," he said, and showed her the slip of paper Miss Burroughs had left with him.

"Is it at all possible?" Sophie asked.

"If I could find four hundred dollars," he replied, "it wouldn't be *im*possible."

That evening after Glicksman went to work Sophie telephoned Bella and told her what had happened. "She gave Pa two weeks to make up his mind about buying the house himself," she concluded.

"That'll be the day," said Bella.

"It's not *im*possible, but if you're going to take a negative attitude there's—"

"Don't get excited, I'm willing to listen."

Sophie outlined a plan whereby their father might become a property owner. And thus — with their father's rise in the world — their mother would be saved from having to go on tippy toe with her crippled feet for fear of disturbing an uppity *balaboosteh* downstairs. "The whole thing was Billy's idea," she finished up. "Now what have you got to say about him taking advantage of Pa?"

"I take it all back. That's one thing about me, Soph, when I'm in the wrong I'm the first to admit it," said Bella; and concluded with asking her sister not to say anything yet to either parent. To save it for Friday night and surprise them with the good news at supper, when she and Henry could be there too.

On Friday night the topic of conversation, naturally, had to do with the forthcoming sale of the house. Sophie said she regretted that the buyer, a stranger, would get the benefit of the work that Billy had put in the house. "Too bad," said Bella, "but that's the way the ball bounces." Henry said it was throwing money away to let the house go to a stranger. "If you could possibly manage the payments," he said to his father-in-law, "I would say you should buy the house."

"The payments I'm pretty sure I could manage. The *down* payment is another story," said Glicksman; and immediately regretted having said it; it sounded as if he was hinting, fishing.

Bella glanced across the table. "Well?" she said to Henry, who was sitting next to her father. "What are you waiting for? Christmas?"

Henry withdrew a cheque from his breast pocket and handed it to his father-in-law. "That's a present from me and Bella. Now all you need is three hundred dollars more and you've got the down payment." The cheque was for a hundred dollars.

Glicksman glanced briefly at the cheque, his face flushing as he did so. Then he folded it and put it beside Henry's plate. "I can't take it, you're not in a position, Henry. Thank you just the same."

"Take it, Pa. If you can't raise the rest you'll give it back to me," Henry said. "I'll take it back, don't worry."

The instructor took an envelope from his pocket and reached it across the table to his father-in-law. Glicksman opened the envelope and found two cheques, one for a hundred dollars, the other for one hundred and ninety-two dollars. "What's this?" he said, bewildered.

Billy gave him to understand that the cheque for a hundred dollars was a gift, and the one for one hundred and ninety-two dollars represented a year's rent in advance, at sixteen dollars a month. "I think sixteen a month is fair," he said, "considering that the house rents for twenty-five?"

"It's more than fair," Bella said, answering for her father, "considering all the money you've already put in the house."

Henry said, "Now you've got three hundred and ninety-two dollars, Pa. Eight dollars more and you've got enough for the down payment."

Bella said, "Phone Miss Burroughs. Tell her that you're buying the house, and to make an appointment for you with the lawyer."

Visibly moved, Glicksman reached for his wine with a trembling hand. He was unable to swallow more than a sip. His eyes filled up. He wanted to express his gratitude and found he couldn't speak. He rose from his chair and moved quickly to the hall. They heard him going into the bedroom.

Mrs. Glicksman came from the kitchen, bringing food. "Where's Pa?" she asked, alarmed. Her daughters told her to sit down.

Billy leaned across the table. "The shock may have affected his heart," he said to Henry. "I think you'd better go and see." And as Henry got up, they heard Glicksman coming out of the bedroom.

Glicksman came in and stopped at Billy's chair. "Thank you," he said, offering his hand. "I appreciate what you did." Billy got up. "You're welcome," he said, shaking hands. Glicksman went over to Henry. "And thank you, Henry, I appreciate what you did." Henry got up. "Forget it, Pa," he said, shaking hands. Glicksman sat down. Looking across the table at his daughters, "And my children," he said with emotion, "I thank you from my full heart."

Bella turned to her mother. "You don't have to worry about having a *balaboosteh* over you. Pa's going to buy the house."

"It's true?" she asked her husband.

"It's true," he replied, and told her that the children had made it possible.

"*Nachess* from his children," she said, nodding her head and speaking audibly to herself. "He earned it, blessings on his head."

A little later that evening, Henry said, "How much are the taxes, Pa? And the water rates?"

Glicksman replied that Miss Burroughs didn't say and he hadn't thought to ask. Taxes. Water rates. In addition to payments on the house, there would be taxes to pay, water rates, telephone, gas, Hydro, coal. . . Now that the possibility of property ownership was practically within his grasp, he was beset suddenly with misgivings. It could be seen by his expression that his thoughts were troubled ones.

"It's going to be a tighter squeeze than you thought?" Henry suggested.

Glicksman nodded. "To buy a house, it's a big responsibility. I'm not so sure now if I can do it. On my pay."

A silence fell. After a while Henry said to his brother-in-law, "Why don't you go in partnership with him, Billy? A piece of property is a good investment. If I didn't owe the bank an arm and a leg I'd go in partnership with him. In five years this house will be double the value. In ten years the house will be paid off and you'll have half ownership with Pa. That cheque you gave Pa for a year's rent in advance? Put up eight dollars more, and that's *your* share of the down payment. If you're a partner with Pa, you don't have to pay rent."

With fingers interlocked on his chest the instructor glanced questioningly at his wife. "What do you think I should do, Soph?"

"I think you should stop cracking your knuckles," she replied.

He took in a breath. "It's a deal," he said, and leaned

across the table to shake hands with his father-in-law again.

Glicksman rose from his chair. "I'll phone Miss Burroughs, maybe I'll catch her home." He went to the hall, searching his vest pocket for the card Miss Burroughs had left with him, with her telephone number.

Presently they heard him saying, "Miss Burroughs? My son-in-laws made me a surprise. . . "

Twenty-Seven

"How does it feel to be a property owner?" Bella asked her father at supper a week later.

He smiled. "I came from Roumania expecting I'll make my fortune here in the New World. Only I didn't expect it will take me so long."

All his years since emigrating from Roumania, Glicksman, untaught, unskilled in any particular craft or trade, had eked out a living of sorts at one job or another. He was a hard and willing worker, and to keep his family from want he took jobs that were not always to his liking. He was a man of short temper, and his pride — a pauper's pride — was a prickly one. Sensitive to a discourtesy, a rebuke, he would on occasion lose his temper and his job. One summer when the girls were small and he was out of work, he invested the last of his money in a supply of needles, thread, yarn, thimbles, measuring tape, chalk, and peddled his wares from door to door. But not in his own neighbourhood; his pride hastened his steps to an outlying district, to do his drumming there. It was a poor living, peddling needles from door to door, but for want of something better, he kept to his course. One day, canvassing a well-to-do district, he rang the doorbell of a

208

prosperous-looking house, and the lady of the house came to the door. After casting a brief glance at his wares, she returned indoors, telling the peddler to wait. She returned shortly, said she was not in need of anything in that line, and offered him a dime. The peddler shut his suitcase, politely raised his hat, and leaving the lady of the house standing on her verandah with a dime in her hand, went home and made a gift of his stock in trade to his wife. He was out of work again, and jobs were scarce. People went on relief; Glicksman hustled to find work. Picking up a short-term job here, seasonal work there, he kept himself employed and his family didn't go hungry.

"What didn't I do to make a living," Glicksman said. "Not to go on relief, I took any job I could find. And my children," he said, looking at his daughters, "they didn't have to go hungry to bed."

True, his children did not have to go to bed hungry. Practiced in economy, Mrs. Glicksman knew all there was to know about keeping a family of four fed on an unsteady housekeeping allowance. And while you didn't sit down to a deluxe spread at her table, you didn't go away from it hungry after a plate of beet borscht, a piece of herring with a boiled potato, a good helping of *mamaliga* topped with sour cream, a cup of tea. A thick barley or bean soup, a stew made of ox heart and lung, a serving of *mamaliga* to go with it, applesauce for dessert, and you left her table replete. *Mamaliga* (corn meal cooked to a thick consistency) was an assured staple at her table. It was filling, it stayed with you. Hot, it went on the plate with a piece of boiled beef and boiled navy beans. When there wasn't any meat it was good on its own with a bit of butter or chicken fat on it. Cold, it was good with almost anything. Glicksman ate it with a raw onion.

"I remember all the different jobs you had," said Bella. "When we were kids, you were always changing jobs."

"I was still a young man," Glicksman replied, "so I looked for an opportunity to better myself."

Seeking to better himself, Glicksman over the years had left several jobs in favour of others, but the changings seldom yielded the advantage he was on the lookout for. If he happened to strike it lucky as he did one year when he changed jobs on two separate occasions (and each time to his advantage) misfortune followed him like a shadow. The first advantageous changeover was when he left a job as marker for a cleaning and dyeing establishment for a promising job in a toy factory. He worked three months for The Original Toy Company, was promoted from worker to foreman, and the plant burnt down. And again when he left a poor-paying job for a job as conductor on a T.T.C. streetcar, that, too, went by the board a few months after he was hired, when the cars with two men operating them were taken off the tracks and new ones put into service, with one man functioning as motorman and conductor. Being let out by the T.T.C. was a blow to Glicksman. He looked for work, cursing his fate.

After being out of work several weeks, he was put in the way of a good job by Mr. Grober, with whom he played pinochle in the back room of Grober's Ice Cream Parlour on Augusta Avenue. Grober's brother-in-law, Moe Blum, owner of Moe Blum's Bargain House Furnishings, a small establishment that sold house furnishings on credit, was looking for a collector, and Grober recommended his friend Glicksman. To qualify for the job, Glicksman had to learn to ride a bicycle. He bought a second-hand wheel and early one evening when traffic had subsided he mounted the wheel and began rockily pedalling, Grober running behind with a fast grip on the saddle.

In a week's time, Glicksman, going on forty-one, had earned how to handle a bike.

"When I first got to know Bella, you were a collector," Henry said. "For a Mr. Blum, wasn't that his name?"

"That's right. When you came to my house for the first ime, I was already working four years for Mr. Blum. A very ine man. He talked like a roughneck," Glicksman said, smiling, "but he was a gentleman."

Bella was fourteen and Sophie eleven when Glicksman vent to work for Blum. And shortly after that, Glicksman, easonably sure of steady employment, moved his family om their lodgings, which consisted of two rooms and a kitchen above a synagogue, and took up residence in a house across the street (the house he was to buy in partnership with his son-in-law Billy ten years later).

The move was effected with the help of his daughters and a coloured man who did odd jobs in the neighbourhood. The girls carried the kitchen table across the street, the kitchen chairs, their clothes, bushel baskets filled with dishes, cutlery, pots and pans, bedclothes, odds and ends. Glicksman and the coloured man carted the heavier pieces across: the stove, kitchen cupboard and the beds. Mrs. Glicksman, too, lent a hand. She took her broom across the street, kitchen mop, pail, washboard, her iron. Her clothes she carried across over one arm, with Glicksman's clothes over the other arm.

There were five rooms in the house, kitchen and two rooms downstairs, two rooms and bathroom upstairs. By a stroke of luck, the house had become vacant at an opportune time, and it gave Glicksman pleasure that it was in his power to decently settle his family. For bedrooms, he apportioned to each of the girls a room upstairs. Himself and wife he put in the room at the front of the house downstairs. The kitchen, and the bedroom he had allotted to himself and wife, were adequately furnished with the furniture he had brought from their former lodgings. To dig up some money for furnishing the girls' rooms and the middle room downstairs, he went to the Mozirer Sick Benefit & Loan Society, of which (on his sister Hannah's advice) he had in the nick of time become a member, and applied for a loan.

The girls meanwhile were clamouring for their rooms to be furnished. (The furnishings of their former bedroom, which consisted of the bed they had shared since childhood, a small table, a chair and a three-legged stool, had arbitrarily been put in the room assigned to Bella.) Neither one knew what it was to sleep in a bed by herself in a separate room, and both were impatient for the experience of sole occupancy.

When the loan was approved, Glicksman with money in his pocket set out to buy furniture. For the middle room downstairs, which was bare but for the picture (left on the wall by the former tenants) of majestically robed Mary Queen of

Scots kneeling with lace-capped head to the executioner's block, he bought a round dining table, two chairs with imitation leather seats, four mismatched mahogany chairs, a white cloth for the table, lace panels for the two windows, and — as a surprise for the girls — a small radio. For the girls' rooms he bought a second bed, two chairs, blinds for the windows, a bureau, and as he was not able to stretch his money to cover the cost of a second bureau, he bought a small chest of drawers.

When he got home he told the girls that he had been able to buy only one bureau, and it was to go to Bella, as she was the oldest. Sophie, in compensation, was given the chest of drawers and the new bed. When the furniture arrived, the bureau — which Sophie was to inherit four years later when Bella got married — went to Bella's room, and the small chest and the new bed, bought at a second-hand store as was everything else, went to Sophie's room. Friday night of that week, Mrs. Glicksman blessed the candles in the dining room, and served the Sabbath meal with a white cloth on the table. In celebration of the occasion Glicksman brought three extra glasses to table and gave his womenfolk a measure of wine to drink. "*L'chayim*," he said, raising his glass. His wife and daughters raised their glasses. "*L'chayim*."

"Ma had tears in her eyes," Sophie said to Bella later that evening when she was in her sister's room. "You didn't notice, but I—"

"I certainly did," said Bella.

"Those were tears of joy," her sister stated.

"Go to the head of the class," Bella returned. "Do you mind getting out of my room?"

Separate rooms, and each with a bed to herself; it had actually come to pass! The sisters revelled in it, visited each other in their rooms (when they were on good terms) and on the whole got along better. Compared with what they had left behind, the house with three bedrooms, dining room and three-piece bathroom was a mansion. And in the excitement and pride of ownership its defects were not at first noticed. A few months after they had taken possession, however, Bella was complaining to her father that the house was falling apart. She pointed out the water-stained cracks in the kitchen ceiling, paint flaking off the walls, the kitchen window with its diagonal crack patched with friction tape, the worn linoleum blistered and rucked up under the sink. The summer kitchen with its rotting roof leaking rain. The faded wallpaper in the dining room coming away from the walls in several places. The linoleum on the uneven floor so worn that its pattern of latticed roses in bloom was almost altogether erased. Window sashes needed replacing; there was hardly a window in the house that you could open without propping a stick under it. The doorbell didn't work. The tap in the bathroom sink didn't work. "I have to wash myself leaning over the bathtub," she complained — the girl who a few months before had been washing herself from a pail of water in the dingy bedroom she shared with her sister. Glicksman said, "I'll have to get a hold of a plumber."

"And a painter and wallpaper hanger too," said Bella.

"One thing at a time," said Glicksman. "I'm still paying off the money I borrowed for furniture."

When he had finished paying off what he owed, and Bella started pestering him again, he reminded her that he had just laid out eighty dollars for the typing and shorthand course she was taking at a high-priced business school. At sixteen when Bella was working in an office and paying board at home, Glicksman, who had been steadily employed two years as collector for Blum, was still saying, in acknowledgement of Bella's complaints, "I'll have to get a hold of a plumber." And left for a game of dominoes or cards, content that the hiring of the plumber and the painter was as good as done.

"He was a gentleman," repeated the night watchman-cum-property owner, nostalgically reminiscing Moe Blum, for whom he had worked six years as a collector. "He gave me respect and I gave him respect."

Moe Blum, thirty-five years old when Glicksman went to work for him, was born in Toronto of immigrant parents. He was a handsome man, arrogant, outspoken, friendly and easy-going with familiars, devoted to an ailing wife to whom he had been married ten years, and father of two children whom he adored. The horn-rimmed glasses he wore had one clear lens that revealed an observant brown eye; the left lens, opaque, concealed the sightless eye he had been blinded in as a boy in a school fight. The small store he rented for his business had a desk, two chairs, a telephone, a makeshift filing cabinet, and was stocked with sheets, pillow slips, bedspreads, blankets, towels, curtains, rugs. From this supply he loaded his car five mornings a week, and set out to canvass old customers and drum up new trade.

His collector Glicksman mounted his wheel six days a week at eight in the morning and went the rounds of the territory Blum had covered by car, collecting payments from customers who bought house furnishings from Blum on a weekly instalment plan. (Glicksman came in for some criticism, riding his bike on the Sabbath; the neighbours called him a *Shabbes goy* behind his back. And six years later when his younger daughter married a *shaygets*, they said: "The apple doesn't fall far from the tree.") Following Blum's instructions, Glicksman rang doorbells and stood his ground till someone came to the door. Where there was no bell he knocked. And kept knocking. Blum had said, "Don't be shy, Glicksman, you're not asking for no handouts. They owe money, let them pay. I'm not running no charity organization."

When Glicksman first went to work for Blum, it worried him when a customer who was down for a two-dollar payment gave him only one dollar; when one who should have given him a dollar gave him fifty cents. These things worried him; and though Blum gave no sign of dissatisfaction and still treated him with the same familiar courtesy as he had the very first day, Glicksman worried that his boss was dissatisfied with his new collector. And at the end of the day's business when they sat down at the desk to tot up the day's take in collections — and Blum made no comment — Glicksman feared for his job.

"What happened to Mrs. Boychuk?" Blum asked him one night. "She drop dead or something?" Mrs. Boychuk was steadily falling behind in payments.

"She told me they're having a hard time but she'll try and

do better. She isn't exactly a rich woman, Mr. Blum. I saw myself how—"

"Mrs. Boychuk isn't a rich woman?" Blum interrupted. "What else is new? I don't go to rich people, Glicksman," he said, fixing him with his good eye. "They don't need me, they can buy for cash. I haven't got any rich customers so don't lose no more sleep over Mrs. Boychuk. Get after her."

Having worked three months now for Moe Blum's Bargain House Furnishings, Glicksman knew his customers didn't get any bargains at Blum's. They paid through the nose, buying on time. A poor man himself, his sympathy was with the defaulter; he tried nevertheless to harden himself, to take a tougher line with a delinquent. But he didn't have the talent for harassing or pressing an overdue account. He took what was offered and said, "Try and do better next week, please."

"That's all you got from Mrs. Andrews, fifty cents?" Blum said to him a couple of days later.

"She promised she'll pay more next week."

"She should live so, the *shikkerteh*," said Blum. "And you didn't get nothing from Mrs. Constantino?"

Glicksman felt his heart pounding. "Her husband was laid off."

"Let him hang himself," said Blum roughly.

I can't work for that man, Glicksman said to himself, riding home on his wheel. I can't work for a man like that. I'll give him a week's notice and look for another job. His heart turned over at the thought that he might not so easily find another job. He was born unlucky, he reflected. When Grober had put him in the way of a steady job with good pay, he thought he had landed on his feet for a change. Counting his chickens before they were hatched, he moved to a house where the rent was twice what he had paid for their rooms above the synagogue, bought furniture on borrowed money — it caused him a pang suddenly to think what pleasure it gave his wife, now that she was able to put a meal on the table without having to pinch and scrape. He put his wheel in the side alley and went in with a heavy heart to supper.

His wife was at the stove. As always when he came from

work, "You're home?" she said, smiling. His glance fell on the pot of soup on the stove, with its lid inverted. This was a habit of hers; a pot was seldom put on the stove with its lid right side up. Testily he righted the lid. "Why must the lid always be *moysheh kapoyr*?" he said irritably.

The following evening after work he sat down as usual with Blum and together they totted up the collections. Then Glicksman got up from his chair. "Mr. Blum—" he began.

"You're sweating," Blum observed. "And you don't look so hot. What's the matter?"

To steady himself, Glicksman sat down. "I'm sorry, but I have to give you a week's notice."

His boss turned in his chair and looked at him. Blum never looked sideways at you or over his shoulder; when he addressed or attended you it was always face to face. The single piercing brown eye made Glicksman uncomfortable. Uneasily he said, "If you can't find a collector in a week's time, I'll stay till you'll find one."

"I can find a man tomorrow. What I want to know is why you're quitting."

"I'm not the right man for the job. I can't fight with a customer, Mr. Blum. For this job you need a harder man than me."

"I had a harder man, he should only rot. The collector before you, a burglar. He clipped me six months hand running, the *goniff*. I could of had him thrown in the hoosegow for the money he took off me. But he had me figured right, the crook — he knew I wouldn't take him to court, a Jewish sonofabitch married with three kids. I fired him, told him to get the hell out. And he had the gall to call me One-Eyed Moe, the bastard. For *that*, I laid him out flat. Right there," Blum said, pointing to the only clear space on the floor. "All right, Glicksman, level with me. Why are you quitting? You got another job lined up?"

Glicksman shook his head. "I'll find one."

"Where are you gonna find work, a man your age? There's a depression going on, didn't you hear? Come on, tell me what's biting you."

"It's like this," Glicksman began. "I have nothing against

you personally, Mr. Blum." Choosing his words and taking care not to give offence, he conveyed as best he could how he felt about being associated with a business based mainly on exploitation of the poor.

"So you think I'm a blood sucker. A con man, a bluffer that takes advantage of poor people that haven't got the money to buy for cash." Glicksman, sitting with his head lowered, made no reply. "Well, let me tell you something about my business," said Blum. "Something which you're too new in the game yet to figure out for yourself. First of all, I buy my goods from a wholesaler. He gives me thirty days to pay. If I want a discount I have to give him cash. Second of all, the goods my customer buys on credit is the goods I already paid for. Let's say a customer buys for twenty-five, thirty bucks. At two bucks a week — if they pay the two bucks — it'll take them thirteen, fifteen weeks to pay up. I'm running a business, Glicksman, so naturally I put a pretty good markup on my goods and take a chance that they'll pay up. Does that make me a monster? There's people in this business a lot tougher than me. They'll bust the door down and go in the house to grab a lousy sheet off the bed if a customer owes. I worked for a man like that before I went in business myself. Me, if a customer pays up half, three-quarters what they owe—" he shrugged "—*ish kabibble*, so I won't make a hundred percent profit on the deal. A customer pays up in full, it's a standoff for the fall I take with a deadbeat. And don't kid yourself, Glicksman, you get plenty of deadbeats in this business. Your Mrs. Constantino — there's a prize deadbeat, the hoor. Her husband was laid off," he laughed. "Which one?"

Just then the phone rang. Blum looked at his watch, rolled his visible eye upward and reached for the receiver. Glicksman heard a woman's voice at the other end, followed by the sound of the receiver being slammed. "That was my wife," said Blum. "She said if I'm not home in fifteen minutes she'll kill me."

He rose, and Glicksman too got up to go. "So," said Blum, "what's it gonna be? Do I have to look for a new collector?"

Glicksman repeated, "I can't fight with a customer."

217

"Who asked you to fight? You're doing pretty good without getting tough. And the customers like you. Especially the deadbeats," Blum said, laughing. He put his hand on Glicksman's shoulder. "Kidding on the square, I respect your type, Glicksman. You're an honest, plain-speaking man. You're no bullshitter and I respect you for that. And I'm not such a bad guy to work for. Stick with me and you won't be out of work so long as I'm in business. Even if times get worse, God forbid. What do you say?"

Offering his hand to the man he had the day before sized up as a man without conscience or heart, plain-spoken Glicksman said with feeling, "I will try and do my best for you, Mr. Blum."

Glicksman worked six years for Blum (who was to go out of business at the end of that time), and as he said he would do, he tried his best for him.

Dissimilar as they were in character and temperament one from the other, a mutual attachment nevertheless developed between employer and employee. On Glicksman's part there was something akin to a paternal feeling in his concern for Blum's welfare; his affection for the man who was six years his junior was that almost of a father's for a son. Blum's affection was expressed in an easier, freer, jocular manner. "Boychik," he affectionately called his collector who was six years older than him. Glicksman, devoted, took no offence at this over-freedom of address. Any employer but Blum calling him boychik, he would have walked off the job without notice. "Deadbeat," a word in Blum's vocabulary, became a word in Glicksman's vocabulary. And Blum, whom Glicksman felt he had wronged by unfairly judging him to be a man without conscience or heart, became in his eyes the victim of the deadbeat. Following up a promise of payment, Glicksman frequently got up from the supper table after a hard day's work, to make a third and even a fourth repeat call on a customer who said she would have money for him if he came back in the evening. And when he managed by sheer perseverance to extract a two-dollar bill from an out-and-out deadbeat, he would mount his bicycle and pedal home rejoicing as if he had drawn a winning ticket on the

Irish Sweepstakes. It keenly distressed him to discover an unsuspected deadbeat in a customer he had taken to be honest. Sadly shaking his head, "She didn't look to me like a deadbeat," he would say of a customer who, after paying on the dot seven weeks in a row, had begun suddenly to give him "the run around" — another of Blum's expressions. Blum would say, "Don't waste no more time on the bitch. Screw her, let her go to hell." And clean-spoken Glicksman would not blink an eye; coming from Blum, coarse language fell on a benign ear.

In the winter he froze going his rounds on the bicycle. He came home blue with cold, eyes watering. In the summer he sweated. In rainy weather he wore a cap and a three-quarter rain cape; the cap kept his head dry, and the cape his body. His legs from the knee down and his arms below the elbow got soaked. Once in a while Blum would telephone his collector early in the morning of a bitter winter's day: "It's a day for the Eskimos, you'd better stay home, boychik. I'm not going out myself, my wife won't let me." Glicksman would reply: "And who's going to make my calls if I stay home?" Blum would come back with: "If you wanna freeze your ass, that's okay by me."

"I remember the first time I came here for supper," Henry was saying. This was a night for nostalgic recall. The *balaboosteh* of the house was in the kitchen washing up; her grandson Philip, a born cadger, was in the kitchen filling himself with sponge cake; and the *baleboss* and his family were sitting around the table, reminiscing. "It was on a Friday night," Henry continued, "and I—"

"The first time you were here was on a Saturday night," said Bella.

When Bella started dating, she grew severely critical of her mother's housekeeping, and of her father's indifference to repairs. Ashamed of the house, she met her date at the top of her street or in a restaurant. Bella's unwillingness to bring a boyfriend to the house did not go unmarked by her father. It disquieted him that she was (unreasonably, in his opinion) ashamed of the house, but for the sake of peace he let her behaviour go without comment.

When she was eighteen she was dating exclusively with Henry Sherman, a pharmacist whom she had met over the counter of a newly opened neighbourhood drugstore. One night she told her father that she was going steady with a pharmacist. Glicksman expressed a desire to meet the pharmacist. And when she made no response he positively forbade his 18-year-old daughter to surprise him with a son-in-law who had not as yet set foot in his house.

When he came home from work one·Saturday a few days after this conversation had taken place, he found his women-folk cleaning house. Sophie, on her knees in the hall, was scrubbing the linoleum and baseboard. Bella, flushed, her expression forbidding, was dusting and mopping in the dining room. He carefully stepped out of the way of her sloshing mop and went to the kitchen, where his wife was sweeping up. She leaned her broom against the wall and laid two fingers on her lips. "Bella's *chossin*," she whispered, "he's coming for supper." On the stove she had a frying pan with hamburgers sizzling in chicken fat, potatoes boiling up in a pot with its lid inverted, covered pots with their contents stewing, bubbling, simmering — by the look of her stove her every pot, vessel and stewpan was engaged. Glicksman righted her upside-down lids without getting cross, and went upstairs to shave.

Punctually at six, 25-year-old Henry Sherman, a man of medium height with a dark complexion, black hair thinning on top, broad face with brown eyes and wide mouth, was at the door with his finger on the doorbell that didn't work. Glicksman, coming out of the bedroom dressed in his second suit, saw him peering through the window. He opened the door and offered his hand, introducing himself as "Bella's father, Mr. Glicksman." He then led him through the hall, calling up to his daughters, who had gone up to wash and change. The girls came down, Bella presented her sister, and Glicksman called to his wife to come out of the kitchen. In clean apron and hair smoothed down with water, she approached with a hand extended to Henry.

Bella sat down, telling Henry to take the chair next to her father's; that way he would be facing the one wall that (by some miracle of paper hanging) had its worn wallpaper still adhering to it.

Mrs. Glicksman served Henry first, apologizing profusely for the second-rate meal she was offering and pressing him at the same time to take more. Sophie, glancing obliquely at Henry from time to time, ate with her head bent to her plate. Bella, too, ate in silence. Leaving it to her parents, who were engaging the guest in conversation, she hardly exchanged a word with Henry.

Interrogating Henry, an educated man, Glicksman respectfully inquired about the course he had taken in pharmacy. How many years did the course take to complete? Did the course involve some training in medical science as well? Was pharmacy a profession that attracted more Jews than gentiles? Things like that. Henry was not a noticeable conversationalist. Questions put to him he answered briefly and to the point. Mrs. Glicksman asked did he come from a large or small family. Replying in Yiddish, he informed her that he was an only child. She sighed. A mother with an only child, she said, was like a woman with one shirt to her back.

Henry got up shortly after supper and said he had to be back at the drugstore before eight. Glicksman shook hands with him, saying he hoped that next time he would be able to stay longer. Mrs. Glicksman, shaking his hand, said, "Don't be a stranger." Sophie got up. "It was nice meeting you." "Likewise," he returned, and Bella went to the door with him.

When she returned, her father, standing, was drinking Henry's untouched glass of wine. "What do you think of him, Pa?" she asked.

Putting down his glass, Glicksman remarked, "He looks to me like a very responsible man." Asked for her opinion, Mrs. Glicksman couldn't praise him enough. She had taken to him right away. She liked the way he conducted himself, like a *haimisher mensch*. And he fairly shone, he was so clean.

Glicksman drank down the rest of Henry's wine and took the glass to the kitchen. Returning, he announced, "He is a man you can go to table with." And having delivered what in his vocabulary of approbation was the ultimate in praise, he left for a game of double-deck pinochle.

"You looked as if the world was coming to an end," Henry was saying to his father-in-law, recalling the night Glicksman had told them that Blum was going out of business.

His father-in-law nodded. "It happened over four years ago and I can still remember that terrible shock I got."

When Glicksman had been working six years for Blum, he entered the store one Friday evening after the day's work and saw Blum sitting at the desk with his face in his hands; his glasses were on the desk by his elbow. He put on his glasses as Glicksman shut the door, turned in his chair and said, "I've got bad news for you. I'm selling out, boychik. I'm going out of business."

Glicksman's knees buckled; he had to lean against the door for support.

"Come and sit down," said Blum kindly. "Take a load off your feet."

Glicksman moved away from the door. Emptying his back pocket, he heaped the crumpled bills and change on the desk and then sat down.

Blum said, "I've got to get the hell out of this country, the climate's killing my wife." (His wife was asthmatic.) "So I'm taking the doctor's advice and moving my family to Arizona."

"I'm sorry to hear that," Glicksman replied, "but you have to do what's best for your wife." From his inside pocket he withdrew a thick stack of record cards bound with an elastic band; each card bore a customer's name and address, and Glicksman's pencilled-in figures of sums collected. Silently he pushed the heaped bills and change towards Blum, took the band off the cards and began: "Mrs. Carter on Roncesvalles, two dollars."

"Did you hear that joke about the cop that found a dead horse on Roncesvalles?" Blum said, smiling. "He had to make out a report but he didn't know how to spell Roncesvalles, so he dragged the horse over to Queen Street."

Smiling, Glicksman turned the card right side down and went on to the next card: "Mrs. Craig on Wright Avenue, a dollar fifty."

Blum opened the Accounts book and recorded under

corresponding headings the amounts as Glicksman called them. He closed the ledger when they were finished, turned to Glicksman and said with a smile, "Did I ever tell you about my old man's bookkeeping system when he ran a grocery store? He bought from wholesalers on credit, and some of his customers bought from him on credit. To keep track of what he owed the wholesalers and what the customers owed him, my old man bought himself a nickel notepad and on one side he wrote, 'I owe pipples,' and on the other side, 'pipples owes me.' "

Glicksman smiled, but from his face it could be seen that his mind wasn't open to light conversation. He bent down to put the bicycle clips on his pants and then stood up. "When are you leaving, Mr. Blum?"

"I'll be out of this place next Saturday. That's a week from tomorrow," Blum said, handing him his Friday pay envelope. "The new man comes in a week from this Monday. But you'll meet him before then. I recommended you and he wants to have a look at you. He'll be here tomorrow when you come from work."

The following day when Glicksman returned from work, a short fat man, with bushy black hair and thick lips, was sitting at the desk beside Blum, in Glicksman's chair. Blum got up. "Mr. Greenberg," he said to the man who was buying him out, "meet Mr. Glicksman, my collector for six years." Remaining seated, Mr. Greenberg offered his hand, and turning at the same time to Blum, he said, with Glicksman's hand in his, "You didn't tell me he was an older man." He then turned to Glicksman. Withdrawing his hand, "How old are you?" he asked in Yiddish, using the familiar thou.

Glicksman was affronted at the man's insolent familiarity of address. Anger accelerating the beating of his heart, he stooped to his bicycle clips to hide his agitation, and took them off with a trembling hand. Then he straightened. "I am not applying for a life insurance policy that I have to tell you my age," he said, trying to keep his voice steady.

Lolling, crossing one short leg over the other, Mr. Greenberg said, "What are you so independent? Do you want to keep the job or not?"

For answer Glicksman emptied his back pocket, heaped

the crumpled bills and change on the desk, took the banded cards from his inside pocket and put them on the desk. "I'll go home now if you'll excuse me," he said to Blum. And added with a smile, "I think you're in this business long enough to know how to check over the cards by yourself."

Mr. Greenberg shot up from his chair. "I asked you a question, Glicksman. Do you want the job or not? Give me a yes or a no."

Glicksman, at the door now, turned to look at him.

"Well?" said Mr. Greenberg. "I don't have to kiss your ass, you know. I can find a man half your age that'll be glad to get the job and be willing to work the same hours for less money."

Glicksman said, "Then you'd better start looking for a collector. Next week when Mr. Blum goes out from this place, I go out too."

Saturday of the following week Blum was on his way to Arizona; and for the first Saturday in six years his collector's wheel remained in the side alley, riderless.

Monday Glicksman was studying Help Wanted ads. There were not many, and the few that were listed he was not qualified for. Tuesday he bought both dailies. In the weeks that followed he presented himself only at places that had openings with no experience required, and found in every case that his age was against him. Which caused him to recall Blum's words: "Where are you gonna find work, a man your age? There's a depression going on, didn't you hear?" The depression was still going on, and he was six years older now than he was then.

One morning when he had been out of work a month, he saw under the Help Wanted ads that Asher Aaronowitz, a *landsman* of his — they had grown up together in Focsani — wanted a night watchman for his tobacco factory. In Roumania they had worked in the same vineyard, and had emigrated within a year of each other. Same age, both immigrants with equal opportunities, neither one of them with more education than the other, or with more money in his pocket — and look at the difference in situation between them now, Glicksman reflected. It would embarrass him to ask Asher for a job. But why should you be ashamed? he argued with himself. You're not going to him for charity. You're looking for work, and he's looking for a night watchman. He went resolutely to the phone.

"Avrom Mendl!" Aaronowitz exclaimed when Glicksman identified himself. "I don't believe it! Only last night we were talking about you. About the old times, when we came here a pair of greenhorns. I said to Fanny I wonder if Avrom Mendl still makes his own wine. Nobody makes wine like you, I still remember the taste. How are you anyway? What are you doing these days?"

Glicksman cleared his throat. "It so happens I'm not doing anything," he said; and then told the factory owner that he had been a collector six years for a very fine man who had to sell out his business last month. "I happened to see in the paper that you're looking for a night watchman, Asher, so I thought I'll give you a call."

"What are you talking about! I wouldn't insult you, Avrom Mendl. It's not a job for you. A night watchman is a job for a *goy*."

"It's honest work," Glicksman said; and argued that a man, even if he was a Jew, did not humble himself taking honest work.

Aaronowitz said, "I won't argue with you. Be here at six. Mr. Frankel, that's my foreman, he'll show you around. I'll see you tomorrow, Avrom Mendl. Give my regards to your wife."

Shortly after this conversation Aaronowitz telephoned his wife and told her about the call he'd had from Glicksman. "It's not right I shouldn't be here when he comes, it's his first day, so I'll be home a little later than I told you." And that evening at six when Glicksman presented himself at the office of the tobacco factory, Aaronowitz was there himself to receive him.

"Avrom Mendl!" he cried, embracing him. "How long since I didn't see you — five years?"

"It could be. Time passes like lightning. . . "

"A very fine man," Glicksman was saying. "We grew up together in Focsani." Having finished crying up Mr. Blum, he was now lauding his present employer, Aaronowitz, the tobacco factory owner for whom he had been working four years now as night watchman. "I came here first, and he came a year after me. He made a success, and I—" he reached for his wine "—I can't complain."

It was getting late. It was time to go home. Bella got up. "We're going, Ma," she called.

Mrs. Glicksman came out of the kitchen. "So soon?"

Twenty-Eight

One morning early in July Billy telephoned his wife from the Y and told her he had just heard over the radio that two more children were in hospital with poliomyelitis. A few days later when he came from work he reported that nine children were now in hospital with the dreaded disease. "Nine children, Soph. That's the beginning of an epidemic. We've got to get out of the city."

Friday morning of that week he engaged a substitute coach to take his classes, took the ferry to Ward's Island, and spent the day there, hunting for rooms. And the following Saturday he moved his family to a three-room apartment in an old house on the lakefront of Ward's Island, where they stayed out the summer, Billy commuting by island ferry to and from work.

The house was owned by Lambert Pollard, a 65-year-old expatriate Englishman called Lambie by everyone. He was a big man, over six feet, bald, flushed face with protruding blood-shot eyes, and a tremor of the hands. He had buried two wives and was married a third time to a woman half his age. Lambie had a houseful of kids; two by his present wife Charmion (whom he called Charm) and five from the previous two marriages. Among the five from the previous marriages was the only child of his first marriage, 29-year-old Pat, a pale hollow-eyed artist who spent his days in a shack back of his father's house, painting.

The Saturday morning Billy with his wife and child came to take up lodgings, Lambie came up shortly after to see how they were settling in. Billy introduced his wife, "This is my wife, Sophie." The landlord bowed and kissed her hand. Emma was dismissed with a pat on the head. "We've seen these before," he said. His breath smelled of whiskey.

Dressed in white flannels, navy blazer, white shirt and bow tie, he came up later in the day and invited them to dinner. "We dine at the unfashionable hour of six. We have fallen on evil days and most of the amenities have gone by the board," he said, "but I still keep a good table."

Billy offered a whiskey. Lambie took it with a trembling hand. "My first today." Sophie invited him to sit.

". . . it was at one of the most distinguished salons in London. I was a lad of twenty, in the Coldstream Guards."

"And you actually met him! Oscar Wilde!" Sophie exclaimed. "What did he look like? What did he say?"

"He was a handsome man, impeccably attired. He made a complimentary remark on our style of dress, but I can't quite remember what else he said. I was a callow youth of twenty."

"Lambie!" It was his wife calling from the foot of the stairs.

Lambie cupped a hand to his ear. "The bell invites me. Hear it not, Lambie, for it is a knell," he said, holding out his glass for a refill, "that summons thee to heaven or to hell." He finished his drink, put his glass down with a palsied hand and rose on steady legs. "You will attend us at six?"

They went down at six and were met at the door by Lambie and his wife Charmion, a thin plain-looking woman with brown hair, freckled skin and no eyebrows. Her youngest, a boy of two, was in her arms, and Araby, her four-year-old girl, was hiding behind her skirt. They went inside and were joined presently by the four daughters of Lambie's second marriage — Miranda, Rosalind, Viola and Imogen; sixteen, fourteen, thirteen and ten, in that order. The guests were led to the dining room, and Pat, already seated, rose at their entrance. "Pat, my son and heir," Lambie said, introducing him, "the Titian of our family. Although at present a poor struggling artist, I am confident that one day we will boast of our connection with him." Then remarked in an aside to Sophie, "Worthless, that one."

After seating his guests, Lambie took up a bottle of wine, went around the table and with a shaking hand poured wine in each glass, never spilling a drop. The first course was a chilled consommé with a slice of lemon on top. The second course, a leg of lamb, was brought to the table by Miranda and put before her father to carve. Lambie refilled his glass and raised it to salute his wife.

"Charm," he said, casting a bleary glance around to see that everyone was taking a sip. "Charm," he repeated, gazing at his wife. "Aptly named, my love."

"Get on with it, Lambie," she said sharply, "and stop playing the fool."

Drunk as he was, and despite a palsied hand, he dexterously carved the leg of lamb, talking all the while of former days in London. Plates were passed to his wife and she served the vegetables. She turned her head suddenly to Pat who was sitting on her left. "You stink of paint," she said and rose quickly from her chair. "Look after your guests, Lambie, I'm not up to it." She hurried from the room, retching. Lambie, talking of an afternoon with Beerbohm Tree, kept on as though nothing had happened. Eyes popping, face mottled and veined, "Beerbohm Tree," he mused, "and I, a callow youth of twenty, was not cognizant of the honour."

Rosalind brought the dessert, a rich trifle, and served it sitting in her stepmother's vacated chair. Viola placed a decanter before her father. "Cognac," he said, removing the stopper, "the elixir of the gods." Imogen lifted the two-year-old from his highchair. "I'll put him to bed." His father blew him a boozy kiss. One by one they slipped away, Pat leading off, till only the host and his three guests were left.

Sophie rose. "Thank you for a wonderful evening and a marvellous dinner."

Lambie lowered his head. "Out, out, brief candle. . . "

The instructor took his daughter by the hand. "Good night, sir."

The host raised his head. "Life's but a walking shadow, a poor player that struts and frets his hour upon the stage. . . ." He paused to lift the snifter of brandy to his lips; Billy slipped away with his daughter. "And then is heard no more," Lambie resumed. "It is a tale told by an idiot, full of sound and fury, signifying nothing."

"That's beautiful," Sophie said. Lambie was quite befuddled now but she had stayed out of politeness to hear him out.

Next morning when Sophie, half dressed, was washing up the breakfast dishes, she heard someone knocking on the door. "Just a minute," she called and went to the bedroom to put something on. When she opened the door, Charm, in the act of turning toward the stairs, turned back.

"I've come to apologize for behaving so badly at dinner last night," she said.

"Please," said Sophie, "don't give it another thought."

"Thank you."

She made as if to go but continued in the doorway. "Lambie's been lecturing me all morning. He insisted that I come up and apologize."

What was Sophie to say to this? Thinking to change the subject, she enthusiastically praised the leg of lamb, the trifle.

"I don't do the cooking," said Charm shortly. "Lambie does."

"Really? He's an extraordinary man. He's—"

"He's a sot," Charm cut in. "And lecherous as an old goat. I'm pregnant again. Another mouth to feed and where's the money to come from," she said and turned towards the stairs.

A minute or so later Sophie heard her on the back porch, talking to Lambie: "She's a stupid ill-bred girl. No manners. She took her own sweet time coming to the door. I felt demeaned apologizing to her, thank you very much."

"Let's keep our distance," Sophie said to her husband later that evening at supper. She had told him about Charm's rudeness, the insulting things she had said about her to Lambie, and that Lambie had not said one word in her defence. "I don't want to get friendly with either of them. They're both hypocrites."

One Friday morning when Sophie was hanging some clothes on the line, she saw Pat on the back porch. Dressed in jeans and undershirt, he was sitting on the daybed he slept in, scratching his pale arms, which were covered with mosquito bites.

He descended the steps and came over to the clothesline. "I am an artist," he said, as if that explained his itch. Looking closely at Sophie, he said he would like to do a painting of her. "I need a portrait head for an exhibition, but I can't pay for sittings." He said if she would sit for the portrait, he would give it to her after it was shown; and a sitting was arranged for ten o'clock next morning.

The following morning she was sitting before a three-way mirror, studying her face. "Oh God!" she cried. "Why did I say I'd sit for him? He must be blind as a bat not to have noticed my cock-eyes."

Billy looked at his watch. "You'd better get going, hon, it's almost ten."

These recurring dramas over the slight cast in her right eye disturbed him. He was well acquainted now with stories of her childhood; the misery she had undergone at being called cock-eyes by kids in the schoolyard, the nightly prayers that her eye would be straight when she woke in the morning, the agony of having to stand facing the whole class during oral composition exams — and while he was not unmoved by her childhood and adolescent sufferings, these periodic outcries, as if an affliction had suddenly descended on her, were getting to be a pain in the neck.

"Three-quarter profile isn't bad, is it, Billy? It's not so noticeable. I'll pose myself and that's how I'll sit. My strabismic eye doesn't show up three-quarter profile, does it?"

She had all the words for it — strabismic, cast, squint, oblique. "You're going to be late, Soph."

Pat was waiting for her outside the shack. He led her into a dank cluttered place, with a high-backed oak chair in the space he had cleared for the sitting. He pointed at the chair. "Make yourself comfortable."

Viewing his subject through half-closed eyes, he rolled a cigarette, put it to his lips without lighting it, and went to work. "Face me," he said irritably from time to time, "don't turn your head." She was giving him her three-quarter profile. He worked about an hour and then put down his brushes. "That will do for today."

"Can I see what you've done?"

He turned the easel to the wall. "Not till it's finished."

The morning of the seventh sitting, there was a note tacked to the door: "I had to go to town. Can we make the sitting for two this afternoon?" Cautiously she opened the door. The easel was not turned to the wall, it was facing outward. Going over to it, she beheld on the canvas a portrait of a beautiful woman with black hair — with the subject's eye dead centre in its socket. Studying the painting, she observed that while the likeness between the face on the canvas and hers was not exactly striking, it unmistakably was a portrait of her, Sophie.

When she came back at two o'clock Pat was mixing paints; and standing before the portrait, viewing it, was a tall man dressed in brown corduroys, with bare feet in sandals. Pat said, "This is a friend of mine, Brian Purtell, an artist," and nodded, indicating she was to take up her position. He left off mixing paints and they stood side by side, both artists, looking several times from subject to canvas and from canvas to subject.

Pat at length turned to his friend. "Well?"

"You've flattered her," was the visiting artist's comment.

"Is that all you have to say?"

His friend shrugged. "Do you want an honest opinion?" he asked, looking doubtfully at him.

Pat pulled his shirt over his head and flung it to the floor. "I didn't ask you here to give me shit-shots," he said, scratching his flea-bitten shoulders.

The other artist looked again several times from subject to canvas. "The flesh tones are good," he finally came out with. "Excellent, but the portrait itself is dead. It's lifeless, there's no expression to it. And you've missed that slight fault in the eyes, that imperfection that gives her face a piquancy of expression. What you have here," he said, looking again at the portrait, "looks like a blown-up reproduction of a chocolate box cover."

Pat took a rolled cigarette from his easel and lit it with a shaking hand. He stooped suddenly to the floor, seized hold of the jam jar in which he kept his turps and hurled it at the painting. He spat the cigarette from his mouth, grabbed up the shirt he had thrown on the floor, bunched it in his fist and applied himself violently to the canvas. His friend moved quickly to the door and stood there a moment, watching the frenzied effacing of the portrait he had criticized. Then he pulled open the door and beckoned Sophie to follow.

With his arm through hers, he walked her quickly away from the shack. Then he slackened his pace, led her to a bench facing the lagoon, and they sat down. "Poor bugger," he said, laughing, "he's long on artistic temperament and short on talent."

He told her that Pat had come barging into his studio eleven o'clock that morning, insisting that he come to the Island to give him an opinion on a painting he was working on. Which was the last thing he wanted to do, he said, but had let himself be persuaded. "He reacts aggressively to criticism, sometimes even violently. Last year around this time he asked Gerry Ross — he's an artist, a friend of ours — to give him an opinion on a painting he was thinking of putting in a show at the Exhibition. When Gerry saw the painting, he advised Pat not to show it. Pat wanted to know why it shouldn't be shown, and when Gerry said, 'Because it'll stink up the ice,' Pat grabbed the painting off the easel and bashed him over the head with it. He nearly brained the guy." Laughing, he said, "I didn't get out of there a minute too soon. When he attacked that portrait, I knew I'd be next in line for a drubbing."

Drubbing — he speaks well, she thought.

"I'd like to do a painting of you," he said. "Will you sit for me?"

She definitely did not want to sit for him. He wasn't likely to overlook that slight fault in her eyes. To give his portrait of her that piquancy of expression that Pat had missed, he'd make her good and cockeyed. She said she had a small child to look after, that it would take hours ferrying across to town and back, that she couldn't possibly leave a four-year-old child alone for that length of time.

"I can't begin myself for a while," he said. "I'm getting some paintings ready for a show. Let's make it the first week in October. You'll be back in town by then?" He brought out a small address book from his pocket. "Give me your phone number."

She gave him her number — October was a long way off; she'd think up some excuse.

"You look very young to be the mother of a four-year-old child," he said.

"I'm almost twenty-three. I was married before I was eighteen."

He said he was thirty-one years old and had been married four years. "I met my wife in a bootlegging joint on Sussex Street," he said. "It used to be a hangout for artists."

"Is your wife an artist too?"

"She's a booze artist. A lovely woman but hell to live with when she gets drunk." The Bluebell's deafening blast signalling its approach brought him to his feet. He ran for the ferry, turning once to look back and wave.

When Billy came from work she told him what had happened that afternoon at the sitting.

"I don't like the sound of that man," he said, "talking like that about his wife. I wish you hadn't promised to let him paint you."

"I've no intention of sitting for him. He's going to phone me first week in October — but that's a way off, I'll think up some excuse."

End of September when they moved back to the city, Sophie began worrying about her commitment to Brian Purtell. And when the month of October went by without a call from him, she experienced a mixture of relief and disappointment. She put the whole episode from her mind and one day in mid-November when the all-but-forgotten artist telephoned, she experienced an unexpected flutter of pleasure.

He said the reason he had not called sooner was because he had been very busy; and then asked could she come for a sitting at three that afternoon.

Three o'clock — she should be home by half-past four. That would give her enough time to get supper before Billy came from work. "I guess I can," she said.

"Good," he said, and gave her the house number of a street in the village.

At a quarter to three she was strolling along Grenville Street, taking in with pleasure its bohemian atmosphere. There were several people on the street, among them a young couple who came suddenly to a stop in front of her. Sophie saw the man open his coat, enfold the girl in it and, oblivious of passersby, they stood embraced in a lingering kiss, he holding his coat around her, she standing inside it with her arms around his neck.

Passing the embraced couple, Sophie wished she were in love again. She felt sad suddenly, remembering how she and Billy used to go to Queen's Park to neck. She recalled their picnics, canoeing on the Humber, bicycling on the Island boardwalk. And the presents he bought her; half a week's pay for a calfskin handbag, next payday a charm bracelet, and the next an expensive compact, then a kimono imported from Japan; all from the same store. "You're my girl," he said, "and I'm going to buy you everything in the window." All this came back to her now, with a sense of loss.

She approached the address and rang the doorbell. Brian Purtell, in beret and artist's smock, opened the door to her.

Twenty-Nine

The artist greeted her with a smile, took off his beret, stuffed it in the pocket of his smock and led her to his studio which was on the ground floor at the back of the house. He helped her off with her coat and then went over to a marble-topped tabouret, with a bottle of gin on it, a bottle of tonic and two glasses. "Let's have a drink before we begin." He fixed two drinks.

Sipping gin and tonic, they sat a long while without conversation, he gazing steadily at her with a half-smile; she, becoming uncomfortable under his unmistakably amorous gaze, drank with her head lowered. She glanced at her watch; a quarter past three, and the sitting hadn't started yet.

"It's getting late," she said. "Hadn't we better get started? I have to be home by five o'clock. My husband will be home at six for supper."

He put down his glass, went over to her chair, brought her to her feet and put his arms around her. Holding her closely pressed against him, he said, "Let's make love first."

She pushed him away. "I don't sleep around," she said severely. "My husband is the only man I've ever been to bed with."

He laughed, and that for some reason made her feel foolish. He sat down in her chair and pulled her on his lap. "Aren't you curious to know what it might be like with another man?"

"Curiosity killed the cat, she said coolly, and felt she had recovered some poise. "Where's your wife, what if she were to come in?"

"She won't. She left me. We're getting a divorce."

He caressed her neck, her arms, his hand wandered to her breast. "Let me make love to you," he murmured, and put his mouth to hers.

His ardour leaves her cold. He doesn't excite her. She is not in the least attracted to him and yet she lets him take her to bed. Why? Is it because she doesn't want him to think her just a housewife whose main concerns are domestic obligations, like getting her husband's supper on time? Probably. Unlike Lambie Pollard who was "not cognizant of the honour" when he was invited to spend an afternoon with Beerbohm Tree, Sophie is definitely impressed with Brian Purtell, a high-ranking artist, a sophisticate, a man of the world. It's not because she wants his love that she goes to bed with him: it's his good opinion she desires.

He takes her — after the briefest possible preliminary wooing — and falls asleep almost immediately after.

We made love, Sophie reflects, studying the sleeping man, but there was no love in it. On either side. Except for money changing hands, that's what a prostitute experiences in her profession: lovemaking without love. Other thoughts come to her mind. She has committed her first adulterous act, yet feels no guilt. She's not by nature promiscuous; shouldn't her first adulterous act be of some consequence to her conscience? After giving this some thought, she comes to the conclusion that the reason she feels no guilt is that her adulterous act has caused no harm to her husband, child or anyone else. Having thus eased her conscience — which is not so free of guilt as she chooses to think — she slips out of bed and gets into her clothes.

That night the instructor came home to one of his favourite meals: salmon loaf, baked potato, creamed carrots, and to top it all, an apple brown betty for dessert.

"Where were you, Soph?" he said, sitting down. "You were out when I phoned."

"I had to go to the library. I didn't realize my books were overdue. They telephoned to remind me and—" I'm saying too much, she thought. "How's the salmon loaf? I think I over-salted it."

"It's perfect," he said and went on to tell her about Alex Teperman, a new friend he had made that day. Teppy (as he was called by everyone) was a baseball and basketball coach who worked with underprivileged kids. He had brought some of his kids to the Y for a workout that afternoon, and that's how they met.

"I admire that man, Soph. He's got a crippled hand—" Interrupting himself, "Chew, chew, chew," he said to his daughter with a smile. Solemnly following her father's example, Emma, a teachable child, masticated slowly before swallowing. "He's got a crippled hand," Billy said, turning again to his wife. "But he doesn't let that get him down; he's a good all-around athlete." He continued talking warmly of his new friend, and Sophie, preoccupied with her own thoughts, attended him with a deaf ear.

He took Emma up to bed after supper, and Sophie cleared the dishes. Washing up, the thought came to her that by giving herself to a man who meant nothing to her and to whom she meant nothing, she had cheapened her husband who loved her. After turning this thought over in her mind, an easier thought, one less troublesome to her conscience, took its place: What she had done was to her shame, not her husband's. It was her person she had shamed, not his.

She put the dishes away, then went to the dining room and sat down in the armchair with a book. She heard a knock on the door, followed by a woman's voice calling "Yoo-hoo!" through the letter slot.

Mrs. Adilman was at the door, and cradled in her arms was a florist's box. "The boy made a mistake. Look, it's for you, Sophie," she said, pointing to the florist's label.

Sophie looked. The label was addressed to her. "What boy?" she said.

"A messenger boy, a young *shaygets* with a bicycle. I

didn't look on the name, I thought it's a surprise for my Lily," Mrs. Adilman said, offering the box. Going down the verandah steps, she turned to say, "I gave him a ten cents tip."

Sophie took the box to the dining room and opened it. The flowers it contained were long-stemmed red roses, and nestled among them was a card. "Dear Sophie," it read, "Forgive me for oafishly falling asleep. Brian."

Reading the card, she heard Billy coming out of the bathroom. She quickly slipped the card inside the top of her stocking, put the lid back on the box and ran down the cellar stairs with the box under her arm. She rammed the box of roses behind a pile of junk. Then she pulled open the furnace door, heaved in a shovelful of coal, and slammed the door shut.

"I just remembered that my father told me to put some coal in the furnace," she said, coming up from the cellar.

"Who was that at the door?" he asked.

Anticipating the question, "Mrs. Adilman," she said. "She came to borrow a spool of thread," and sat down with her book, acutely conscious of the card inside her stocking.

Later, when they were undressing for bed, Sophie took off her dress, and with her back to her husband who was taking off his shoes, slid her hand deep inside her stocking; the card had worked itself below her knee. Palming the card, she approached the bed and slipped it under her pillow. Then she took off the rest of her clothes, got into bed and fell asleep almost as soon as her head touched the pillow. . .

Billy woke her up. "Soph," he said, shaking her by the shoulder, "did Emma have a bowel movement today?" Waking her in the middle of the night to ask whether Emma had moved her bowels: annoyed, she shrugged his hand off her shoulder. "I only asked you a civil question," he said. Piqued, he turned his back on her. Then he turned and put his arm around her waist. "Are you awake, hon?" She tried to say no but there was no voice in her throat. He switched on the bedside lamp and came over to her side of the bed. "Let's dance," he said, pointing to his naked self and making lewd gestures.

She heard the furnace being stoked. That meant her father

was home: he fired the furnace first thing when he came from work. He'd see the roses! The pile of junk she had shoved them behind was adjacent to the coal bin. She lay back the covers and with effort dragged herself out of bed. Her father was sitting on a crate in the dimly lit cellar, reading his morning paper. He put down his paper and took off his glasses. "Is this the way I brought you up," he said severely, "to go naked around the house? Go put something on." She boldly told him not to order her around. "I'm not a child, I'm a married woman now." He took off his belt. "You're not too old for me to give you a licking," he said, and advanced menacingly towards her, belt in hand. And she for once stood up to him. "I defy you to hit me." And as she hung her head, dismayed at having uttered such words to her father, her shoulder received the blow of his belt. She cowered and let out a cry of pain, though she felt none. He hit her on the buttocks. Again she felt no pain but she squealed nonetheless, in acknowledgement of the blow, and seized hold of the belt. "Let go," he commanded, tugging at the belt. Acting out a remembered childhood scene, "Don't hit me, Pa," she beseeched him, at the same time kissing the hand that held the belt.

With her words "Don't hit me, Pa" echoing in her ears, she woke to find herself pressing her sleeping husband's hand to her mouth. Letting go his hand, she felt under the pillow for the card. She got out of bed and, in the dark, opened her bottom dresser drawer and slipped the card between the pages of her diary.

The following morning shortly after eleven a telegram addressed to her was delivered to the house. Above the signature Brian, the message read: Am I forgiven?

She smiled, reading the message: that he had fallen asleep was obviously of some concern to him. And this somehow altered the complexion of yesterday's happening. It put a different slant on things. In short, it soothed her pride that he did after all have some regard for her. Not that his regard was of any interest to her; it mattered only insofar as she now saw her position — her position in relation to him, that is — in a different light from how it had appeared to her yesterday.

She went up to her bedroom and put the telegram — the first she had ever received — between the pages of her diary, next to his card. Then she went down to the cellar and, from a purely practical motive rather than an act of ill will towards the sender, picked up the box from behind the pile of junk and consigned his roses to the fire.

Coming up the cellar stairs, she heard the telephone. That's him, she thought. And for some reason that she would have been hard put to define, her heart quickened.

"I thought it might be you," she said offhandedly.

"How eh — how are you fixed for time this afternoon?" He sounded ill at ease.

"Time for what?" she rudely returned. "Another sitting?" And when he made no reply, "I'm sorry," she said. "I didn't mean to sound so crude."

"That's all right." Hesitantly he said, "I thought perhaps I could see you sometime this afternoon? Just to have a drink together and talk."

She said she would "consider it." And then primly gave him to understand that if she did come, there was to be "no furthering of yesterday's escapade."

A few minutes after three, Sophie, sitting in the chair she had briefly occupied the day before, was drinking gin and tonic.

". . . standing naked before my father! By the very nature of its bizarreness I should have known I was dreaming," Sophie was saying, having told him about her dream. "My sister Bella and I — even as kids — didn't dare show ourselves in a petticoat."

Brian said his father was every bit as puritanical. "On my thirteenth birthday he came up to my room after I'd gone to bed and woke me up to tell me about the facts of life. It was all I could do to keep a straight face when he described the sexual act, which was not to be casually indulged in, he said, for fear of venereal disease and so on, and made me promise I would keep myself pure for the girl I would eventually marry. When I was twenty, he showed me the watch he had bought for my birthday, but before he would give it to me he wanted to know if I had kept the promise I'd made about keeping myself pure. I said, 'Yes, Dad—' "

241

"And got the watch under false pretences," Sophie put in, smiling.

He continued: "Just about that time I quit the job I had at the Post Office on Front Street and registered for a course in art classes at the Grange. My old man nearly had a fit. He said I had taken the first step towards going to the dogs, and predicted I'd end up in the gutter."

"The first time my father caught me smoking a cigarette — I was about sixteen — he warned me that I'd be smoking opium next," said Sophie, laughing.

She was enjoying herself. Today she felt easier in his presence, less constrained than yesterday, and surer of herself. He had chafed her hands, which were cold when she arrived, and then kissed them. Other than that he had made no overtures. Attentive, solicitous of her comfort, he had not done a single thing that could in any way be construed as an act associated with sexual familiarity. They conversed, he attending her remarks with obvious pleasure and amusement. From their manner they might have been old friends who, after a long absence from each other, had been brought together again through some fortuitous circumstance.

Nonetheless at five minutes past four (the transition from comradeship to physical intimacy having in some way or other come to pass) she was in his embrace, and a few minutes after that, in his bed. Wooing her, he aroused an excitement in her she had not experienced yesterday. They lay embraced afterwards until Sophie, rousing herself, announced that she had to go home. He, too, got into his clothes and accompanied her to the streetcar stop.

"When is the best time to call you?" he asked.

"Don't call me," she said. "I'll call you."

"When?"

"Tomorrow. If I can."

"I'll wait for your call. I'll be at the studio all day," he said, and kissed her as the car approached.

Several people boarded, she last among them. Hanging onto a strap, she looked out the window and saw him still standing at the streetcar stop. He smiled when he saw her, snatched off his beret and held it in the air, high above his head. I have a lover, she said to herself, and her heart skipped a beat.

As the car went into motion, a sudden depression came over her, and with it a sense of guilt. Yesterday she had experienced only a twinge of conscience, but today — though she had been just as guilty yesterday of wrongdoing — she felt a positive sense of guilt. Did the repetition of a wrongdoing result in compounded guilt? she asked herself. A single theft made the perpetrator a thief, she reasoned. Committing a second theft did not make him doubly a thief. Working it out in her mind, she came to the conclusion that the reason she felt guilty was due simply to the fact that this time she had taken pleasure in the adulterous act, whereas yesterday she had not.

Brian returned to the studio, poured himself a drink and sat down to read again the Special Delivery letter from his wife, which he had received a few minutes before Sophie's arrival:

"Dear Brian, Mother fell down the stairs a few days ago and broke four ribs. She's in bed taped like a mummy and in pain, poor dear. I'm looking after her, she won't have a nurse. Daddy's getting to be a bore, grumbling about Phoebe who's getting old, poor thing. Her sight's failing and she's losing her memory. She takes out her teeth when she's cleaning house or cooking, and forgets where she's put them. They're apt to turn up in a fruit bowl, in a jam jar, on a windowsill, an old tea caddy, or in a kitchen canister. The other morning when she served breakfast (without her teeth) Daddy wouldn't eat his porridge until she found them. He thought they might have been cooked in with the oatmeal. I've been rationing myself, I haven't taken a drink in the morning since I've been here, and one day I managed to go the whole day without a drink. A victory which I celebrated by tying one on the next day. I bawled afterwards and cursed my inner demon. Mother and I had a long talk last night about us, you and me. She's unhappy about our getting a divorce and thinks we ought to give it another try. Barkis is willing. How do you feel about it? Love, Anne.

"P.S. How many women have you had since I left? Don't

243

answer that question (as if you would), I don't want to know. Jealousy is an inferior emotion and I behave very badly under its influence. What I'm getting at is that I'm sorry about dashing that drink in your face. I positively *writhe* when I think of it. Give my love to Gerry and Kay. Love, Anne."

Making a scene over another woman, packing up, threatening divorce and entraining for Vancouver, where her parents lived, had become a dependable pattern of his wife's behaviour. These exits would be followed by a series of drunken, abusive long-distance calls. In the middle of the night Brian would be roused from bed to hear himself called a son of a bitch and whoremaster.

But neither of them gave serious thought to divorce. It was a game they played; with a trip to Vancouver for Anne, and for Brian a welcome respite from the surveillance she kept him under. A respite which afforded him some freedom for amorous exploit. Women were attracted to Brian, and he to them. But he was a devoted husband and would have been, but for a wandering eye, a faithful one as well. He loved his wife and if it were not for the unqualified fidelity she demanded of him (of which he was physically incapable) their marriage in his view would have been a perfect one. Apart from love, another tie that bound him to Anne was his financial dependence on her.

Brian was not the high-ranking artist Sophie had taken him to be. A friend of his, a picture framer, hung a few of Brian's paintings in his shop from time to time, where they sold now and then. His one dependable source of income was the T. Eaton Company who commissioned him fairly regularly to decorate their display windows with papier-mâché models. But this didn't bring in enough to support him and his wife. Anne, an only child, received monthly dividends from the several investments her father, a stockbroker, had made in her name. She paid the rent, bought the groceries, her husband's canvases, his paints and brushes, and put money in his pocket without stint. She seldom asked for an accounting; and Brian was a spender. He owed for the roses he had sent Sophie.

In the early days of their marriage, Brian, who had been brought up in a household where every dollar spent was accounted for, was alarmed at his wife's wastefulness, the impressive sums she trifled away, and at the same time respectful of her unconcern for money, her ease in dealing with it. Later, when he became accustomed to her extravagances, he began to spend her money as freely as she did herself.

Brian poured himself another drink and sat down to answer his wife's letter. "Darling Anne," he began, and paused to consider the problem her letter posed.

Anne was reliably consistent in her behaviour. She had been gone a week. As expected, he had received several nocturnal calls since her departure. Being roused from bed to hear himself abused came as no surprise. But the inevitable letter (which usually arrived about four weeks after her departure) had come as a surprise. She couldn't have chosen a more unfavourable time for a reconciliation. Her arrival at this time would interfere with his plans.

He read the letter again. Anne said she was nursing her mother — surely she wouldn't leave until her mother was fully recovered? It wouldn't be like her to come back and leave her mother in old Phoebe's care. How long did it take for an old person's ribs to heal? he wondered. Two weeks? Three? That would give him a breather.

Brian resumed his letter to his wife: "Thank you for your sweet letter. If Barkis is willing, so am I. I have started two new paintings. I think you'll like them. I've been working steadily on them, and except for Gerry and Kay I haven't seen a single soul since you left. Give my love to your mother. I hope she gets well soon and is on her feet before long. Write again and let me know how she's getting on. And how are you, love? I hope you're sleeping better. I'm so glad you haven't been drinking in the morning, keep up the good work. And take care of yourself. I love you and think of you all the time. Love, Brian."

Thirty

"Do you like it?" Brian asked Gerry. And without waiting for an answer, "Do you, Kay?" And again without waiting for an answer, "I think I'm on to something," he said, smiling with pleasure.

"You sure are," Gerry said, reaching for the gin.

Gerry Ross, whose studio was on the second floor, and Kay Beamish, who shared his studio and bed, had been invited down for a drink. Brian, whose belief in himself as an up-and-coming artist was sustained by an unshakeable and cheerful confidence, was showing them his new painting. He genuinely admired his own work, took pleasure in showing it and in viewing it himself.

"Sign it Wassily Kandinsky," said Gerry, "and you've got a winner."

Brian took no offence. He was good-natured and had a cheerful disposition. Everyone who knew Brian liked him. And Brian liked everyone he knew.

"How much longer will Anne have to have her leg in a cast?" Kay said to Brian.

When her mother was able to get around without help, Anne, who had been cooped up four weeks, accepted an invitation to spend a weekend at Grouse Mountain. Skiing with a party of friends, she had broken a leg on the slopes and was now back in Vancouver with her broken leg in a cast. She had been away seven weeks.

"From what her doctor said, Anne thinks she'll have to have it on for at least another two or three weeks. She wanted to come home and have it taken off here but her doctor advised her against it."

Kay laughed. "Doctor's advice or not, if Anne got wind of Sophie she'd come back on the next train and wipe up the floor with her." And you'd get what's coming to you, was the malicious thought she did not give voice to.

Gerry said, "How would Anne get wind of Sophie? We're the only two who've met her."

The subject made Brian uncomfortable. To change it, he said to Kay, "Has Anne written you? She said she was going to."

"No," said Kay. "She hasn't."

Anne's letter was in her purse. Received that morning (and concealed from Gerry) the letter read: "Dear Kay, Brian's last letter said he was working hard and doesn't see anyone but you and Gerry. He said the new painting he's working on is so engrossing he can't tear himself away from it — but I smell a rat. I may be wrong but I suspect I'm right. Am I? Love, Anne."

And in the post was Kay's reply: "Dear Anne, When the cat's away the mice will play. Enough said. A word to the wise is sufficient. Love, Kay."

Kay Beamish, also an artist, was thirty-one years old, short, dumpy, with freckled skin and reddish frizzled hair. A little over a year ago she came uninvited to a studio party Gerry was giving, stayed all night and wouldn't go home the next day. Or the next. Having failed to dislodge her, despite having employed all means within his power short of assault, Gerry resigned himself to her presence and made use of her. Kay paid half the rent, cooked, cleaned, did Gerry's laundry, ran his messages, and was repaid by being badly used. He referred to her as his limpet, his leech, his mollusk, his barnacle, his Old Man of the Sea, and thumped her head against the wall when his work wasn't going well.

Brian, who felt sorry for her, treated her with extra courtesy. His manner in general with Kay was the engaging one he assumed in the presence of an attractive woman. Anne, who was indignant on Kay's behalf for Gerry's abuse of her, treated her with affection and sympathy. Kay responded by doting on Anne, and falling in love with Brian.

Late one night seven weeks ago when Anne had stormed out of the studio, Kay, who happened to be in the upstairs hall, saw them going out the front door, Brian carrying Anne's case. She returned to the studio and told Gerry that Brian was seeing Anne off on her ritual trip to Vancouver.

"When he gets back he'll be home free and ready for the plucking," said Gerry. "Here's your chance to score. You've got the hots for him," he said, laughing, "and Brian's easy."

Kay daring to say, "You really are contemptible," angered him; she never talked back. He shoved her out of the studio and locked the door.

When Brian returned to the studio after putting his wife on the train, he found Kay in his bed. She said she and Gerry had had a fight; Gerry had kicked her out, it was late and she had no place to go.

Brian was dumbfounded, dismayed; an unattractive woman in his bed for the taking was an uninviting prospect. "Gerry's my best friend," he said; and if she were not Gerry's mistress he'd pop into bed with her like a shot. Ill-favoured Kay was not fooled: if she were a good-looking woman he would not have scrupled about his friendship with Gerry. Brian handed her her clothes, coaxed her to get dressed, and taking on himself the role of mediator, escorted her upstairs and made Gerry let her in.

As of that night, Kay's love for Brian had come to an end. She now nursed a deadly grudge against him.

"When did you do that?" Gerry said, pointing to a charcoal sketch tacked to the wall. "It's Sophie, isn't it?"

"Yes. Do you like it?" said Brian eagerly.

Just then there was a knock on the door. "Sophie!" said Brian, opening the door. "What a nice surprise." He kissed her, helped her off with her coat and went to the kitchen to get another glass.

Gerry got up and gave her his chair. "Brian wasn't expecting you," he said. "We came down to keep him company."

"How are you, Kay?" said Sophie.

"Fine," said Kay, smiling. "Just fine."

Brian returned with a glass, fixed a drink for Sophie and poured one for himself. Standing, Gerry finished his drink, put down his glass and glanced at Kay. "Two's company," he said, "three's a crowd, and four is an assembly." He moved towards the door, then turned and looked at Kay. "Move it," he said unpleasantly. Kay put down her unfinished drink and followed him out.

"He treats her brutally," Sophie said. "They're not married, why does she stay with him?"

"The secret heart has its reasons," said Brian.

"The secret heart," said Sophie, laughing. "Have you a secret heart? Have I?" She knew him better now and was no longer impressed by his talent or intellect. She liked him, enjoyed sex with him, and privately thought he talked a lot of nonsense.

Brian got up and locked the door. Sophie finished her drink. "I can't stay long," she said. "I want to get home before Billy."

An hour or so later, when they were getting dressed, Sophie said, "I always get so depressed going home. No, it's not depression," she said, testily correcting herself. "It's guilt. I'm *corroded* with it!" To herself she said, It's not worth it. I'm not in love with him. I come here with a heavy heart and leave with a heavier one — why do I do it?

"Billy doesn't suspect anything," she went on. "I don't know how he'd react if he did — I don't want to think about it!" She finished combing her hair, put the comb back in her purse and glanced at her watch. "Oh God!" she cried. "I'm going to be late again."

Thirty-One

The beginning of Sophie's love affair coincided to the day with Billy's first meeting with Teppy. The meeting of the two men resulted in a spontaneous friendship, and before long they were seeing each other almost every day. One night Billy told Sophie he had met Teppy's wife Judy, who also was a good all-around athlete. She was captain of a ladies' basketball team, a softball pitcher, and a hundred-yard-dash sprinter. "She's a lot taller than Teppy," he said. "I told you he was a little guy?"

Another night he said, "I was telling Teppy about you. He didn't know I was married to a Jewish girl. They'd love to meet you, Soph. How about our getting together?"

Friday night of that week they went to Shopsy's after Emma had been put to bed, to have supper there with Billy's new friends. Teppy and Judy were waiting for them. "Here's my wife," Billy said, presenting her. Without getting up, Teppy, a dark-complexioned plump little man, introduced his wife. "And here's my wife," he said, placing on Judy's shoulder a puffed fingerless shiny brown hand which looked, with its cicatrixed cross in the centre, like an overbaked hot-cross bun.

Hot dogs and a variety of sandwiches were brought to the table. The husbands ate, joking and kidding with each other. The wives ate, exchanging smiles. Sophie observed that while Teppy ate with his good hand, the misshapen one he left resting obtrusively on the table. Whenever the dills, mustard or coleslaw had to be passed, Teppy, with a prod of his maimed hand, was quick to send them moving.

After an exchange of several smiles, Judy said to Sophie, "Teppy never stops talking about Billy."

"And Billy never stops talking about Teppy," Sophie returned.

"It was love at first sight," said Judy.

Sophie leaned confidentially forward. "I read somewhere that most athletes are homosexually inclined," she said, and saw from Judy's change of expression that she had got off on the wrong foot.

"What are you two talking about?" Billy said, turning to the ladies.

"Nothing worth repeating," Judy said indifferently.

"What were you saying about athletes?" Billy asked his wife.

Sophie shrugged. "I was saying I read somewhere that most athletes are fairies."

Teppy thumped the table with his nipped hand. "Hey! Let's keep it clean."

After supper they got into Teppy's car and, as had been planned, went to a downtown roller skating rink to finish the evening.

Before the evening was over it was apparent to Billy that the chemistry existing between him and his friend was non-existent between the wives.

"Why didn't you like Judy?" he asked later when they were preparing for bed.

"I don't dislike her. It's just that I've nothing to say to her and she has nothing to say to me. I tried to be friendly but you saw what happened when I made that remark about athletes. It was only in fun — and you saw how she clammed up."

"Don't get mad at me, hon, but why do you say things

like that? You're sweet and loveable and people like you right away. You don't have to be smart to impress them."

"If that's what you call being smart let's forget the whole thing," Sophie said, and turned her back on him.

He turned her around. "Let's not go to bed mad, Soph. But you did like Teppy? I could see you were getting along with him."

"He's all right."

"He's a wonderful guy. He's overcome a terrible handicap and—"

"And never lets you forget it," she put in. "The way he keeps flaunting that hand."

"That's a cruel thing to say, it doesn't sound like you." He sighed. "I was sure you'd get along with them. They're nice people and we haven't got that many friends. I was hoping we could make a foursome now and then—" he shrugged "—but you've taken such a dislike to them."

"I haven't taken a dislike to them. Dislike is a positive feeling. I found them dull, uninteresting and boring."

"You read too much," he said. "It's gotten so that you take more interest in people you read about in books than real people. I was hoping the four of us could have supper out again next Friday and go bowling afterwards — but I guess that's out now?"

"Why can't you go without me? You enjoy their company."

"It's not the same, going without you. Come too, Soph," he coaxed, "to please me."

The following Friday when they met at Child's for supper, Teppy was friendly and Judy was noticeably standoffish. All through the meal the three athletes talked about sports. After supper they went bowling. After bowling they went to a restaurant for coffee, and again the talk was of sports.

Teppy dropped them off and as soon as they were inside the door Sophie said, "Please, Billy, don't ask me to go out with them again."

He shrugged and went to the bathroom to brush his teeth. Then he got into bed and lay back with his hands behind his head.

252

"They're my friends," he said, staring at the ceiling, "and you didn't even try to be friendly. You sat there without a word—"

"No one spoke to me."

"You could have spoken up. I've never known you at a loss for words. You usually have something to say."

"Not when it comes to sports. And that's all you three ever talk about. I'm not interested in sports."

"You used to be."

"Oh come on, Billy, that was in the beginning. We were in love and I — well, naturally I was interested in everything that concerned you."

He sat up as if suddenly alerted to danger. "What does that mean? Are you out of love with me? Since when?"

She looped her arms around his neck. "Don't get so solemn, Billy. Be realistic. We've been married five years — how can it be the same as it was in the beginning?"

He unlocked her arms from his neck and lit a cigarette without offering her one. "It is for me."

"It's not the same for you any more than it is for me. We know each other too well, we get on each other's nerves. But that doesn't mean we don't love each other. We have a child, and if anything we're closer now than we were in the beginning—" she paused "—but that's not what I'm talking about."

"What are you talking about?"

"I'm talking about being in *love*. And that's not the same thing. Loving is one thing and being *in* love is another."

"And I suppose I'm to blame."

"No one's to blame. It's the day-to-day living together that does it. It doesn't only happen to us. And if you can sit there and tell me that it's still the same for you — then all I can say is you've forgotten."

"And you forget all the times you turn me down when I want to make love." He stubbed out his cigarette. "Where do you get your kicks?" he demanded, coarsely, unlike him. Her heart took fright. He knows! she thought wildly. He snatched up her book from the bedside table and threw it to the floor. "Is that where you get your kicks, from all these books you read?" He caught her roughly by the shoulders and pin-

253

ned her back. "Spread your legs!"

"Stop it," she gasped. Fighting him off, she was struck suddenly with the absurdity of the situation. The command "Spread your legs" was more in keeping with his style on the gym floor: "Heads up! Legs apart! Hup two three."

"Don't give me that cave-man stuff," she said, giggling. "It doesn't suit you."

He took her in his arms afterwards. "I'm sorry, Soph. I didn't mean to get rough with you."

After that night there was no more talk of making a four-some Friday nights with Teppy and Judy. Friday night, for-merly his and Sophie's night for going to a movie, Billy spent with his new friends. "Sure you don't mind, Soph?" he'd say on leaving.

Saturday when he was off work he took Emma with him to his friends' house to spend the afternoon. Teppy and Judy had a child, a girl a year older than Emma; and the two chil-dren got along well.

Two or three nights a week the instructor brought Teppy home with him after work and Sophie made sandwiches and coffee. (Membership at the Y had doubled since Billy had become physical instructor, and Teppy had been hired, on Billy's recommendation, as assistant coach. He now worked four nights a week with Billy, from seven till ten.)

Teppy's manner with Sophie continued friendly and at times even mildly flirtatious. Suddenly there was a change in his attitude towards her. He stopped speaking to her; he hardly acknowledged her presence. When she spoke to him he mumbled a reply and looked away. When their glances met, his was positively hostile. Sophie observed that the mis-shapen hand, in her presence, was put out of sight — in his lap when he sat, behind his back when he stood. His Achilles heel, was the thought that came to her mind. He hides it from me as if I'm his enemy.

One night she said to her husband, "What's the matter with Teppy? He's become very unfriendly."

"He has his moods like anyone else," Billy replied, avoid-ing her eyes. He himself had unwittingly been the cause of his best friend's ill will towards her. . .

In the early days when Sophie began her love affair with the artist, she conducted herself with caution. Stealing out for an afternoon at the studio, she took care to be home at least an hour ahead of her husband. Overstaying an evening at the studio, she hurried home trembling at the thought that he might have preceded her. And then gradually, as if under compulsion to lay herself open to exposure, she began taking risks she never would have dreamt of in the beginning. Overstaying an afternoon at the studio, she would glibly telephone home: "I'm downtown. There's a big sale on at Eaton's. I'll be home soon." And having kept him an hour late for supper, would arrive with nothing to show for an afternoon's shopping. Coming home empty-handed was not in itself cause for suspicion. She was a hopeless shopper. She got lost in the aisles, blundered from one department to another, and after losing herself in wrong exits would come home with a purchase she felt had been palmed off on her, or with nothing at all. She hated shopping downtown and never went unless there was no help for it.

Suddenly she had become a devotee of the downtown stores, hunting bargains. And came home with stories of triumph, success: "I bought a pretty pair of pajamas for you, Emma, but they won't be here till tomorrow. There was such a mob I couldn't wait for the salesgirl to find the right size." And employing a craftiness altogether outside her nature, she would go next morning to Bloor Street and buy the pajamas she had promised Emma, taking care to remove the telltale wrappings and tags.

Lying became a habit, an addiction. With no need for a lie, she told one. With no necessity for a cover-up, she spoke double talk. But she was a poor thief. Where she was careless, she was confident that she had been discreet. Where there was no discernible evidence of misconduct, she went to elaborate lengths at concealment.

Coming home late, she came prepared. If the excuse for being late was that she had been to a movie, she was prepared — like an auditioning actress with a set piece — to give him the title of the picture, the cast, the story line. Generally he asked nothing. Without querying her further he accepted the fact that she was late getting home, having been to a double feature. This made her uneasy; she felt she had slipped up somewhere. She would then proceed to make up lines she hadn't learned: Coming from the movie she had witnessed a terrible accident — a collision, two cars, police, ambulance. "My name was taken as one of the witnesses. I didn't actually see how it happened. If I'm called up in court I won't be able to swear to anything."

And pretended next day to wait for the post, a summons, a subpoena; and the day after, forgot all about it.

One night, timing herself to be well in advance of her husband, she came home early from her lover's studio, carrying under her arm a large illustrated book on the new movements in art. As she flicked on the overhead light, a groan issued from the bed, and her husband sat up. He was wearing a woollen scarf around his neck and he smelled of menthol. Blinking, rubbing his eyes, he told her he had had to leave the swimming meet before it was over.

"I'm sick as a dog, Soph," he said. "I'm coming down with something."

He had doctored himself; he was mentholated, aspirined, and all he wanted from her now that she had wakened him was a little sympathy. And if she had used the good sense she was born with, she would have put her hand to his forehead and remarked on its heat, or something like that. Instead, she came up with a cock-and-bull story of an encounter with Pat Pollard.

"You remember him, Billy? Lambie's son Pat, that crazy artist who did a painting of me and then destroyed it. I was coming out of the library," she said, exhibiting the book, "and I bumped into him at the corner of St. George and College. I hardly recognized him, he looks so prosperous. His work is selling. He's got a studio now on St. George near the library." He had asked her to come back to his studio with him, to see the large abstract he was working on.

Next day Billy stayed home from work and his wife looked after him. She rubbed his chest with Vick's Vapo-Rub, gave him aspirin and brought him his breakfast in bed. Waiting for his lunch, he took up the book she had left on the bedside table — the illustrated book on art she had brought home last night from the library — and saw at a glance that it was not from the library. It was privately owned and on the flyleaf was the name Brian Purtell. Who's Brian Purtell? he wondered idly. An artist·friend of Pat Pollard's probably. Pat must have loaned it to her. But she said she had got it from the library. Why would she lie? He began to doubt the story of her encounter with Pat Pollard. And the story of her having been to the library — that, too, was a lie; she never came empty-handed from the library. Why would she lie about where she had been?

All at once everything fell into place. He wondered at his blindness. His own wife, and he hadn't observed the change in her: downtown sales, double-feature movies — lies, all of it! She was cheating on him. As he lay in bed anguished, it came to him after a while that he could be jumping the gun. Actually, there was nothing positive to go on. His weakened state was making him morbid and suspicious.

"You're sweet to me, Soph," he said when she brought his lunch, and secretly searched her face for signs of guilt.

He became alert to her every change of expression, her every change of mood. Desperately wanting to believe in her, he attended her excuses and alibis, fearful always that he might in spite of himself catch her out in a lie. Unwilling to face up to the conclusion that his wife was deceiving him, he continued to listen with a deafened ear to the stories she told. But there was no way of blinding himself to a love blemish on her neck, a hickey on her shoulder. And still he held off from speaking; and the more he delayed the more he shrank from it. Sophie was clever, she'd have an answer for everything. Or worse, she might admit she was having a love affair: she might even ask for a divorce. He loved his wife, more now than ever it seemed to him, and he was afraid that by his own act he would bring down on his head the most dreaded of consequences — a confession. He didn't want to hear a confession from her. He felt he would break under it. To keep his head buried in the sand was the lesser evil, and so he maintained an outward composure and suffered in silence. From time to time a desperate urgency to con-

257

fide in Teppy took hold of him. But he fought against it. To talk against his wife — even to his best friend — was unthinkable. An inherent sense of decency forbade it.

Late one night, bringing Teppy home with him for coffee, he went upstairs first to see whether Sophie was home. At the sight of the empty bed, a feeling of utter hopelessness descended on him. He went downstairs to his friend.

"Teppy," he said, trembling, "I think my wife's cheating on me."

That was the beginning of Teppy's ill will towards Sophie. Repeated confidences culminated in a positive hatred of her. He began badgering his friend to do something about it. He made repeated representations to him: devising schemes for trapping Sophie, he advised putting a private eye on her. Get evidence of adultery. He, Teppy, would take oath on it in divorce court. The father would be awarded custody. Emma would be better off without a mother like Sophie. And his friend, too, would be rid of her once and for all.

Where Teppy was dogged, eager, the betrayed husband was reluctant, indecisive. He loved his wife, he couldn't conceive of a life without her. The very thought was intolerable but he was ashamed — for the sake of his manhood — to own up to his friend that the last thing on earth he desired was to be rid of his faithless wife.

He had no heart for trapping, spying out his wife. And so he gave lip service to his friend, but his heart's secret design — that Sophie would stay with him — he kept to himself. The outcome of having reposed his confidence in Teppy was more than he had bargained for; the comfort derived in the beginning from a sympathetic ear was outweighed now by the constant harassment he was under. He wished he had never spoken.

Thirty-Two

A few days after Kay had posted her letter to Anne, she received a long-distance call from Vancouver. Firing questions, Anne began: "How long has he been whoring around? Since I left? Who is she? Anyone I know? Does she come to the studio? Does he go to her place? Tell me everything."

"I'll have to make it fast," said Kay. "Gerry will be back any minute. He had a woman in here the week you left. You don't know her. We've met her a few times. She's married and has a kid. Brian sees her two or three times a week. She's here Friday nights as a rule, and Saturday afternoons. She's here other times too, but not as regularly."

"Friday nights and Saturday afternoons? I'll catch him red-handed this time. I'll break my crutches over his head, the son of a bitch. I'll demolish both of them. Thanks, Kay, I'll be seeing you," Anne said and hung up.

Two days later, around a quarter past eleven on a wintry Friday night, Brian and Sophie were startled by a pounding on the door. Then a woman's voice: "Brian? Let me in!"

"Good heavens!" Brian whispered. "It's my wife."

Sophie, in the act of putting on her shoes, froze. "Your wife? You said she had left you—"

He put his finger to his lips. "Put your coat on," he whispered, handing it to her. "Quickly. She mustn't find you here."

Sophie got into her coat. "Where can I *go*?" she whispered, glancing frantically around the room.

Anne pounded on the door, violently, with her crutch. "Brian! I know you're in there. Let me in!"

"Who *is* that?" Brian called querulously, as if just roused from sleep. Beckoning Sophie, he went over to the window and opened it.

"It's me, you son of a bitch. Anne."

"Anne!" Brian cried in a welcoming tone, as if he had just this minute recognized her voice. He lifted Sophie under the arms and lowered her into the back yard. "Come in, love," he called to his wife. "The door's open."

"It isn't," she said, rattling the knob.

Brian leaned out of the open window and handed Sophie her purse. "There's a back door," he whispered, "it—"

"My galoshes. Give me my galoshes," Sophie said, but he had already closed the window and was drawing the curtains.

With her hand pressed to her heart to still its beating, Sophie stood a while, glancing around. The back yard he had put her in was a big yard, fenced in, and heaped with snow. A garbage can, which stood against the wall next to where she had been set down, was half submerged in snow. And she herself stood in snow almost to her knees. She trudged miserably through the snow, in search of the back door he had mentioned. She found the door but it wouldn't open. Frantically she turned the knob one way and another several times. The door was either stuck or locked; she couldn't get it to open. And there was no other way out of the yard. Except to climb the fence, which looked to be about five feet high. She went back to where she had been set down. With her hand she swept off the piled-up snow on the lid of the garbage can, sat down with her back against the wall and lifted her feet out of the snow. Sitting forlornly on the garbage can with her heels on the rim of the lid, knees drawn up and clasped against her chest, she wept piteously for herself.

Presently her thoughts turned to her husband. She had to

get home. But how was she to get out of the yard? All at once it came to her how it could be done. She got up, took hold of the garbage can by its handles and trudged through the snow with it to the fence. Standing on the garbage can, she was able to straddle the fence. Once astride, she eased the other leg over, then dropped down on the other side and landed on her hands and knees in a parking lot.

Billy at the same moment was sitting dejectedly on the bed. It was almost half-past eleven and Sophie was not home yet. Bitter thoughts passed through his mind. How much longer could he put up with it? He wasn't made of stone. A man could only take so much and no more. He was sick and tired of listening to her alibis. He should take Teppy's advice and divorce her. Which would be easy enough if he didn't love her. By rights he should hate her for all the misery she had heaped on him. He had had enough. He'd have to talk with her. Get it off his chest. Tonight. I don't want to know where you've been, he'd say to her, but we can't go on like this. I want a divorce.

He got into bed, lay wearily back on the pillow and fell into a troubled sleep from which he woke suddenly at the sound of Sophie calling his name. He sat up and switched on the light. He had been dreaming; her side of the bed was empty. He looked at the clock. A quarter past twelve. She had never been this late before. She's been in an accident, he thought; and his heart turned over. No, she couldn't have been; he would have been notified by now; he had been home since eleven. She was with him. He got out of bed and paced the floor, cracking his knuckles against his chest. A murderous anger flamed up in his heart: against him, Brian Purtell, his wife's seducer. (As of a few weeks ago when he first saw the name on the flyleaf of the book she said was from the library, the name Brian Purtell had been branded in his memory.)

Unsteadied by the violence of his emotion, he had to sit down; he was shaking. He sat still a while, his tired heart beating thickly. Suddenly he got up and clenched his hand. "Hands off!" he said, shaking his fist menacingly at his invisible rival. "She's my wife."

Fiercely shaking his fist in the air, he caught sight of himself in the mirror. The reflection shocked him: the face in the mirror was one with his father's. His father's face as he had last seen it in a coffin at Taylor's Funeral Parlour. He stared, unbelieving; but it was not himself he beheld in the mirror, it was his father's ghost. He turned away from the mirror. My head's in a muddle, he thought. I'm seeing things. He rapped his head sharply with his knuckles several times — to clear it of cobwebs — and turned again to the mirror. His father, pale and drawn, stared back at him.

Trembling, he went over to the window. "Dear Lord," he prayed, looking up at the sky. "Send her home. Come home, Soph," he implored his absent wife. He turned away from the window and as he went towards the bed he felt the blood leaving his brain.

Presently he heard Sophie calling his name. Slowly he opened his eyes. He wasn't dreaming; he was lying on the floor and Sophie, kneeling over him with an arm under his head, was caressing his face and calling his name.

"You're here, thank the Lord. I prayed that you'd come home. I can't make it without you, Soph," he said brokenly.

"You've got a temperature," she said, putting her hand on his forehead. "Can you get up? You should be in bed, dear."

He took her face between his hands. "You called me dear. Do you love me, Soph?"

"I do," she said earnestly, with emotion.

"I thought I saw my Dad. In the mirror. But I must have been — what's that word when you think you see something that isn't there?"

"Hallucinating," she said, helping him up.

"I'm so tired I could sleep forever." Getting into bed he said drowsily, "Come to bed, hon," and fell asleep almost at once.

Sophie lay awake, giving her thoughts over to the indignity she had been subjected to. She had never been so humiliated in her life. That Brian's estranged wife had chosen this night to come back — the very night she had made up her mind to tell him she was calling it quits — made her feel she was the pawn of some diabolic force. She was going to tell Brian that she was breaking it off because of the increasing sense of guilt she experienced, that the guilt she felt was beginning to prey constantly on her mind. Things had come to such a pass (she was going to say) that she was incapable of normal behaviour in her husband's presence. But before she herself had had a chance to tell him she was calling it quits, he had put her out in the back yard. With the garbage.

Next day being Saturday, Billy, as had become customary since the beginning of his friendship with Teppy and Judy, took Emma with him after lunch to spend the afternoon at his friends' house. Shortly after they left, Sophie went to a store on Dundas Street and bought herself a pair of galoshes. A half hour after she arrived home, Brian telephoned.

"I'm awfully sorry about last night," he said, and uneasily added, "I wasn't expecting my wife." She made no reply. "You left your galoshes—" Receiving no reply, he offered to put them in a cab. "I'll pay the driver at this end."

"Don't bother, I have another pair. Put them in that garbage can outside the window. Where you dumped me." Delayed anger rising in her, "Listen," she said tensely, "I deeply regret my association with you. I deplore it. I can't think of it without shame. I want to wipe it out of my mind. Expunge it from memory. I — that's all I have to say," and slammed down the receiver.

She went up to her bedroom, got her diary out of the drawer and removed from between its pages the card he had sent with the roses, and his wire. She laid open the wire, took up her pen and beneath the message Am I forgiven? she wrote in an unsteady hand (under the signature Brian): "Am keeping this to remind me of a shameful episode in my life — namely, my first and *last* extramarital affair. I've seen B.P. for the last time, thank God. Never having loved him, he won't be hard to forget."

She folded the wire, put it and the card in an old envelope, wrapped her diary in a tea towel and returned it to the drawer, with the envelope between its pages.

Three weeks later Sophie was writing in her diary: "I haven't given B.P. a single thought. I don't miss him and I never think of him. But my peace of mind isn't altogether restored — and that's because I'm pretty sure that B knows I had an affair. He's been buying me presents — an angora sweater, stockings, chocolates. He acts as if he's vying with a rival for my favour. That makes my heart ache for him. But the anger I feel against myself for taking up with B.P. I feel at times like letting out on B for letting me believe he didn't know. I know he knows, but he doesn't think I know, and so we keep up the pretence. In time it will be forgotten, I hope."

Thirty-Three

"What do I owe you, Mr. Biderman?" Sophie said, opening her purse.

This was one afternoon early in December. Sophie had come to pick up the plaid jumper she had bought for Emma, and had left with Mr. Biderman a few days before, to be shortened. (Emma, eight years old now, was smaller in size than most children her age.)

Mr. Biderman, the proprietor of Biderman's Cleaning & Pressing, a small store on Spadina Avenue near College, was a middle-aged man of medium height, pockmarked face, fleshy nose, and carefully combed sideways on his balding head was a sparsely spread show of hair. In answer to Sophie's question, he leaned over the counter and pinched her cheek. "For you, my little lady, a dollar fifty."

Sophie handed him a two-dollar bill. Mr. Biderman was scrabbling in his pocket for change when the door was suddenly thrust open and in came a tall, exceptionally good-looking young man. "Pa!" he cried on entering, went behind the counter, took Mr. Biderman in a bear-hug embrace and kissed him on the mouth. Then he stood back to look at him. "How are you, Pa?" he said.

Watching, Sophie was struck by the contrast between the two: whereas the father was plain ugly, the son who had a dark-skinned complexion, black hair, dark eyes, a beautifully shaped mouth with a rather feminine fullness to the lips, and a smile revealing even white teeth, was strikingly handsome.

Mr. Biderman pursed his lips. "You remembered I'm still living?" he said, pouting and at the same time gazing lovingly at his son.

"Don't make a drama out of it, Pa," said his son; and Sophie observed it was not his father he was looking at now, he was looking at her.

From the smile, coupled with the questioning look he gave her, she understood that he was waiting for a sign of recognition. He was unknown to her, she had never met or even seen him before, yet she sensed almost instantly that there existed between them a bond of mutual understanding: she knew him, and he knew her. She returned his smile.

Mr. Biderman extracted two quarters from his pocket, put them on the counter, then quickly wrapped up the jumper in brown paper. Handing Sophie the parcel he made an abrupt gesture of dismissal with his hand, turned and said fretfully to his son, "You know how long I didn't see you?"

For answer his son came around from behind the counter, opened the door for Sophie and followed her out, saying over his shoulder, "I can't stay, Pa, I'll see you tomorrow." He shut the door behind him and put his arm through Sophie's. "Let's go somewhere where we can talk," he said, and at the same moment Mr. Biderman in shirtsleeves came running out.

"What are you in such a hurry?" he demanded of his son.

"Go inside, Pa," said his son. "You'll catch a cold."

He let go Sophie's arm as they approached the intersection at Spadina and College, and flagged down an approaching cab.

"Where are we going?" Sophie asked.

"To my place," he replied, then got in beside her and gave the driver his address.

They were let off at a four-storey apartment house on Bathurst near Bloor. There was no elevator in the building, and as they ascended the stairs to his apartment, which was on the third floor, the thought going through Sophie's mind was: If he thinks I'm getting into bed with him just like that, he's got another thought coming.

He took off his overshoes, put them on the rubber mat beside his door, then turned to Sophie. "Give me your foot," he said, kneeling before her on one knee.

With parcelled jumper under one arm and purse in hand, she lifted her foot, resting her free hand on his shoulder. Before rising, he took her hand off his shoulder, removed the glove and brought her hand palm upward to his lips. He then unlocked the door and stood back for her to precede him. The door opened on a living room, and Sophie entered the room acutely conscious of the pleasurable sensation his kiss had left in the palm of her hand.

He helped her off with her coat, opened the door to his bedroom which was off the living room, and as he was putting their coats in the closet, Sophie observed a violin case on the seat of a chair. She remembered then that Mr. Biderman had once boasted of having a son who was a violinist. "A beautiful boy," he said. "He plays in the Massey Hall and on the radio too." And she remembered thinking at the time: Beautiful? A son of his?

He came out of the bedroom, smiling. "My shoulder," he said, placing a hand on his right shoulder, "is still warm where you touched it. In the hall," he explained, noting her puzzled expression. "You put your hand on my shoulder when I was taking off your galoshes. Would you like a drink of brandy?"

"That would be nice," said Sophie, and irrelevantly followed with, "You don't look in the least like your father. There isn't even a trace of family resemblance."

"I look like my mother. She's a beautiful woman," he added offhandedly, as if he meant only to point a fact. He proceeded to the kitchen, and as he did so Sophie noticed the passing glance he gave to his reflection in a mirror that hung on the wall above a side table.

He returned presently with a small tray, two wine glasses on it, and a half-full bottle of brandy. He set down the tray on a bookcase (which contained more records than books), filled both glasses and handed one to Sophie. Then he sat down in an armchair opposite the one she had taken and raised his glass. "To you." Sophie raised her glass. "To you," she returned. Keeping his eyes on her, he brought his glass to his lips. "To us," he said. He finished his drink and set the glass down on the floor. "I'm so happy I met you." He reached for her hand, dropped it suddenly in the act of raising it to his lips and pointed a finger at her wedding ring. "You're married!" he charged.

"You didn't ask me whether I was married," said Sophie, "or I'd have told you." She took a sip of brandy. "I've been married nine years. And I have a daughter who's eight years old."

He fell moodily silent. After a while he said, "Who's your husband? What sort of person is he? What does he do?" And without pause, "Don't tell me, I don't want to know anything about your husband. I'm not interested in him. He's of no concern to me. I want to know about you." And having thus cast off her husband, he took up his glass from the floor, put some brandy in it and returned to his chair. "Are you happy with him?"

"Reasonably."

"What do you mean, reasonably?"

Sophie shrugged. "I'm not excessively or ecstatically happy with him. I'm reasonably, moderately happy. Except for a child we've nothing much else in common, but we live together fairly amicably. I get bored with him. But that's only natural," she put in quickly. "I'd probably get bored with any man I'd been married to nine years."

"Were you in love when you married him?"

"I thought I was. But I was very young — not yet eighteen — and I mistook sexual attraction for love. . . What *is* love?" she pondered, sipping brandy. Supplying the answer, "Love is a much over-used word," she said. She finished her brandy and held out her glass. He filled her glass and brought it to her. "Love," mused book-learned Sophie, accepting the glass, "is what Heloise and Abelard experienced. Love is what Dante felt for Beatrice. . . " Coming down to earth, "And what my mother feels for my father," said Mrs. Glicksman's stepdaughter, smiling, "that's love."

He took the hand he had a few minutes ago rejected and kissed it on the palm. Gazing at her he held her hand a while in his, and before releasing it kissed it again on the palm, then on the back.

"What's your name?" he asked.

"Sophie James. What's your name? Your first name, I mean."

"Shelley."

"For the poet?" said Sophie, smiling.

He said he wasn't named for the poet. He was named Solly, for his grandfather. "When I was eighteen I changed my name from Solly to Shelley. Did you say your last name was James?"

She nodded.

"That's not a Jewish name."

She told him she had married a gentile; that they were married secretly, by a minister. "I lived at home three months after we were married — no one in the family knew I was married — and my husband had a room on Jarvis Street. When I became pregnant I packed my suitcase, left a letter telling my father I had been married three months to a gentile — for which I asked his forgiveness — and moved in with my husband. My father telephoned a few days later and said unless my husband was willing to become a Jew, I was never to darken his door again," she said, laughing. "And so my husband became a Jew. He was circumcised, and—"

"Circumcised!" he cried. And suddenly, as if he felt the pain of it in his own groin, he sat tensely hunched a moment, with hands clenched at the join of his legs. Pain subsiding, he reached for his brandy. "Go on."

"We were remarried by a rabbi and — and that's all there is to it."

He remained silent a while, then began talking about himself. He began studying the violin, he said, when he was seven years old. When he was thirteen he was playing at weddings, bar mitzvahs, Purim celebrations, the B'Nai Brith, the Hadassah and other Jewish organizations. When he was sixteen he was invited to give a recital at the Conservatory. "I played an all-Beethoven program to a packed auditorium. My father," he said, laughing, "had papered the house with *mishpocheh, landsleit*, neighbours, friends, storekeepers, pushcart peddlers and members of a pressers' union he used to belong to." As of the last two years he had been playing fiddle in the Toronto Symphony Orchestra. He also played on radio shows that were sponsored in part by Swift's. The musicians referred to the show as the Swift's Back Bacon Symphony, he said, smiling. He got up from his chair. "I'll play something for you," and went to the bedroom for his violin. Returning, he positioned himself a few feet from her chair, put the bow to his violin and began. Varying expressions fleetingly crossed his features as he stood with eyes focussed on Sophie, playing his violin. "That was 'Nina,'" he said when he finished, "by Pergolesi. It's a love song. One of the most beautiful love songs ever written." He put his violin back in its case and returned to his chair. "Have you ever heard Heifetz?" he asked; and without waiting for a reply, "He's the prince of fiddle players," he said. "He plays like an angel. I'm a good fiddler, but compared with him I play like a pig." He praised Heifetz, lauded, extolled him; and Sophie, deriving pleasure from studying his lovely face, attended him with a smile.

Billy meantime was saying to his daughter, "Where's Mummy?" He had come home for supper and Sophie was not at home.

Emma said she didn't know where her mother was. "She wasn't here when I came home from school."

At that moment Sophie was freeing herself from the violinist's embrace. Both of them with their clothes on, she had lain in his arms a few moments with flushed face and wildly beating heart. She had never before experienced such intense desire; yet the minute he began undressing her she swung her legs over the side of the bed, said she had to go home to get her husband's supper, and busied herself buttoning up the blouse he had started to unbutton.

He sat up and put both arms around her. "You're not going to leave me now?" he said. "Stay. Please. I've got a radio

270

show at seven o'clock. I'll have to be out of here myself at a quarter past six." (It was half-past five.)

Sophie freed herself from his embrace and stood up. "I can't. I'm late now," she said.

What had passed through her mind when he began undressing her was simply the state of her underwear. That he would see the brassiere she was wearing, which was none too clean, and her slip with its hem held up on one side by a safety pin — that was by far a more pressing consideration than keeping Billy waiting for his supper.

"I'm sorry," she said and went to the closet to get her coat.

"So am I," he said glumly. "I wish I'd never met you."

Coated, Sophie went to the living room. He followed and stood silently watching as she gathered up her parcel, purse and gloves. "I'm sorry," she said, moving towards the door. He made no reply. "Well, I — I guess that's all." She was at the door now, with her hand on the knob.

He came over to her and took her hand off the knob and kissed it. "When am I going to see you again?"

Just then the telephone rang. "Wait," he said, and went to the phone which was on a telephone table next to the bookcase. "Yes?" After listening a few seconds, impatiently tapping his foot, "For Christ's sake!" he shouted. "Leave me alone. Stop phoning me!" and slammed down the receiver. Almost instantly the phone rang again. He put his back against the wall and flung his arms wide. With the telephone ringing, he stood a while with arms outstretched in the attitude of Christ on the Cross, then jerked the receiver violently off its hook. "What do you want of me?" he demanded. And without waiting for a reply, "I'm not going to see you again. I don't *want* to see you again. And that's final. We're finished. Can't you get that through your head?" He slammed down the receiver, waited two or three seconds, then lifted it and put it to his ear. On hearing the dial tone he put down the receiver, off its hook. Having put the phone out of commission, the glowering expression disappeared from his face and he approached Sophie with a smile.

"Can you come to the symphony concert tomorrow

night? I'll leave a ticket for you at the box office under my name. The concert will be over—" He stopped without completing the sentence. "You're upset," he said, looking closely at her. "Because of that phone call?"

Sophie was not upset so much as taken aback: the caller was clearly a woman he had been intimate with; how could he speak so brutally to her? "It's none of my business," she said, looking at the floor, "but you did say some awful things to — whoever she is."

"That was Jane Macklin," he said, as if that explained everything. Sophie made no reply. "I met her a few weeks ago," he went on, "and I've been trying to get her off my back since. But she keeps hounding me. She phones or comes uninvited and knocks on my door." Sophie remained silent. He flung up his arms. "You don't know what I've suffered from that woman. She called me at Massey Hall one morning last week — during rehearsal, for Christ's sake! — and said she was going to commit suicide. She's nuts. She's got a thing about fiddlers. Any fiddler," he said with indignation; and that won a smile from Sophie. He smiled and said, "I'll tell you about her some other time," and without pause, "The concert will be over around half-past ten. We leave by the stage door on Victoria Street. Wait for me there."

The following evening at twenty past eight Sophie, freshly bathed, wearing spanking-clean underwear and a brand-new slip under her best dress, was sitting in a ground-floor seat at Massey Hall, tenth row from the front.

Presently the musicians came on stage, the women wearing long dresses and the men in dress suits. Shelley Biderman, scanning the row she was sitting in, was among the first of the violinists to come on stage. He smiled when he saw her, and in taking his place saluted her with a touch of the bow to his forehead.

When the concert was over, he was first among the musicians to emerge from the stage-door exit. He took her under the arm and led her across the street, where a cab was waiting.

"Did you enjoy the concert?" he asked when they were on their way.

Sophie said, "I'm not familiar with classical music. This is the first time I've been to a symphony concert, but I did enjoy it."

The pleasure she had taken in the concert was purely a sensory one, from gazing at his lovely face. The music itself had fallen on an untrained and thereby unreceptive ear.

He was pleased she enjoyed the concert. "You probably have an instinctive ear for good music."

"Why was that violinist — the one who came on stage last — why was he applauded?" Sophie asked.

"He's the concert master."

"Concert master? Does that mean he's the best violinist in the orchestra?"

"Not always. And certainly not in his case. I'm a better fiddler and I know a hell of a lot more about music than he does. But there's a lot of snobbishness in our profession. I don't mean racial snobbishness. He's a Jew too, but he comes from an upper-crust Jewish background and I'm only the son of Hymie Biderman the presser."

When they were let off at his address he inquired whether she would like something to eat. "There's a restaurant on the corner," he said, pointing to it.

Sophie said she wasn't hungry. He said neither was he. He opened the front door of the building, and with a unanimity of purpose they ascended the three flights of stairs to his apartment.

"It was destined that we should meet," the violinist was saying. "I didn't intend to see my old man yesterday. I happened to be passing the store. I wasn't even thinking of him, and I saw you through the window. That's the only reason I came in."

Sophie looked at her watch; it showed twenty past eleven. Billy was at a board meeting. Board meetings took two hours, from ten till twelve. And on occasion broke earlier. If she left now there was a good chance she might get home ahead of him.

"It's late, I'll have to go," she said and reached her hand to her underthings, which she had put over the back of a chair by the bed.

He took her in his arms. "Don't go. Not yet," he murmured with his lips on hers.

Returning his kiss, all thoughts of her husband fled from her mind. She relinquished her hold on her underthings. Her brand-new slip and clean underwear, which she had laid out in showable array over the back of the chair, fell in a heap to the floor.

A half hour later Sophie, coated, and Shelley, wearing slacks and turtle-neck sweater, were standing inside the front door of the building, waiting for the cab he had ordered.

"Can we have lunch together tomorrow?" he asked.

"Call me at ten o'clock. I'll know by then whether my husband is coming home for lunch or not."

He embraced her as the car drew up. "God, I love you," he said, and in slippered feet accompanied her to the curb. "Don't pay the driver. I've got a charge account. It'll go on my bill."

When Sophie got out of the cab she saw Teppy's car parked in front of their house. Tonight's meeting had obviously broken before twelve. Passing through the hall, she heard Billy saying, "I'd better leave a note for Sophie."

Coming into the kitchen, she saw Teppy sitting at the table, with his coat over the back of his chair. An open suitcase lay on the table, with Billy's dressing gown in it, his underwear, socks, some handkerchiefs and his first-aid kit. His navy-blue suit was draped over the back of a chair, and on the seat lay his white shirt and black tie.

Sophie stared, her attention fixed on the navy suit, white shirt and black tie: her husband's funeral attire.

"Aunt Margaret passed away," he said, putting his arm around her. "The funeral won't be till three o'clock tomorrow afternoon but I want to get there tonight. Mother's terribly upset. Teppy's driving me to Galt."

"I'm sorry," Sophie said. "But she was quite old — almost ninety, I think?"

He nodded. "Poor Aunt Margaret, she died two days ago and no one knew a thing about it." He told her that the superintendent of the building where Aunt Margaret lived had called Mother around ten-thirty this evening and told her he had been doing a routine check — knocking on doors where the tenant was an old person living alone. Knocking on Aunt Margaret's door he heard the cat mewing; other than that there was no sound. "He opened the door with his pass key and found Aunt Margaret lying on the floor of her bedroom, in her nightgown. He called a doctor and the doctor said she had been dead at least forty-eight hours."

He took up his white shirt and black tie and put them in the suitcase. He folded his jacket, put it in the suitcase, then closed the case and put it on the floor. Teppy gave him a prod with his maimed hand. "You forgot your pants." Billy opened the suitcase. Putting the pants in his case, he said absently, "Where were you, Soph?"

"Ruby telephoned and asked me to come over — Lou's out of town." She had left the house shortly after eight, she said, and didn't get to Ruby's till almost nine. "The streetcars are so slow in this weather." Eleven o'clock when she got up to go, Ruby said she would drive her home. "It took her almost half an hour before she could get the car started, and then it stalled halfway down the street." She and Ruby left the stalled car and walked two blocks to a restaurant, where Ruby used the phone to call a tow truck. "The streetcars had stopped running so I called a cab and left Ruby in the restaurant, waiting for the tow truck."

Teppy got up from his chair and put on his coat. With his nipped hand concealed in his pocket, he took hold of the case with his good hand and said, "I'll wait for you in the car. Don't be long, Billy," and with pointedly intentional rudeness, he brushed past Sophie without a glance in her direction.

Billy winced. His friend's rudeness to his wife had not gone unnoticed by him, despite the troubled state of mind he was in. "You look so pretty in that dress, Soph," he said, then went to the hall and came back with his coat on. "I'll be away all day tomorrow. I promised Mother I'd stay for supper and a visit. Teppy will be taking my classes. All my classes as well as his own. He'll have a tough day of it," he smiled.

"When will you be home?" Sophie asked, accompanying him to the door.

"I should be home around nine o'clock." On hearing the sound of Teppy's horn, he kissed her and said, "So long, hon. Kiss Emma for me."

Thirty-Four

"Where's Daddy?" Emma asked when she was wakened by her mother instead of her father.

Sophie told her he had to go out of town and would not be home until nine o'clock this evening. "Don't be long getting dressed, it's late," she said, then kissed the child. "Daddy told me to kiss you for him."

Going down the stairs, Sophie saw her mother passing through the hall with a glass of tea in one hand and in the other a few lumps of sugar.

Aware that her presence was not pleasing to her son-in-law, Mrs. Glicksman saw to it that she did not unnecessarily intrude her person on his presence. When Sophie served him his meals in the dining room, she kept to the kitchen. And latterly had begun taking her morning tea to her bedroom before he came down to his breakfast. With her back to her sleeping husband, she sat at the window with her tea and did not emerge from the room until she saw Billy leaving for work.

More than once she had caught the expression that fleetingly crossed Billy's features when their glances happened to meet, an expression that plainly bespoke his dislike of her.

Because of that look she was not deceived by the courtesy he showed her, or taken in by the smile on his face. But she bore him no ill will; he was her daughter's husband and the father of her grandchild.

Pondering on his dislike of her, she would now and then put the question to herself: "What have I done to him that I'm like a bone in his throat?" And in answer to her question, would ask herself: "Where is it written that he has to like you?" Musing on her husband's care for her, a smile would come to her face. "He likes me, God bless him. And that's enough for me."

"Isn't it time you put a stop to this foolishness?" Sophie said, stopping her mother in the hall. It caused her a pang to see her mother hurrying out of her own kitchen to put herself out of Billy's sight. "You've talked yourself into something. It's all in your imagination that Billy doesn't like you," Sophie said, knowing better herself. She took the glass of tea out of her mother's hand. "Come back to the kitchen. He isn't home anyway. He had to go out of town last night."

Mrs. Glicksman followed her daughter to the kitchen. "Where did he go, your husband?" she said, taking her chair. She seldom spoke Billy's name. Speaking of Billy to her husband, she referred to him as he or him.

Sophie told her Billy's mother telephoned last night and told him his aunt had died.

"She was an old woman, his aunt?"

"She wasn't young. She was ninety."

Mrs. Glicksman nodded. "Ninety," she observed, "is not nineteen."

Shelley telephoned at ten, and Sophie said she would be able to have lunch with him. He said he'd have a cab pick her up at noon. "Don't send a cab to the house," Sophie said, speaking quietly into the mouthpiece (her father was asleep). "Tell the driver to pick me up at the corner of Nassau and Bellevue."

A few minutes before twelve she went to the kitchen and said to her mother, "I have to go out, Ma. Will you give Emma her lunch?"

"With pleasure," said Mrs. Glicksman.

The cab was waiting for her when she arrived at the corner; and fifteen minutes later she was knocking on the violinist's door. He opened, drew her in and at once took her in his embrace.

Presently there came a knock on the door, followed by a woman's voice: "Shelley?"

Sophie's heart stopped. Revisited by the panic she had experienced four years before when Brian Purtell's wife came knocking on the studio door, she went limp in her lover's arms.

"Who's that?" she whispered, drawing away from him. "Jane Macklin?"

He laughed. "It's a waitress from Mark's, that corner restaurant," he said. "I ordered a goulash for our lunch," and went to the door. "Thanks, Marie." He took from the waitress the covered stewpan she held out to him by its handle. He put the pan on the sidetable, brought out a bill from his wallet and gave it to the girl, telling her to keep the change.

"You'll like the goulash," he promised. "Mark's has a reputation for the best goulash in town." He took her coat to the closet and returning he asked, "How long can you stay?"

"I'll have to be home before six."

"Then we don't have to hurry with lunch," he said. "Unless you're hungry. . . ?"

It is now a quarter past two and the goulash, unsampled as yet, is in the oven being kept warm. Another ten minutes and Mark's goulash, which is said to be the best in town, will be dry as cuttle bone. The percolator is still perking. Full to begin, it now contains perhaps two meagre cups. If it remains much longer on the stove, the coffee pot will yield only the dregs.

The lovers are in bed. Having made love — twice — they are now lying in each other's arms in languorous embrace. "I think we should have lunch," Sophie suggests after a while. "If you're hungry. . . " he stipulates, seeking her mouth. Both of them in the same instant are taken with renewed desire.

A half hour later Shelley clothes himself in a dressing

gown and brings a robe from the closet for Sophie to wear. He wraps her in the robe, kissing her hands as he rolls back the sleeves, and both proceed to the kitchen for a late lunch. He takes up the bottle of wine that's on the table and fills both glasses. "To you," he says, raising his glass. "To you," she responds, raising hers. "To us," he says. "To us," she agrees.

Shelley puts down his glass and goes over to the stove. "The percolator's run dry," he says. Sophie says it doesn't matter; he agrees; they'll drink wine, he says. He slips his hand into an oven mitt, opens the oven door, takes hold of the stewpan, puts the pan on the table, and the oven mitt on a chair. "It smells burnt," he says, sniffing. He lifts the stewpan lid by its hot metal knob, lets out a howl of pain and flings the lid violently across the floor. The violence of his action causes Sophie to start.

"That's my bowing hand," he explains. "I've got a rehearsal call at nine-thirty tomorrow morning." He holds his hand up to his face and scrutinizes the thumb, the index and middle finger of his bowing hand. He lays his hand palm up on the table, for Sophie to see the injured fingers. His fingers show a faintly perceptible trace of burn. "Will they blister?" he anxiously inquires.

Tutored by her husband in the rudiments of first aid, Sophie says that a mixture of baking soda and water should be applied to the burns. "That'll keep them from blistering."

He says he hasn't got any baking soda; he'll go down to Mrs. Gutcher, the superintendent's wife. "She bakes, she'll have some baking soda." He goes to the bedroom, blowing on his fingers. He returns shortly, wearing slacks under his dressing gown, a scarf around his neck, a handsome pair of suede slippers, and leaves for Mrs. Gutcher's. He returns in ten minutes and the balls of his fingers, all five, are plastered with a paste made of baking soda and water. Sophie refills the wine glasses, slices the pumpernickel, dishes up the goulash (which she has moistened with wine), and they sit down to eat. With his injured bowing hand resting palm up in his lap, the violinist applies himself to his goulash with his left hand.

When Billy came home at nine o'clock, his wife was in bed, reading a book. "Mother and the girls sent their love," he said, and sat down on the edge of the bed, saying he was dead beat.

He and his mother had spent the morning clearing out Aunt Margaret's place. "Aunt Margaret's always been a magpie," he said, smiling sadly. "She never threw anything away." Her closets and drawers were crammed full with a hodgepodge of odds and ends, empty chocolate boxes, worn-out slippers, old shoes, clothes that were falling apart, a stack of magazines dating back to the year ought, Uncle Dan's love letters, his valentines, empty cologne bottles, threadless spools of thread, dried-up sachets, an Ouija board, and in an old hatbox they found seven empty gin bottles. "Who would have thought that Aunt Margaret, of all people, was a secret drinker," he said.

Sighing, he went on to talk about the funeral, which had been attended by his mother, sisters, Roger, himself, the superintendent of the building where Aunt Margaret lived, his wife — and who should arrive at the last minute but Marjorie with her mother, Mrs. Ward. "It's always touch and go with Mrs. Ward," he said, "but apparently this must have been one of her good days. She didn't create any disturbance." He said she cried a little during the burial, then kept them all waiting while she stood at the graveside, reciting some poetry from memory. Other than that, she had behaved more or less normally.

"It's sad about Aunt Margaret, isn't it," he concluded.

It is sad, Sophie thought, that Aunt Margaret — but for the few tears shed by a crazy woman — went to her grave unwept.

Billy unpacked his suitcase, hung his navy suit in the closet, took off his clothes and got into bed. "I missed you, hon." Fondling her, he whispered, "Let's make love."

His advances were mistimed.

During the time of Sophie's love affair with Brian Purtell, it had eased her conscience (to some extent) that not even once had she had sex with her husband the same day she had been with Brian. Because she felt that to make love with

Billy the same day she had been with Brian would be an act of discredit on the person of her husband, she had scrupulously kept the occasions separate.

To make love with Billy now — when just a few hours ago she had lain in her lover's embrace — was unthinkable. Apart from her high-minded concern for her husband's good, she was not stimulated at this particular time by his caresses. She lay unresponsively in his embrace, pleading fatigue, a headache.

Next morning at half-past ten she was in the downstairs hall, monitoring the telephone. Shelley said he would call at ten-thirty, during a rehearsal break, and at ten-thirty the phone rang. Speaking quietly into the mouthpiece, she told him she would not be able to get away before a quarter past one. And he understood that her husband was coming home for lunch.

"I'll have a cab pick you up," he said. "At twenty past one? On the same corner?" She told him to make it half-past one, on the corner of Bellevue and College. (Where there was less likelihood of encountering an immediate neighbour.)

Emma left for school at ten past one; but Billy, who usually left at the same time, was in the bathroom spraying his nose to clear his nasal passages. He came out at last — it was already half-past one — and went into their bedroom where Sophie, impatiently idling time, had a dresser drawer open, affecting to be in search of something.

"I think Emma should be told about Aunt Margaret," he said, sitting down on the edge of the bed, "don't you?"

I'll go out of my mind, said Sophie to herself. To him she said, "Yes, I think she should."

He sighed and said, "It'll be a sad Christmas this year without Aunt Margaret." As of the last four years they had been going to Galt for the Christmas holidays. "We should start thinking about Christmas presents, Soph. If we wait much longer the stores will be mobbed. Let's go downtown this Saturday."

"Okay. Aren't you going to be late for work?"

Thirty-Five

Sophie looked at her watch. "I have to go home," she said.

"It's only nine o'clock," Shelley protested.

"I don't want to take any chances. If I leave now I'm sure to get home before him."

This was a Wednesday night, December 23. They had been lovers three weeks and Sophie, as she had done during the early days of her love affair with the artist, was conducting herself with caution. Although she and the violinist had been seeing each other three and even four times a week since December 2 when they first met, Sophie had seen to it — but for that one night when she got home to find her husband packing his case — that she arrived home before he did.

"Am I going to see you tomorrow before you leave?" Shelley asked.

"I won't be able to get away. Billy's getting the afternoon off tomorrow."

"That means I won't see you till Sunday?" He lifted his shoulders in a shrug and went to the phone to call a cab.

Sophie had told him they would be leaving for Galt the following evening on the six o'clock train.

"Mr. Biderman here," Shelley said, speaking on the phone

and at the same time gloomily eyeing Sophie who was putting on her coat. "I want a car here in five minutes."

With a forbidding expression, he put on his coat and accompanied her down the three flights of stairs. Waiting for the cab, he stood beside her in silence, looking away from her with his head held high.

Sophie was becoming used to his sudden shifts of mood. We're going to be separated for three days, she was thinking, but if this is the way he wants to part — acting like a spoiled child — that's all right with me. Then, with the confidence of a woman who knows she's loved, she put her head down to hide a smile.

When the cab arrived, he held the door open for her and then got in beside her.

The cabbie asked, "Where to, Mr. Biderman?"

"Drop me off at the corner of Spadina and College," he replied, then turned to Sophie. "Do you mind if I ride part way with you?"

Sophie laughed. "Help yourself."

He took her hand from her lap, removed the glove, brought her hand to his mouth and kissed it on the palm and on the back.

Coming into the kitchen when she got home, Sophie saw her mother sitting at the table with Glicksman's daily, studying news photos. Seeing Sophie, she pointed to a photo of a young woman crying with her hands partially covering her face. Why was the woman crying? Mrs. Glicksman wanted to know. Next to the photo of the weeping woman was one of a smiling child with a doll in her arms.

Sophie, who had read an account of the tragedy earlier in the day, pointed to the picture of the child and said, "This was her child. She was run over by a car and killed."

Mrs. Glicksman put her hand over her heart. "A Jewish child?"

"Why do you always ask was it a Jewish child when you hear of a child being killed?"

"A Jewish child — I pity the mother."

"You pity the mother. This was a gentile child." Pointing to the picture of the mother, Sophie said, "What makes you think she feels less pain than a Jewish mother would?"

Sophie went upstairs and Mrs. Glicksman turned her attention again to the newspaper. She was moved, studying the photo of the grieving mother. Reflectively nodding her head, she conceded to her invisible auditor: "A mother's heart is a mother's heart." By that she meant that when it came to grief over the loss of a child, a mother's heart, whether it resided in the breast of a Jewish or a gentile woman, was, after all, one and the same.

Billy came home a few minutes past ten and found his wife in bed, asleep. (When Sophie heard him coming into the house, she had put down the book she was reading, pulled the bedclothes up to her chin, turned on her side and closed her eyes.)

He sat down on the edge of the bed, took off his shoes, then stood to take off his clothes. Through half-closed eyes Sophie saw him go over to the dresser, and leaning into the mirror, stick out his tongue to see if it was coated. He had developed various hypochondriacal habits over the years, and this one in particular irritated her. But tonight for some reason it caught at her heart to see him standing naked at the mirror with his tongue out.

Shortly after five the following evening Sophie, with Emma following, came into the kitchen. "Good-bye, Ma," she said to her mother who was clearing Glicksman's dishes. "We're going."

"God go with you," her mother replied.

Billy came down the stairs carrying two suitcases, one packed with Christmas presents, the other with their clothes. Putting on his coat, "Come on, Soph," he called from the hall. "We're going to be late."

"Did you call a cab?" she asked, coming into the hall.

He stooped to the suitcases. "There's no point in spending money on a cab. A streetcar'll get us to the station in just as good time."

Comparing him unfavourably with her lover who taxied to rehearsal, taxied to the grocery store for a bottle of ginger ale, kept a cab waiting while getting his shoes shined, she followed her husband out, giving his back an unpleasant glance.

When they arrived in Galt, Louise's husband Roger was at the station to meet them. "Season's greetings," he said, shaking his brother-in-law's hand. He gave Sophie a cold wet kiss on the cheek, bent down to Emma and kissed her.

On arriving at the house, they were warmly received by Billy's mother and his two sisters. Louise and Roger's six-year-old daughter Mary Ann had eyes only for her cousin Emma.

They sat down to a supper of shepherd's pie, peas, carrot coins, and for dessert, rice pudding. During the meal, Aunt Margaret was fondly reminisced. With affection they spoke of her forgetfulness, her habit of mislaying things, the tizzy she got herself into hunting for something that was under her nose. Mary recalled one morning three years ago when Aunt Margaret, who had spent the night at their house, wouldn't come down to breakfast because she couldn't find her teeth. She said to her mother, "You went up to help her look for them, remember?" The mother smiled and said, "We turned the room upside down looking for her teeth, poor dear — and for the life of me I can't think what made me look in her bedroom slippers, but that's where they were, wrapped up in a hankie."

Going through Sophie's mind was the picture of Aunt Margaret drinking straight gin from Uncle Dan's christening cup, and then going tipsily to her room, forgetting to take the dentures she had wrapped up in a handkerchief. But she made no mention of this incident; she had been cautioned by her husband not to: Louise and Roger didn't know, nor did Mary, that Aunt Margaret had been in the habit of tippling on the sly. For the sake of keeping their memory of Aunt Margaret unclouded, Billy and his mother had thought it best not to mention the seven empty gin bottles they found in her old hatbox.

Louise and Roger left shortly after supper, leaving Mary Ann to stay overnight at "Gram's."

The children were put to bed in Louise's old bedroom, and on waking early next morning each found a Christmas stocking on her pillow. Emma got out of bed right away — she loved going to Gram's for Christmas. Before getting dressed herself, she helped Mary Ann to get dressed. "I'll tell you a secret," she whispered, doing up her cousin's dress. "There's no Santa Claus — *Gram* is Santa."

Mary Ann stared at her cousin, with a hand over her mouth as if she herself had spoken the blasphemous words. Eyes popping, she retreated a few steps, turned and ran from the room with her dress unbuttoned, leaving her Christmas stocking behind.

Presently Billy came in. Emma, dressed, was sitting on the bed. Her Christmas stocking lay unopened in her lap. He sat down beside her and kissed her. "Merry Christmas, sweetie."

"Merry Christmas," she returned, and followed with, "Did Mary Ann tell on me?"

He put his arm around her. "You mustn't let that spoil your Christmas."

"Did she *tell* on me?" The child was almost in tears now.

"Mary Ann said you told her there was no Santa Claus, and Gram said you were just teasing." He took her closer in his embrace. "Don't let it worry you. Let's go down and have breakfast and then we'll have the tree."

"Can I go to church, Daddy?" Emma asked, coming to the living room. "Mary Ann's going."

Waiting for his mother and sister who were getting ready for church, Billy was clearing the floor of discarded wrapping, ribbon, string, Christmas seals. He was touched by the child's eager face. "You'll have to ask Mummy," he replied, hoping Soph wouldn't be contrary about it.

Sophie was upstairs putting away their Christmas gifts. Emma came into the room. "Can I go to church, Mummy?"

The little *shiksa*, said Sophie to herself. To the child she said, "Go if you want to, but don't say anything about it to *bubbeh* when we get home."

Billy came up shortly after. "Thanks, Soph," he said, "Emma would have been terribly disappointed if you had said she couldn't go."

A half hour later when he and his daughter were at church attending a Christmas service, his wife was writing in her diary: "Making love with B last night I tried to imagine it was S I was making love with. But it didn't work."

Saturday evening after supper the resident family were gathered in the hall, bidding the visiting family Godspeed.

Sunday, Sophie's lover telephoned at ten o'clock. "Welcome home. When am I going to see you?"

"Not before one," she replied.

Sundays, Billy seldom found time to come home for lunch. He ate at a restaurant near the Y, and once in a while called home before or after lunch. And Sophie, careful not to give him cause for suspicion, made a point of being on hand should he call. This Sunday he called a few minutes before one, and at five past one Sophie was getting into a cab at the top of her street.

Ernie, a cabbie who had driven her several times to and from the violinist's address, turned as soon as the car was in motion, and said, leering at her, "You getting much these days?"

The expression was new to her. She had not read it anywhere or heard it spoken, but its meaning she intuitively sensed.

"Let me out!" she cried.

The driver made as if he hadn't heard.

"Let me out!" she commanded, clubbing the back of his seat with her fist.

He brought the car to a stop, turned and said with a nervous smile, "What are you getting so excited about?"

She wrenched open the door and got out of the car.

Ernie sat a minute at his wheel. "Bitch," he said, watching her as she walked towards the Bathurst and College streetcar stop. Abruptly he got out of his car and caught up with her.

"Please, Miss," he said, walking meekly beside her. "Please get back in the car." She continued walking.

"Have a heart, Miss. I'm a married man with two kids. This could cost me my job."

"Good," said Sophie; the same Sophie whose concerns, when she was a member of the YCL, were compassionately concentrated on the improvement of the workingman's lot.

"Where the hell have you been?" her lover greeted her. "I phoned the taxi station and they said Ernie reported that you refused to get in his car."

"The liar. I refused to get *back* in his car," said Sophie; and told him what had happened.

"The son of a bitch." He went over to the phone and called the taxi station. "Let me speak to eh — the manager, whatever the hell his name is." The manager came to the phone. "Mr. Biderman here," said Shelley. "Close my account. I won't be using your cab any more," and hung up.

The manager immediately called back. He wanted to know why Mr. Biderman, a good customer of three years' standing, was closing his account. "Is there anything wrong with the service?"

"You're goddamn right there is when one of your drivers thinks he can insult a friend of mine and get away with it. My friend is a lady!" the violinist bellowed. "Who the fuck did Ernie think he was talking to!"

He hung up and went over to Sophie. "God, I love you," he declared, taking her in his arms.

Thirty-Six

Late one Friday night in mid-March Sophie and the violinist were standing inside the front door of the apartment building, waiting for the cab that was to take Sophie home. "What's keeping him?" she said, looking nervously at her watch. If she were late tonight, it would be for the third time this week.

They had been lovers almost four months and Sophie had begun repeating the incautious behaviour she had employed during the latter weeks of her love affair with the artist.

"Oh God!" she wailed (the taxi was drawing up). "Where will I say I've been?"

"You said he never asks."

"He hasn't so far, but what if he does tonight?"

"Tell him the truth. Let him sue for divorce and name me corespondent. Give him my name and phone number. If he wants to speak to me, I'll talk to him."

Just like that, Sophie said to herself.

In the cab she recalled a conversation they had had a while back. "We're mentally and temperamentally unsuited to each other," she had said, speaking of her husband. "We never should have got married."

"Divorce him," he said, "and marry me. You don't love him."

When she made no reply, he demanded, "Or do you? Tell me."

And she had cautiously replied, "I'm not exactly indifferent to him—"

He looked at her a long minute, then turned his back. "Go home to your husband." And then had stopped her from getting dressed.

Getting out of the cab a few minutes before twelve, she looked up at their bedroom window. The room was dark. Billy was asleep or not home yet (he had gone to a wrestling match with Teppy and Judy).

Billy was not asleep. Unseen by Sophie, he was standing at the window in the dark, keeping watch, as he had done several times in the recent past, to see if she would come home again by cab. He came away from the window when he saw her getting out of a cab, and got into bed, sick at heart.

Sophie turned on the hall light and saw Billy's coat on the rack. She hung up her coat, flicked off the light and went up to her bedroom on tiptoe. She undressed in the dark and fell asleep almost at once.

With beleaguered heart beating tiredly in his breast, Billy lay open-eyed in the dark, grudging his wife's repose. She's not going to get away with it this time, he said to himself. I'm not going to go through that again, I've had it. I won't ask any questions. I'll just lay it on the line. Let her leave me. If she wants a divorce she can have it. I'll be better off without her. . .

His thoughts went back to what had happened to him two weeks ago, during a swimming class for Juniors. With his mind on his wife's carryings-on, he hadn't noticed that a boy, a beginner, was in the deep end and in trouble. Because of her he had been negligent. For the first time in his life. He was held to be one of the best swimming instructors in Toronto, and if a drowning had occurred in one of his classes it would have meant curtains for him.

He got out of bed, wrapped a towel around his middle, went downstairs and poured himself a stiff drink from

Glicksman's bottle. The drink relaxed him and eased his heart. He poured himself another.

Drinking whiskey from a kitchen tumbler, he sat half-naked at the table, firming his resolution to have it out with Sophie. He had waited long enough. Tomorrow would be the logical day for a showdown; he didn't work Saturdays. He'd never forget the anguish she had caused him four years ago. He had let her get away with murder because he was afraid of losing her. He felt different about it now.

Several times he had been on the verge of confiding in Teppy and was glad now that he hadn't. Teppy was a good friend and had his interest at heart, but this was a matter concerning himself and Sophie. He would handle it himself. Soph, he'd say to her tomorrow after breakfast, it's time we had a talk. We can't go on like this. A man can only take so much and no more. And I've had it.

He woke before eight next morning; she was still asleep. The thought that she was running him ragged yet could sleep so peacefully filled him with bitterness. Moved by an impulse to wake her, talk turkey to her instead of beating around the bush, he leaned over the bed. "Soph?" She didn't stir. He put his hand on her shoulder. "Soph!"

Half asleep, she opened her eyes. "What is it?"

His heart began to beat violently; he could feel the beat in his ears. He took his trembling hand off her shoulder and moved away from the bed. "I'm a bundle of nerves," he said, moving towards the door. "My sinuses are acting up—"

Sophie put on her dressing gown, combed her hair and went downstairs to make breakfast. Coming into the kitchen, she saw that her mother's chair was empty. At the sight of the empty chair, a feeling of rancour welled up in her heart.

"My mother asked to be excused," she said sarcastically to her husband when he and Emma came down to breakfast.

"Where did *bubbeh* go?" Emma asked.

"She's hiding in her bedroom," Sophie said tightly. "Ask Daddy to tell you why."

"That's not fair," he protested. "It's not my fault that—"

He put his spoon to his cereal without completing the sentence. He didn't want to argue with her in front of the child.

291

Besides, he had other things on his mind.

Shortly after breakfast he left to visit a fellow athlete who was in hospital, and returned a few minutes before noon. "Emma?" he called from the foot of the stairs. As she came running down wearing her best dress, he smiled. "You're all dolled up."

"Blanche is going to wear her new dress, and Mum said I could wear mine too." Blanche was Teppy and Judy's daughter. "Good-bye, Mum," the child called, getting into her coat.

Sophie was upstairs tidying her room. "Good-bye," she answered, "have a good time."

They were going to Teppy and Judy's for lunch, and afterwards — as a treat — the children would be taken to see Shirley Temple in *Heidi*.

Half-past twelve Sophie was at the top of her street, getting into a cab.

"I won't have any, thanks," Billy said. Smiling apologetically to Judy, he passed his strawberry shortcake to Teppy.

He rose abruptly from his chair. "Excuse me. I don't feel well, I feel punk — I think I'd better go home." He went over to Emma and kissed her. "You don't mind if Daddy doesn't come to the movie?"

Teppy got up and offered to drive him home.

"Teppy," Billy said as they were getting into the car, "don't bring Emma home after the movie. Take her back to your place, please."

Teppy turned his head. "What's wrong, Billy?"

"Nothing. It's just that—" He took a cigarette from his pack and lit it with a shaking hand. "I'm a mess, Teppy. I don't know whether I'm coming or going."

Teppy said nothing.

"I'm a nervous wreck. Remember that kid that nearly drowned two weeks ago? That's still preying on my mind."

"Forget it," Teppy said shortly. "A near drowning is something that can happen to the best swimming instructor."

They drove the rest of the way in silence. Drawing up before his friend's house, Teppy asked him, "Do you want Emma to stay at our place overnight?"

"I don't know," Billy said vaguely.

Teppy gave him a searching look. "What's on your mind, Billy? Is it Sophie?"

The instructor lowered the window, threw out his butt then turned to his friend. "You guessed it, Teppy. It's my wife," he said, cracking his knuckles against his chest.

Teppy turned off the motor and waited for his friend to speak.

"Sophie's been seeing someone." Speaking rapidly, he said that as of the last couple of months — maybe longer — Sophie had been going to Massey Hall Tuesday nights. One Tuesday night a few weeks ago, when he—

Teppy interrupted. "How do you know that's where she goes?"

"She doesn't make any secret of it." He said she had told him some time ago that she had bought a season's ticket to the Tuesday-night concerts. Besides, he had seen a couple of programs lying around. "I know for a fact that that's where she goes. But I don't know where she goes after the concert. She always gets home late." One Tuesday night a few weeks ago, when he was coming home late, he saw her getting out of a cab. "She didn't see me." He was halfway down the block, he said, when a taxi stopped in front of their house and Sophie got out. He had found out that she went out other nights too and came home in a taxi. "I've been keeping tabs on her," he said despondently. "She also goes out Saturday and Sunday afternoons. She's never at home Sundays when I phone from the Y. My mother-in-law gives Emma her lunch. Two Saturdays ago when I phoned from your place she wasn't at home. And last Saturday she came home long after Emma and I got back from your house — wait a minute, Teppy." He got out of the car, ran up the verandah steps and opened the door. He came out again immediately and got into the car, wiping sweat from his face. "She's not at home. Her coat isn't on the rack."

"What are you going to do about it?"

"I don't know. I honestly don't know, Teppy. But I can't go on like this. I'll have a nervous breakdown. If I knew who the man was at least, I'd—"

"Find out," said Teppy. "Put a private eye on her."

"I was going to speak to her this morning," Billy said. "But I lost my nerve. I'm a weakling, Teppy, a spineless weakling."

"You're not a weakling," Teppy said kindly; and added with a smile, "You're just a sucker for punishment. Speak to her, Billy. Don't put it off any longer — or you *will* have a nervous breakdown."

Firmly Billy said, "I'm going to have it out with her today. Actually, that's the reason I asked you to take Emma back to your place." A rush of blood coloured his face. "I don't have to put a private eye on her to find out who the man is — I just thought of something." It had come to him that a clue to the man's identity might be found among Sophie's things. He thanked his friend and got out of the car with his heart eased somewhat of its burden.

He went upstairs to their bedroom. It was against his principles to go into his wife's private things, but he hesitated only a short minute. With rapidly beating heart, he pulled open the bottom drawer of the dresser. There was a pile of stuff in the drawer — old birthday cards from school friends, comic valentines, newspaper clippings, pages of a novel she had started, several copies of the Zangwill two-sheeter, poems she had written for the Zangwill, letters of praise from the editor, a few programs of concerts she had recently been to, and copies of letters she had written. Among the letters was one to Thomas Wolfe in praise of *Look Home-ward, Angel*; to Ben Ruskin, disavowing Darwinism; to Avrom Bochner when she resigned from the Zangwill; to Ronnie Swerling when she quit the YCL; and the one to her father, telling him she had been married three months to a gentile. He returned the letters to the drawer and continued his search. What he was looking for he found wrapped up in a tea towel: her diary.

He folded the towel and laid it in the exact place where he had found the diary. He rose from his squatting position and, taking the diary, went over to the window seat. Between its pages was an envelope, unsealed, the flap tucked in. He lay the open diary face down on the window seat and took from the envelope a florist's card and a wire. On the card was written: "Dear Sophie, Forgive me for oafishly falling asleep." The signature was Brian. The telegram read: "Am I forgiven?" And under the signature Brian, in Sophie's hand: "Am keeping this to remind me of a shameful episode in my life — namely, my first and *last* extramarital affair. I've seen B.P. for the last time, thank God. Never having loved him, he won't be hard to forget."

B.P., he knew, stood for Brian Purtell.

That Sophie had not been in love with the man was of no comfort to him. If anything, it made it worse. He couldn't quite figure out why, but it did. And he hated the man more now than ever, for all the misery he had suffered at his hands. His thoughts went back to the night he had gone in search of him. . .

Sophie had started coming home later and later. One night he decided to take a stand. He looked up the name in the telephone directory, and found a Brian Purtell on Grenville Street. To see the name listed in the directory made him weak in the knees. To steady himself he took a drink of whiskey from Glicksman's bottle. Then he set out on a freezing-cold night for Grenville Street, not clear yet in his mind what he intended to do. He found the house, strode purposefully up the steps to the front door, and as he made to ring the bell, his hand failed him. He descended the steps and crossed the street. Chilled to the bone, he stood gazing with suffocating heart at the house across the street.

Recalling that night, he was gripped again in the pain he had known four years before.

He put back the card and wire in the envelope and took up the diary. Returning the envelope to the place where he found it, his eye fell on an entry dated January 26, four years ago: "I haven't given B.P. a single thought. I don't miss him and I never think of him. But my peace of mind isn't altogether restored — and that's because I'm pretty sure that B knows I had an affair. He's been buying me presents — an angora sweater, stockings, chocolates. He acts as if he's vying with a rival for my favour. That makes my heart ache for him. But the anger I feel against myself for taking up with B.P. I feel at times like letting out on B, for letting me believe he didn't know. I know he knows, but he doesn't think I know, and so we keep up the pretence. In time it will be forgotten, I hope."

He found it hard, suddenly, to breathe. He opened the window, put his head out and filled his lungs, gulping air. When he was able to draw breath, he shut the window, sat down again and said miserably to himself: It can't be forgotten. I've been through hell.

He took up the diary and turned the page. Three months later she had written a detailed account of a quarrel she had with her father. The next entry, six months later, was given over to comments on a book she had read. He turned the page to find a vivid description of a dream in which she had found herself walking along their street without a stitch of clothes on. "I was horrified," she had written. "With one hand spread over my tits, and the other covering my pubis, I turned back to go home — and couldn't find our house. Neighbours passed me on the street, not noticing that I was naked."

He went on to the next page, and the next, glancing only at the dates: he was looking for what had been written as of December three months ago when she began going to symphony concerts.

His eye fell at last on the date he was after. On the page dated December 2 she had written: "Went to Biderman's Cleaning & Pressing this afternoon to pick up E's jumper. Mr. Biderman's son came in while I was waiting. A strikingly handsome man, Circassian in appearance. It's incredible that so ugly a father could have sired him. He followed me out when I left. We taxied to his apt, drank brandy and had an interesting conversation. He played his violin for me. A love song called Nina. Then made a play for me. Beauty combined with sexual magnetism — as it is in S's case — is a powerful combination. It took some effort on my part to resist him. Am going to Massey Hall tomorrow night. S plays violin with the Toronto Symphony Orchestra."

The man was a musician. He had guessed as much.

December 4: "Taxied to S's apt after the concert — and the inevitable happened. S said it was destined that we meet.

Stayed too late, B was home when I got in. His mother had telephoned with news of Aunt Margaret's death. B was packing his case, and Teppy was waiting to drive him to Galt. Will have to be more careful in future."

December 11: "S is affectionate, irrational, generous, temperamental, warm-hearted, impetuous, dictatorial, loving, arrogant and conceited — a complex personality."

Galt, Xmas day: "Making love with B last night I tried to imagine it was S I was making love with. But it didn't work."

His throat felt as if it were in the grip of a strangling hand. He got up from the window seat and sat on the bed. His heart beat violently a few seconds, then turned to stone. After a time he went back to the diary.

January 10: "S has expensive tastes in food, clothes, shoes, ties, scarves, lounging robes, toiletries — he indulges himself in all things. He's a Sybarite. He's also narcissistic. I've noticed that he can't resist taking a glance at himself when he passes a mirror."

January 31: "S is passionately devoted to music. He's ambitious to become a conductor."

February 15: "S has a cruel streak in him. His volatile mood shifts are truly alarming. He becomes abusive, insulting. Yesterday I walked out on him. He came chasing after me. He said it tears him apart to quarrel with me — and talked me into coming back. He can charm the birds out of trees."

March 2: "S told me he's had several mistresses but has never been in love till he met me. He wants me to divorce B and marry him. I said that marriage would soon put an end to his love for me. He said I didn't know what I was talking about. Never having been married himself, he doesn't know what day-to-day living together does to love."

He turned the page. It was blank. He got up, pulled open the dresser drawer, wrapped the diary in the tea towel and returned it to its place. Before closing the drawer he took out one of the symphony concert programs and turned to the page on which the musicians were listed. Looking for the name Biderman, he found, under violinists, the name of his wife's lover: Shelley Biderman, the man she referred to as S in her diary. He put the program back in its place and shut the drawer.

Emotionally he felt nothing. His head was in a turmoil; he couldn't think straight. He paced the floor, trying to put his thoughts in order. Gradually his head began to clear. The last thing he wanted was a showdown with Sophie. He would just leave her. High and dry without support. Let her boyfriend support her. He would clear out and take Emma with him. He'd find a furnished apartment and — no, that wouldn't do. Who would look after Emma? Come to think of it, Teppy and Judy had a spare room. He'd speak to them about renting the room to him. Emma could bunk in with Blanche. It was a big room and could easily accommodate a second bed. The children were more like sisters than girlfriends. Teppy and Judy loved Emma. Judy, as a matter of fact, showed as much love to Emma as she did to her own child. He was fond of Judy. Several times in the recent past, the thought had come to him that he would have had a happier life married to a girl like Judy. She was a good wife and a good mother. . . Here a guilty smile came to his face: the erotic dream he had had a few days ago about Judy had come unbidden to his mind.

He blotted out the picture of his best friend's wife lying naked in his bed and went on with his plans. Emma would be transferred to the school Blanche attended. He wondered how wise that would be — to transfer the child, midterm, to another school. She was doing so well. She brought home report cards with marks between 80 and 95 in all subjects. Sweet little soul, she was a clever child. She liked her teacher, and it would upset her to be transferred just like that, without any preparation, to another school. The move would have to wait till the summer holidays. Three and a half more months — this was only March 18. Could he stick it out? For the child's sake, he'd have to.

His thoughts turned to his wife. This time she wasn't giving him any alibis. He had had his fill of them four years ago. And they had been hard to take. He was being spared that, at least.

These thoughts evoked a picture in his mind: his wife in

298

bed with her lover, the man she had tried to imagine she was with when he was making love to her. He took out his wallet, removed the snapshot he had taken of her in the early days of their marriage, and slowly tore in half the picture of his wife sitting on a park bench in the dress she wore when they were married. "We're finished, Soph," he said to his absent wife, covered his face and wept despairingly for himself.

"Let's have some music," Shelley suggested. It was five o'clock of the same afternoon, and the cab he had ordered for Sophie was not expected before five more minutes. "What would you like to hear?" Without waiting for an answer he took a record from the bookcase and put it on the phonograph. Presently there came the sound of orchestral music.

"What's that?" Sophie asked.

"The Mendelssohn Violin Concerto." He lifted the needle arm off the spinning disc and carefully repositioned it. At the sound of a solo violin, he put a finger to his lips. "Listen to him. That's Heifetz," he said reverently. With raised head he stood motionless beside the phonograph, staring into space as if he were spelled. When the solo violin subsided, he lifted the needle arm off the disc. "He inspires me," he said, returning the record to the bookcase, "and also breaks my heart." He turned to face her. "If I can't play like that by the time I'm twenty-five I'll cut my bowing hand off at the wrist."

By the time he's twenty-five? "How old are you?" she asked.

"Twenty-three."

They heard the sound of a horn; the taxi had arrived.

When Sophie got home at a quarter past five, she noted with relief that the rack was bare of both Billy's and Emma's coat.

At half-past five Billy telephoned. "Don't get any supper for us, Soph. Judy invited us to have supper here."

"I've already started supper," she said, "but that's all right, it'll keep."

"I'm sorry," he said, "I should have phoned earlier."

Thirty-Seven

"It's a perfect day," Billy remarked. He turned to Teppy. "A perfect day," he repeated, smiling broadly.

Teppy took a quick look at his friend; he smelled whiskey on his breath.

It was May 6, a Saturday afternoon, and they were on their way to the Riverdale Zoo. Judy was in the back seat between the two children, and Billy was riding up front with Teppy.

On arriving at the zoo, the children began clamouring to see the monkeys. "Count me out," said Judy; she didn't like monkeys.

Teppy said, "You take them, Billy. We'll wait."

Billy proceeded to the monkey cage, holding each child by the hand.

"He's been drinking," Teppy said.

"That's what I thought. Drinking isn't going to solve his problems."

"It's getting serious. A couple of guys in Business Men's Class noticed it."

Judy gasped. "You'll have to speak to him, Teppy. If he gets fired for drinking, he's finished."

Judy was unnecessarily alarmed; their friend wasn't in the way of losing his job because of drink. He took a drink or two on Saturdays and occasionally on other days too. And while it's true that in his troubles he had come to rely to some degree on the bottle (with a drink in him, things didn't seem so bad), he wasn't the boozer his friends feared he had become. The two guys Teppy had mentioned were partners in business. One night, in celebration of some event, they had opened a bottle in the locker room after classes, filled several paper cups with whiskey and passed them around.

When Billy came to lock up, he too was offered a drink. He accepted and as he drank down the whiskey, they jokingly remarked, "Billy sure knows how to knock it back." And next day in class they kidded him about knocking back the booze.

Seven weeks had passed since that Saturday on March 18 when Billy had returned his wife's diary to the drawer and began making plans for his future. Firming his plans, he had already made arrangements to take his holidays from June 29 to July 12. On June 29 he would take Emma to Galt, spend his two weeks' holiday there, and leave Emma to stay on for the duration of the school holidays. Emma had spent the last two summers in Galt, and it was understood that she would be going there again this summer. As had already been arranged with Teppy and Judy, he would return from Galt July 12, pack his things and move to the room Judy had readied for him. If Sophie happened to be at home, he'd tell her that — he wasn't quite sure yet what he'd say to her — he'd cross that bridge when he came to it. A day or two before the school holidays were over, he would go to Galt and bring Emma back to his friends' house. He wouldn't have to explain anything to the child; Judy had offered to break the news to her. He was relieved that he wouldn't have to deal with it himself, but was worried that Judy, who had no use for Sophie, might turn the child against her.

As it turned out, it was Judy who had stressed the point (in subsequent discussions) that Sophie must not on any account be discredited in her child's eyes. The child would be given to understand that she could see her mother, and her grandparents, any time she wanted to. As for the separation between the parents, Judy would find a reason other than the existing one, and the child would be given a plausible explanation.

Meanwhile, Billy was biding his time. In a little more than seven weeks he and Emma would be on their way to Galt. He had stopped keeping tabs on his wife. There was no need now to check up on her; her diary had told him all he needed to know. He knew the name of the man she was seeing, and knew where he lived: on Bathurst near Bloor. He had looked it up in the telephone directory. Seeing the name Shelley Biderman had not caused him the agitation he had experienced four years before on seeing the name Brian Purtell in the directory. He had already been through the mill, he reflected, and it hadn't hit him so hard this time.

It still bothered him though — in fact it drove a knife through him to see her side of the bed empty when he came home late. But he had found a way of dealing with that too. Instead of working himself into a state at the sight of the empty bed, he took a stiff drink of whiskey from the bottle he kept in his drawer, got into bed and before long was dead to the world. He paid for the drink he had taken by waking next morning with a hangover. On nights when he came home and found her in bed, he undressed and, to avoid physical contact, lay down on the far side of the bed; he couldn't trust himself to be close to her without becoming physically aroused. He hadn't been with her for over two months now. That cruel blow he had been dealt — reading what she had written about the night she tried to imagine she was making love with S — that more than anything kept him from approaching her.

One night when he had reached the limit of physical endurance he got out of bed, shut himself in the bathroom and, to still himself, put into practice a habit he had not indulged in since boyhood.

On Tuesday night, May 30, the instructor made short work of clearing the tank. A few minutes past ten he boarded an eastbound streetcar instead of going home, and got off at Jarvis and Carlton. He walked a few feet south on Jarvis

302

Street, lit a cigarette and leaned in a casual manner against a lamppost, as if waiting for someone. Which in fact he was.

He had taken a drink of whiskey last night before going to bed and, as a result, went to work this morning with a hangover. Teppy, who had noticed the condition he was in, gave him a talking to. "Drinking isn't the answer," he said. "You're heading for trouble, Billy."

It was easy enough for Teppy to talk. He went to bed every night of the week with a wife who loved and respected him. But Teppy had a point just the same; whiskey wasn't the answer. It was a woman he needed, not a drink. He had boarded a streetcar on leaving the Y, got off at Jarvis and Carlton (which he had heard was a red-light district) and was now leaning against a lamppost, waiting to be approached.

Several women passed him, some young and some not so young. Two or three of the younger ones had given him a glance in passing, but none of them had stopped. Deciding he'd try the other side of the street, he went back to the intersection, crossed over, and as he stepped onto the curb he was clipped by a car that was making a right turn into Carlton, and sent sprawling. Shaken but unhurt, he got to his feet and began dusting himself off. Several people came running, among them a girl who appeared to be more shaken than he was.

"Are you all right? It's not my fault, I didn't see you." She was trembling, he noticed, and very pretty. She turned to the few people who had gathered. "It's not my fault, I didn't see him," she repeated, appealing to them, the witnesses. Then she took the instructor by the arm. "Let's get away from here," she whispered, leading him to her car. "I haven't got a driver's licence."

"This isn't my car," she said when they were in the car. "It belongs to the superintendent of our building. He's got a new car and said he'd sell me this one at a bargain if I was interested. I've got it out on a trial run but I don't want any part of it now. Sure you're all right?"

"Never felt better in my life." She was very pretty.

"I'm still shaking," she said, drawing up to an apartment house on Carlton. "I could use a drink. How about you?"

"That suits me fine."

"You remind me of someone," he said, following her into a ground-floor apartment, "but I can't think who—"

"Ginger Rogers?"

"That's right. You're her double."

"So I'm told." She shrugged, making nothing of it. "Sit down, I'll just be a minute."

Her living room was furnished with a cretonne-covered sofa, an end table on either side, two low-slung wicker chairs, a lowboy with a glass vase on it containing artificial flowers, a floor lamp with a fluted parchment shade, a few landscape pictures and some scatter rugs.

She returned presently, bearing in each hand a kitchen glass filled to the brim. "I hope you like coke in your rye? I didn't think to ask. Some people don't," she said, handing him his glass. "Here's mud in your eye." She raised her glass, drank down a good portion, went over to the sofa and sat down. "What's your name?" She was holding her glass in both hands between her knees.

She had lovely legs. "Billy James," he replied.

"Mine's Christine Brady. But you can call me Christie, everybody else does."

"Do you mind if I sit beside you?" he asked, half rising from the wicker chair.

"I don't mind so long as you keep your hands to yourself."

"Wait a minute," Christie was saying, "I'll show you what he looks like." She put down her glass, left the room and returned shortly with a framed photograph. "Meet Nick Brady, the ladies' man." She sat down and together they studied the photo of her estranged husband, a blond, good-looking, smartly tailored young man.

This was a half hour later and they were on their second drink. He had learned that she was a married woman, separated two months from her husband, a car salesman. They were married a year ago when she was eighteen.

"When we were married eight months," Christie said, putting the photo face down on the end table, "he started playing around. I was still in love with him but I kicked him out. He stayed away a month, then he came back, got down on his knees and swore he'd be good if I took him back. I took him back and kicked him out after a few weeks when he began fooling around again. He's phoned a couple of times since. He wants me to give him another chance."

"How do you feel about it?" Billy asked.

"About giving him another chance? With two strikes against him? I'd have to have my head read."

Passing through Billy's mind was the thought that Sophie too had two strikes against her. He was enjoying himself for the first time in two months; thinking of Sophie put a damper on his pleasure. He turned his thoughts to Christie. He admired her independence, among other things, and wished he had her strength of character.

"You're wonderful," he said warmly. "I've never met anyone like you."

She put down her glass and said, "Would you like to kiss me?"

Billy set down his glass, took her in his arms and as he put his mouth to hers he feared his heart would give out, beating so wildly.

She withdrew from his embrace. "Would you like to make love to me?" she said, rumpling his hair.

He couldn't believe his luck. "Oh yes," he murmured.

They got up from the sofa and passed through the hall to her bedroom. Christie shut the door and without ado took off her clothes and got into bed. "You've got a marvellous physique," she remarked as Billy was putting his clothes on a chair.

Naked and in a manly state, he approached the bed, smiling.

Thirty-Eight

"Sit down, Soph," Shelley said, coming away from the phone. "Your cab won't be here for ten minutes. I want to talk to you."

Sophie knew what was coming. He had recently begun talking of leaving Toronto for New York. He had already made inquiries about getting work in New York and had received several promising replies.

"The symphony season will be over in three weeks," he said, "and I'm not going to renew my contract. What am I doing in Toronto playing one night a week at Massey Hall for a short season, and picking up an extra buck fiddling for Swift's Back Bacon Symphony on the radio? There's no future for me here."

Sophie said nothing.

It was Thursday night, June 8. Six months had passed since they first met, and the passage, companioned as it had been by quarrels, threats, retaliatory fault finding and the inevitable reconciliation with its aftermath of impassioned lovemaking, had been a stormy one.

"I've got a big talent," he went on, "and it'll die if I stick around here much longer."

"Stop grinding me down, Shelley. If you want to go, go. I'm not holding you back."

"Come with me," he said, "and let your husband sue for divorce."

As of the last few weeks he had begun threatening to leave her unless she divorced her husband. He wanted her for his wife, he said, not his mistress who ruined every bit of pleasure they had together, always worrying about getting home late.

Not for a minute did Sophie consider divorcing Billy to marry him. Living together as man and wife, he'd be out of love with her in a year. Or less. She wanted things to go on as they were — for as long as it lasted. It was to keep the peace that she had been promising to speak to her husband.

"Are you going to tell him or not?" he demanded. "You keep saying you'll speak to him. When are you going to do it?"

She was four years older than him and the mother of an eight-year-old child. To break up her home and run off to New York with him would be an act of lunacy on her part.

She kept silent.

"If that's the way you want it, I'll put my notice in to-morrow at rehearsal," he threatened.

"It's the way *you* want it," she returned. Changeling, she said to herself (yesterday he said he couldn't live without her).

He called her next morning at nine-thirty and told her that Boris Jellinek, the principal cellist in the symphony orchestra, had called ten minutes ago and invited him to replace Mischa Ortenberg, a violinist who was leaving the quartet Jellinek had formed three years before.

"It's a great honour, Soph. Of all the fiddlers he could have asked, he wants me."

"When do you start?"

"This Sunday. We'll be playing at Jellinek's studio Sunday mornings from ten till half-past twelve. I've got to go, Soph, I'll be late for rehearsal."

Sophie hung up the phone, smiling; she knew him well, her lover. What a boost to his ego to be singled out by Jellinek.

This coming Sunday he'd be taking his rightful place, sitting in the first violinist's chair. Pride of place was the breath of life to him. The promising letters he had received from New York would be replied to at his convenience, if at all.

That Sunday Sophie taxied to his apartment at her usual time, eleven o'clock, and let herself in with her key. She took off her dress, her slip, and put on one of his many dressing gowns. Waiting for him, she roamed the apartment, read, played the radio. The sensual pleasure she derived wearing something of his was vaguely reminiscent of a similar sensation experienced in the past. . . It came to her all at once that she was repeating a pattern of former days. As she had done on Sundays nine years ago at Mrs. Todd's — waiting for an unrevealed husband with his scarf around her neck for the sensual pleasure it gave her — so she was doing now, waiting for a secret lover, wearing his dressing gown.

She brushed aside the memory of those long-ago Sundays. It saddened her to think of them, and at the same time confirmed her belief in the impermanence of married love. She had been in love with Billy then, and he with her. Would things have been different if she had been a faithful wife? She doubted it. Love being the transitory emotion it was, particularly in a marriage situation, fidelity on her part would not have made a scrap of difference in their relations.

Did Billy suspect she was having a love affair? she asked herself for the hundredth time. If he did, it didn't seem to bother him. He showed no interest as to where, or with whom, she spent her time. Billy had his own interests, she reasoned. He enjoyed his work and took pleasure in the company of his friends.

Did Sophie actually believe that her doings were of no concern to her husband? No, not for a minute. It was to lull her conscience that she told herself Billy had his own interests, that he had a life apart from hers. And suffered pangs of guilt just the same. Constantly.

"That's okay," Teppy said and hung up. "That was Billy," he told Judy. "He's not coming with us."

"What else is new?" said Judy.

This was Friday night, June 16, and they had planned to go bowling. Last Friday too he had phoned at the last minute to say he would not be accompanying them to a movie. Last Saturday, and the Saturday before, he brought Emma to their house as usual, but did not stay himself. And on both occasions had phoned at six o'clock and asked Teppy did he mind driving the child home.

"Where was he phoning from," Judy asked, "her place?"

"I guess so. When we were locking up I heard him phone Sophie that he wouldn't be home for supper, so he must have gone to her place right after work."

"Then why did he say he'd come bowling with us?"

"Because he's on cloud nine. I've never seen such a change in a man. He's slap-happy."

"Is he serious about her?"

"He's gone overboard, Judy. He's planning on divorcing Sophie and marrying Christie — when she gets her divorce. He wants us to meet her. He'd like to bring her here tomorrow afternoon, if that's okay with you."

"Is he out of his mind!" Judy said indignantly. "Did he forget that Emma's going to be here?"

To which Teppy mischievously replied, "Maybe he wants Emma to meet her future stepmother?"

"Future stepmother," Judy scoffed. "She herself isn't much older than Emma."

"I told you they were Jewish," Billy said, speaking of Teppy and Judy.

Christie solemnly nodded her head. "I've never been in a Jewish house before. What'll I wear?"

It was half-past seven Friday night, June 23. They had been invited to spend the evening with Teppy and Judy. They were not due there before half-past eight; and Christie was sitting in Billy's lap, in her dressing gown.

"Wear the dress you had on the night we met."

"You're the romantic type. I like that in a man," said Christie. "Nick never noticed what I wore."

He wished she wouldn't mention Nick. Her husband's name went through him like a shaft when she spoke it.

"Do you love me?" she said, rumpling his hair.

He loved it when she rumpled his hair. "More than anyone in the world," he said with emotion.

"More than you loved your wife when you first met her?"

"I think so." He took her face between his hands and kissed her. "That was a long time ago, and I really don't remember."

"Does she know about me?"

"I haven't told her yet, but I will."

"What does she think when you come home at all hours? Isn't she jealous?"

"We haven't got that kind of relationship," he said carefully. Christie didn't know the true cause for his alienation from his wife. It wasn't in him to blacken Sophie in Christie's eyes, so he had given her to understand that he and his wife were incompatible.

"We're not very close," he went on, "and haven't been for some time. But we don't quarrel, and we don't hate each other or anything like that. She has her friends and I have mine. There won't be any trouble about divorce. We both realize that we can't go on like this."

"What about your kid? Will your wife want custody?"

"Emma stays with me," he said firmly. "With us," he corrected himself, smiling. "You'll love her, Christie."

An hour later they were being received by Teppy and Judy.

"Nice to meet you," Judy said on being introduced to Christie.

Smiling, Christie turned to Teppy. "I feel as if I know you. Billy talks about you nonstop," she said, her eyes involuntarily dropping to his maimed hand.

Teppy gave Billy a mock bow and led them to the living room. Christie sat down on the chesterfield, with Billy next to her. Seated, a silence fell on them.

Directing her glance to Christie, Judy broke the silence. "Billy wasn't exaggerating when he said you looked like Ginger Rogers."

"Thank you," said Christie. "Her figure's better than mine."

"That's a matter of opinion," said Billy, smiling.

Judy rose abruptly from her chair. "I'll make some coffee. Or do you prefer tea?" she asked Christie.

"I don't mind," Christie replied.

"I'll give you a hand, Judy," Teppy said and followed her out.

"They're not very friendly," Christie said to Billy when they were alone. "I can't think what to say to them."

"Just be yourself. They don't know you yet. They'll loosen up."

In their midst, she had the appearance of a child, he thought, and was beset suddenly with misgivings at the disparity between his age and hers. Not noticing that Judy had returned bearing a tea tray, he took Christie's hand in his and said, "Tell me honestly, Christie, does thirty-three seem old to you?"

To which she promptly replied, "Thirty-three isn't old." Smiling, she turned to her hostess and, in all innocence, qualified her assertion by saying to Judy (who was thirty-four), "Not for a man, it isn't. . . . It's a mature age," Christie commented, accepting a cup of coffee.

"What's a mature age?" Teppy asked, returning at this point.

"Billy's age," said Christie. "He's thirty-three."

"You call that mature? It's what I call over the hill," Teppy said, giving her a broad wink.

"Not for a man," Judy put in, smiling. "For a woman it's over the hill."

They're making fun of her, Billy thought. And making a joke of his relationship with her. Why would they do that? They were his best friends. They knew what he had been through. Didn't they realize what Christie meant to him? He was happier now than he had been in his whole life. And it wasn't as if he was just having an affair with her; she was going to be his wife.

"Sorry," he said to Christie; she was asking him for a cigarette. "I forgot to bring them," he said, feeling in his pockets.

"Try the grocery store," Teppy suggested (he didn't

smoke, nor did Judy). "They might be open."

When Billy returned, Christie, leaning back in a relaxed attitude with her hands in her lap and lovely legs crossed, was saying, addressing herself alternately to Judy and Teppy: "I met him through my best friend. He had taken her out a couple of times and when he started dating me she warned me that he wasn't the marrying kind."

She smiled at Billy as he resumed his place, turned to her hosts and continued: "Then when she heard we were getting married she went around telling everyone that I vamped Nick away from her. She was gaga about him. And she wasn't the only one either. Well, they're all welcome to him so far as I'm concerned. I don't want any part of him. My mother told me that Nick's been to see her. She thinks I should take him back." Here she turned to Billy. "That'll be the frosty Friday."

"What did you think of her?" Teppy asked his wife. It was half-past ten. Their guests had just departed and they were clearing up.

"What does it matter what I think of her," said Judy. "She's not for him. It's out of the frying pan into the fire."

"He's a born loser," Teppy said.

"He's infatuated. You said yourself he's on cloud nine. But he'll get over it. Between now and the time she gets *her* divorce and he gets *his* divorce, he'll come to his senses. Billy isn't dumb."

Billy wasn't dumb; he was in love. Not an hour had passed since that Tuesday night when he had made love to Christie for the first time that he hadn't thought of her. He went to bed thinking of Christie. And woke thinking of her. Naturally he was disappointed when he learned that Teppy and Judy didn't approve of her. Teppy had made that clear to him last Saturday, the day after he and Judy had met her.

"We've nothing against her personally," Teppy said (speaking for both of them), "it's just that she's not right for you, Billy. Can't you see that yourself?"

Thirty-Nine

"I was twenty-four last week. Twenty-four years old, Soph," Shelley said moodily, "and getting nowhere fast."

This was Tuesday night, June 27.

Last Sunday he had played for the third and last time in Jellinek's quartet. It had been an affront to his pride when he had been summarily informed last Sunday that Mischa Ortenberg (who had been laid up a few weeks in hospital with infectious hepatitis) would be returning to the quartet. When Shelley, who was under the impression that Ortenberg had resigned from the quartet, angrily protested that he had been invited to replace Ortenberg, not to sit in for him, Jellinek coolly apologized for having misused the word "replace."

"You remember Moe Edelstein?" Shelley said.

"Moe Edelstein?"

Impatiently he said, "He used to play fiddle in the orchestra — you met him that night I gave a party for Primrose. He quit the orchestra two months ago and went to Europe. And do you know what he's doing now? He's associate concert master with the Paris Symphony. Moe Edelstein, for Christ's sake! The Heifetz of the Bar Mitzvahs," he said in accusing tones, as if she had been instrumental in promoting Moe Edelstein over him to his present enviable position.

"I began studying the fiddle when I was seven," he went on. "When I was sixteen my teacher called me a virtuoso. That was eight years ago — and what am I doing now? Fiddling my future away, Soph, that's what I'm doing."

"Stop it," said Sophie wearily. "You poison every bit of pleasure we have together."

"Look who's talking about poison. How do you think I feel when you leave my bed to go home to another man?"

"There's nothing between us."

"But you won't leave him."

"It's Emma I can't leave. I'm not the best mother in the world, but to leave an eight-year-old child is something—"

"She'll survive," he interrupted, "didn't I? I wasn't much older when my mother left my father."

He had told her sometime ago that his mother had left his father when he was nine years old and that he had been brought up by his 80-year-old grandmother.

"What was your mother like?" Sophie asked, to divert him.

He loved talking about his mother. Speaking of her, he never failed to mention what a beautiful woman she was. Except for her beauty, he didn't seem to remember much else about her.

"She's a beautiful woman," he said. "Wait, I'll show you a picture of her. My uncle gave it to me a couple of days ago." He got out of bed, rummaged through a drawer, found the picture and brought it to her.

"She *is* beautiful," Sophie said, studying the photo of his mother.

"Do you think I look like her? They say I do."

"Exactly," said Sophie; he did in fact bear a striking resemblance to his mother.

He took up a hand mirror from the dresser. "I'm getting fat," he said, gazing severely at his image. He put down the mirror and got back into bed.

"Are they still together, your mother and the man she ran away with?"

"Of course. They live in California. My father wouldn't give her a divorce but that didn't stop her. And it took some courage in her day to do something like that. She was a daring woman and I admire her for it."

Daring woman, thought Sophie. She ran off with her lover, leaving her nine-year-old child to the care of her embittered husband and a senile old woman. He makes it sound as though she had performed a feat of heroism.

"And you've no feeling whatever of — of resentment against her?" she asked.

"None whatever," he said without hesitation. "Her life with my father was a misery. And I admire her because she had the guts to make a new life for herself. Which is more than can be said for you."

Sophie shrugged. "My life isn't exactly a misery."

"That's because you've got me. But not for much longer, Soph, I mean it. I've definitely decided to go to New York, and I'm asking you for the last time — are you going to speak to him or not?"

She made no answer.

"You're an intelligent woman," he went on, "and in some ways you're so dumb. Don't you think he knows what's going on? You come home twelve, half past, one in the morning, and he doesn't even ask where you've been. I'd throw you out on your keester. He doesn't ask because he doesn't care. He's not doing without, he's getting it somewhere else."

Sophie sat up. "Getting it somewhere else," she said. "What an expression to use."

He looked keenly at her a second, then he reached to the dresser and grabbed hold of the hand mirror. "Look," he said, holding the mirror to her face. "Look at that expression on your face. You're jealous. Of him! Christ, what have I left myself in for!"

He slammed down the mirror and got out of bed. Turning his back to her, he put on his dressing gown, belted it, put his hands in his pockets and then turned to face her. "Get out of here."

Sophie was used to his outbursts, his suddenness of mood. It was nothing new for him to order her out and then prevent her from leaving. And nothing new for him to let her leave and then come running after her. But the expression on his face in this instance was unlike the one he ordinarily wore in pique. It was hostile, unyielding. Hands in his pockets, he stood adamantly before her, waiting for her to put on her clothes and get out.

Unwanted, Sophie felt shame suddenly at her nakedness. She reached for her clothes, pulled the sheet over her head, and with her unclothed body concealed under the tent she had made for herself, hastily got herself dressed. Clothed, she emerged from under the sheet and picked up her handbag. He went to the phone and called a cab. Without a glance in his direction, she opened the door and went down the stairs.

As Sophie expected, the phone rang next morning at ten o'clock, his usual time. "That's for me," she said to her mother. "Answer it, Ma, say I'm not home," and went upstairs to make her bed. She would speak to him when she was good and ready.

She heard her mother answering the phone; it was Aunt Hannah calling. Making the bed, she listened with growing impatience to her mother gabbing with Aunt Hannah. "Ma!" she called from the top of the stairs. "Are you going to be on that phone all day?"

Mrs. Glicksman bade her sister-in-law a hasty good-bye.

The phone rang shortly after and Sophie ran down to answer it. It was Bella. "Let me speak to Ma."

"She's busy," said Sophie, "call her later."

"What's she busy with?" Bella wanted to know, but her sister had hung up.

To intercept a possible second call from Bella, Sophie stayed downstairs a few minutes to monitor the phone. Then she went upstairs, gathered up a few things that needed washing and took them to the bathroom. Listening for the phone, she scalded her hand under the hot-water tap and didn't feel the pain.

When Billy came for lunch, he noticed that the back of her hand was red. "What did you do to your hand?" he asked.

She told him she had scalded it washing some clothes.

She served lunch to her husband and daughter; sat at table with them while they ate, eating nothing herself. The burn, she said, had spoiled her appetite.

When Billy left for work, an agitation such as she had never known before took possession of her. To still herself, she took up a book, opened it at its marker and put it down again. She could not settle to anything. But for the silent phone, nothing held her attention.

With heart-sickening slowness the ensuing hours passed until half-past five, when the phone rang.

"How's the hand?" Billy asked, calling from work.

"It's better, thanks." She hoped he would say he was coming home for supper; his presence would be a welcome distraction.

"Don't bother getting supper for me," he said. "And look after your hand. Keep it out of water."

"What time do you leave tomorrow?" Teppy asked his friend. He and Billy were having supper at a restaurant near the Y.

"We're taking the nine o'clock train," Billy replied.

After classes they locked up together, and taking leave of each other warmly shook hands. "Have a good holiday," said Teppy.

Billy thanked him, asked to be remembered to Judy, and at a quarter past ten was boarding a streetcar, with a pair of earrings in his pocket for Christie.

When he came home shortly after twelve he found his wife in bed. Lights on, she was lying on her back, her open book face down on the covers. Her eyes were red; he wondered if she had been crying.

"Does your hand hurt?" he asked.

"No," she replied, got out of bed suddenly and hurried from the room. He heard her shut the bathroom door; and a little later thought he heard her crying.

"Soph?" he said, knocking on the bathroom door. She didn't answer so he opened the door.

Naked but for her underpants, she was sitting on the toilet seat with her hands clasped between her knees. Her head was bowed and she was sobbing. Tears were dropping on her hands.

He went over to her. "What's wrong, Soph?"

"My hand hurts," she said, like a child.

They've quarrelled, he thought. Poor Soph, she looks the picture of misery.

Loved, and in love himself, his heart went out to her in pity. But as there was nothing he could do about it — to comfort her was beyond his power — he took the Ozonol out of the medicine cabinet, uncapped it and gently salved her hand.

fore I knew him. I should have my head re
lf into a state over Solly Biderman.
one?" she asked her mother on coming into

ss of high spirits, Sophie had a sudden urge
ther a hug for her obtuseness. "Who?"
hat man who phoned."
sman took up the pot she had been scouri
oned. Who's to phone? You scared Pes

e pot against her breast with one arm around
a spoon from the table and began scraping at
uck to the bottom of the pot.
vered her ears. "Stop that!" she cried. "
to lie down for a while and you're drillin
head scraping at that pot. Soak it, for Go
ot water in it!" She seized the pot from
it in the sink and ran from the room.
vake that night brooding, pondering, recap
ogression of her love affair with the violi
nning to the present time. When had he fal
vith her? At what precise moment had it h
e finished, we're quits. How dare he speak to
o did he think he was! Dressed in white tie a
onscious of admiring glances from women in
e knew the real Shelley Biderman; Solly, son
nan the presser. His arrogance, his lordly m
ers, taxi drivers, clerks. And in contrast with
anner with service people was his toadying
people who "counted." Like William Primro
who had come to Toronto a few months ba
ement with the T.S.O. The day of his arriv
ked, was at the station to personally welcom
attendance on Primrose, he carried his suitcas
his hotel, and the night before the concert ga
for him at his apartment, with champagne a
from a French restaurant. She remembered t
h which he treated him. Maestro, he called hi

Forty

Sophie woke next morning at half-past nine. When she saw Billy's side of the bed was empty, she remembered that it was Thursday. He and Emma would be on their way to Galt; they had left without waking her. Getting out of bed she noticed that Billy had left a note for her on his pillow. The note read: "Didn't like to wake you, you were fast asleep. I made some porridge for brkfst, and left yrs in the double boiler. Billy."

She was touched at his concern for her. Which she didn't deserve. He was her true friend. To keep in mind who her true friend was, she pulled open the bottom drawer of her dresser and appended to that accretion of memorabilia never looked at from one year to another her husband's note. She then took her Japanese kimono from the closet, the one he had bought her when they were in love, and put it on for the first time in years. It was stained, spotted, and its belt was missing; but a talisman nonetheless, a token of love. Wrapped in the kimono she descended the stairs, deriving meagre comfort in its embrace.

The telephone rang at ten minutes before ten. "Can I speak to Chayele?" a man's voice said in Yiddish; it was Mrs. Glicksman's cousin Pesach.

"Chayele's busy," Sophie told him in Yiddish, "she can't come to the phone."

Her mother, passing through the hall, heard her. "Who did you tell I was busy?" she asked.

"Pesach," said Sophie irritably. "I'm expecting an important call."

At noon she decided that if he hadn't called by half-past twelve she would have to swallow her pride and call him; she was wearing herself out waiting for his call. At half-past twelve she nervously lifted the receiver and heard a woman's voice; their party line was using the phone. She put down the receiver and stood waiting a while, then tried again.

". . . she swore up and down. She said, 'May I hope to die, I shouldn't live to see my mother again if I told you even one word of a lie.' "

"So what did you say?"

"I told her straight out, 'You're a liar,' and showed her the door. Next comes the waterworks—" there was a pause "— wait a minute, someone's on the line." In polite tones the woman said, "Do you mind getting off the line please? This is a personal conversation."

Keyed up as Sophie was, it was not humanly possible to wait another minute. She went next door to the Adilmans. Mrs. Adilman was on her knees, cleaning the oven. "With pleasure," she said when Sophie asked if she might use the phone.

Sophie sat down at the phone, took in a deep breath, then dialled his number. She let the phone ring twice; then she hung up, waited a short second then dialled again, cuing him. He had recently taken to giving over the hours between twelve and two to practising the violin, and except on signal from her did not answer the phone during practice.

He always answered at the first ring after the signal, but this time he let the phone ring and ring. He's punishing me, she thought, how childish.

He answered at last. "Who's that!" he shouted.

Her heart suspended its beat. "It's me."

"We're finished!" he bellowed. "We're quits! Forget this number. Put it out of your head because the next time you

call I'll be out. O-U-T," he
Do you hear me!"

She hung up the phone an
Mrs. Adilman's back; then t
phone and got up.

Her mother was in the hal
as Sophie came in. "A man ph

"A man?" said Sophie dul
echoed in her ears, *we're q*
couldn't have been him. Over
went up to her bedroom an
Her heart felt tender; the sl
to her like a blow. A car
laughed, a peddler called h
pain. She got out of bed a
was just getting up from hi
leave, then said to her mo
when did he phone, how long

"The same minute. I put
in."

It must have been him.
was nothing new for him to
ogize. Never before though
had he spoken such words to
Forget this number. But he
meant what he said, he wo
that why he phoned? Becau

A surge of anger rose up
room, took the key out of
of paper and put it in an
dressing the envelope, how
led with a name like Biderm
ley, and above it wrote in
minutes to one; if she coul
he'd have the key in tomor
raced two blocks to the mai

The key dispatched, a w
of her, a feeling of vigour, e
New York. The sooner the

was happier
working mys

"Did he p
kitchen.

"Who?"

In an exc
give her m
mimicked. "

Mrs. Glic
"Nobody p
away."

Holding t
she took up
burnt food s

Sophie c
tired. I wan
hole in my
sake! Put
mother, flun

She lay a
lating the p
from its beg
out of love
pened? *We'*
like that! W
tails, vainly
audience —
Hymie Bide
ner with wa
patronizing
haviour with
for example
for an enga
Shelley, una
him. Dancin
taxied him t
a small party
food catered
reverence wi

sitting at his feet after supper. Primrose had a concert to play next day, so the party broke up early. Shelley ordered a cab, escorted him down and came back flushed with pleasure at the privilege of seeing the violist into the taxi he had paid for.

"Why do you humble yourself like that?" she said when they were alone. "Sitting at his feet, calling him Maestro — you'd think the Messiah had come."

"Who said I was humbling myself? That was plain ordinary ass-kissing," he said, laughing. "Primrose is a man who can do me some good — if I ever get to London."

Chalking up to his discredit every incident from her first meeting with the violinist to the present time, she fell asleep towards morning, brooding on the unthinkable probability that he might actually be through with her.

When Sophie came into the kitchen next morning, her mother was preparing the Sabbath meal. "I woke you up?" she asked, putting down the meat cleaver she used for chopping fish.

"No," said Sophie, and poured herself a cup of tea. Determined to keep her thoughts off Shelley, she went upstairs after finishing her tea, took a pile of neglected wash from the clothes closet, filled the bathtub with hot soapy water, and leaning over the tub washed every piece on a washboard till her hands were raw. She then washed the toilet bowl, the basin, cleaned the window and scrubbed the linoleum on the bathroom floor till it shone. Then she went downstairs. "I'm going to clean out the kitchen cupboard," she announced.

Mrs. Glicksman looked up in alarm. Knowing from past experience that her daughter cleaning out the kitchen cupboard could only lead to trouble for her, she hastily put aside her own task in hand and cleared out of the kitchen.

The cupboard done, Sophie looked for more work, and found it. She worked hours without pause, her thoughts all the while revolving with unyielding persistence on her lover. I can live without him, she told herself. I was happier before I knew him. Her mood changed from one minute to the next; from strength she went to weakness, from indignation to despair.

At the end of her labours, her thoughts took a philosophic turn. Love comes to an end, she reflected. I accept that. But not overnight. Let him tell me to my face what happened between us that made him fall out of love with me overnight. I have to know that for my own peace of mind.

At half-past eight she was standing at the door of his apartment, screwing up courage to knock. What if he slammed the door in her face? He wouldn't dare, she thought. She held her hand to her heart a second, to still its beating, then knocked. There was no answer. She knocked again and put her ear to the door. There was no sound from within; all she heard was the erratic beat of her heart.

Regretting she had been so hasty with the key, she descended the three flights of stairs and knocked on the superintendent's door.

His wife came; Sophie knew who she was from having seen her in the building cleaning halls. "Hello," said Sophie, as if greeting an old friend.

The woman returned a blank stare.

"I'm a friend of Mr. Biderman's. He's expecting me but I guess I'm a little early — he isn't home yet. Can you let me in with your pass key, please?"

"We're not supposed to let nobody in if the tenant is out," said the superintendent's wife, slowly closing the door.

"Wait a minute, please. There won't be any trouble. I'll take full responsibility." Sophie took a two-dollar bill from her purse and offered it through the partially open door. "For your trouble," she said, smiling.

The woman took the money and went to get the keys.

Sophie followed her up the stairs, reflecting bitterly on how low she had brought herself; wheedling and bribing to gain access to his apartment, when heretofore she had had independent use of it.

Inside at last, she leaned against the door a few seconds. Then she roused herself and roamed the apartment. The bitterness against her lover began slowly to subside. And her heart for the first time in three days was at peace. She took a glass from the sideboard and poured herself some brandy from a half-full bottle of Remy Martin, and drank it slowly down. She at once felt strengthened, and hopeful of the future. With or without him. She filled her glass again.

It was almost eleven o'clock before the violinist returned. Lights were on and Sophie half asleep was reclined in an armchair.

"What are you doing here?" he said curtly. "How did you get in?"

She primly arranged her skirt over her knees, bent her head and peered blearily under the chair for her shoes. The floor rose, the room began to spin. She closed her eyes and leaned back in her chair.

It was not till then that he noticed the bottle at her feet. He picked it up and held it to the light; there was a heel of brandy left in it. "You're drunk. You'd better go home," he said and went to the phone to call a cab.

"Don't be so fast with your taxis—" She felt a rise of nausea. Stomach heaving, she staggered to the bathroom and vomited in the toilet bowl, dimly aware that he was at her side applying a wet cloth to her forehead.

After a while he led her back to her chair. "Would you like some coffee?" he asked.

"No, thank you, I didn't come here for a social call."

"What did you come for?" he said coldly.

"I came because—" She paused, trying to gather her thoughts. "I came because we have something to talk over. You said we're finished, quits. For what reason?" she said tearfully. "I have to know that for my own peace of mind." Her head was aching and she was conscious of blurring her words. "We have something to talk over," she said, trying desperately to gain control of herself. Her stomach rose. She put her hand over her mouth and lurched to the bathroom.

He was leaning against the fireplace when she returned, with an elbow resting on the mantel shelf. "We've nothing to talk over," he said as she sat down. "It's pointless."

"We certainly have something to talk over. It's over seven months that we've known each other intimately. It isn't as though—"

"It's late," he interrupted. "Do yourself a favour — and me too. Go home," he said, and went to the phone.

"Put that phone down. I'll go when I'm ready, not before." Her face was white and she was trembling.

He put down the phone.

"I came here to tell you a few things," she said, forgetting altogether — her head was so muddled — that the purpose of her call was to obtain an explanation from him. "You're not dealing with that woman — the woman who telephoned you the first time I was here. I've forgotten her name but I haven't forgotten how you spoke to her. It was brutal! Well, you're not going to speak to me like that because I have a few home truths to tell you before we're finished." She paused for breath. "You're vain of your looks. And you have an overweening conceit about your talent. You said your teacher called you a virtuoso. That was eight years ago and you have been deluding yourself ever since that you're a talented musician."

"Are you finished?"

"Not yet," she said grimly.

He loosened his tie and sat down in the chair opposite hers, head back, legs extended and crossed at the ankles.

"Stay all night if you like," he said, "but nothing you can say will make any difference."

"Don't flatter yourself. I didn't come here to ask you to take me back."

He lit a cigarette, formed an O with his lips and blew a smoke ring towards the ceiling.

Watching him, she searched her mind for a barb, a thrust, something to hit him with: she wanted desperately to give him partnership in her pain.

"You said if you couldn't play as well as Heifetz by the time you were twenty-five you'd cut your bowing hand off at the wrist." She leaned tensely forward. With her left hand she made a chopping motion at the wrist of her right hand. "You might as well do that now," she said, eyes alight with malice.

He tilted his head and blew smoke rings one after the other towards the ceiling.

A weariness descended on her, an overwhelming fatigue, and with it an awful sense of futility: she was powerless to hurt him. She put on her shoes and rose from her chair. "Call me a cab. Don't treat me to your charge. I'll pay for my own taxi."

He went to the phone and called a local taxi station. She remembered then that she had given the last of her money to the superintendent's wife.

"I'll need some money," she said, staring at her shoes.

He drew out several bills from his pocket and held out the lot to her in the palm of his hand. She scrupulously picked out a two-dollar bill from the generous offering, then delivered a stinging slap to his hand, scattering the remaining bills to the floor.

The superintendent's wife was in the downstairs hall, stacking newspapers for disposal. At the sight of her, Sophie was overtaken by a feeling of repugnance. My evil genius, she thought. Head averted, she passed by the woman and rode home miserably huddled in a corner of the cab, unable to stop her tears.

Forty-One

Wednesday afternoon, July 5, Billy posted a letter to Christie. "Dear Christie," he had written, "The five days that I've been away from you seems more like five years. I can't wait to see you. I think of you all the time and go to bed hoping I'll dream about you. I wish I could express my feelings, but this will have to do for the time being. Do you think of me once in a while? With all my love, Billy."

"It isn't that we quarrel or anything like that," Billy was saying. "It's just that things aren't right between us. We never have anything to say to each other. We live together like strangers almost. I'm not happy in this situation, Mother, and Sophie isn't either."

Billy and his mother were in the back garden. It was Monday, July 10. Two more days were left of Billy's holidays; he was due back at work Thursday morning. He hadn't meant to burden his mother with his cares but had found himself nonetheless opening his heart to her (making no mention of course of Sophie's infidelity or of his own physical intimacy with Christie).

"We can't go on like this, Mother. And it isn't because I

328

met Christie that I want to divorce Sophie. . . Well, yes, in a way it is. I have something to look forward to now. And Soph will make out. We're not together that much anyway."

"How long did you say you've known each other?" his mother asked.

"About six weeks."

"That's not very long, Billy. And she is rather young."

"I'm not kidding myself, Mother. I realize that I'm almost twice Christie's age, but we suit each other. I love her and she loves me."

His mother looked up; she had been sitting with her head bent, turning her wedding ring around and around on her finger. "Don't say anything to Mary," she said, "or to Louise and Roger."

"They'll have to know sooner or later."

His mother smiled. "There's many a slip between the cup and the lip," she said, giving him a tap on the knee.

Billy felt as if he had lost his last friend. Teppy had tried to discourage him, and now his mother had let him down. Many a slip between the cup and the lip — that showed how lightly she had taken the whole thing. He longed more than ever to see Christie. His heart ached to be with her. That decided him; he would leave tomorrow instead of staying over till Wednesday. Accordingly, he packed his case that night. And next day when he told his mother he had decided to take the five o'clock train home instead of staying over another day, he was relieved to see that she did not take it amiss.

"Don't do anything rash, dear," she said as he was leaving. "Think it over very carefully."

"I have thought it over very carefully, Mother. Now it's just a matter of speaking to Sophie."

Emma and Mary Ann were on the verandah, cutting out paper dolls. He kissed his niece, then took his child in his embrace. "Let go, sweetie," he said after a while (she had fastened her arms around his neck). He loved Emma with his whole being, but it was Christie who occupied his thoughts. "Let go, sweetie," he said somewhat fretfully, "or I'll miss my train."

Billy got off the train at six-thirty. A half hour later he was emerging from a jewellery store on Yonge Street; in his pocket was the watch he had bought for Christie. The one she wore didn't keep time. Apart from that, it was the watch her husband had given her. It was twenty past seven when he arrived at her apartment.

"Who's there?" she called in answer to his knock.

"Guess," he replied; she wasn't expecting him till tomorrow.

She opened the door wearing a dressing gown and the earrings he had given her the night before he left for his holidays.

"I just couldn't wait another day," he said, smiling.

As he made to enter she gently pushed him back and stepped into the hall. "I can't let you in, Billy," she said. "Someone's here."

"Your mother?" he said, disappointed; she had kept him out once before when her mother was visiting.

Christie shook her head. "Nick's here. I've made it up with him."

He remained speechless a moment. Then he put his suitcase on the floor and interlocked his fingers against his chest. "Don't do this to me, Christie," he said, cracking his knuckles. "It's cruel. You said you'd never take him back."

"I'm sorry, Billy. Nick is my husband," she said, "and I was brought up to respect the marriage vows as sacred."

He gazed mutely at her.

Cajolingly she said, "Make it up with your wife, Billy, and let's part friends." She turned to the door, then back again to him. "No hard feelings?" she said, rumpling his hair.

He stooped to his suitcase and left without a further glance in her direction. Numbed, he walked slowly along Carlton Street. If she was brought up to respect the marriage vows as sacred, how does that tie in with going to bed with another man? he said bitterly to himself. She was a liar. She had never intended to divorce her husband and marry him. She had just been making time with him while waiting for Nick to come back — and he had fallen for it like a ton of bricks.

He'd have to get Christie out of his system, put her out of his mind, forget about her. Perhaps he'd go in to work tomorrow instead of waiting till Thursday. Taking classes required concentration and would keep his mind off Christie.

He would go to his friends' house and spend the night in the room Judy had prepared for him. Take a stiff drink (he had a bottle in his suitcase), flop into bed and forget everything. The last time he had a drink was the one he had with Christie the night before he left for his holidays. He groaned, remembering how loving she had been.

Eleven o'clock the same evening Teppy, putting out a garbage can in the driveway, heard the hum of a motor coming from his garage. He opened the door and saw Billy's suitcase beside the car. The ignition was on and his friend, mouth open, was slumped sideways on the driver's seat.

Teppy shut off the motor and ran back to the house. "Judy," he shouted, "call a doctor, get an ambulance!" and ran back to the garage.

On the seat beside his dead friend lay a half-full bottle of whiskey and a small package wrapped in blue paper. On the wrapping was written in Billy's hand, "For Sophie."

THE NEW CANADIAN LIBRARY LIST

McCLELLAND AND STEWART LIMITED
publishers of The New Canadian Library
would like to keep you informed about
new additions to this unique series.

For a complete listing of titles and
current prices – or if you wish to be added
to our mailing list to receive future catalogues
and other new book information – write:

BOOKNEWS
McClelland and Stewart Limited
25 Hollinger Road
Toronto, Canada M4B 3G2

McClelland and Stewart books are
available at all good bookstores.

Booksellers should be happy to order from our catalogues
any titles which they do not regularly stock.